BAD DEMON

HELL ON WHEELS SERIES

SHERILEE GRAY

Visit my website at: www.sherileegray.com
Cover Designer: Natasha Snow Designs, www.natashasnowdesigns.com
Editor: Jovana Shirley, Unforeseen Editing,
www.unforeseenediting.com
Proofreading: Marla Esposito, Proofing With Style, www.
proofingstyle.com
& Shelley Charlton

This book is a work of fiction. Names, characters, places, and incidents
either are products of the author's imagination or are used fictitiously. Any
resemblance to actual persons, living or dead, events, or locales is entirely
coincidental.

ISBN: 978-1-0670019-4-0

CONTENT NOTE

BAD DEMON contains scenes that include medical and body horror, non con (not between the hero and heroine), extra large penetration, knotting, blood drinking, blood, gore, violence, explicit sex.

Although I don't consider Bad Demon a dark romance, there are dark themes and scenes that may be disturbing to some readers. Your mental health is important to me, so please proceed with caution.

PROLOGUE

FERN

SEVENTEEN YEARS AGO

I WHIMPERED when Mommy cut my finger with her special knife. I didn't cry though. Mommy never cried when she made herself bleed, and neither would I. She pressed the cut on her finger to mine, whispering a spell I didn't understand, then she lifted my sleeves and smeared blood on the inside of both my wrists then across my feet. I squeezed my eyes closed and bit my lip because it hurt really bad. Mommy cupped my cheek, staring down at me. She looked scared and sad.

I breathed heavily because my throat was tight, my eyes were stinging, and my belly hurt. "I don't feel good."

"I know, baby, and I'll give you something to make you feel better soon," Mommy said.

The sound of the back door in the kitchen opening and banging shut echoed down the hallway.

1

Mommy spun away and then back to me. "Quick, under here."

"Why are you scared, Mommy?" I asked, positive I was going to throw up now.

"It's going to be okay, baby," she whispered, then pressed a kiss to my forehead. "Promise me, no matter what happens, you won't move from this spot."

"I promise," I whispered back and crawled under the hall table.

"Don't make a sound, okay?"

I nodded.

She stood, quickly arranging the lace tablecloth in front of me so I was hidden, and rushed down the hall toward the kitchen. The door opened before she reached it—

A monster stood there, his eyes glowing red.

"Get out of my house," Mommy said, her voice loud but trembling.

"Give me the child," the monster said.

"Never." Magic sparked across her fingers.

"Don't make this harder, Eleanor."

Daddy!

He was here. I started to crawl out from my hiding place under the table because Daddy was strong. He'd protect us from the monster. But then Mommy lifted her hands, aiming them at him as well.

"You dropped the ward; you let him in. How could you do this?" Mommy said.

Daddy looked angry. "Yes, I let him in. This has gone on long enough."

"What the hell is wrong with you? She's our daughter. She's your—"

"That abomination is not my daughter."

"How can you say that? You were there when I had her;

2

you held her in your arms. She's our little girl." Mommy's hands were trembling. "She's still young. Give her time—"

"There's no magic in that child, no trace of witch. It would be bad enough if it was only your grandmother's tainted blood running through her veins, but it's much worse than that, isn't it, Eleanor? We've pretended long enough. I will not have her polluting my family name, or my coven."

"She is your flesh and blood—"

He laughed, but I didn't like the way it sounded. "You're a lying whore. That child has her father's eyes."

"Gerald—"

"No," Daddy said. "She's not staying in this house. You're not keeping her."

Sparks burst from Mommy's hands, fire dancing on the tips of her fingers as she screamed.

The monster standing beside Daddy lifted his hand and slashed it through the air. Blood sprayed across the floor, and everything went quiet.

Mommy hit the floor—hard.

Daddy roared, and I covered my mouth with both hands so the monster didn't hear me screaming.

Daddy knelt on the floor and lifted Mommy in his arms. "Goddammit, Grady, this wasn't supposed to happen. You weren't meant to kill my fucking wife."

"She gave me no choice," the monster said.

Mommy needed to wake up. Why wasn't she waking up?

Daddy yelled at the monster to leave as magic buzzed through the room. The monster hissed and snarled as Daddy's magic wrapped around him, and the monster was dragged by invisible hands from the kitchen and tossed outside.

I crawled out from my hiding place. "Daddy?"

His head shot up, and his eyes glowed bright. "You did this. You killed her!"

I shook my head. "No, I didn't do it. It was the monster."

"Go to your room," he hissed.

"Daddy?"

"Now," he yelled.

I spun and ran up the stairs and shut myself in. Curling into a ball on my bed, I cried and cried until my eyes were puffy and sore, and I couldn't breathe through my nose.

There were noises downstairs. Voices.

My door opened, and I sat up. "Grandpa?"

He looked at me. "We need to pack your things, Fern."

"Where am I going?"

He took a bag from my closet and started stuffing my clothes inside.

"I don't want to go."

He grabbed my arm, pulled me off the bed, and shoved my coat on. Then he took my hand and dragged me from my room and down the stairs. I searched, but Mommy was gone. I could hear Daddy talking to someone, but I couldn't see him.

"Daddy!" I called as Grandpa opened the door and led me out.

We got in his car, and we drove away. No matter what I said or did, he wouldn't look at me or talk to me. I was scared, and it was dark. We drove for so long that, eventually, I fell asleep. When I woke, the sun was starting to come up.

I sat straighter and looked around. "Where are we?"

He didn't answer, he just got out of the car, got my bag, and opened my door. "Out," he said.

I climbed down, and he grabbed the back of my coat

instead of my hand as we walked toward a big old building. We took the stairs, and he banged on the door.

I didn't like this place. I didn't want to be here.

"Grandpa?"

He looked down at me but said nothing as the sound of footsteps echoed from the other side of the door.

"Mommy's dead, isn't she? And it was my fault?"

"Yes," he said.

"What's an abomination?" I asked him.

"You are, Fern."

CHAPTER
ONE

FERN

PRESENT DAY

THE TRUCK BOUNCED OVER POTHOLES, and I gripped the steering wheel tighter. I wouldn't be able to drive much farther. Pretty soon, I'd be forced to go on foot. The forest was oppressively dark, my dull headlights doing a shitty job of illuminating the horror show that was Oldwood Forest ... or what was hiding in it.

The next pothole was so deep that my head almost hit the roof.

"Fuck."

If I didn't stop now, I'd get stuck, and I wouldn't be able to drive back out. That wouldn't be good, not at all.

The demons who lived in this part of the forest were always on the lookout for breeders. Females went missing all the time in Seventh Circle—the demon part of the city—

and were brought out here. If they had no one in their lives who gave a fuck—like, for example, me—then no one went looking for them. Unfortunately, not all the demons who lived out here were idiots. They might not be able to pass as human, but they weren't stupid. There was a thriving black market for orphaned demon females of breeding age for a reason.

Was I taking a huge risk coming out here? Fuck yes. But there was no way I was giving up or going home now. I had to protect myself. I wasn't going to end up in another prison with a different jailor. Sadly, strolling through a forest full of sick and twisted demons was the only way to make sure that didn't happen.

Pulling the truck over, I turned off the engine, and the cab was submerged in darkness.

Don't freak out. Don't do it. Breathe.

I fucking hated the dark. *Hated it.* And as soon as it closed in around me, my mind tried to fuck with me, throwing up memories—so vivid that I was sure I could hear that slow drip, that I could feel the coldness against my skin, that I could hear the screams. I bit my lip hard enough to break flesh, and the flash of pain chased the memories away. Forcing myself to keep breathing slow and steady, I sat still and utterly silent as I listened and let my eyes adjust to the pale moonlight.

You've got this. You can do this. You need to do this—

A groan from the back of the truck interrupted my little pep talk.

Time to move.

Quickly getting out, I bounded up onto the cargo bed and pulled the pouch of herbs from my pocket—a mix I'd created that was strong enough to take down an elephant.

Speaking of the creeps who kidnapped and sold females, I crouched beside the bound demon, flailing against the bindings around his wrists and ankles.

He hissed, cursing me out. "That wasn't very nice," I said and pinched his nose closed. His eyes widened, and he started jerking and twisting. Climbing on his chest, I slid forward, using my thighs to keep his head still, and waited him out. Finally, he opened his mouth for a desperate breath. I quickly sprinkled my special tranquilizing mix onto the back of his tongue, and he gasped it right on down his throat. He coughed, and I snatched up the water bottle from my bag and poured some into his mouth. He gulped greedily to wash away the nasty shit.

Success.

I smirked. "Night-night, fuckface."

His eyes flashed red, a growl tearing from him, and then he slumped. Out cold. Thankfully, before he could fully recover from the first dose I'd given him and use his powers to take me out.

Following this prick and slipping my sedative into his drink had been the easy part. Getting him out to the truck before he passed out had been a little trickier, but I'd gotten there in the end.

Jumping down from the cargo bed, I opened the tailgate, unfolded the tarp I'd thrown back here, and laid it on the ground. Then, grabbing the demon by his ankles, I hauled him off the back and onto the tarp with a thud. This prick wasn't your average run-of-the-mill demon. He was powerful, strong, and high up on the food chain. If Rune caught me doing this, I'd be fucked. Lights out, all over for Fern—or worse, I'd be sent to Hell. Rune was in charge of the demons who'd been granted sanctuary and given permission to remain topside. There were rules, of course, and I was currently breaking a big one.

But that couldn't be helped, and this asshole deserved what he was about to get.

As for why I'd chosen this particular demon? Well, his function, for me, was threefold. First, I'd seen him talking to a couple of demons who'd been hanging around my street, creeps who had been watching my store. This slimy fucker had sent breeder scouts to watch me. It was only a matter of time before they made their move, and I wasn't going to just sit around and let that happen. No fucking way. So, I'd gotten in first.

Second, I needed an offering of value if this was going to work, and third, he was my ticket to get safely through this forest. With the stench of power rolling off this prick, along with the come-closer-and-die demon aggression seeping from his pores, even while unconscious, the others around here would stay the fuck away.

I'd estimated my success rate at about seventy to eighty-five percent. No matter how you looked at it, those were some pretty spectacular odds.

Far-off calls and cries echoed through the trees, and I shivered, but as long as whatever nasty breed of demon making those noises stayed where they were, everything would be okay. Grimacing, I got down on the tarp and rubbed up against the unconscious bastard so his scent mingled with mine. If any demon did come across me on my own, I'd smell as if I'd been taken by someone they wouldn't want to mess with.

"Let's go, fuckstick." Grabbing the edge of the tarp, I trudged on down the path, heaving my comatose buddy with me.

As I walked, the sounds of branches cracking, of rustling, had me stopping to listen over my huffing and puffing. Yes, they were definitely closer, but my unconscious bud was obviously doing his job and stinking up the place because if he wasn't, the others would already be here.

It was hard to see the landmarks I needed to find in the dark, but there was an overgrown track, and I was pretty sure I'd managed to stay on it.

Magnolia Thornheart—the witch I'd gotten the information from—was a regular at my store. She dabbled in dark magic, yes, but she'd seemed trustworthy enough, I guessed, and even warned me about several traps that I should look out for. Good thing too—there was a snare up ahead, one I could have easily missed if I hadn't known to look. She'd definitely be getting a discount the next time she came by the store.

Gritting my teeth, I heaved the heavy demon off the track and around the snare, his head bouncing off rocks and fallen branches as we went. The scent of wood smoke finally reached me, and I searched the forest ahead. There was a glow in the distance. Almost there.

My fingers were cramping, and my thigh muscles and biceps were trembling by the time I stopped at the end of the path that led to a compact, storybook cottage—but not the cute kind, the kind the evil-child-eating witch lived in. The place had been all but swallowed by the forest. Trees butted up against its walls, and one seemed to have gone right through it, its branches forming a canopy over one side of the roof. Light shone from its windows, and where I stood, at the end of the path, was bracketed by two tall trees.

They were decorated with a variety of offerings that had been tied to their branches with twine. Bones with rotting flesh still hanging from them; demon skulls; jars filled with unknown, floating organs; one with pieces of fabric; another with fingernails and a larger one with a wad of matted hair in various shades.

There was only one way to get the witch's attention and hopefully be granted admittance—blood. It told the crone who you truly were, and revealing who I was would either be a help or a hindrance. I had no idea what reception I'd get. I hoped the witch would listen and agree to help me, but she could just as easily send me away—or worse, I'd end up in her pot. From what I'd learned about the female, all three options had an equal percentage of probability.

A sixty-six percent chance of survival was not the best, but it wasn't completely terrible either—at least compared to the alternative.

Turning on my phone's flashlight, I rounded one of the trees at the top of the path and searched for the marking Magnolia had told me about. I spotted a knot midway up it, the color deeper in the center and worn smooth. Slipping my knife from my pocket, I pricked the tip of my finger right over the tiny scar I'd gotten when I was seven. Something in my chest tightened as I watched the blood bubble to the surface, then sent ice shooting down my spine. I shook off the feeling—along with the memory I tried to avoid whenever it surfaced—and pressed the tip of my finger against the knot.

Stepping back, I waited while nerves went manic in my belly. I didn't know what I'd do if she turned me away. I snorted. *Maybe you should be more worried about ending up in her pot.*

The cottage door swung open, and I straightened. Not

sure what to expect, I braced for anything. A very short female stepped out, stooped low, with wiry gray hair and wrinkled skin. She started down the steps, and a raven cawed, flying from the house, swooping around her several times before settling on her shoulder. As she drew closer, I felt her power. Her blue eyes traveled over me from head to foot and back again, her mouth clamped shut.

Finally, she was standing in front of me, the ward she'd surrounded her cottage with the only thing between us.

"Agatheena?"

Her eyes flashed red, and I let mine do the same. She snorted exactly like I had a short time ago.

"Go on then, child." She held me trapped in that piercing gaze. "Say it."

My mouth was dry, and my heart slammed in my chest, but I straightened my spine. "I go by Fern Honeycutt, but my birth name was Estelle Gannon. My father is Gerald Gannon, and my mother was Eleanor Burnside." My birth name felt, gods, foreign on my tongue. I wasn't her anymore, and I never wanted to be her again. Ever. "And I believe you are my great-grandmother."

The raven let out another caw and bobbed up and down on her shoulder.

"Oh, yes, I'd know that tainted blood anywhere, but why are you darkening my door now?"

I bristled. *Tainted blood.* I huffed a laugh, even as stupid fucking hurt filled me. "Am I not even good enough for you, Agatheena? Will you send me away as well?"

"I send beings away due to character, not blood, and I say yours is tainted because it's the same blood that runs through my veins. Some see it as bad or undesirable, but I've learned to see my mixed blood as an enhancement, a gift." She looked at the prone demon behind me. "Is that for me then?"

I blinked down at her, stunned by her words. No one had ever called my contaminated DNA a gift.

"Speak, child," Agatheena snapped.

"Yes, he's an offering."

She waved her hand, and I felt the hum of power drop between us. "Bring him in."

Gathering up the ends of the tarp, I dragged him down the path, following her around the side of the cottage and into a small ramshackle shed. She held out her hand, and the demon lifted from the ground as if by invisible hands. He was spun upside down, and then a rope lashed out of nowhere and coiled around his ankles, yanking him higher and over a thick metal hook, suspending him from the low rafters.

The demon's eyes snapped open, and he snarled and thrashed. Agatheena slashed her hand through the air again, and his mouth slammed shut. Then she kicked a bucket under him, grabbed a massive dirty knife from the scarred wooden bench beside her, and sliced his throat.

The demon jerked, his cries muffled behind his tightly pressed-together lips as blood gushed from his throat, over his face, through his hair, and into the bucket.

Agatheena walked out of the shed, and I stared, stunned, as the demon went limp.

When demons died, we turned to ash; nothing left. Agatheena had the ability to prevent that from happening though. Our organs held power, but due to the whole disintegrating-into-nothing thing, they were rare and highly sought after. Not just anyone could harvest them.

This had to be seriously lucrative for the old witch.

"Are you coming?" Agatheena said as she walked away.

I jolted out of my stupor and rushed after her as she rounded the cottage and followed her up the stairs. When she opened the door, the scent that flowed out was like nothing I'd ever smelled in my life. It wasn't bad, but it was intense.

"Don't touch anything," she said and waved toward the kitchen. "Sit over there."

I did as she'd said—I didn't dare do anything else—and tried not to stare at all the weird shit she had hanging from the rafters and sitting on shelves. There was what you'd expect in a witch's cottage—herbs, books, bottles of potions, and elixirs—but there were also shriveled limbs, dried entrails, skulls and other bones, and more organs floating around in jars.

Agatheena was preparing us tea by the looks of it, and her raven turned on her shoulder, facing me, his beady black eyes staring a hole through my head.

I avoided making eye contact. "What's your raven's name?"

"Dolores, and she's an excellent judge of character." Agatheena set a delicate floral teacup in front of me. "She likes you."

"How can you tell?" I subtly sniffed the vapor drifting up from my cup. I knew herbs better than most. If she was attempting to sedate or poison me, I'd know.

"It's safe." She sat, studying me, and I could be wrong, but I thought there might be a look of approval in her eyes. "And if Dolores didn't trust you, your eyeballs would already be in that jar over there."

Yep, there was indeed a jar full of bloody eyeballs. "Well, I'm glad she likes me then."

Agatheena chuckled. "You know herbs," she said, not a question, and motioned to my tea.

Nope. She hadn't missed the way I'd been scenting it.

"I do. I have my own store in Seventh Circle."

Her gaze sharpened. "The need to be among herbs, to learn about them—that's the witch in you, girl."

A stab of hurt sliced through me. "The witch gene bypassed me almost entirely. I don't have a familiar or any magical ability. That's why I'm here actually. I was hoping you could help me."

She noticed my fingers tapping against the table. "What kind of help?"

I quickly dropped my hand, but finished counting in my head. *One, two, three, four. Four, three, two, one.* "I'm being watched. Breeder scouts." I'd been free from the hell my grandfather had dumped me in for five years, and I would turn myself to ash before I ended up at the mercy of another fucked-up monster.

"What about your family?" Her stare didn't falter, but her eyes flashed red momentarily.

"My mother was murdered when I was very young, and then my father had me taken away. Apart from you, I have no family. I'm the perfect target. A lone female with no ties."

Her fingers curled, tightening into a trembling fist. "I sensed Eleanor's soul in the afterlife, but I could never reach her." Her eyes flashed red again, but this time, they stayed that way. "It was as if someone was keeping her from me. Just like my Hazel. The coven—has to be—they bound their souls so I couldn't reach them, even in death."

Hazel was my grandmother and Agatheena's daughter.

"Why? Why would they do that to you?"

Agatheena sipped her tea, and I could see her mind ticking over, as if she was deciding what she should tell me.

"Please."

16

She blew out a breath and sat forward. "Because my mother dared to fall in love with the wrong male. As you know, her mate was a demon, but when her parents found out, they had him killed, then forced her to marry a widower—a coven elder who had too much money and no heirs. I'd been conceived before the marriage though, and when the coven realized what I was—that I was half demon—they told everyone my father had forced himself on my mother. They lied, and then they cast me out. It didn't help that I was far stronger than them." She took my hand and turned it over, searching the lines on my palm. "But you know exactly what that's like, don't you, Fern? Our stories are almost identical."

Yes, eerily so. It was almost like history had repeated itself.

"Except for the bit about my father. Mine was a witch, and I can only guess that it was the demon DNA—passed down from you—that terrified him, which is why he got rid of me."

Agatheena held my gaze, her glowing red eyes boring into me. "Not just any demon DNA runs through your veins, one of the most powerful and most feared. But that wasn't the only reason they cast you aside, child."

"What do you mean?"

"You say it was your father who cast you out?" she asked.

Anger—which I'd refused to let in for a very long time —slammed into me, and my eyes changed. They were glowing red, just like hers now. "With the help of my grandfather."

"Who murdered your mother, Fern?"

My mouth went dry as the memory of that night flashed through my mind, as the terror I'd felt flooded me.

Agatheena kept hold of my hand when I tried to pull away, her grip far stronger than it should be.

"A demon named Grady." I couldn't suppress the shudder, but forced myself to share more when that wasn't something I ever did. "That's why I'm here. My freedom was taken from me. I ..." I shook my head. "I was a child when I was handed over to a monster. I escaped, and I made sure they couldn't come after me, but alone, powerless, I'm still vulnerable. I need to know how to protect myself, Agatheena. I refuse to be a victim again." And seeing those breeder scout creeps around my store had brought home just how vulnerable I was.

Her grip on my hand tightened. "You are a target, great-granddaughter, because you are unique. Evil is drawn to you because of what you are. You are magnetic, you are special, and in the wrong hands, you are incredibly dangerous."

I scoffed. "Dangerous? No. Despite my parents, I don't have a magical bone in my body. My demon blood is dominant. I'm not a witch, and sadly, as far as demon powers go, I'm unremarkable. I'm definitely not dangerous."

"You were lied to. You're more than remarkable. You're a threeling, Fern. Extremely rare and, yes, extremely powerful."

She'd obviously lost it, living out here all on her own for the last fifty years.

"Perhaps coming here was a mistake."

Her grip tightened again. "Your father was not the male your mother married. You are no Gannon; that coven is not yours, and it never was. Like my mother, her mate was an undesirable in the eyes of her coven."

I straightened in my chair. "No ... that's not—"

"It's the truth."

18

"How do you know?"

"Your blood, child. My tree knows all. I know exactly who and what you are."

Magnolia had told me about the tree. She'd told me what it could do. I didn't think Agatheena was lying. She had no reason to.

"That child has her father's eyes."

The words filtered through my mind, pulled from the past, words I'd locked away, like a lot of things from that awful fucking night. The male I thought was my father had said it to my mother the night she was murdered, the night I'd been taken.

"If Gerald Gannon isn't my father, who ..." No, that was the wrong question. "What ... was he?"

"You can't work it out?"

Without thought, I swiped my tongue over my teeth, over the longer-than-normal canines I had. They were sharp as hell, but despite the name, I didn't think my father was a shifter. Something coiled in my belly—a shameful part of me, urges I kept locked down, which I'd ignored but now couldn't deny.

"Vampire."

She grinned, flashing rows of sharp demon teeth. "No. I get why you'd think that though. No, child, you are a soul collector, a deal maker, but, yes, the breed is closely related to the vampire, which means they are blood drinkers. You're a potent mix—witch from your mother, demon from my bloodline, and also one of the most powerful demon breeds there is from your father—so, no, you're definitely not unremarkable. You are so much more than you think you are."

My blood was rushing too fast through my veins. "Witches mate with others all the time—maybe not demon, not as often, or at least not always out in the open. But still, I can't be the only one with mixed blood."

"You're right; you aren't. There are many like you, but what makes you special, Fern, is that when your mother conceived you with her demon mate, you were one of three."

What now? "No, that can't be—"

"Stop interrupting me," she said, a flash of fury in her eyes.

I forced myself to clamp my mouth shut when the urge to call bullshit was overwhelming, but again, why would she lie? Even if what she'd said seemed utterly insane, I wanted to hear what she had to say. I also wanted to get out of here in one piece.

"I might have been exiled, but I've kept tabs on my family," she said. "Until you vanished, that is. Your mother mated in secret, and she conceived soon after, right before the coven found out about her mate."

A cold blast hit me, making me shiver.

"They would've had to have murdered him, like my own father. A demon as powerful as that, he would've wiped out the entire coven before he let them take his female away from him. Your mother didn't know she was with child though, and the pain of losing her mate was unbearable, enormous, so incredibly strong that it created violent magical and demonic power surges inside her. She was forced to lock them down, to hold it in, or risk exile. Your sisters didn't survive it, but their powers, their magic, did, and with nowhere else to go, you absorbed them all."

I couldn't believe what I was hearing. "That can't be true ... it can't be."

"I don't tell pork pies, child."

Fear churned inside me. "But I don't have any powers."

20

"They're untapped—that's all. And for now, that's what's keeping you safe."

"Safe? Without powers, I'm a sitting duck. I have no real way of protecting myself."

"Is your store and your home warded?"

"Yes."

She nodded. "Good, because until I know more about the kind of power you have, it's far more dangerous to set them free. Luckily, with all that powerful demon blood, you're immortal. Just don't lose your head, and you'll be okay."

I'd already figured out the immortal part for myself. A being couldn't go through all I had and survive, but death wasn't the worst that could happen to someone—I knew that firsthand. And everything else she'd told me? It definitely wasn't the information I'd come here for.

I came here for help; now the ground under my feet felt even shakier than before. "What do I do?"

"No idea. Never thought I'd encounter a threeling. In this, my knowledge is limited. I'll need to do some poking around. Come back this time next week, and maybe I'll have something for you." She stood.

My mind was in a whirl with everything I'd learned. "Thank you, Agatheena."

"You can repay me by bringing me another offering," she said, then shoved something into my hand. "Protection. Carry it when you move through the forest or when you leave the safety of your ward. It needs to have contact with your skin."

She opened the door. Magic coiled around me tight, and then I was dragged out by invisible hands.

I all but flew down the path and was expelled from her property, tossed onto the ground.

Oof. I quickly got to my feet and brushed the dirt off my ass as I searched the trees around me.

A roar echoed through the forest close by. Agatheena said the charm she'd given me would keep me safe, but I wasn't risking it, and I took off at a jog, heading back the way I'd come.

TWO

RELIC

WARRICK'S PHONE CHIMED, and our alpha frowned down at the screen.

"What's going on?"

"Lucifer." Warrick glanced up, running a hand down his beard. "He wants to meet, says he'll come to us."

That wasn't normal. Lucifer didn't leave Hell often, not after his son had locked him out a while back, trying to overthrow him.

"I'll contact Maddox. He might know what this is about," Warrick said.

Maddox commanded our brothers in Hell for our alpha. War made regular visits, keeping an eye on things, but we'd left in Lucifer's absence, refusing to serve his twisted son. After spending my entire life in Hell, it turned out I liked it up here a whole lot more, and so did my brothers. War had made a deal with the king of Hell; some new hounds were created, and we'd hung around, training them up so there were enough of us to keep the demons there under control.

Now, we took shifts, ensuring we always had several of us older hounds in Hell to make sure nothing went tits up below ground.

I planted my hands on my hips. "He say when he's coming?"

"Tonight," War said, still frowning.

Jagger, Warrick's lieutenant, leaned against the wall. "I'll make sure everyone's here and spread the word that the clubhouse is off-limits to everyone else."

I grabbed my phone when it vibrated in my pocket. A text from Zinnia. The witch was a good friend and family since she was cousin to Warrick's mate, Willow.

Zinny: Hey, so I need to swing by the demon part of town and wondered if you wanted to tag along.

No fucking way would I let her go to Seventh Circle on her own. It wasn't safe for any female, especially a witch.

Relic: When?

Zinny: Now, if you're free?

Relic: I'll text when I'm there.

Zinny: Awesome, thanks.

I shoved my phone back into my pocket, striding out of the clubhouse and to the line of bikes parked just outside.

We'd been living in Linville, just out of Roxburgh, New York, for long enough that the locals had gotten used to us. The people here thought we were a human motorcycle club, and that suited us just fine. They mainly gave us a wide berth, and we were free to live the way we wanted.

Swinging my leg over my bike, I kicked up the stand and started the engine. It roared to life, vibrating through my chest and echoing around the parking lot. Riding was nowhere near as good as going hound and running free, but it was a pretty close fucking second. I quickly tied my hair out of the way, walked my bike back, and opened her up, speeding out onto the street.

It took thirty minutes to reach the city. I parked and fired off a text to Zinnia, telling her where I was. Humans naturally avoided Seventh Circle. It was swarming with demons, and their flight instincts tended to keep them away without any extra help.

Ten minutes later, Zinny was striding down the street. The witch was beautiful, tough, loyal, and currently dealing with some seriously fucked-up shit. So, if she needed me, I was there.

Hounds had limited emotions, yes—some of us more than others—but when it came to females, we all had the same endless protective streak, probably because all hellhounds were male.

"Just couldn't stay away from me?" I said to her when she stopped in front of me.

Her familiar—a tiny rat named Hemlock—poked his head out of her bag, and I gave him a scratch.

Zinny snorted. "You wish."

"You have no idea. But since sex is off the table, I'm happy to display my superior fighting abilities and protect a damsel in distress."

"I'm not a damsel."

No, she wasn't. She'd proven herself a warrior time and again.

Instead of agreeing though, I planted a hand on top of her head and mussed her hair. "Whatever you say, princess."

She rolled her eyes. "You've been going to Willow's movie nights, huh?"

I laughed. She was perceptive. "Of course. Can't you see

how evolved I've become? My emotional education is coming along nicely. I'm almost like a *real boy*."

Humor came more naturally to me than my brothers, but they'd been learning since we'd left Hell. Lucifer gave us the ability to understand emotions, but having them ourselves wasn't necessary. Tender emotions were considered a hindrance. And because most hounds were created full-grown, we didn't have the same familial connections as some beings.

"So, what are we doing here?"

"I need some ingredients for a job I'm doing today." She quickly looked away, avoiding making eye contact.

Yeah, she was full of shit and up to something. I could literally smell the lies.

Still, it fucking pleased me that she recognized my strength and that I was her first choice when she required protection, even if she wasn't ready to share what this was really about. Lucifer had given us a deeper knowledge of loyalty—along with anger and lust—and I was glad she not only saw that loyalty, but also accepted it from me.

I scanned our surroundings while we walked and talked. The demons on the street looked our way as we passed, but as soon as they got an eyeful of me, they quickly turned away.

Not surprising since, the only demons allowed to live openly in this part of the city had to be able to pass as human, and they also needed to know how to follow rules. If not, either the knights of Hell would take care of them, or the hounds would collect them and drag their asses below ground to answer to Lucifer and receive punishment for their crimes.

"Just up here." Zinnia motioned to a store ahead.

Malicious Brew was painted on a sign above the door. I

strode in and was instantly assaulted by so many different scents that my fucking skull was buzzing. I snarled, shaking my head, my beast rearing up inside me, as I scanned the room, then tilted back my head, forcing myself to scent the air.

"This shit is burning my fucking nostrils." A growl built in my chest as a sensation I didn't recognize rolled through me and had me curling my fingers into tight fists. "I don't like this, Zinny. It's too much. I can't smell anything else. No nose, no idea what the fuck's coming …"

A beaded curtain hung at the back of the shop, and I braced as it was drawn back.

A tiny female walked out, and I narrowed my eyes at her, wrestling control of the beast as it fucking leaped forward.

Demon.

She was short as fuck, curves for days, and had wavy blood-red hair that reached her round ass. Her face was humanoid but reminded me of a pixie or one of the fae with that upturned nose and those full pink lips.

She stopped abruptly. Her yellow-green eyes landed on me, and they widened. Her gaze shot to the Devil Dogs MC patch on my leather vest.

"I didn't do anything," she said. "Whatever they told you, I'm innocent." She lifted her hands, backing up like she was ready to bolt. "I didn't do anything. Don't take me away, please … don't …"

"Not here to take you to Hell, demon," I said before she took off, and Zinnia was left empty-handed. "So, slow your roll and take a fucking breath."

She blinked those wide eyes up at me. "You're not?"

"Nope." I subtly sniffed. There was something familiar

in the air, but it was hard to place with all the other scents saturating the room.

"He's just keeping me company," Zinnia said quickly, obviously afraid the little demon would take off as well. "I'm here for a couple of ingredients—that's all."

The demon's alarmed expression changed, and she scowled. "What the fuck is wrong with you, witch? You brought a freaking hellhound into my shop? I almost pissed myself." She turned her scowl on me. "And you should know better." She shook her head. "Hounds, man. Meatheads, the lot of you."

My head jerked back at all that attitude and fire she was throwing at me. "What did you call me, demon?"

"You heard me." She straightened, puffing up like a feisty little gerbil. "Lucifer didn't send you for me. You can't do shit, so save the intimidation bullshit for the next demon you drag to Hell."

"Well, this has gotten off to a great start," Zinnia said.

I ignored her and strode up to the ballsy female, still scowling at me. She tried to step back, but I grabbed her arm, stopping her retreat while she squirmed, trying to pull away. The familiar scent was stronger now that I was closer to her. I dipped lower and scented her.

"What the hell do you think you're doing, mutt?" she yelled and flashed a set of fangs. They didn't look like vampire, not really, but I still couldn't place the demon breed. "Let me go."

There was something else there. The demon blood was strong. She was an immortal—I could smell it on her. So, yeah, definitely demon dominant.

"You're not just demon." I scented her again.

Her fight stopped instantly, and she blinked up at me. "How do you know that?"

"I can smell it." I curled my lips into a smirk. "Can't quite make out what else you are, but looking at you, I'd say a gremlin or maybe a troll."

She shrieked and slammed her knee up, aiming for my nuts, but was too short to get anywhere near them.

Zinnia said something, but I didn't hear her because all my focus was on the squirming demon in front of me.

"Meathead," she muttered again while she tapped her pink-tipped fingers against her thigh, one after the other, over and over again.

I wasn't quite ready to let her go for some reason. "You couldn't handle my meathead, gremlin." I flashed my fangs, enjoying myself.

"So, do you have any white snakeroot?" Zinny asked.

"You do realize that gremlins don't actually exist? They're a myth," the demon said.

She pressed her hand against my chest and shoved. Something sizzled through me, lifting the hair on my arms and on the back of my neck.

"It's pretty cringe that you don't know that," she added.

She shoved again, but I didn't budge. No, I still wasn't ready to back up just yet—I was enjoying myself too much —but I did release her.

I tilted my head to the side. "You have a very smart mouth for someone so small and annoying."

Images filled my mind with all the ways I could occupy that smart, pouty mouth of hers.

"And you have a giant head and ridiculous ... muscles." She flushed. "You look like a deformed Sasquatch."

She thought I was strong. The demon was admiring my muscles. I didn't know why, but I liked that.

"Now, I'm embarrassed for you, *Gremmy*, if we're talking about things that don't exist," I said, teasing her.

Some females liked being teased, and I found I wanted to see those pretty eyes light with pleasure.

"Don't call me Gremmy," she fired at me, her pretty fingers still tapping against the side of her thigh.

"But it suits you"—I flashed her a grin, the one I knew females liked—"Gremmy."

The demon crossed her arms, bristling. Cute.

"Leave," she said, her unusual peridot-colored eyes darting around the room.

"I don't think so."

How was it that I was enjoying this interaction more than the one I'd had two nights ago, in the office of the Hellfire, when a female eagerly sucked my dick?

She looked down, her thick lashes fluttering rapidly, and then she drew in a breath through clenched teeth and looked back up. "I want you to leave, you giant pain in the ass," she fired at me. "I want you to leave my shop now."

I wanted to tweak that upturned nose. "If I were in your ass, Gremmy, I promise it would only hurt for a minute, and then I'd make it feel real good."

She hissed, and my abs clenched. Those little fangs were doing things to me.

"Okay," Zinny said. "If you could just get the ingredients I need, we'll leave. Right, Relic?"

I winked down at the pissed-off demon in front of me. "Sure."

She spun away, and I had to force myself to stay put and not grab her and pull her back or follow her as she rushed down one of the aisles crowded with ingredients.

She snatched something off the end, then strode up to Zinnia and shoved it into her hand. "Now, leave."

Zinnia took money from her pocket. "I need to pay you."

"I don't care, just leave," the demon said.

Zinny dropped a wad of cash on the counter, then grabbed my arm and tried to push me from the store. For some fucked-up reason, I was reluctant to leave, but she was persistent, so I let her have her way.

The sound of the bolt being thrown came as soon as we walked out. The demon stood behind the glass and quickly flipped the Open sign to Closed before she disappeared into the back of her store.

"What the hell was *that*?" Zinnia said when we started walking.

"What?" I was still grinning. No, I hadn't enjoyed myself like that in a very long time.

"You terrified that female, then sexually harassed her," Zinny said.

The fuck? I stopped in my tracks and stared down at her. "No, I didn't. That's not what happened."

"I've never heard you speak to a female that way."

She couldn't be serious?

I glanced back at the shop, then at Zinny. "No ... she wasn't afraid. She was—"

"She was shaking. You're a hellhound, and she's a demon. She was trying to hide it, but she was terrified. I thought she was actually going to cry for a moment."

Nausea slammed into my gut.

"Cry?" My voice was like sandpaper. "No ..." I looked back at the shop. "No," I repeated, not wanting to believe it.

"Yes," she said.

"Fuck." That would not fucking do. No fucking way.

I started back toward the shop, but Zinny grabbed my arm, stopping me.

"What are you doing?"

"I don't make females cry. I don't scare them, and I

31

don't"—the sick feeling in my gut increased—"sexually harass them."

"Going back there now will only make it worse. She wants you gone, and you need to respect that," Zinnia said.

She was serious. I'd known her a long time, and I knew what that looked like. I might be a little more evolved than the hounds that had come before me, but I wasn't that fucking evolved. If Zinnia said I'd scared the little demon, I'd fucking scared her.

"Fuck," I said again and let her tug me back toward my bike.

We parted ways, and I headed for the clubhouse to await Lucifer, but it was the last place I wanted to go. I wanted to head back to that store and demand that the little female hiding inside not be afraid of me. Which made no fucking sense whatsoever.

You need to stay the fuck away.

I should. But I didn't think I could.

CHAPTER
THREE

FERN

Zipping up my sweatshirt, I lifted the hood, checked the coast was clear, slipped out, and locked up behind me. After my run-in with that hound, I didn't want to hang around the store. I hated that he'd scared me so badly, but I hated more that I'd let him.

It didn't help that my fear response was to go on the offensive, no matter how afraid I was. It'd served me well in the past. In my experience, showing fear or weakness to a predator only excited them. When you showed fear, when you cried or cowered, they got off on it, and the pain that followed was even worse.

I yanked on the door to check it was locked—*one, two, three, four* hard yanks. That hound had thrown me off completely because the more shit I'd given him, the more he'd seemed to enjoy it.

I shook my head. I needed to learn when to shut my damn mouth, but it was no use because fear was a trigger. When given the choice of fight or flight, most chose the former. But for most of my life, flight hadn't been an option, so as soon as my fear spiked, it was muscle memory, and I automatically switched into fight mode.

Cursing under my breath at my stupidity, I glanced over my shoulder to make sure I wasn't being followed by the pricks who'd been hanging around or a giant meat-head of a hellhound. Dipping my head, I started along the street.

Fuck. Did I lock the door?

Yes, you locked the fucking door.

But what if I hadn't?

Cursing, I jogged back, gripped the door handle, and yanked it again—*one, two, three, four.* Definitely locked.

I headed back down the street. Agatheena had said she'd have information for me when I went back to her cottage, but it wouldn't hurt to do some research of my own. The more I knew about what I was, the better.

There was only one place I could go that might have the information I needed. It took me twenty minutes to reach my destination, but finally, the massive building loomed up ahead. Back in the 1800s, it'd been known as the Sunnydale Insane Asylum but had been decommissioned in the early 1980s. Nothing about the monstrosity looked like it belonged here. It was as if it'd been transported here from another country and plonked in the middle of the city two hundred years ago.

It was massive, with dark, slick stone walls and arched windows, like a medieval cathedral. Its name implied warmth and light, but this place was the complete opposite.

I walked through the gateway, which opened out to a large garden area out front. Pulling my hood lower, I glanced over my shoulder again and jogged across the lawn. I rushed up the steps and banged on the heavy, wooden double doors.

The chilly wind blew around me, and I rubbed my arms as ice slid down my spine and goose bumps prickled the back of my neck. The feeling that I was being watched sent frozen tendrils through my veins, and I scanned the area around me again.

The door opened, and I turned back as the demon standing there gave me a once-over, then grinned.

"Hey, gorgeous. What's up?"

"Hey, Berkley. How's your sister?"

"Yeah, good, honey. Behaving herself, for now."

I laughed. Berkley came in to my store with her from time to time.

"So, I was hoping I could use the library this afternoon."

"Let me check with Rune. Should be okay though."

Rune, the demon in charge of all of us here in Seventh Circle, had been selected by Lucifer to run things. He was scary as hell, but if you toed the line and followed the rules, he let you be. If he ever found out what I had done with that demon a few nights ago, he wouldn't be happy with me, not at all.

Berkley put his phone to his ear and opened the door wider for me. My boots thudded against the old, stained, and cracked linoleum as I strode in, goose bumps lifting all over my body.

Breathe. You can leave at any time.

I curled my fingers into tight fists. I'd been here several times, but I'd never get used to that goddamn smell. The scent of hospital still lingered, along with a few other unpleasant things that caused a visceral reaction and made every cell in my body fucking contract in terror. Forcing myself to breathe slow and easy, I stood in the cold and stark hall and waited while Berkley muttered down the line.

Finally, he hung up and gave me a chin lift. "You can head on up."

"Awesome, thanks."

I headed along the hall, passing door after door. I didn't know what they used the rooms down here for, but the upper floors had been converted into accommodations for Rune's brethren. They followed orders and were a pretty tight-knit group. Rune had the very top floor to himself. The other floors were used for various things—things I wasn't privy to but had heard rumors.

I rounded the corner and onto the ancient-looking elevator.

Gripping the strap of my bag—and still thankfully managing to keep it together—I hit the button for the fifth floor. The elevator moved slowly, and when the doors finally slid open, I rushed out and down the hall to the library. It wasn't a huge room—not as big as, say, the witches council's library. I'd never been, of course, but I'd heard about it. A lot of our demon texts had been taken from us, mainly by witches, and were locked up out of our reach. I wasn't sure what this room had been used for in the past—maybe an office of some kind. At least it smelled better and the old radiators still worked and kept most of the rooms warm. It had started to rain outside, and surprisingly, it felt kind of cozy in here.

Turning slowly, I tried to decide where to start. We didn't have a system as such, but over the years, someone had taken the time to put the modest collection in some kind of order. Dumping my bag on the table, I ran my finger along the spines.

A slow drip came from the eave outside, and I shivered.

I closed my eyes and tried to breathe as an unwanted memory rushed forward.

Drip. Drip. Drip.

The sound came from a small basin in the corner of my room. I stared at it, focusing on that noise, counting in time with it—up to four, then back again, over and over—while I shivered and my skin burned like it had been set alight. It helped; somehow, the counting helped.

The door opened, and my raw nerve endings had me jolting.

"How are we doing this morning, Essie?"

I couldn't answer; my jaw was clenched too tightly to speak.

The Chemist moved around the bed, staring down at me as he slid on black latex gloves. "The virus has taken hold, I see." He tilted his head to the side. "This one definitely shows promise. I'd like to know how contagious it is. I have high hopes for it. You are eighteen now, Estelle, old enough for what must be done. I've found a suitable demon for you to copulate with so we can test how easily this virus passes via bodily fluids."

I stared up at him in horror.

"Don't look so alarmed. Demons are, after all, filthy, rutting, and base, which is why this form of transmission is best. It's your nature to enjoy such endeavors. I'm sure you'll take pleasure from it." He leaned over me. "I'm sure a whorish creature like you will relish the chance to have a male between your thighs."

My entire body convulsed, rejecting his words. It wasn't the first time he'd called me a filthy whore, of course, and he'd told me this was coming, but I had hoped it was just a threat.

"But before we get to that, Ghoul needs feeding," he said, his eyes sparkling with glee. "He's very hungry, and having you a

37

little weaker during the next phase of my experiment is probably for the best."

No. *The word screamed through my mind as Grady walked in, a smirk on his face.*

The Chemist untied me, and his pet demon—the fucker who had murdered my mother—scooped me up and carried me from the room. I wanted to fight, to kick, and bite, but I was far too weak. He shoved open the basement door, and we descended into darkness. The Chemist flicked on the light, and the red bulb did little to illuminate the room. A snarl came from the corner, and the familiar rattle of chains made everything inside me recoil.

Grady dumped me on the ground as The Chemist took the cattle prod from its place on the wall. Sparks and a cracking sound came from the thing as he tested it. It was the only way to make Ghoul stop. The Chemist nodded, and Grady used his foot to nudge me closer.

Ghoul's chains rattled again before his hand shot out of the darkness. A bony hand grabbed my ankle and dragged me into the shadows. Red eyes flashed, and then sharp, cold fangs sank into my flesh, agony slicing through me as he greedily gulped down my blood.

My jaw unclenched and I opened my mouth and screamed.

"Looking for anything in particular?" A deep voice resonated through the room, startling me from the memory.

I spun around, and Rune stood in the doorway.

He slid his hands into his pockets and tilted his head to the side. "I haven't seen you in a while, Fern." His eyes—a yellow-green, so similar to mine—studied me closely.

I dipped my head. "No, I guess not." My voice came out all trembly—and not just from the memory.

The top few buttons of his dark shirt were undone, revealing his ink and the brands scarring his skin, and power oozed from every single pore, so heavy and thick that just being in his presence had goose bumps breaking out all over me. I needed to pull it together.

If anyone could sniff out bullshit, it was Rune.

"So, what brings you here, little one?" he asked, those eyes penetrating my freaking skull, as if he could see my mind spinning, searching for what to say, how much to reveal.

He wasn't here as only an enforcer; he was here to protect us as well, but showing weakness around him was definitely not a good idea. Lying outright wouldn't work either. Whatever I said now, I had to mix in truth if I wanted to get out of here without any trouble.

"I found out more about my family history. I was hoping something here might give me some insight."

Rune scented the air, then grinned, flashing a set of fangs very much like mine—demon, not vampire. "You're afraid. Why is that?"

My spine straightened without my say-so. "No, I'm not," I said with way more attitude than I should have.

His brow arched. "No?" He stepped closer and scented the air again.

He was the second arrogant goddamn male to do that to me today. My fear spiked, and heat flushed through me as reflexive, uncontrollable, irrational, stupid fucking anger hit me. I choked it down.

"I mean, yes, okay, fine. You scare me. But I assume you scare everyone," I forced myself to admit. Again, it was the truth; I'd just omitted a few of the reasons for my fear.

"There are a lot of females who enjoy my company very

much," he said, that grin still in place. "You don't feel that way though?"

"I don't doubt it's true," I said. "But I'm more in the shit-scared than turned-on camp."

He chuckled, low and, yes, sexy. "Fair enough. Is there anything you'd like to ask me? I know the books in this library well."

"Blood drinkers—do we have a compendium of all the demon breeds?" I asked. Because what the hell? He was one himself. It wasn't like it was against the rules if you did it responsibly, left humans alone, and used one of the drinking clubs.

"Finally figured out those cute little fangs aren't just for show, have you?" he asked, his gaze moving over me.

My face heated again. "Um ... yes."

He studied me, his tongue sliding over one of his own fangs. "Have you fed yet, little one?"

I shook my head, unable to lie to him now, even if I wanted to for some reason, and I was terrified he'd ask me something that would get me into a whole lot of trouble. "No."

"I sense your hunger. Don't leave it too long. I wouldn't want you to lose control and do something you shouldn't."

He reached out like he was about to touch my face, and I flinched. I couldn't help it. He dropped his hand.

"It would be a shame if you let that happen. Take care of it—and soon." He stopped by one of the shelves on the left, slid a book out an inch, and then walked out, shutting the door behind him.

———

RELIC

Lucifer sauntered in, carrying his cat, Mini. He was flanked by two of his handmaids, Ursula and Roxy. Both warriors sauntered in—one carrying an axe, the other a long blade. The king of Hell was well over six feet and covered in tattoos, and if he were human, he would pass for a male in his mid-twenties. He had a twisted sense of humor and liked to fuck with people. He could make a being feel at ease, like you were his best bud, and also fill you with the kind of terror that turned your blood cold. And he, of course, excelled in the art of torture.

Thankfully, we didn't often piss him off.

Jagger clasped hands with the king of Hell, and they exchanged greetings. Warrick would usually be here to greet Lucifer himself, but his mate and her family had received some bad news tonight, and Wills and their baby, Violet, came first—always.

Lucifer handed Mini to Roxy, ran his fingers through his slicked-back hair, and then aimed his yellow eyes at his audience—a roomful of curious hellhounds.

"Brothers," he said, his eyes glinting. He was pissed off —no, he was fucking furious. "I come bearing seriously fucked-up news. You know how I feel about betrayal." He bared his teeth. "It makes me stabby. And before you freak out, it's not Diemos. My son is where I put him, and he's not going anywhere." He cracked his neck. "One of my lords, Faron, has up and fucked off. He didn't ask for permission, and he's not answering my summons."

Menace transformed his features and saturated the room. Unlike us, the lords couldn't be summoned by force, a show of loyalty Lucifer had offered a very long time ago— something I could see he regretted giving now.

"Faron might look fucking stupid and more interested in spending his days being a gluttonous sex pest, but there is more to him. Not much, but enough to make him dangerous. I want him found and his ass dragged back to Hell. This is top priority. His disappearance—his blatant defiance—can mean only one thing. He wants to take what's mine, and he's got a bead on the means to do it. Faron is in this realm, but he's concealed himself. Brothers, I want him found ASAP."

"We'll find them," Jag said.

"I know you will," Lucifer said, then looked at another of our brothers, Lothar. "But right now, I need a fucking drink." He held out his hand. "Hit me."

Loth tossed him a beer as the music was turned up, and Brick, one of our young hounds, rushed to throw open the clubhouse doors, which didn't surprise me. His sire, Dirk, and his mate had several pups, but Brick was our oldest. He was nineteen, and all about fucking and fighting, and there were always females hanging around outside. A group of them sauntered in. There was only one reason they came here, and the group that just walked in was no different. I could smell it.

Lothar strode over and handed me a beer. "You think Faron is really that fucking stupid?"

"Faron doesn't strike me as the kind of demon to attempt a takeover. He's powerful, yes, but weak of character. He's always been lazy and ignorant. He enjoys his comforts and the respect he gets as a lord, but if he's gone, then perhaps I read the male wrong."

Lothar nodded, scratching his beard. "If Lucifer said Asmodeus or that fucking dick Beelzebub were planning a takeover, I wouldn't even question it, but I agree; Faron isn't who I was expecting."

Loth was four hundred years my senior and my sire, but we'd never had the kind of relationship War or Dirk had with their pups.

Roxy headed over. The handmaid was cute and sweet— and fucking deadly.

"Hey, Relic." She gave me a quick hug. Then she turned to Lothar and actually fucking blushed. "Loth, it's been a while." Her smile turned shy.

Lothar frowned down at her. "Rox." His gaze sliced down her body and then back up, and his nostrils flared. "How you doing, sweetheart?"

"Um ... yeah, really good, excited. It's been a while since we've been above ground, you know? Lucifer said he'd take us shopping tomorrow before we go home, and I'd literally slaughter everyone in this room for some In-N-Out Burger, so hopefully, that'll happen as well."

Lothar flashed her a grin, and I didn't know if it was because she was flashing her pearly whites at him and he'd worked out that was what was expected or if he was genuinely feeling it. Like all of us, his emotions were extremely limited, but with War's mate, Willow, determined to help us feel more, things had slowly been changing. I knew they had for me.

Yes, I still had massive holes in my emotional range, and that wouldn't change—couldn't change—until certain things happened. But pleasure—not just the physical—was something I'd been feeling more, and I'd seen it in my brothers more often as well. I guessed it wasn't surprising that pleasure was an easier emotion for us to truly understand since we'd always enjoyed the physical side of it, whether it be fucking or just a simple touch. All I knew was there were a lot more smiles and even laughter around the clubhouse now than there ever had been.

"Yeah? You'd even slaughter me, Rox?" Loth said.

There was a light in Lothar's eyes that made me think that smile had definitely been genuine.

She blushed harder and laughed, a light musical sound. "Fine, maybe not you."

"What about me?" I said because Rox was too fucking sweet for her own good, and we all loved making her blush and squirm whenever we had the chance.

She shook her head. "Oh, no, definitely not you."

"Why definitely not me?"

Her smile grew softer. "Because you're my favorite." She patted me on the chest. "My little Scrappy. My favorite snuggle pup." The look in her eyes could only be described as warm. "You used to curl up in bed with me when you were tiny and shove your furry nose into my neck to sleep." She shook her head. "I'd never hurt my sweet little Relic."

Lothar kind of stilled beside me. We didn't talk about that time. Honestly, I didn't know all the details surrounding my birth, and I had no recollection of my mother. All I knew was that Lucifer had decided to try something new. I was the result, and he decided not to do it again, probably because the handmaids had been the ones to take care of me—at least until I was big enough and strong enough to train—and Lucifer did not like sharing them with anyone.

I looked down at the little handmaid, who had somehow hung on to all that sweetness despite how old she was and what she did for Lucifer, and grinned. "Haven't been called Scrappy in a while, Rox."

She smiled. "You'll always be my Scrappy."

I leaned in. "Don't tell Urs, but you're my favorite as well."

She wrapped her arms around me and gave me a tight

hug; she knew how much hounds craved contact, and she gave me what I needed—affection without expectation.

I planted a kiss on top of her head. "Don't ever change, Rox."

She looked up at me. "Promise."

Then she looked at Loth, and bit her lip. She had a thing for him—had for a really fucking long time—but as far as I could tell, nothing had ever come of it.

"Do you wanna hang out tonight, Loth?" she asked, sounding breathless.

Lothar pulled her from my arms and took his own hug, and I knew it was to cushion his rejection. "Would love to, sweetheart, but I already got plans. You have fun though, yeah?"

He kind of screwed up his face, gave her a quick pat on the back, then walked away. Rox watched him go, her smile slipping when she saw the she-wolf standing just inside the door waiting for him. Loth and Asher, an alpha female from the Silver Claw Pack, were friends. He'd helped her build her bike, and they hung out a lot, but I didn't think it was more than that.

Rox turned back to me when they disappeared through the clubhouse doors. "Did you know Lothar named you?" she said, surprising me.

"He did?"

Lothar had never told me that.

She nodded. "He argued with Lucifer and everything. Said he sired you, that he should get a say." She grinned up at me. "He said he chose Relic because, one day, others would look back on your creation with reverence, that you would be of historical significance as the first hound born, not made."

"I never knew. We don't talk about that time."

Her gaze slid back to the doors he'd walked through. "He used to come and check on you when you were a tiny pup. He'd watch you sleep with this ... look on his face. I'd never seen it on him before, and I've never seen it since." She looked back at me, her smile soft. "And when you got a little bigger, he'd wrestle with you on the floor and bring you meat he'd caught himself. I think he was feeling things he never had before." She chewed her lip. "It was a confusing time for him."

I didn't know what to say. I had no idea. None.

Then Fender was there, our brother grabbing her hand and getting his own hug. She waved to me as she was led away.

I sipped my beer, scanning the room. Lucifer was already surrounded by females while a scowling Ursula stood beside him, Mini in her arms. I lifted a hand, and the handmaid gave me a chin lift.

I should stay. Lucifer was here, and it'd be rude to leave, but the beast was restless—that dominant part of me wasn't enjoying the confines of this room right now. There was this feeling in my chest, so tight and persistent, that I couldn't keep my feet planted to the spot even if I wanted to. So, I left the clubhouse and headed for my bike, the destination cemented firmly in my brain.

This was a mistake. I should stay the fuck away, but the call to go back—the driving need of the beast to seek out that little demon—was far too intense to resist. A hound never ignored their instincts. Ever.

It seemed to take forever to reach Roxburgh, especially with the beast rumbling in my chest the entire way.

Finally, I parked my bike, kicked down the stand, and swung off.

I stared down the street at the closed door to Malicious Brew.

Zinnia would be pissed if she knew I'd come back here, but I couldn't get the witch's words out of my fucking head —that I'd scared the little demon, harassed her, that I'd almost made her cry. That shit did not sit right with me, not at all, but I also didn't want to terrify her even more.

Which meant I was standing in the middle of the street with my dick in my hand like a fucking moron, not sure what to do.

Fucking move.

Growling at myself, I headed down the street toward the store we'd visited earlier that day. It was late on Saturday night, but the bars and clubs were a couple of streets over, which meant this street was dead. She probably wouldn't even be here.

Still, I ran through the list of movies Willow had played for us, desperate for help, for the words that would make what I had done right, but nothing came to me. How did you apologize for terrifying someone—someone who wanted you to keep the fuck away from them—without freaking them out even more?

The door to the store opened ahead of me—

I stopped in my tracks as she walked out, locked the door, popped in earbuds, then started down the street. I was fighting my urge to follow when she stopped, muttered something, walked back to the door, unlocked it, locked it again, tested it with several hard pulls, then turned and marched back the way she'd come. She got no farther than last time when she stopped once more, turned back, and did the whole thing again. Then, finally, apparently satisfied, she strode away, fingers tapping against her thigh as she walked—the same way she had when we were in the store earlier.

I had no idea what that was all about, and I should absolutely turn around and leave, but instead, I couldn't stop myself from following. She was on her own at night in an area swarming with demons. Yes, she was a demon as well, but still, I didn't fucking like it, especially since she couldn't even hear if someone was approaching her.

Scanning her from head to feet, I growled low. She was wearing tight jeans that hugged her round ass and thick thighs and made my mouth water. Her blood-red hair was tied back high on her head, and my fingers twitched to feel those silky strands wrapped around my fist.

I shook my head, trying to shake off the haze of lust pulsing through me. Hounds were always ready to fuck, but I'd never felt like this before—an uncontrollable drive to rut like a fucking animal. Christ, my palms itched with the need to touch. To lift her up, toss her over my shoulder, and take her back to my den with me. To swat that round ass when she wriggled to get away. To tear off those jeans and grip that soft flesh in my hands …

I shook my muddled head again, swallowing hard. Why was my mouth so fucking dry?

She passed two demons leaning against a shop front, and they watched her walk by. One of them grinned and pushed away from the wall, following, and the other chuckled and jogged to catch up.

Nope.

Scooping up an empty soda can from the pavement, I crushed it into a ball and fired it at the grinning demon's head. It found its mark, connecting hard enough to make a dent in the fucker's skull. The demon went down, hitting the ground. His friend spun around, teeth bared. I flashed my fangs and shook my head, and the demon quickly averted his gaze, grabbed his unconscious friend by the arm, and dragged him around the closest corner.

And my little demon saw none of it. She hadn't even looked behind her once. No, her ponytail swished as she walked with a bounce in her step to whatever music she was listening to.

How the fuck had she survived this long? She couldn't be trusted to be left alone.

She turned off the main street and into a motherfucking dark, dank alleyway. I rounded the corner in time to see her jog across the street and then turn another corner.

Her scent hung in the air, and I drew it deep into my lungs, then exhaled on a low rumble. Fuck, I wanted to lick her all over. Would she taste as good as she smelled? I really fucking wanted to find out.

FOUR

FERN

TAKING A DEEP BREATH, I released my tight grip on the rock that Agatheena had given me and dropped it into my pocket—no more contact with my skin, no more protection. Thank the gods, my potion had finally kicked in. There were so many things I had to do tonight that I did not fucking want to do, and I needed all the help I could get. Physically, I knew what I was capable of. I was strong; I could fight, but my mind tried to sabotage me constantly.

After I'd escaped five years ago, after I physically healed and the rage finally burned out, all that was left was fear. So much goddamn fear. I needed that fear that I carried around on my back like a boulder to piss right off, and my potion did that. For a couple of hours at least, there was no anxiety, no intrusive thoughts, no compulsions, and my fear was at a normal fucking level. It wasn't something I could take all the time though, or I'd be pouring that shit down my neck all goddamn day.

Unfortunately, it gave me one hell of a hangover—and

not just a headache. When I'd gotten home from Agath-eena's last week, I'd puked for three hours straight, but it was worth it, and I'd tell myself that when I was hugging the toilet again later tonight and all the things I'd taken the potion to avoid for that short time, came back even worse for hours, sometimes days, afterward.

I subtly glanced over my shoulder. The demons who'd been hanging around the shop most of the day were nowhere in sight. They'd been watching me—I was positive of it. Where had they gone? I only needed one of those breeder scout fuckers. Not only would they be an excellent offering to Agatheena, but it would get one more of those assholes off the streets.

I really hoped Agatheena had some answers for me. What did being a threeling truly mean?

If I showed up empty-handed though, she'd send me away, and I'd get nothing.

The library at the asylum had been no help, there'd been no mention of a threeling or even triplets, not that I could find anyway. There wasn't much about soul collec-tors either. The book Rune had pointed out hadn't really been a demon compendium, but it had contained a basic ritual, and there was mention of a tithe that Lucifer paid when a soul was claimed. Nothing that I'd ever need to know. I was more interested in the blood-drinking side of it, like the dos and don'ts and how often, because the idea of hurting someone that way made me sick to my stomach. There had to be a way to do it that wasn't painful though, right? Or there wouldn't be donors lining up to get bitten at the feeding clubs ... unless they were into pain.

I had no idea. All I knew was my own experience, and being fed on, drained by a starved being in a desperate frenzy, had been the stuff of nightmares.

Cursing under my breath, I stopped beside my truck and pretended my bootlace had come undone. Those pricks had to be here somewhere. They'd been watching me all freaking week. How easy did I have to make it for them to make their move? I had earbuds in, for fuck's sake. I'd made myself appear as vulnerable as possible.

Approach me, assholes. Fuck.

All week, I'd been running from them, hiding with the help of Agatheena's stone, and now, I was out in the open, all but asking them to come get me—and nothing.

Goddammit.

Cursing repeatedly, I straightened and scanned the street again. Those two assholes had completely vanished. Walking around my truck, I got in, started it up, threw her into gear, and headed out.

Agatheena wanted an offering, which left me one choice —I'd have to get one on the way.

Twenty-five minutes later, I was bumping along the forest track I'd driven down the week before. There'd been some rain the last couple of days, and the ruts and dips in the "road" were even worse. A few times, I had to go as fast as hell so I didn't get stuck. I didn't make it as far into the forest as I had last time, but I found a spot that wasn't too boggy and parked.

Grabbing my pack and the charm Agatheena had given me, I locked up and started along the track. Gripping the charm tight, I tried not to jump at the demon shrieks and calls. Yes, I was a demon as well, and I'd doped myself up on courage juice, but some of the breeds in these woods were savage, totally feral—the kind of demons I did not want to fuck with. Even my potion couldn't take away what I considered a healthy dose of fear—you know, like what normal people lived with.

I quickened my pace, walking as quietly as I could. Protection or not, I didn't want to risk bringing any of them closer—not yet anyway.

I didn't stop until I'd trekked almost all the way to the cottage. If I didn't have to drag dead weight the entire way, I sure as hell wasn't going to. The sound of demons still echoed through the trees, but they were more distant now —and something I'd been counting on. Agatheena's wards were unbreakable, and any demon who had good instincts would stay the fuck away, but those capable of more critical thinking would use the area surrounding the cottage to their advantage—that was, avoiding the ferals.

I ran my thumb over the smooth charm. It was warm from being held, and I was positive I felt a vibration of some kind coming from it. If I were a true witch, I'd feel the magic inside it; I'd feel its power. Those kinds of thoughts used to hurt. I'd felt like a failure the majority of my life, until I got tired of trying, until I got sick of the self-pity and embraced my demon nature instead, but after seeing Agatheena and hearing the things she'd said, those thoughts had been creeping back in all week.

Gritting my teeth, I shoved them back down. I didn't have time for self-pity right now.

Slipping the charm she'd given me in my pocket, I pulled my blowgun from my pack and loaded it. I might not have magic or powers of any kind, but I could brew a good tonic or elixir, and my poisons and sedatives were second to none. I also had excellent fucking aim.

It didn't take long before I heard something moving through the undergrowth. The demon coming sounded large and heavy-footed. I screwed up my face, smelling the creep before I saw him. He smelled like he'd puked up horse shit.

He finally strolled out. I'd been expecting some ugly, deformed bastard. Instead, I was confronted by a male who could absolutely pass as human, and whatever that smell was, it was all over his clothes. I hid my blowgun behind my back.

"What's a pretty little thing like you doing out here, all on your own?" he said, tilting his head to the side.

I kept my breathing even and hoped he couldn't hear my heart racing, though thanks to my potion, it wasn't from fear as much as adrenaline. "I could ask you the same thing."

"Why, thank you." He batted his lashes and chuckled, then shrugged. "I like to hunt every once in a while."

"Right. Yeah, same here," I lied—well, kind of. That was exactly what I'd planned to do tonight. "Just FYI, that shit all over you smells seriously rank. You might want to wash it off before you head back to the city." In other words, *fuck off and leave me to do my thing*.

This guy wasn't the right offering. Taking out another male with sanctuary would be a really bad idea.

"But I'm not finished getting dirty." His gaze moved over me in a way I did not fucking like.

This male was trouble, and I doubted he was alone. He probably had buddies not far behind him.

"Well, I'll leave you to it then. I have somewhere I need to be."

He took a step closer and shook his head. "I'm sorry, sugar, but you have to know that everything in this forest is fair game."

I fucking hated pricks like him. Twisted bullies, and he obviously didn't give a fuck about the rules. "You think you can catch me?"

He grinned. "Oh, I know I can."

"And what happens when you do?" I asked, my adrenaline spiking higher.

"Well, that's for you to find out." Hateful lust glinted in his eyes.

He'd hurt me, and he'd enjoy it.

He took another step closer—

I whipped out my blowgun from behind me, pressed it to my lips, and fired.

My dart hit him right between the eyes. He stopped in his tracks, blinked at me several times, and then reached up, pulling the dart out of his skin. "The fuck—"

He went down hard, hitting the ground with a thud.

Quickly pulling my charm from my pocket, I searched my surroundings again, listening, watching. Nothing.

I couldn't hold the charm and drag the massive stinker on the ground, but Agatheena said the charm needed contact with skin, so I shoved it into my bra. Then I took a rope from my pack and hog-tied him. I'd dosed him good, but the male was big, so I needed to get moving.

Gritting my teeth, I dragged the demon behind me, and thanks to my excellent forethought, it was only a short hike to Agatheena's cottage. As soon as I reached the pathway, I sliced my finger and pressed it to the marking on the tree to let her know I was there.

The door to the cottage opened a few minutes later, and she shuffled out. You didn't need to be a witch to feel the buzz of power this close to her wards, and they didn't drop as she made her way toward me. Dolores flew out and landed on her shoulder, its black eyes on me as she got closer.

"I brought your offering," I said when she finally reached me.

Her eyes narrowed on the demon at my feet. "Toss me the rope."

"Did you find anything out? I was hoping—"

"Toss me the rope, child," she said again, more sharply.

I did as she'd said, right as the demon gasped in a breath, then slammed himself into the back of my legs, knocking me down. I spun around, diving on top of him, then pulling another dart from my pack, I stabbed it into his thigh. He shrieked, then collapsed back into unconsciousness.

Pushing away from him, I stood, shoving my hair off my face. "So, did you find anything out about this threeling thing—"

"I have no information for you yet. Come back next week, and don't forget your offering," she said.

Then, she tugged on the rope, and like the demon weighed nothing, his unconscious body shot across the ground and through the wards, and she dragged him down the path.

I stared after her, stunned.

She had nothing?

She was Agatheena Burnside, one of the most powerful witches in this city—if not the most powerful. And she had nothing at all for me?

My fingers curled into fists. Was this all some elaborate load of crap so I'd bring her demons to harvest? I wouldn't put it past the old witch. She was my blood, but she felt no loyalty to me. I doubted she felt loyalty to anyone.

Brushing the dirt off my jeans, I cursed under my breath. I had no choice but to head back to my truck.

I needed answers. Maybe Agatheena was full of crap or using me for a steady supply of demon organs, or maybe it was hard for even her to find the information I needed, but in the meantime, demons *were* watching me, and the awful, dark feeling I kept getting—that monsters were coming for me—was real. It was so real.

I hugged myself against the chill and walked faster. The forest was creepy as fuck at night. My potion was starting to wear off, and charm or not, I just wanted to get back to my truck and get out of there.

I was over halfway to the truck when I heard something walking toward me. The trees rustled to my left, then my right. Dread shot through me so hard and fast that my nerve endings spiked as three demons stepped out of the trees. They were big and ugly and smelled worse than whatever Agatheena's new friend had all over him. The one in the front grinned, flashing slimy, pointed green teeth, while the one beside him sniffed the air.

"She's unmated." He sniffed again. "And she'll be in season soon."

"I've been looking for another breeder," another said. "I'll take her."

"I saw her first," the third one said.

My hand flew to my chest. The charm was gone.

It must've fallen out back at the cottage when that demon knocked me down.

Fuck. I was in serious trouble.

Yanking my blowgun from my pocket, I loaded it with a dart. I couldn't take them all down at once. Maybe two if I was quick enough, but that would still leave me with the third to deal with. My only option was outrunning him, but a chase like that through this forest would only draw more demons.

One of them charged me. With force, I blew air through the blowgun. The dart got him in the throat. He took two more steps and went down with a ground-shaking thud.

The other two roared, then ran at me as well. The closest demon reached out, claws about to swipe across my face—and then he was gone. Something huge and black tore the demon to shreds with only a couple of swipes of its massive claws.

What the hell was that? A wolf?

The second demon tried to run, but the beast jumped on him and wrapped its huge maw around the male's head. Its vicious fangs crunched through the demon's skull before its head was torn completely off, leaving only a bloody stump.

The beast spat out the head, and the moment it did, the demon's remains turned to ash.

Then, the beast turned to me.

Holy fuck.

Its eyes glowed red, and ash coated its mouth. No, not a feral wolf—or any kind of wolf. Running from this beast would be pointless.

"Easy," I said softly, lifting my hands. "I'm no threat. I'm not—"

The beast contorted. No, not a beast, a dog ... on steroids.

A hound.

A fucking hellhound.

He shifted suddenly, transforming into the big, arrogant male who'd been in my store. He stood tall and imposing—and completely naked. His hair was down and wild around his face. His wide, tattooed chest was covered in demon ash, and a decent dusting of hair trailed *all the way down*. His thighs were braced apart and bulged, and his abs—which looked like thick ropes slung across his stomach—were clenched tight.

He said nothing; he just strode to one of the trees,

snatched up a pair of jeans, pulled them on, and then advanced on me.

I backed up. "What are you doing?"

He growled, as if the beast was still there and actual words eluded him.

"Stay back."

He ignored me, and when I turned to run, he hooked me around the waist, hauled me off my feet, and flung me over his shoulder.

"Let me the hell go," I yelled.

I tried to wriggle out of his hold while my heart exploded in my chest, and fear choked me so tightly that I struggled to drag in the next breath. I fought harder, but it was pointless. He had me pinned down with one tree trunk-sized arm.

"Where are you taking me?"

"You've been a very bad demon," he said, his voice vibrating through my body, all the way to my bones.

"I've done nothing wrong. You said I wasn't in trouble when you came into my store," I rushed out.

"That was before," he bit out. "This is now."

"What the fuck are you talking about, Sasquatch?" I snapped, then quickly slammed my mouth shut.

The potion had worn off, and I was scared out of my mind, which meant going on the defensive. Even though pissing off a hellhound was just plain idiotic.

"What I'm talking about, Gremmy, is you kidnapping a demon—a demon with sanctuary—and delivering him to the crone to harvest for parts. That's not allowed, or have you forgotten the rules?"

Shit. He knew.

"It was self-defense."

"If he threatened you? I'd get it. But you dropped him

before he laid a hand on you. Can't scent any blood on you, except for that tiny slice on your finger, which means you took him down before he could touch you, and instead of walking away when he was out cold, you dragged his unconscious ass to Agatheena."

"How do you know he had sanctuary?" I fired at him, grasping on to anything that could get me out of this.

His other hand lifted. He was holding a wallet. "He dropped this when you were dragging him to his death. He has sanctuary ID from the knights of Hell, like you do, along with everyone else living in Seventh."

I was screwed. If he decided to enforce the rules, I was on my way to Hell. "Why didn't you stop me then? You're just as bad as me."

A rough sound rumbled from him. "I found the wallet first and tracked you to the cottage just as Agatheena took him, but thank you for confirming what I suspected."

Goddammit. "What are you going to do?"

"Lucifer's in town, at our clubhouse. I could carry you out of this forest and take you straight to him." He sounded angry again.

"You'd like that, wouldn't you?" I bit out.

If I came face-to-face with Lucifer, I'd piss myself, then blackout.

"I don't relish the idea of taking you to a place where you'll suffer horrifically because you freaked out and chose your victim unwisely."

The prick was far too perceptive.

He put me down suddenly, and I shoved my hand in my bag and pulled out the pepper spray I always carried, aiming it at his face. He'd be on me again in a heartbeat by the time I grabbed out my blowgun and loaded it.

"Okay, back the fuck up, or I'll blind you, you fucking psycho."

"You sure that's the way you want to play this?" he rumbled.

No, I was not, but I was all out of options.

CHAPTER
FIVE

RELIC

MOTHERFUCKER.

I'd followed her out here, and now I had a real reason to haul the little demon to Hell. Demons killing demons? That shit happened all the time—of course it did. But a demon selling their own kind to a witch—I assumed for her own gain, especially a demon with sanctuary? Not fucking okay.

The last thing I wanted to do was take her to Hell. She was too small and weak, and that smart mouth of hers would get her into all kinds of trouble—the kind that would make her scream in agony. I didn't like the thought of that. Not at all.

"Fuck," I growled, and she startled. I didn't like that either.

She waved her pepper spray around like that could protect her from me if I meant to cause her harm. That shit wouldn't work on me, but I wasn't going to tell her that if it made her feel safer to hold it. Despite the real threat I posed to her right then, I didn't want her afraid of me.

"I went to your store earlier to apologize for scaring you. Then, you came out of your shop, and I—"

"You followed me?" She lifted her can of pepper spray higher. "You're a fucking stalker. And you don't know what you're talking about. That demon had every intention of hurting me. It was absolutely self-defense."

I didn't doubt her. I believed one hundred percent that she'd defended herself. When it'd stopped being self-defense was when she trussed him up and delivered him to Agatheena.

I shoved my fingers through my hair and did my best to get some control over my anger. Because I was fucking pissed that not only had she put herself in this fucked situation, but me as well. The idea of taking her to Hell made me feel physically ill.

"Don't know if you know this about hounds, Gremmy, but we're extremely protective of females." The urge to explain myself was impossible to choke back down. For some reason, I didn't want this little demon thinking I was a fucking stalker. "I didn't like what happened when I was in your store, though to tell the truth, I had no idea I'd scared you." I flexed my fingers; my palms itched to snatch her up again. "I thought you were enjoying it until my friend corrected me."

Her eyes widened. "You thought I was enjoying it?"

Zinnia had been right; the only one of us who'd enjoyed our sparring was me.

"Hounds aren't the best at reading emotions." Why was I telling her any of this? I had no idea, only that I didn't want her to think I was some fucking creep. "I was coming to say sorry, and then I saw you walking down a dark street on your own, and my protective side kicked in."

She was shaking. It could be anger. I hoped it was. It

could also be fear. What did I know? I'd gotten it completely fucking wrong last time.

"I don't need your protection. I've been looking after myself my whole damn life, and I've done just fine."

"So, you clocked the two demons following you then?"

Her chin jerked back.

"I'll take that as a no."

Her cheeks darkened. "I didn't see any demons."

"Because I strongly encouraged them to fuck off."

The pepper spray lowered a little. "Are all hellhounds egomaniacs?"

"We don't have an ego. We know what we're good at— it's just a fact. We don't need to prove shit."

"And what exactly are you good at? Because you're a terrible conversationalist, and you didn't need to tell me that you're bad at reading people because it's obvious. Like, right now, I'm giving off a whole lot of *get the fuck out of my face*, and you're missing it completely."

No, I hadn't missed it, not with all the attitude she was giving me. I saw that as clear as day. But then, I'd thought that was all it was last time, and I'd been fucking wrong.

"Hounds are unmatched when it comes to tracking, fighting, and fucking. You want me to demonstrate any of those things, just say the word." I snapped my mouth shut. Fuck. I hadn't meant to say *fucking*, but she had me saying all kinds of shit I shouldn't.

Her cheeks darkened even more, and her eyes flashed from yellow-green to red. "I'll pass on all three, thanks." She took a step back. "Now, I'm going to walk away, and you're going to go in the opposite direction and leave me alone."

The wind shifted, carrying her scent right to me. There was anger, but the bitter scent of fear was fucking strong.

I slid my hands in my pockets, trying to look as unthreatening as possible, and shook my head. "You think I should just let you go? That the rules don't apply to you?"

Her lips parted, giving me a little flash of those sharp, tiny fangs, her breathing coming faster. "You owe me—you said it yourself."

"An apology for scaring you, not letting you off for harvesting demon organs for profit."

"That's not what that was. No money changed hands."

"No? But you get something out of it, right?"

Her gaze darted around, as if she was searching for help. "I wasn't breaking Lucifer's rules because they don't apply to me."

"You're special, are you?" I should just let her go because there was no way I was taking her to Lucifer or Hell —I couldn't bring myself to fucking do it—but I wasn't ready for her to leave yet either.

"I'm not just a demon. I have witch blood."

More lies. I'd thought I scented something else on her when I was in her store, but my scent had been off with all the herbs and other shit in that place fucking with me.

"You live in Seventh Circle."

"Are there *rules* that say I can't?"

I leaned in, scenting her again.

"Stop fucking sniffing me," she bit out.

Like last time, I thought I had caught something else, but I wasn't getting witch. Maybe because it was so heavily diluted? I veered more toward her lying through her teeth. Everyone knew our alpha's mate was a witch and she obviously thought saying she was as well would save her ass.

I crossed my arms. "What's the name of your coven?"

She bristled. "I don't have one."

"You're gonna need to talk, Gremmy, so I can help you."

If she had witch blood, it was definitely fuck all. The female was demon through and through.

She crossed her arms as well. "Don't fucking call me that, and FYI, my coven didn't want me." Her eyes flashed red. "For obvious reasons."

Nah, I wasn't buying it.

"I still need the coven's name."

"I'm not giving you that information."

She was afraid—seriously afraid now; the scent of it grew stronger. She was terrified and lying through her teeth to save her ass, and I was going to let her get away with it.

"Then, give me your name."

Her jaw tightened. "Fern."

"Fern what?"

"Honeycutt."

Her peridot stare held mine, silently begging me to let her go.

"Okay then, Fern Honeycutt, if you say you have witch blood, then I guess I have to believe you." I didn't, not at all, but I couldn't stomach the alternative.

Her shoulders lowered, and she blew out a breath. "I-I appreciate your ... understanding."

A weird feeling curled inside me. I blew out a long breath as well, and something like pleasure moved through me, but it was ... different. My muscles, which had been tight as fuck, relaxed.

"What are you feeling right now?" I asked her. I thought I knew, but I didn't trust myself since I'd kept getting it so wrong with her. I needed her to spell it out.

She blinked over at me. "What?"

"Tell me the emotion you're feeling."

"You want to know what I'm feeling?"

I nodded. "You blew out a breath; your muscles relaxed."

"You really have no fucking clue, do you?"

"Tell me," I said, my voice so damn rough.

She released another long breath. "Fine. Relief. What I'm feeling is obviously relief. I'm not being dragged to Hell in the jaws of an arrogant hellhound."

That was what I'd assumed, but relief wasn't something I'd ever felt before—or maybe I had and not really thought about it—but I knew what the definition of relief was. What I didn't know was why I cared that she wasn't scared anymore or why I gave a shit whether this little female went to Hell or not. No, I didn't like the idea of her being hurt, but why I reacted this strongly was fucking confusing.

"You're still a demon, witch blood or not—those eyes give you away, Gremmy. Demon rules apply, which means I'll be watching you."

Her eyes flashed, her spine straightening. "Are we done?"

"We're done," I said. "For now."

"So fucking arrogant," she muttered.

"You're welcome."

Fern spun around and stormed off, and I followed.

She looked over her shoulder, and those pretty eyes flashed again. "Stop following me."

"Not following you, Fern, just going the same way you are." I was definitely following her. If I left her now, the demons would be all over her in fucking minutes.

She growled.

I chuckled. The sound was cute. I was very much going to enjoy keeping an eye on Fern Honeycutt.

———

I wiped grease off my hands, and the human female smiled up at me when I handed over the keys to her car that I'd just serviced.

"All yours."

My brothers and I all took turns doing shifts here at the garage and at the bar next to it. To stay above ground, we needed the humans to see us as legit.

Her gaze slid down my front and lingered on my dick. She quickly looked up, cheeks pink. I could smell her pussy. She was wet.

"So, um, I was wondering if you were free tonight."

The female was nice to look at. Not enough meat on her bones for my liking, but that had never stopped me before. Usually, I'd take her up on her offer, but I wasn't feeling it. I hadn't been feeling it all week. Instead of partying at the clubhouse, I'd been hanging around Seventh like the stalker Fern had accused me of being.

"Thanks for the offer, but I'm busy."

She moved closer, licking her lips. "What about tomorrow? I promise, I'll make it worth your while."

The only thing she'd be able to do was give me a hand job or maybe suck my dick if she was really committed. Not many humans could handle a male my size. Yes, there were some who could manage it. But hounds were hung—we were just made that way—and not just anyone could take us, no matter how determined they were. We were used to it, and yeah, sometimes, I just wanted to fuck, but unless we took another shifter to our beds, since they were built a little differently, more times than not, my brothers and I were shit out of luck.

An image of Fern's ass in those tight jeans filled my head, and a growl slipped out. The human took a step back, and I quickly grinned and winked as if I'd done it on purpose. She giggled nervously.

"Sorry, but I gotta work. Thanks for the offer though, yeah? Drive safe," I said, dismissing her, and walked out of the garage.

"Are you coming down with something?" Warrick said, just outside the roller doors.

I hadn't even seen him walk over. "Nope. Why?" Brick was with him, carrying Vi's unicorn baby bag. He'd obviously done something to piss War off.

Baby Violet was against War's shoulder, and he was gently patting his tiny daughter's back while she fussed. My alpha shrugged. "She seemed like your type, brother."

"What can I say, War? I'm six hundred years old. Random pussy doesn't hold the same appeal as it used to."

He gave me a look that felt like he was trying to invade my brain.

"Shit, I'll take her number," Brick said, a shit-eating grin on his face.

War gave Brick a hard stare, and the pup snapped his mouth shut and quickly looked down. Oh yeah, he'd definitely pissed off our alpha.

Violet gave me a toothless grin, and I brushed my hand over her soft, peach-colored hair. She made a gurgling sound, and protectiveness filled my chest. "That's right; tell your favorite uncle all about it."

War snorted. "I think you might be, you know. Whatever you do, don't tell Rome. He thinks it's him."

Roman was a brutal fighter, a skilled tattoo artist, and like the rest of us, the hound would lay down his life for Vi and Willow, in a heartbeat. My lips curled up. "I knew it." I didn't see the need to fill War in on the little demon currently driving me crazy, but he still might be able to help me another way. "So I need to talk to someone at the witches council. Any suggestions?" I asked him.

"Nathan Trotman. He's a good man. Definitely your best bet. Why? What's going on?"

"Just a demon I've been keeping an eye on. Told me her mother was a witch, not sure I'm buying it."

"She causing trouble?"

"Nothing I can't handle."

Warrick trusted our judgment, but I wasn't sure how he'd feel about me protecting this female after what she'd done, so that was as much information as I was willing to share right then.

"So if she has witch blood, whose responsibility is she?" Brick asked. "The hounds or the witches council?"

"That's where the lines can get blurred. If she's telling the truth, and she's causing serious trouble, it could involve a meet with a council member," War said.

I was the one who'd let the demon go, which meant she was my responsibility as far as I was concerned.

"Let me know if you need anything else," War said, then he motioned to the clubhouse. "It's Vi's nap time." He strode off, then barked Brick's name when the pup didn't follow immediately.

Cursing under his breath, he rushed after Warrick.

I chuckled. The pup had a lot to learn; luckily, he had brothers to set him on the right path, whether he liked it or not.

Pulling out my phone, I called the witches council and spoke to Trotman.

There was no record of a Fern Honeycutt, not in any of the coven records.

Of course she'd lied. I'd hoped like fuck she was telling the truth. If the little demon pulled that shit again, she might not be so lucky. One of my brothers might not be as forgiving as me.

What the fuck was Fern up to? She was reckless and fucking fearless, except when it came to me. I seemed to scare her, no matter what I did or said. She acted tough and threw attitude, and that confused me when the unmistakable scent of fear was there underneath it all.

Getting on my bike, I started it up and took off. Why I was going back to Seventh Circle, I didn't fucking know, only that there was this pull, and I just I had to.

Whatever she was doing, she was afraid and vulnerable and desperate enough to seek out Agatheena for help and take down a demon twice her size in that forest to get it.

I hit Seventh a short time later. The street Fern's store was on was busy during the day, but a fucking ghost town at night. She lived above her store—I knew that because after she closed up, the light would come on upstairs, and last night, I'd seen her from my spot across the street through the window when she shut her curtains.

I stood in the same spot now, under the eave of an empty store, and shoved my hands in my pockets. I'd just wait until she was asleep, and then I'd go over there and guard her door. With the shit she'd pulled, she was a sitting target, and I still felt guilty for scaring her. That was why I was doing this. That was why my protective instincts were off the fucking charts.

I could see her now through the window, moving around the store, serving customers, and doing whatever else it was she did in there during the day.

It eventually grew dark, and I stepped back into the shadows when she locked the door and flicked the Open sign to Closed. A short time later, the light came on upstairs, and I could see her moving about up there. She'd pulled the curtains, but they weren't very thick, and her shadow drifted by every now and then. It grew later, and finally, her light went off ... then it came back on. It flicked on and off three more times. What the fuck?

Then the room went dark, and it stayed dark. I waited a few minutes. I was about to cross the street and stand in front of her door—just so anyone thinking of coming for her saw that she was protected—when it opened, and she walked out, gave the door four hard tugs, then headed off down the street at a fast clip.

She had on spiked boots, and instead of tight blue jeans, these ones were black, and she wore a short black leather jacket, zipped up.

Where the fuck are you going, Tinker Bell?

Pushing away from the wall, I trailed after her. If she was going back to that forest, if she was thinking about taking out another demon for Agatheena, she was fucking mistaken.

Fern darted down the same alleyway she had the last time I followed her, and I growled under my breath as I rushed after her through the alleyway and out the other side.

I didn't spot her right away, and then I saw her, somehow sprinting at full speed in those fucking boots. She'd made me.

Fuck.

If I didn't set her straight now about what I was doing, she'd think I was stalking her again. I took off after her. It wasn't hard to catch her. Not only was I fast, but her strides were tiny compared to mine. The sound of my boots echoed off the storefronts as I closed in on her.

She spun on me suddenly, her hand flying up. She was holding a blowgun, and she lifted it to her lips and fired. I dodged the dart, forced to veer around her, so I didn't run the fuck right over the top of her.

"You cannot be serious," she said through gritted teeth as she reloaded the blowgun. "What the hell is your problem?"

I lifted my hands and took a step back. "You're not in danger from me." I curled my lips in an attempt to defuse the situation. I'd never felt more fucking confused and out of my depth than I did with this female.

Her eyes widened. "You followed me—again—and then chased me down the fucking street," she said, panting. "What else am I going to think?"

"It's not like that."

"You're a fucking *stalker*," she fired at me.

I bit back my growl. "There's nothing about you in the records at the witches council, Fern."

She froze, blinking those wide, peridot eyes at me. "You had someone look into me?"

"That's my job, and so is keeping an eye on bad, murderous little demons who lie about what they are."

She backed up, and I stepped forward, like there was a tether connecting us, and I had no other choice but to follow.

"What the hell are you doing?"

I didn't know. All I knew was I had to go with this feeling—there was no other choice. "No, Fern, what the hell are you doing?"

The attitude dropped, just for a moment, and she looked up at me with an expression I had no hope of reading.

"I promise you don't need to do this. I-I'll stay away from demons with sanctuary. The other night in the forest, that asshole, he scared me. I needed an offering for Agatheena. I was running out of time, and I-I panicked, okay? That's the truth."

"Running out of time for what?"

She shook her head. "I'm not telling you that."

"Why?" I wanted to know everything there was to know about this female. Everything.

"Because it's none of your business. I'm none of your business." She chewed her lip. "Unless, of course, you plan on sentencing me to Hell. But you're not going to do that, are you?"

There was no use in lying. I shook my head. "I told you I wouldn't if you behaved."

She blew out a breath, and her shoulders slumped, like they had in the forest. She was feeling relief again. "All right, good. And you'll stop following me?"

"I'm not demon, and I'm not human. I am beast. The beast's instincts are second to none, and that part of me insists I go where you do. I don't know why, but I listen to my instincts. I also don't like that I scared you. To tell you the truth, I fucking hate it."

Her eyes flashed red, and she gritted her teeth. "You're being unreasonable. You're just looking for an excuse to punish me. You're getting off on this shit."

I shook my head. That smart mouth—she couldn't fucking help herself. What she'd done was wrong, yes, and I could tell myself I was only here because I wanted to make sure she wasn't breaking any more rules, but the truth was something else.

"You keep doing dangerous shit, Fern. So, I'm going to make sure you don't do anything else you're not supposed to, and I'm also going to make sure you don't get yourself killed."

She huffed out a breath. "You're not only arrogant, but

you're insane too. I don't need a minder. I can take care of myself."

I shrugged. "You don't have to like it; that's just how it is."

Her hands trembled at her sides. She was scared now. I didn't want that. What could I do to ease her fears? All I could do was show her how strong I was, how I could keep her safe. Eventually, she'd realize I would never hurt her, that the idea of it—of anyone hurting her—made the beast snarl and hunger for blood.

"Fine, whatever," she snapped. "Trail after me like a sad fucking lapdog all night if you want, but stay out of my damn way." Then, she spun on a pointed heel and strutted off down the street.

I growled in approval; the sound vibrating in my chest.

No, I wasn't letting her out of my sight.

CHAPTER
SIX

FERN

SHIT. Shit. *Shit.*

I glanced over my shoulder as I walked into The Bank, a popular nightclub, especially among shifters and witches, and true to his word, the hound was right on my tail. I shivered. The male fucking terrified me, and telling my giant hellhound stalker to get lost to his face had not been very clever on my part. Not that I had personal experience with stalkers, but it was common sense. Under any normal circumstance, pissing off anyone bigger, stronger, with more power than you would be dumb, but a hellhound? Then, bruising his giant ego had been just plain fucking stupid. I'd known this—of course, I had—but my self-preservation responses were seriously fucked up and deeply ingrained, and no matter how hard I'd tried, I couldn't get it under control, not without my potion anyway.

I didn't want to encourage him either though, so what were my choices here? He'd looked down at me like I was a snack that he had a serious craving for, and I refused to be that male's next meal.

Maybe I could lose him?

He knows where you live.

He'd checked up on me at the witches council or had someone do it for him. I hadn't expected him to do that for some stupid reason. He didn't have my real name, so no, there wouldn't be any record, but then, even if he had, I doubted anything about me was there. My family, my coven, would have wiped all traces of me from public record.

I glanced back. The hound was still there watching me. What the hell was I going to do? Agatheena said I was powerful—pity I couldn't harness all that power right now because I could seriously use it.

Searching the room, I looked for somewhere to hide, and spotted the door to The Vault on the other side of the club—the real reason I'd come here tonight. My belly swooshed. The Vault was a private club below this one that catered to blood drinkers and live donors who willingly offered up a vein. I'd never been there, but after what Rune had said about feeding, I couldn't think of anything else. I sure as hell didn't want to hurt anyone, and I knew first-hand the damage that could be done when a blood drinker was starved and out of control.

All my life, I'd resisted the gnawing hunger for blood, positive there was something seriously wrong with me. I never wanted to be like Ghoul, who'd hurt me so many times, but there was no denying it now. My father's breed were blood drinkers. And so was I. It was horrifying and confusing, but I also felt like a weight had been lifted, one I'd been carrying around for far too long. I craved blood because of who I was, because I needed it. I'd been anemic my whole life; I'd had bouts of extreme weakness and chronic tiredness and never known why. Now, I knew no amount of herbs or tonics or elixirs would make it better. What I needed was blood, and I assumed the only reason I'd survived this long without feeding was because of the small amount of witch and other demon DNA I had diluting it.

Tonight, I'd planned to finally give in to the unshakable need inside me. My mouth actually watered at the thought, while my stomach twisted with self-loathing. My pulse sped up, the anticipation making me shake, and I felt sick to my stomach at the same time. I wished I didn't need this, but I did, and I'd never forgive myself if I hurt someone because I'd ignored my hunger.

I knew what that looked like, what it felt like.

When I glanced over my shoulder again, my eyes were instantly drawn to a pair of golden ones, almost freaking glowing from across the room. But even if he didn't have those beast's eyes, it wouldn't exactly be hard to find him; he stood a head taller than everyone else in the club. I quickly looked away. I'd finally gotten rid of the breeder scouts hanging around my place—the last week at least—and now, I had the hound to deal with.

Screw this. I didn't care what he thought of me, and with any luck, knowing I needed blood would put him off.

Lifting my chin, I rushed across the room, through the heavy crowd, and over to the big male guarding the entrance to The Vault.

He took me in from head to toe. "You here as a donor or to feed?"

I shook my head. "I'm here to … to feed."

"Never seen you here before, honey. You got your membership card?"

With shaky hands, I opened my bag and pulled out two thousand dollars cash—the amount required for a visitor's admittance and almost all my savings. "I'm here to check the place out for possible membership."

I didn't need to turn around to know the hound was close; I felt his eyes burning into me like laser beams. The big male guarding the door took my money, counted it, and then handed me a black card with Guest scrawled on it in gold lettering.

"No need to be nervous, honey," he said with a smirk. "They'll be lining up to offer you a vein." He licked his lips. "I finish here in thirty; if you wanna wait, you can sink those pretty little fangs into me."

Without my say-so, I was drawn to the fat, pulsing vein in his thick neck, and I swallowed audibly.

A growl rolled over me from behind. My stalker. The fear and nerves, already rioting inside me, shot through the roof. Still, I refused to look back. The guy in front of me darted a glance over my shoulder though, and instantly, he dropped his gaze when he saw who'd made the sound.

My heart sank. Everyone was afraid of the hellhound, which meant there was literally no one who could help me. I was on my own—nothing new, I guessed, but I had no idea what to do. How to make it stop. If the male decided to do more than just follow me around, there wasn't anything I could do and no one I could turn to. The unsettling thought had my pulse racing wildly, followed quickly by a familiar helplessness. I shoved it down fast. I wasn't that same terrified little girl—in pain all the time, achingly lonely, and utterly broken—and I would not let him fuck up the life I'd risked everything for.

"Ignore him," I said to the male in front of me, and I was

pleased when the tremor vibrating through me only made my voice shake a little bit. "I'd like to go in now."

He nodded, his eyes still averted as he opened the door.

Unless the hound had two grand in his back pocket, the asshole was shit out of luck and would be forced to wait out here.

The door closed behind me, and I quickly took the stairs down to the lower level and over to the huge, round steel door at the bottom. This whole building had been a bank in a previous life, and this was the original door to its vault— or so I'd been told. I glanced back up the stairs. No hound. I felt a small amount of relief until I turned back to the door and remembered what I was about to do. Grabbing the steel bars, I turned them and pulled it open.

I was instantly hit with sounds—voices, music, a low and throbbing beat that pulsed through me. The scent of blood and sex hit me at the same time, and my legs started to shake as a buzz of excitement filled me, and my hunger grew.

I didn't want to stare, but there was a lot going on. A female on a couch, writhing in ecstasy, while a male drank greedily from between her thighs. There were donors strad-dling blood drinkers, grinding while they were fed from— more than one couple straight-up fucking. I swallowed thickly. I wanted to feed, yes, and, horrifyingly, the idea of it kind of turned me on, but I didn't want to fuck some random asshole. Right now, I was more nervous than anything else.

The throb between my thighs intensified, and I squeezed them together to stop it. I didn't want it. This was about the feeding, that's all.

Or maybe you're just a twisted whore, like they said you were.

I shoved the voice out of my head.

No, I could do this. I needed to do this.

But what if I hated the taste? What if I hated everything about it? It could happen, right? I wasn't a full soul collector. I had no idea what to expect.

I turned away from a bloody threesome and realized a lot of eyes were on me. Not the vampires or other blood drinkers. The donors. They saw it; somehow, they saw what I was when it had taken me most of my life to learn the truth, and I still hadn't figured it out for myself.

A younger male, who looked to be around my age, broke away from a small group and walked toward me. He kept his gaze down—trying to be respectful, I assumed—but I didn't miss the way he trembled slightly. As he drew closer, my senses narrowed in on the rapid thump of his pulse without even realizing I was doing it—that I could do it.

He dipped his head. "Mistress, I'm at your service. It would be my honor to feed you tonight, if it pleases you?"

My mouth went dry, and my fangs tingled in a way they never had before. It had to be the scent of all the blood in this place; it was seriously getting to me.

I cleared my hot, scratchy throat, swallowing several times so I could speak. "I'm here to feed, not fuck. I don't want to be touched, and I don't plan on touching you."

He nodded, then looked up at me from under his lashes. He was disappointed. "May I touch myself, mistress?"

I glanced around the room again, and, yeah, there was a lot of that going on as well. My stomach felt weird. This felt ... wrong. I hated myself for needing this, wanting it, but I was so incredibly hungry, in a way I hadn't been my entire life. Now that I knew the truth, now that I'd surrendered to the idea, there was no suppressing the hunger, not anymore.

"I, uh ... I guess that's okay."

I didn't know the rules or what was expected. I didn't want to feed out in the open, and I was terrified I'd kill this guy, that I'd go into a feeding frenzy and drink until there was nothing left.

"I'm very hungry," I confessed, my face heating. I hated this feeling, being in over my head, being perceived as weak in front of this male, in front of everyone else. "Is there someone here who can stop me if I get, um ... carried away?" The only reason I chose this place was because I assumed it was safer, controlled.

I expected him to look frightened, to maybe change his mind and skedaddle back to his buds. Instead, his heart rate quickened, and the front of his pants literally tented before my eyes.

"Is this your first time here?" he asked.

"It is."

He nodded, breathing heavily now. "Someone is always watching. If you have trouble stopping, they can intervene."

"Right. Okay, that's good."

He motioned to a vacant couch.

I looked around. Did I really want to feed for the first time in front of everyone? What if I fucked up or did something wrong?

He led me to the couch and sat down, looking up at me expectantly.

Shit. I felt like an idiot.

I sat and shifted so I faced him. I had to be honest with this guy. He needed to know what he was signing up for. "Look, this is the first time I've done this. You're my first." I cringed. "I'm feeling a little out of my depth here, so you wanna tell me your name?"

His eyes flared. "Oliver."

"Hey, Oliver. I'm Fern, and I've recently learned I need to drink blood." I didn't know why I was telling him this, only that it made me feel better to have some kind of connection with this guy—flimsy as it was. "I don't think I need to feed as often as some, but I have this ... craving, and I can't resist it any longer. I think it's only fair you know up front that I don't know what will happen when I have my first taste of blood. I really don't want to hurt you. The idea of doing that ..." I rubbed my clammy, trembling hands on my thighs. "I really don't want to do that, but I can't guarantee you won't get hurt either. If you want to get up and go now, I'll totally understand."

Oliver shivered. "I'm your first?" His hand went to his erection, and he squeezed, then shuddered again.

Gross. But then I was literally about to suck the blood from his vein, so if he wanted to jerk off, I guessed it was only fair.

"Yes."

"Where do you want to bite me?" he said, voice trembling but definitely not from fear.

"Is there somewhere you'd prefer?" I asked, so nervous now that I felt queasy.

"My throat. I really like being bitten on the neck. I showered before I came, using unscented soap so there's nothing to interfere with my scent or taste." He squeezed his dick again, then kept massaging.

This was so fucking weird. Yes, nauseatingly, I'd been kind of turned on when I walked in here, but I wasn't anymore. Far from it.

"Sounds good," I said, but had no fucking clue.

He licked his lips and tilted his head, exposing his throat for me. I slid closer on the couch, my hand curling around the back of his neck, and leaned in. I blew out a nervous breath, ruffling his hair—

Oliver jerked and shuddered, a low groan leaving him.

I stilled, looking down. There was now an obvious wet patch on the front of the guy's pants. I looked back up, and his face was bright red.

"Did you just ..."

"It's okay," he said breathlessly. "Bite me. Oh, fuck, please bite me. I want to be your first. Let me be your first, mistress."

I wasn't a fan of this whole mistress thing, not at all. "Fern. Call me Fer—"

A *thump* invaded my brain, pulsing through my skull. Not Oliver. His heartbeat was racing like a wild hare being chased by a fox. This was steady, strong, the beat heavy. Whoever it belonged to was big. They had thick veins, thick enough to pump blood around a large frame. I turned to search the room, but I knew exactly who I was looking for, didn't I? And I didn't need to look far.

A pair of golden eyes locked with mine from across the room.

The hound—he'd gotten in. His lips were peeled back, his canines bared, extended. He didn't move, keeping his distance like he'd promised, but he didn't have to come closer. His hard stare sliced to Oliver, who was looking at him as well now, eyes wide, and the hound shook his head. *Feed her and die*—it was all there in that look, in that subtle shake of his head.

Oliver stumbled to his feet, and a moment later, he was gone, disappearing into the crowd. I turned back to the hound. This wasn't good. This was the absolute fucking opposite of good. Somehow, I'd caught the attention of one of Lucifer's pet beasts, and he'd decided I was the toy he wanted to snatch up in his jaw and toss around for his own entertainment.

Our gazes still locked, I stood slowly. His chest was rising and falling heavily, and his eyes were glowing. I took a step back, and he took one forward. Not closing the space between us, staying the same distance away. Everything in me screamed that I needed to run, like I had earlier, but I knew that was the worst thing I could do. For some reason, my getting close to Oliver had awakened the beast in him, and I didn't want to find out what would happen this time when he caught me—because he would catch me.

Keeping my movements slow and measured, I backed up several more steps. He took several toward me.

Fuck. Breathe, Fern. Turn slowly and leave. Walk. Don't run.

Taking another steadying breath, I turned, and keeping my steps unhurried, I made my way to the exit. Another burly male opened the door for me, and I walked out, then up the stairs. I tried not to, but when I reached the top and heard the now-familiar sound of his heavy boots, I turned back. He was at the bottom of the stairs, unmoving again, stopping because I had.

If anything, he was breathing even more heavily now.

"You don't need to walk me home, hound," I said, trying to assert some authority in my voice.

He growled. No words, just a guttural rumbling sound echoing up the walled stairwell.

"Good talk."

I pushed the door open and walked into the upstairs club, then rushed into the crowd. I moved quickly now, shoving my way through the people on the dance floor and out the other side.

When I hit the pavement, I sucked in the cool night air

and headed briskly down the street. I glanced back as he walked out.

Don't run. Do not run.

This street was busy and had a lot of bars and clubs, but when I rounded the corner, it was instantly quieter. The soft thud of my boots, followed by the heavy thump of the hound's, were the only sounds around me. The tension inside me was climbing higher and higher until I was ready to jump out of my skin. I couldn't take it. I had to do something. Stopping suddenly, I spun around. The hound stopped as well, watching me, waiting.

Getting to know your tormentor, abuser, torturer—sharing details, pretending you cared—could save your life. I knew that firsthand, and it was all I had right then.

"What's your name? If you're going to follow me everywhere, I should at least know your name." My nerves were fucking choking me. My fingers tapped against the side of my thigh. *One, two, three, four. Four, three, two, one.* Over and over again.

His nostrils flared, that massive chest expanding. "Relic," he said on a rough exhale.

"Well, Relic, you've done your job; you've kept me safe. I appreciate it. Thank you. So, how about we let bygones be bygones, okay? You can leave now. I'm good from h—"

"Drink my blood. You need blood. You're hungry. I'll feed you," he said so deep and growly that my belly quivered.

I wrapped my arms around myself. I wasn't drinking from that fucker. I was trying to discourage this guy, this psycho, and he wanted me to take his vein? Not fucking likely.

"Thank you," I said cautiously. "But I'm not hungry anymore," I lied.

"Yes, you are."

No, I wasn't fooling him, but it was never going to happen.

"I just want to go home and sleep." I aimed my thumb over my shoulder. "So, I'm gonna head home, and maybe I'll see you around sometime, yeah?" Or not. Hopefully, never again.

He said nothing.

Cool. This wasn't fucking terrifying *at all.*

If he felt bad for scaring me earlier and this was his way of making up for it, he was even more clueless than I'd thought.

I started walking, and the sound of his boots on the pavement echoed after me. I walked faster, and so did he.

Do not fucking run.

This late at night, I never used the alleyway, and the only reason I had earlier, and was about to use it again, was because I had a giant, unwanted stalker/bodyguard behind me. I rushed through it—anything to get away from this guy.

My shop was just ahead. Rummaging around in my bag, I pulled out my keys. My hand shook, and it took several tries before I managed to shove it in the door. My place was warded strongly—I'd paid a witch to do it for me, and she came back regularly to keep it that way. Still, I wasn't sure if it was strong enough to keep this guy out or what kind of powers he had.

Breathing deeply, I turned to him. He stood several yards away, his gaze still locked on me.

"This is where we go our separate ways, okay, Relic?"

He shifted in his big boots, from one foot to the other, then dipped his chin.

"Thanks for the protection tonight, but I've got it from

here. I promise not to fuck with demons I'm not supposed to, and you've made up for scaring me. We're even now, yes?"

He gave me another nod.

"Goodbye, Relic," I said to make sure he understood we were severing all ties—*for good*.

His nostrils flared, and his fingers curled into fists at his sides. "Night, Tinker Bell."

I paused. I guessed it was an improvement on Gremmy, but still. *Asshole*.

I shoved the door open, rushed in, and locked it tight after me.

CHAPTER
SEVEN

RELIC

MINE.

She was *mine.*

Her door closed, shutting me out, and a snarl erupted from me, echoing along the dark street. Her scent was branded on my senses, swimming in my head. The sound of her heart beating—I'd fucking felt it. I wanted to strip her down and rub my scent all over her. Mark her, brand her, claim her. I wanted to snatch her from that store, plant her ass on my bike, and take her home with me.

I wanted her in my den.

In my bed.

My fangs in her throat while I was deep inside her, marking her as mine. And I wanted her to bury those cute little fangs of hers into me. I wanted to feed her until she was satisfied. I wanted to be the one to satisfy her in every single fucking way.

The little demon was mine.

My mate.

How had I not seen it?

I shook my head, trying to clear it.

I'd never expected to find her, not fucking yet. It wasn't my turn. I had brothers almost twice my age, still waiting to find their mates. I hadn't believed it—that she could be mine. I hadn't let myself believe it. I was undeserving. Jagger, Roman, Fender, Lothar—they were all more deserving than me.

But she was here, and she was mine. Until that piece of shit at the feeding club had bared his throat, offering his vein to her, I'd had my head lodged up my own fucking ass. Then, she touched his neck, and it all clicked into place, sharp and with force. Honestly, if he hadn't gotten up and walked away from her, if she hadn't walked out of the feeding club when she had, if she'd let anyone else feed her, that place would have been even more of a bloodbath because I would have torn anyone that tried, limb from limb.

My feet had me moving to her door without thought, and I pressed my hand to it. Power vibrated through my palm from her ward. At least she had that.

My lips peeled back, and I bared my teeth. I wanted to be in there with her, upstairs in her apartment. I wanted to pick up my Tinker Bell and feel her pressed against me while I nuzzled her pretty neck and tasted her skin. I wanted her naked and draped over me in bed while she fed and I made her come until she collapsed with exhaustion, then snuggled up against me all night, warm and soft.

My growls were constant now, every indrawn breath and every exhale, because I'd have to wait. For some reason, she wasn't feeling it, not yet. She should want me close, but she'd told me to leave her alone. Her pussy should be weeping for me, but she didn't smell of arousal; she smelled of fear. I didn't know what to do. How to make her see who I was, how to make her want me like I did her.

I shoved my fingers through my hair. I'd never had to work at making a female want me. The ones who hung around the clubhouse were always ready, always willing. My fingers curled around the door handle, and I tested it. Locked. Of course it was. I could break it easily—one hard twist and it would snap right off.

Power from her ward hammered into me, pain slamming through my arm, knocking me back a step. If I were anyone else, I would have been thrown across the street. The ward was strong, but it would be nothing for me to get through. A little pain wasn't enough to bar me from my female.

Not when she was right there, on the other side.

If you break in, you'll only scare her more.

I cursed. She wouldn't like it, would she, if I let myself in? Tensing every muscle in my body, I battled for control, resisting the urge to force my way inside.

I gripped the door handle again. "Fuck."

———

FERN

I paced my apartment. He was still down there. I walked to the window and looked out. I couldn't see him, but I could hear him. Hunger gnawed at my belly, and I couldn't stop shaking.

Because of him, I was down two thousand dollars, and I still hadn't fucking fed.

The door handle rattled downstairs again.

Fuck.

Relic was growling and cursing. Every now and then, the handle rattled; he'd be hit by a blast of power from my ward, and he'd curse again. He should be unconscious, flat on his back on the other side of the street by now. The male wasn't only insane; he was *strong*. Stronger than anyone I'd ever met. I guessed it shouldn't be surprising; he was a motherfucking hellhound.

He growled again, and I startled, then cursed under my breath. I needed to do something. He wasn't going to leave me alone—that much had become obvious.

My phone rang, and I yanked it out of my pocket but didn't recognize the number. Shit, it was probably Relic. Ignoring it, I paced away from the window and back. My phone started ringing again.

How had he gotten my freaking number?

Fucking hell.

I was about to turn away when something moved on the roof of the building across the street. I moved closer as a dark figure stepped out of the shadows and into the moonlight. A male. I couldn't see his face. He wore a hooded sweatshirt and lifted an arm, holding up a phone. Not Relic. The male tapped at the screen and put it to his ear. Mine started ringing again a moment later.

He was one of the demons who'd been watching me— he had to be. Why was some lowlife breeder scout calling me?

Was I some kind of psycho magnet? First, this asshole standing on a roof across the street and his buddies, and now the hound. Though I hadn't actually seen anyone hanging around my place this last week.

My phone stopped ringing, and the male on the roof took the phone from his ear, tapped the screen, and lifted it again. Mine instantly started up.

Shit.

Stepping back from the window, I stared down at my phone. He wasn't going to stop, not until I talked to him. Gritting my teeth and my hand shaking, I answered. "Who are you? What the fuck do you want?"

"Come back to the window, and I'll show you," a distorted voice said down the line.

Fear dug its hooks deep into my flesh. That voice—the clipped tone, the pauses at odd places was horrifyingly familiar.

I didn't want to go back to the window. *No. He was dead.* I'd killed him. He burned to ashes. No one came out of that building. No one. He'd fucking burned.

I didn't want to see the truth, but my feet obeyed his order as if I were still under his power. I stood there and looked across the distance between us, watching in horror as he lifted his other hand and shoved back the hood, revealing a face I'd prayed to Lucifer that I'd never see again.

Grady.

And if Grady knew where I was, that meant … The Chemist had sent him.

No. No, no, no.

I couldn't speak, couldn't move.

They were dead. They were supposed to be dead.

"Hello, Estelle. It's been a long time."

I shook my head. This had been my deepest fear for the last five years. I'd told myself it couldn't happen, that I was safe. I'd convinced myself that the demons watching me had been sent by someone else, but of course, it was The Chemist. Of course it was.

He hadn't burned to death in that fire and neither had Grady. No, they were like roaches. Nothing could kill them. I should have stayed longer after I lit it. After I barricaded them in that building and set it alight, I should have stayed. I should have made sure there was nothing left, that they were nothing but ashes.

The Chemist said he'd find me if I ever left, and he meant what he said—always.

"You're going to get rid of the hound, Estelle, and then you're going to let me in."

It was as if my soul left my body at his order; my physical form locked solid, but everything else in me jerked to obey, to do as I'd been told.

"Do it," he hissed. "Now."

It physically hurt to ignore him. My body and mind had been conditioned to do as I was told, reminding me what disobeying would mean—all the awful, horrific, degrading things he had done to me, the things they'd both done to me.

"What d-do you w-want?" I hated the terror in my voice.

"You didn't think we'd just let you leave and never come for you, that we'd let you get away with what you did? It's over, Essie. It's time to come home."

I shook my head and stumbled back from the window.

"Get rid of the hound, Essie, right the fuck now," he hissed.

The sound of his voice was low, hushed. He was worried about something. Grady never spoke in hushed tones. Ever.

He was afraid the hound would hear him.

He's afraid of the hound.

Of course he was. Any demon with half a brain cell would be.

Adrenaline jolted through me, and it was incredibly

hard to disobey him—it was so fucking hard. But I would never go back. Never.

The shock of seeing him, though, of hearing his voice had my defenses dropping, and the past rushed forward like it was yesterday.

The door to the surgery opened, and a young male—a demon—was dragged in. He was crying, beaten bloody, and shaking.

"Please, let my brother go. Please."

Grady ignored him and dragged him over to me. "I told you, you just need to fuck her, and we'll let your brother go."

He cried harder, shaking his head. "I won't do it."

The front of his track pants was tented, and he was trying desperately to cover himself.

Grady noticed as well. "Excellent. The potion's finally worked. It's time."

The male tried to fight him off, but Grady was stronger and much older. A scream came from down the hall.

"Did you hear that? I don't think your brother's having fun here."

The male cried out, "Stop it! Don't hurt him. Please."

"Then do what you're told."

He looked down at me. "I'm sorry," he choked out. "It's ... it's my brother."

I said nothing. There was no stopping this. There was no fighting it. I was strapped down, sick from The Chemist's virus and weak from blood loss after Ghoul almost drained me.

Shaking and crying, the male climbed on top of me. I turned my head away while he apologized over and over again as he forced himself inside me.

When it was done, he climbed off the bed and threw up. Grady grabbed him and dragged him from the room.

I lay there in silence for several moments, numb. Every part of me felt disconnected.

A slow thump reached me, a repetitive sound over and over again. I turned my head. The door to the other room was open. He'd done it on purpose—it wasn't the first time. The Chemist wanted me to see him.

He was on his favorite gurney, fucking his medical mannequin while he stared at me, his gaze locked between my thighs.

I turned away again as his grunts grew louder, flinching when he finally groaned my name.

My phone started ringing again, and I jumped. I quickly hit End, put it on silent, and shoved the phone into my pocket.

I clenched my teeth. Grady was scared of the hound. Relic was the only thing standing between me and a fate worse than even Hell itself.

Rushing out of my apartment, I took the stairs back down to the shop and peeked around the doorframe. Relic stood with his face so close to the door at the front of the shop that his breath was fogging up the glass.

He growled suddenly, so loud that I startled.

Was Grady still on the roof across the street? Without a doubt. If he'd been told to come for me, he wouldn't leave until he did just that. The demons who'd been hanging around, they'd stopped, and now I had a feeling I knew why.

I hurried back upstairs and grabbed my laptop. I logged in to my security software and opened the files from the last week.

I hadn't really been checking the footage; all I'd had to do was look out the window, and I'd see them. The demons had stood just a few shops down, and either they were terrible at stealth operations, or they hadn't really been trying to hide because they were constantly looking this way. Every night, they got closer, getting bolder. Now, I knew they'd wanted me to see them so I knew *he* was coming for me. They'd been toying with me at Grady's order.

I clicked around, searching through the footage.

One night, they were out there, and the next, they weren't, as if ... as if something or someone had scared them off. I opened the next file, fast-forwarding to after closing time, and froze.

There.

Relic.

Standing across the street. Then, later, outside my freaking shop door, like a giant sentry.

It was him. He was the reason they were staying away. He was the reason Grady had come himself and why even he was too scared to come closer.

Then I remembered what he said in the forest, about the demons I'd planned to bring to Agatheena, well, when he asked if I'd seen the them following me, and I said I hadn't.

"Because I strongly encouraged them to fuck off."

Holy shit.

My giant stalker had inadvertently saved my ass—at least for now. Like a humongous, deranged bodyguard that I had absolutely no control over.

I chewed my lip. Now, I knew The Chemist was alive, and I knew he wouldn't stop. Now that he'd finally found me, he wouldn't leave, not until he had me at his mercy again. The demons, now Grady—they were waiting for Relic to leave. And as soon as my stalker hound got bored and left, I'd be screwed. I could leave, I could try and run, but where would I go?

I chewed my lip. If I had control over him though—over that big, powerful male—I could make sure he didn't leave.

You've lost your fucking mind.

Ten minutes ago, I'd wanted him gone. Now, I was trying to think of ways to make him stay—and fetch, and sit, and beg like a good boy. Was I really contemplating this? What choice did I have?

Agatheena still didn't have any information for me on what a threeling was and, more importantly, how to unleash all the power she'd said I had.

I needed protection, and the hellhound could give me that.

There was only one way to make sure he couldn't leave my side.

The demon blood that ran through my veins was ancient and powerful—a soul collector, according to Agatheena. It was the only way to ensure I had control over him, but Relic wouldn't just sign away his soul to me because I asked him to. He was a hellhound; he'd know what that meant more than most. I didn't like tricking people or deceiving them, but this was life and death—mine.

I needed to get him to drop his guard, to convince him this was a good idea—his idea. But to do that, I'd have to let him in. This was insane. I guessed I only had a fifty percent chance of this working. He could absolutely turn on me. He'd said hounds were protective of females though, and he'd seemed genuinely unhappy that I was scared of him. So, maybe my odds were fractionally better. Maybe around a sixty-five percent chance of success. Compared to the alternative, which was a one hundred percent chance of losing everything and suffering horror and agony for the rest of my life—then sixty-five percent didn't seem that bad at all.

Are you really going to do this?

I needed protection, and there was no one better—he'd been right about that. So, yes. Yes, I was.

I left my apartment, and jogged down the stairs. Then, taking a deep breath, I stepped out into the shop.

Relic straightened, his eyes narrowing on me as I walked up to the door.

"Are you planning on standing there all night?" I didn't have to pretend I was shit-scared to play on his protective instincts because that's exactly what I was.

"Yes," he said in that deep, rumbling voice.

"Why?"

"Because your ward is flimsy."

For some reason, the hound was fixated on me, had singled me out as the damsel he needed to protect, and I planned to use that to get what I needed.

"Well, then, if you're not planning on leaving, can I get you a drink?"

His eyes narrowed again. "What are you doing?"

"Dude, you're standing there with your nose pressed to the glass, like a sad dog that's been kicked out in the rain. I could ask you the same thing."

He licked his lips. "Will you drink with me?"

"Sure, but you'll be out there, and I'll be in here."

He nodded, grinning wider. "Okay."

That grin was way too freaking handsome for someone so deranged.

"Back in a sec."

I headed out the back of the shop to my small break room. I grabbed two glasses and filled them both with bourbon, more in his than mine. I needed him a little loopy

—tipsy, at the very least. Drunk would be even better. Going by the size of him though, that would take a lot more than a glass of bourbon, but that was fine because that wasn't what the bourbon was for. I just needed something to mask the other things I was putting in it.

I kept my dangerous herbs and other ingredients back here, and I quickly pulled down the bottles I needed. Four drops of highly concentrated valerian—six would drop an elephant, so that was probably about right—a pinch of black oak root, a spoon of witch hazel elixir, and a small spoonful of my own personal healing tonic. It was slow release and should kick in after the other ingredients did their thing. It wouldn't kill him—it couldn't since he was immortal—but if I wasn't careful, I could put him in a coma for a few weeks or even longer, and I definitely didn't want to do that.

I sniffed the contents of his glass, then mine. Perfect.

I strode back out, and he tracked me the whole way. Placing the glasses on the counter, I braced and unlocked the door. He didn't move when I opened it, staying just on the other side of my ward, like I'd told him to.

Picking up my glass, I took a sip, then handed him his. "I hope you like bourbon."

"I like bourbon." He took a sip. "Surprised you do though. Thought you'd be more into those fancy cocktails."

"Me? Nah." I stayed well back from the door so he couldn't grab me if he decided to.

"So, why the change of heart, Tinker Bell? A little while ago, you were telling me to get lost, and now, you wanna have a drink."

I shrugged. "A demon can change her mind, can't she?"

He took a big gulp. "This is good."

Valerian worked almost instantly and would kick in at

any moment now. He grinned again, for no reason, but this time, it was a little goofy. The valerian was a go.

"How're you doing over there, big guy?"

He flashed his teeth, and his eyes sparkled with humor. "Really fucking good. What was this stuff again?"

"Bourbon—my own special blend. Drink up."

He downed the rest and swayed a little to the right. "Nice."

"You know, I really appreciated you protecting me tonight."

His brows lifted. "You did?"

"Oh, yeah. I've never felt so safe. It's a pity you can't be here all the time."

He leaned in. "You want me here all the time, Tinker Bell? You got it."

"That's so nice of you. But I have to confess, I am a little scared of you," I said, steering the conversation carefully.

"I'd never hurt you, Fern," he said, slurring a little.

It was now or never. The size of him, he'd metabolize my sedative quickly and be back to his old window-licking self in mere minutes.

"Do you want to stay close to me, Relic?"

"Yeah, babe." His eyes darkened. "I want that—really badly."

"There's a way you can. And you'd only have to do this tiny, teeny-weeny little thing. If you did it, you could come inside. You could come up to my place and stay as long as you'd like. Do you want that?"

The grin dropped, and he looked as serious as a heart attack. "Name it, and I'll do it."

"Will you make a deal with me, Relic?"

He nodded. "What kind of deal?"

"You offer me your soul and promise you'll do what I

say, you know, just so I'd feel safe, and then I'll let you come in and be with me all the time."

He smiled wide. "Deal."

"You'll do it?"

"Sure," he said.

"I'll need to cut you. The deal needs to be bound in blood. Is that okay?" My heart was banging in my chest.

I was going to have a hellhound at my beck and call, under my command. I could do anything, go anywhere. No one would ever hurt me again.

He lifted his hand. "Cut me, Tink."

Pulling my knife from my back pocket, I made a slice in my palm. I'd read the ritual only once, but I'd taken a picture of it before I left the demon library. It was simple enough. Taking a breath to steady my nerves, I uttered the words to drop the ward. I expected him to surge forward, but Relic didn't move; he stayed where he was.

His stare didn't waver, was fixed on me as I made a slice in his palm. His skin was thick and calloused, forcing me to slice deeper. He didn't even flinch.

"Ready?"

"Yep."

He was still grinning, and it was so freaking infectious that I had to bite back my own. I felt guilty as hell, but also giddy with relief. I hadn't felt truly safe in a very long time, and in a few minutes, I'd have my own hellhound protector. Grady wouldn't dare come near me with Relic here. I opened my phone and double-checked the ritual, then pressed our palms together.

"Repeat after me. *Fern Honeycutt, I offer you my soul.*"

He licked his very nice lips. "Fern Honeycutt, I offer you my soul."

"*This deal made in blood is binding until death.*"

102

"This deal made in blood is binding until death," he repeated, his voice nothing but a growl now.

"You don't need to repeat this next bit," I said. "In exchange for your protection, I will allow you to remain by my side." My heart humped heavily in my chest. "The deal is done," I finished as sparks, little zaps, shot down my arm and through my body from where we touched.

I released his hand and stepped back, feeling breathless, my belly all weird and swirly—and, yeah, between my thighs was hot and slick and achy. I had no idea how it felt to claim a soul, no point of reference. I didn't know what to expect, but I had to admit, this felt really freaking good.

CHAPTER
EIGHT

FERN

"Can I come in now?" Relic asked.

I chewed my lip. "You understand what just happened? You know I own you, and you have to do what I say?"

"I understand what just happened perfectly, Tinker Bell."

Owning his soul obviously hadn't stopped him from being a smart-ass.

I tugged at my sleeves, nerves running wild inside me.

You did it. He's yours. Now, you need to lead. You need to take charge.

I motioned to the stairs. "Let's go then."

He stepped over the threshold, and I led him upstairs and into my apartment.

"You can sit down on the couch," I said, trying to insert as much authority in my voice as I could.

He tilted his head back and scented the air. Then, his eyes darkened when he looked around the small living room and kitchen area, taking in everything before walking to the couch and sitting, doing as I'd said.

I rushed to the window, yanking the curtains closed. Then strode to the small island that separated the lounge from the kitchen, like that would protect me from Relic if this thing hadn't worked.

"How are you feeling?"

He looked around the room again, this time blinking several times before he frowned. "What did you put in my drink, demon?"

My pulse fluttered wildly. "Nothing that'll cause any permanent damage." I straightened my spine. I was a deal maker, a soul collector, and I needed to act like one. "You can growl and yell all you'd like, but you belong to me now."

His nostrils flared, and he released another of those growls with his next exhale. "That was a fucking devious move, even for you."

"Make me a cup of tea," I said, forcing myself to stare him in the eyes.

Yes, I needed to assert my authority—quickly. The sooner he came to terms with his new situation, the better.

He bared his teeth but stood and walked to the kitchen. He filled the kettle, turned it on, then opened cupboards until he found a cup and the tea.

"I take it with milk and sugar."

His gaze sliced to me, and the muscle in his jaw jumped several times, but he made the tea. When he was done, he handed me my drink, then went back to the couch and sat. "I thought you wanted me here for protection. Not to fetch you fucking tea."

"Put the tea away," I said, fighting back the nerves

zipping wildly through my belly, but I had to be sure I had control over this male.

He narrowed his eyes, but he stood, stalked back into the kitchen, put the tea back in the cupboard, then turned to me, brow raised.

"Move that pillow." I pointed to the pink one on the end of the couch. "Put it on the chair."

"Are you fucking serious?" he said, but he was already moving to do it because he had to, because I had control over him. I had all the control.

When he put the cushion in the chair and sat back on the couch, I walked around the island, my heart pounding, but I was feeling a little bolder now and sat across from him. Placing my cup on the small table beside me, I crossed my legs. "Take off my boots, hound."

His eyes flashed, but he stood instantly, then dropped to his knees in front of me, taking my foot in his hand.

"You may not hurt me, not in any way."

"Never had any plans to hurt you, Tinker Bell," he said as he slid a hand over my ankle and up my calf.

His hand was huge, bigger than my foot. Then he gripped the zipper and slid it down slowly. The heat of his palm radiated through the leather, and I barely suppressed my shiver as he reached the bottom, slipped the boot off carefully, and placed it on the floor. He took the other foot, and as instructed, he dragged one of those big mitts up my leg again, slower this time, and I swore I felt a pull low in my belly when he tugged on the zipper. I actually held my breath as he slid it down slowly and eased it off.

"Anything else?" There was a whole lot more growl to his voice.

He was pissed off, but obviously under my control. Completely.

I was safe, and for the first time in a very long time, I allowed myself to relax, and as soon as I did, I realized how tired I was—no, how utterly exhausted I was.

It'd been a long time since I'd had a proper night's sleep. I never felt completely safe, and on my worst nights, my memories turned into nightmares. But now, I had a hellhound protector, and no one could touch me.

I stood. "I'm going to bed, hound, and you're going to protect me while I sleep, understand?"

He bared his teeth in a vicious smile. "As you wish."

I went to my bedroom and quickly changed. I should have been nervous that he was there, crowding my place, but weirdly, I felt the complete opposite. I owned him; he was mine to command. When he'd said he never planned to harm me, for some reason, my gut had told me to believe him.

I wasn't sure how this soul-owning, deal-making thing worked, but that feeling—the zaps and tingles—they were still there. This was obviously how it felt to make a deal—this buzz of euphoria, followed by a crash so hard that I could barely keep my eyes open.

After ordering a new phone, because this one was obviously compromised, and ignoring all the missed calls, I drowned my old one in a basin full of water. Try calling me on that, asshole.

The last thing I wanted to do was my bedtime routine, but I had no choice. I didn't miss a step, even in a daze, then climbed onto my bed, crawled under the covers, and passed out.

———

Blinking groggily into the darkness, I reached for my phone to check the time, then remembered I'd destroyed it. Something caught my attention—

A pair of glowing golden eyes, watching me through the shadows.

My heart leaped into my throat. "What the fuck are you doing?"

"Protecting you," he said.

"I never said you could come in here—"

"Sleep, Tinker Bell. You're safe now."

My eyes were too heavy to hold open, and his voice, it slid over me, soft and rough, somehow soothing. I should tell him to leave, to get out, but I was too exhausted to say the words.

The next time I woke, I was hot. I kicked off the covers with a groan. It was still dark, and those glowing eyes were closer, right there beside me.

"It's okay," he said. "Go back to sleep."

That low rumble in the dark, it was a soft blanket wrapping around me. How could a voice make you warm? How could that rough-as-gravel voice be comforting? But it was, and unbelievably, I drifted back to sleep.

Yawning, I stretched, and my hand hit hot, bare skin. My eyes flew open, and I shot up, spinning around. Relic was sitting on my bed—no shirt, boots off, pillows propped behind him, leaning against the headboard. He was reading one of my romance books.

"Why are you in my bed, Relic?" I tried to sound confident and in charge, but my voice came out all jittery and breathless.

He turned the page. "You kept tossing the covers off, and I got sick of getting up and down all night to put them back over you, so I sat here to make it easier. Then, when the sun came up, I thought I'd kill time with a little light reading, but I gotta say, Tinker Bell, this shit is hot as fuck. I'm only a quarter of the way in, but it's good stuff. This male—he knows what he's doing." His gaze slid to me. "His female danced with his enemy, so he carried her out of the club, spanked her ass, then finger-banged her." He looked back at the book. "Respect."

I snatched it out of his hands. "Put that down and get the hell out of my bed."

He grinned. "Not in it, babe, on it, and thanks to me, you slept like the dead. Seemed like you needed it."

I hadn't slept that deeply in five years. Still, I shoved his shoulder. "Get out of my bed." The sight of that wide, muscled, tattooed chest was making me feel … funny. "Make me a cup of coffee," I snapped, desperate to get him out of my room.

"No, I won't be doing that. I did that shit last night because I could see you were freaking out over what you'd done, but I'm here to protect you, not clean your toilet and do the dishes."

"We have a deal." Unease filled me. "You agreed to protect and obey."

He shook his head. "No, you swindled me out of my soul, and in exchange, you demanded I protect you. That means if someone scares you, I will fuck them up. If you need me to reassure you, soothe you, I'm your hound. When it comes to anything to do with your safety and well-being, I don't need to be told what to do; I'll already be doing it. Anything else? You need to say please, like everybody else."

"No, that's not what the deal was. I said—"

"You said—and I quote—'In exchange for your protection, I will allow you to remain by my side.' You said nothing about obey."

"Yes, I did."

He grinned. "That was before. You skipped that bit during the actual ritual."

Did I? Oh, fuck, I did.

"I still own your soul. You have to do what I say," I said desperately.

"How many souls do you own, Tink?"

My face heated. "What does that have to do with anything?"

"For future reference, you need to spell that shit out during the ritual; otherwise, you end up with an extremely protective hound on your hands who does whatever the fuck he wants."

He grabbed my wrist when I tried to scramble out of bed, stopping me. I gasped in a panicked breath, trying to jerk out of his hold, and he quickly released me.

A deep frown rearranged his features. "I have sworn to protect you, Fern, from everything, even from me. Not that I would ever hurt you."

"Right," I said.

"Take a breath." He picked the book back up, but the muscle pulsing in his jaw gave away his unhappiness. "Didn't hurt you last night, did I? And like I already told you, hounds don't harm females in any way." He flicked back to the page he'd been on, and then he glanced over at me. "Go get ready. It's almost time to open your store."

He was fucking with me. Pretending he was cool with me *swindling* him out of his soul when he was actually furious.

"Whatever you have planned, you might as well forget

it. You said yourself, you have to protect me, even against you."

He looked up from the book again. "I know what I said, and I've got nothing planned, Tink. I'm yours. Whatever you need, whatever will help you sleep at night, just ask, babe. I got you."

He sounded so sincere. How did he do that? He had to be a freaking psychopath. He didn't *have me*. He was trying to lull me into a false sense of security, and then he'd make his move.

"I think I want you to leave."

"Can't do it. I've sworn to protect you, and that's what I'm going to do." His gaze stayed on me as he placed the book down on the bedside table. "Wherever you go, Fern, I'll be right there, by your side."

My swallow was audible. "Is that a threat?"

He shook his head. "Not a threat. I'm just doing what I promised."

"And what's that?" I needed him to spell it out because he'd proven that he was good at twisting my words and being tricky as hell.

I might have forced him to be my protector, but he'd been my stalker first.

He licked his lips, and his eyes flashed red the same way mine could. "To make sure nothing and no one ever hurts you."

My heart jumped in my chest at the look in those intense eyes and the growl in his voice.

"If any fucker even looks at you wrong, Fern, I will make them regret it. If someone does somehow manage to hurt you, I'll gut them. I'll make them scream for mercy, and then I'll tear them to pieces. That clear enough for you?"

I backed up, climbing off the bed. "Crystal."

He nodded. "Glad we got that straightened out." He got off the bed. "I'll let you get ready. You have sugar in your coffee as well?"

I blinked over at him. "Uh ... yeah."

"Cool." He walked out.

CHAPTER
NINE

FERN

TRUE TO HIS WORD, Relic didn't leave my side all day. He stood behind the counter, arms crossed, eyeing everyone who came in and—I assumed—assessing them and the level of threat they possessed. I tried to convince him— order him—to move to the back room, but the stubborn hound refused. I had literally no power over the asshole, and he was loving it.

I'd totally screwed myself, but this was still better than the alternative, thanks to Relic's humongous and threatening presence. There was no sign of Grady or the other demons—I checked for them throughout the day, scanning the street outside the store, as well as the security footage of the previous night, and nothing. As fucked as my situation with Relic was, it was working.

Still, I was on edge, and it didn't help that my giant stalker decided to pepper me with questions. He wanted to know every single thing there was to know about me. I didn't give him any answers because I didn't need to give this male any more ammunition. I already felt exposed in a way I fucking hated.

But despite all of that, and though it made no sense, I also felt incredibly safe.

I didn't know if I should trust it—that feeling. I probably shouldn't, but he'd had ample opportunity to hurt me if he wanted to. Yes, he was a behemoth pain in the ass, but I could get used to this feeling. I'd spent so much of my life afraid it felt nice to know that someone had my back, even if he was unpredictable and there because I'd forced him to be. Even if he hated me for what I'd done, he was here, and unless I ended the deal—which I had no idea how to do even if I wanted to—he wasn't going anywhere.

"What do you want for dinner?" he asked, surprising me while I locked up.

"Dinner?"

"You gotta eat, Tink. Unless you're thirsty. You want some blood?"

My gaze slid to the thick veins in his forearm, then up to the one pulsing at the side of his throat, and without my say-so, my hearing intensified, tuning in to the swoosh of his blood as it pumped through that massive body. My mouth went dry.

"I'm not thirsty," I lied.

He tilted his head to the side. "No?"

"Nope."

"So, how often do soul collectors need to feed, Fern?"

The way he'd said my name made my belly all swirly.

"We're all different." I had no freaking idea, but no way was I telling him that.

"Okay, then, how often do you feed?"

I shrugged. "Not often." *Not ever.*

He nodded, and his eyes narrowed a little. "But you still gotta eat food, right? So, what do you want?"

"I'm not picky. What do you want to eat?"

He licked his bottom lip before his teeth sank into it, flashing one of those sharp canines. Then his thick throat worked as he swallowed. "What I want is currently off the menu, Tinker Bell. So, for now, I'll have to make do with a nice, juicy steak."

I pretended like I hadn't caught his meaning or the way those words had alarmingly affected me—and not in a bad way—as I rounded the counter. Grabbing the stack of takeout menus, I dumped them on top. "Take your pick."

"Nah, we're going out," he said, not even sparing them a glance. "My treat."

"You don't need to do that."

Why would he want to do that? And what if Grady was out there?

"I'm hungry, female. I want meat; don't read more into it. There is no ulterior motive other than feeding me."

If I insisted we stay here, he'd want to know why. And I was safe, right? With him, I was completely safe.

"Okay, fine." I snatched up my keys and slid my new phone into my back pocket. It'd arrived earlier that morning, and Relic had watched, brow raised as I'd opened it, but at least he hadn't peppered me with questions about that as well.

As soon as we hit the street, the big hound reached out and took my hand.

"What are you doing?" I tried to pull free.

"You're my responsibility," he said without looking my way.

"I'm not your responsibility. I'm the owner of your soul."

I tried to pull my hand free again, but he wouldn't let go.

"We've talked a lot about what you get out of this bargain, but my soul wasn't free, Tink. In exchange, I get to be by your side, and I'm in the mood to hold your hand while I protect you. So, win-win. We both get what we want."

"I don't want to hold your hand," I bit out.

"You'll get used to it," he said, then stopped beside a very large motorcycle.

He pulled me close to it, so I was all but pressed against him when he swung his leg over the seat. When he started it, the growl of the engine made me jump and echoed off the buildings on either side of the street.

"Get on," he said.

"No fucking way."

He grinned. "You drugged a hellhound and stole his soul, but you're too scared to get on the back of a bike? Never thought you'd be a chickenshit."

"I'm not a chickenshit." But I was. I was the biggest chickenshit in existence, and the idea of getting on there, of being so ... so close to him—gods, not only panicked me, but it also made me feel all out of breath and weird.

"It's just a short ride, Fern. Just a few blocks, and then we'll be eating a nice, juicy steak."

The way he'd said it, like he was talking an unstable person down from a ledge, had me bristling. "Your arrogance is insufferable."

He grinned wider, as if I'd just told him he had pretty eyes—which he absolutely did, and the fact that I recognized that pissed me off more.

"You getting on or what?"

Cursing, I jumped up behind him, not letting myself think too much about it or the way my hands trembled when I searched for something to hang on to. Relic reached back, taking my wrist with one hand while the other went to my lower back, and he jerked me forward so I was *plastered* to his back, my groin snug against his ass, my legs spread *wide*. Then he pulled both of my arms around his waist. Hell no, this was way too fucking close. I was about to scoot back, but he took off, and I was forced to hold on tighter instead.

Adrenaline spiked through my veins as we roared down the street. He wasn't going fast; he was taking it easy—for me, I was sure—but my heart was still pounding in my chest.

True to his word, the restaurant was only a few blocks out of Seventh but still close. He parked, and I quickly jumped off and forced myself to breathe normally, to appear utterly unaffected. Relic took his time, swinging one long, muscled leg over the seat, the leather of his vest creaking. Before I could step back, he grabbed my hand again and led me into the steak house.

He towed me along to a booth, motioned for me to slide in, and then followed, trapping me in.

"There's a seat on the other side."

"Wouldn't be doing my job if I sat over there. Plus, this side has a better view of the rest of the room and the door."

The male had an answer for everything. "Let's just get this over with."

He handed me a menu from the middle of the table.

"Aren't you going to pick something?" I asked when he didn't even glance at it.

"Already know what I'm getting."

Of course he did. He probably came here all the time. He probably brought his dates here. Did hounds date? Why was I even thinking about that? Why did I care? I didn't. I

117

opened the menu and scanned what was on offer while he scanned the room like he had laser beams coming out of his eyes and was ready to slice someone in half if they dared look at me wrong.

A server came to our table and smiled at me. "Can I get you something to drink?"

"Don't look at her," Relic said before I could open my mouth. "Look at me."

The guy went pale. "Uh ... sorry. What can I get you?"

"Beers."

The guy dipped his head and rushed off.

"That was so freaking rude."

Relic tracked the guy all the way back to the bar. "He looked at your tits."

I froze. "No, he didn't."

"Yeah, Tink, he did. When we walked in and while you were looking at the menu."

"Oh."

"Yeah, oh. Now, let me do the protecting."

The guy delivered our drinks, and this time, he kept his head down. We ordered, and as soon as we were on our own, Relic turned and faced me.

"So, what's going on?" he asked.

I blinked up at him. "What do you mean?"

"Fern, you literally drugged me and bartered me out of my soul. You're fucking terrified of something even more than you are of me. So, what gives? Who's the big bad? Who am I fighting? Point me at them, and I'll take them out. Deal done."

"I'd rather not say," I said. "And if the big bad comes, you won't miss them. You'll deal with them then."

"Fern—"

"I'm not talking about it."

No, I couldn't talk about any of it. I couldn't take the looks of disgust or pity that were sure to follow. Or worse, if I talked about it, the nightmares would definitely come, the memories would invade more than they already had been, and I'd spiral out of control all over again.

My fingers tapped against my thigh before I knew I was doing it. *One, two, three, four. Four, three, two, one.* Always fours. Everything in fours.

Our dinner arrived, and thankfully, Relic let his line of questioning go.

We didn't talk much while we ate, and after he paid for the meal, he took my hand again, led me back to his bike, and took me home. If I hadn't tricked him out of his soul and if he wasn't being forced to protect me, it'd almost be like we'd been the ones on a date. I'd never been on a date. I'd never had a boyfriend.

But it hadn't been a date, and he wasn't my boyfriend. I didn't want or need either of those things.

We walked into my place, and I left him in the living room to take a quick shower and dress for bed.

I went through my bedtime routine and my current list of things I *had* to do before I could sleep. Moisturizing first, brushing my hair second, then I sat on the edge of the bed and had a sip of water before placing my drink bottle on the coaster on the bedside table, tapping the bottom of the cup against it just right. *Front, back, left, right. Twist left, twist right.* Then I slipped off my slides, making sure they were lined up perfectly. *Not quite right.* I adjusted them. *No, still not right. Fuck.* I did it again, using my thumb to make sure they were lined up perfectly. *Good.* Then I climbed into bed and pulled up the covers. Some rituals came and went, but this particular line-up had lasted years.

I could hear Relic moving around in the living room, and then he knocked on my door and walked in.

"You can sleep on the couch."

He chuckled. "Not sleeping on that fucking small couch, and that's too far away from you."

He tugged off his shirt, kicked off his boots, and then undid his jeans.

"Whoa."

He shoved them down so he was standing in only a pair of black boxer briefs, which hugged his monster thighs, muscled ass, and the intimidating bulge at the front.

"You can't sleep with me."

He ignored me, rounded the bed, and got in. "Not trying to fuck you, Fern. I was awake all night last night. Yes, I am fucking superior in all ways, but I still need sleep, and I won't get it on your couch."

"You're too big. You're taking up all the room." I jerked away. "Did you just touch me?"

"Hard not to in this tiny fucking bed. But again, not trying to get all up on you. I just want some sleep." His golden eyes came to me. "Wouldn't say no to a hug though."

"Are you insane?"

"Nope, hounds need contact; we're tactile. At the club-house, I get those needs fulfilled. It's not me being a creep; it's a biological need. If I don't get to be close to someone, I get antsy, then snarly, and then I want to bite something."

"You can't be freaking serious right now." I huffed out a breath. "You're harder work than an actual dog."

He shrugged. "Even dogs need to be petted, Fern. Just one hand—"

"I'm not touching your dick," I shrieked.

His brows lowered. "Did I ask you to touch my dick? Get

your head out of the gutter, Tink. I know what I got packing is hard to ignore, but you're gonna have to try."

I shoved at his chest, and he grabbed my hand and held it there, right over his Devil Dogs MC tattoo, and his lids slid shut for a moment. I tried to pull away, and his eyes opened.

"That's all I need. Just that—your hand on my chest— and I'm good. You're forcing me to be here, Fern, so you gotta help me out."

What had I gotten myself into?

"Fine, but my knife is right beside the bed. You try anything during the night, I'll stab you—repeatedly."

His eyes closed. "Sounds good." His voice was husky, like he was blissed out and on the verge of sleep already.

I rolled away to turn off the lamp, and he growled.

"I'm just turning off the light," I bit out.

It went out before I could even flick the switch.

"Did you do that?"

"Yes."

"You have powers?"

"Yes."

"What else can you do?"

"Burn shit, pick up shit and throw it around, you know, manipulate things, move stuff, bend it." He shrugged. "Lots of things. Not just the hound stuff."

"What's the hound stuff?"

"Best trackers in existence, obviously. See in the dark, hear really fucking well, fight really fucking well, heal really fucking fast, and we got poison-tipped claws."

I stared at him, kind of shocked. I knew some of the hound stuff, but I had no idea about the other powers.

"Hand, Fern," he muttered.

I quickly pressed my hand onto his enormous chest

again. It was hot—hotter than your average being—and hard. The hair there was actually soft. I'd expected it to be coarse, but it felt kind of nice.

No one had ever slept in this bed with me before, and as his warmth radiated over me, I could admit, just to myself, that I kind of liked it. I felt the cold; my feet were always like ice. It was nice to feel warm.

As soon as he was asleep, I'd take my hand away.

My eyes drifted closed.

CHAPTER
TEN

RELIC

I DIDN'T FUCKING MOVE; I was barely fucking breathing because I didn't want her to wake up. Not yet. As soon as she woke, she'd shove me away and put distance between us, and I needed this. I needed her close in a way that made me feel fucking feral.

But that wasn't the only reason I didn't want her to wake up. She'd had a nightmare not long after she fell asleep, and she'd been restless on and off for most of the night. She'd finally stilled in the early hours of the morning. Fern needed rest.

My precious little female, she was fucking terrified of something or someone, even more than she'd been of me. She'd tried to drug me, then claim my soul for protection, for fuck's sake. And I'd been standing at her door, growling and rattling the door handle like the big bad wolf trying to blow her fucking house down, as out of control as I'd ever been. Still, I'd been the safer bet, the lesser threat than whatever evil was terrifying her.

I was her mate—born to protect her, to take care of her, to give her everything she needed—and she had no fucking clue. I would kill for her without a second thought, protect her with my life, but she didn't trust me—not yet—and it was near impossible to contain everything I felt blazing inside me. Every time I scented her fear, I wanted to tear the motherfucking walls down. I wanted to drop to my knees in front of her and beg her not to be afraid of me.

I couldn't do any of those things, not while she was still so skittish.

If I told her the truth now, she'd run. I didn't doubt that for one second.

I pressed my nose to her hair and breathed her into my lungs. Her scent was deeper in the morning when she was all warm and soft. My hand rested on the small of her back, and I wanted to smooth it over her body, to feel every curve, but I didn't dare move.

She made a cute little snuffling sound, and I studied her features. She was stunning, like a curvy little pixie. The thought of her being afraid raised my hackles and made me thirst for blood.

When she'd handed me that glass of bourbon, I'd known she was trying to drug me, just not why. I'd scented the herbs and whatever else she'd put in it before she even carried it from the back room. Hounds were not only immortal, but we also had a metabolism that was incredibly fast. I'd gotten a high from it for a few seconds, and then my body had burned it right up.

As for my soul, she didn't own shit. Fuck knew where she'd gotten that bullshit from, but that wasn't how soul ownership went down. First, not only had the ritual been all wrong, but you needed to use your true name, and I got the feeling Fern Honeycutt wasn't it. Second, even if she had gotten the ritual right, I didn't have a soul for her to claim—no one Hell-born did. Hellhounds had a kind of equivalent created by Lucifer. Some still called it a "soul" because it was an easier way to explain it to others. Instead, we had a kind of life force—an essence, I guessed—something that meant if we died, we weren't gone forever. It worked in a similar way to a soul, but it wasn't what Fern was hoping for, and it wasn't something she could own. There were only two places our life force could go if we died —back to Hell, or if something went wrong or we deserved it, Limbo. Either way you looked at it, you couldn't claim what didn't exist.

While I'd sat on her couch, she'd been waiting for her drug to wear off, anticipating when I'd realize what she'd done. I was no actor, but I'd watched enough movies to know she'd expect me to be pissed off, enraged that she'd taken my freedom and made me her guard dog. It wasn't easy, and at first, I wasn't sure I was selling it. It was hard when, instead of being angry, I was over the fucking moon. My mate might not realize who I was just yet, but she knew I could protect her. She knew I was the only male strong enough to keep her safe, and the satisfaction I felt was heady as fuck. I'd been fighting not to puff out my fucking chest and howl.

So, yeah, she could believe she owned my soul for as long as she needed to—whatever my Tinker Bell needed to make her feel safe and whatever ensured I could stay close.

I breathed her in again. The name she'd chosen for herself fit her well because her scent was like an open field covered in honeysuckle. Fuck, I wanted it all over me.

She jolted on top of me suddenly, a gasp coming from her before her eyes flew open, and she lifted herself with a jerk. Her eyes widened when she looked down at me.

"You're okay," I said, giving in to the need and sliding my hand up her back and down again. Then, I had to choke down my growl and force myself not to grip the back of her neck and tug her down for a hard kiss because her full lips were extra puffy from sleep, like I imagined they'd be after she—

Her hand flew up, and she slapped me across the face. "What the fuck do you think you're doing? Did I say you could touch me, hound?"

Cute. She was all flushed and pissed. I liked it when she got all worked up. The scent of her anger made my dick hard. Better that than the bitter scent of her fear.

"If you're going to hit me, do it like you mean it." I grinned. "That was just a little love tap, Tinker Bell."

She growled, but I noted she still hadn't moved. She stayed draped over me, her body all up on mine. She was also shaking.

My little female was seeking comfort from me, and she didn't even realize it.

"You have another nightmare, Fern?" I didn't know how I knew it, but I did. That slap was more about releasing tension than hitting me.

Her gaze darted away from mine. "I'm fine, just ... don't do it again," she said.

I noted again how she still hadn't moved.

"Do what?"

Her soft belly was against my abs, and every now and then, her tits grazed my chest.

"This ... touch me." Her face turned pink. "Pull me on top of you."

"Didn't touch you, and you crawled up there all by yourself. I woke and found you on me." I shrugged. "You looked comfortable, so I left you where you were." I pressed my hand more firmly against her back, unable to stop myself.

Fuck, I wanted that mouth.

She stiffened, and I saw the moment she realized I wasn't holding her there, that she was free to move however she wanted, and she hadn't. She quickly scrambled off me and off the bed, and I wanted her back instantly. But in her hurry to get away, her sleeves had come up, and I could also see a strip of her belly. Silvery scars marred her smooth skin—some vicious-looking slices, burns, and fuck knew what else.

My grin slid away.

Immortals—demons—didn't scar. Which meant someone had hurt her and made sure she was left with those on purpose, and going by the way she quickly yanked down her sleeves and straightened her shirt, she didn't want me to see.

"I'm taking a shower," she said, not meeting my eyes. "Could you put a pot of coffee on … please?"

I nodded, my throat too fucking tight to speak. Someone had hurt her. Someone had cut and burned her. Someone had tortured my female so badly that she was terrified all the time, to the point that she had nightmares and had tried to claim the soul of a hellhound for protection.

Gritting my teeth, I sucked in a sharp breath and forced myself to stay perfectly still while anger seared its way through me so hotly that a roar built in my chest, burning deep. If I opened my mouth right then, it would burst free. If I stood, if I moved, I would punch a hole in something— several somethings. I couldn't do that. I would not give Fern another reason to be scared of me, so instead, I locked it down tight—so fucking tight that it caused physical pain.

After taking several more deep breaths, and getting a handle on my control, I swung out of bed, got dressed, and went to make my female her coffee.

When she finally walked out, she was dressed in a way that covered every bit of skin. I'd never thought about it, but she always did. Every time I saw her, she was covered completely. She wasn't looking at me right then; she was checking something on her phone.

I slid her coffee across the counter, and she took it with a mumbled, "Thanks," but still no eye contact.

No, I couldn't read emotions very well, but what she was feeling wasn't good—I knew that much.

"Talk to me, Fern," I said before I could stop myself. "Tell me what you're feeling?"

Her yellow-green eyes sliced to me. "What I'm feeling?"

I nodded, but I didn't add anything else because she knew why I was asking.

"I don't know. Irritated that the humongous hound in my tiny apartment keeps asking me stupid questions." She grabbed her boots and sat on the couch to put them on.

I wanted to scoop her up and sit her on my lap. I wanted to do that so fucking badly. Then, I wanted to bury my nose in her hair while we cuddled, and I played with her pussy to make her feel better.

"Something's bothering you."

Her chin jerked up, and her eyes flashed red. "Do not forget that you belong to me, Relic, and I'm ordering you—as the owner of your soul and for your own protection because these boots could make mincemeat of your balls—to stop acting like you give a shit about me when we both know you'd end me in a heartbeat if you had the chance."

She'd gotten one thing right; I fucking belonged to her. I was hers, and she was mine.

I shook my head. "You don't know me very well yet, so I'll forgive you this time for saying that shit, but I will repeat this because you don't seem to be paying attention. I have no intention—and never had any intention—of hurting you, Fern, in any way. And you suggesting that I would—that I want to hurt you, *end you*—makes me seriously fucking grumpy." I grabbed her coffee off the table beside her and held it out. "Now, finish your drink, and let's go open the shop."

―――

"Why are you doing this to me?" Fern said as she climbed off the back of my bike, her gaze darting around the clubhouse parking lot as she tugged at her sleeves.

"Not doing anything to you, Tink."

I took her hand, and she dug in her heels when I started toward the clubhouse.

"Nope. I changed my mind. I'm not going in there."

"What's the problem? You don't think I can protect you? You think that my brothers would dare lay a fucking hand on you?" My voice came out rougher than I'd intended because the beast in me did not like that my female questioned my ability to protect her.

"They're hellhounds. I'm a demon."

"We don't hate demons, Fern. If they're up to no good, then, yeah, we let them see our mean side, but we don't just see a demon and immediately want to fuck them up."

She didn't look convinced, she was still searching our surroundings, over the row of bikes, then to the garage, where a couple of my brothers were working. "They won't like me. They'll sense I'm a demon and see me as a threat."

I stopped trying to pull her after me and stepped close

to her instead, forcing her to tilt her head back. I grinned down at her. "No one here will see you as a threat, little demon."

"Asshole," she muttered.

"You're cute when you get all feisty."

She tried to shove me. "Why are you like this?"

"Like what? Charming? Sexy? Handsome? No idea. I was just born this way, Tink."

She tried to fight it, but a small smile curved her lips, which was exactly what I'd been going for. She was scared as hell, and the bitter scent surrounded her. I fucking hated it.

"So, why was it so important that we come here?" she asked, this time letting me lead her toward the door, albeit reluctantly.

"Willow—the alpha's mate—got some bad news this week, and I wanted to pay her a visit."

She frowned up at me. "What kind of news?"

"She's losing someone close to her."

"Oh."

She didn't say anything more as I led her into the clubhouse. Jagger and Rome were at one of the tall tables across the room and gave us a chin lift. A couple of other brothers were sitting on the couches in the back with females and didn't even notice we'd walked in. The door to the dens opened, and Warrick walked out. He spotted me and headed my way.

His gaze slid to Fern when we stopped, and she stepped behind me, pressing against my back. I fucking hated that she was afraid, but I fucking loved that she instantly sought protection from me.

War looked at me and lifted a brow. "What's up?"

"Wills home?"

"Yeah."

"How's she doing?"

Warrick's expression grew heavy. Before he'd met Willow, before they mated and he gained the ability to truly feel, he hadn't done that; his face had given away nothing. Sometimes, when I looked at him when he was with his family, he'd have this look that even I could tell expressed a whole lot of really fucking good things, and I wanted to know what it was like, what those good things felt like. This time, though, it was obvious. I didn't need to ask what this one meant.

"She's not doing too well. She's heading back out soon."

"You good if I stop in and see her?"

War looked back at Fern, and she actually whimpered.

"Who's your friend?"

I reached back, curling my arm around her to reassure her. "Brother, you're freaking her out."

He looked back at me, and there were questions, but thankfully, he didn't voice them.

"I've got her," I answered.

Fern was no threat to his female or their pup.

Warrick nodded. "If you go now, you'll catch her before she leaves, and then I need you back up here. We leave in half an hour."

War had texted earlier—something I hadn't told Fern. We had a couple leads on Faron, and he wanted all hands on deck.

I felt her stare burning into me, and I ignored it. I jerked up my chin and carried on toward the door that led below ground. War's orders weren't the only reason I'd wanted to bring Fern here. The faster she got used to my brothers and to the clubhouse, the better. But most of all, I wanted her in my den, in my bed. Fuck, I wanted her honeysuckle scent all over my sheets.

———

FERN

I'd never met Willow, but I knew of the witch's family, and I'd met a couple of her sisters. Magnolia was one of my regulars and the one who'd told me how to find Agatheena's cottage. And, yeah, okay, I'd checked out their profiles on Nightscape—a social media app for non-humans—but I never thought I'd be in one of their houses, never in a million years. Nor the hellhound's den, and definitely not in the alpha's private quarters. I sure as fuck hadn't thought I'd be standing by the door, trying to be invisible, while Warrick's mate distractedly offered me fucking tea.

"No, thank you."

She'd barely looked at me when we walked in, and I got the feeling when we left, she'd forget I existed. She was definitely preoccupied; grief etched her lovely face. Good thing she wasn't in the mood to chat because right then, I was busy working at keeping my breathing even and not hyperventilating. I didn't like confined spaces, and knowing we were below ground was making it hard for me to remain calm.

You know where the exit is. You're not locked in. You can leave at any time.

Relic was holding her baby in his big arms—rocking her gently, murmuring low, and occasionally scenting her tiny head—while the witch rushed around, putting things in a bag covered in sparkly unicorns. The baby had been fussing but calmed seconds after Willow handed the child to Relic.

Relic and Willow talked about someone I didn't know in reverent, hushed tones, and I barely heard a word, focused inwardly now, trying really fucking hard not to freak out.

Relic placed the baby in her car seat and buckled her in, and then he pulled the witch into his arms, hugging her and dropping a kiss to the top of her head. Something sharp and painful tugged in my chest. It was unexpected and weird, and I didn't like the way it felt. Not at fucking all.

"You need anything, Wills—any of you—I'm here, babe."

She smiled up at him. "I know—we all do, and we love you for it."

We left and carried on down the main tunnel.

Fuck.

The walls were stone, and torches lit the way, giving everything a golden glow. There were more caves branching off here and there. The dens were obviously vast. The clubhouse was nothing compared to what was down here.

Finally, Relic stopped in front of a door, unlocked it, and then opened it.

His scent was stronger in this room. This was where he slept.

He led me inside and closed us in.

"Why are we here?" I asked, wrapping my arms around myself. My heart was pounding, my palms were sweaty, and every inhale had my body tightening and heating.

"I need some more of my shit if I'm staying at your place," he said, his gaze really freaking intense.

I quickly looked away, taking in the large room. There was a big bed to one side, a dresser, and a couch off to the side with a flat-screen TV on the wall. I assumed the door beside the bar fridge across from me was the bathroom.

I desperately searched for a window, but of course, there wasn't one. There were grooves between the edge of the wall and the ceiling. What looked like natural light filtered in from somewhere, and that helped ease the pressure in my skull a little. It wasn't exactly like the dark dungeon I'd imagined. Still, I didn't want to be down here.

"What do you think?" he asked.

"Uh, yeah, it's fine, I guess." I didn't know what to say, and he was watching me closely.

"War and Dirk—our two mated brothers—have bigger quarters. The rest are like this one."

"Oh ... right."

I crossed my arms, still feeling on edge and off-balance from being in this place, being below ground, being stared down by the alpha, seeing Relic with that witch and her baby, and now this. My fangs tingled, and my heart pounded. I was a volatile mix of thoughts and feelings, and my hunger was growing again, rearing its head, reminding me of what I was. I was torn between curling up on the floor in fear, running like fuck out of here, and launching myself at Relic and sinking my fangs into that thick vein at the side of his throat.

"Can we go now?"

He was studying me, and I wondered what he could sense, how many of my fucked-up emotions and desires were being broadcast to the hellhound.

"My brothers need my help first. You can stay in here —"

"No, you need to take me home first."

Relic shook his head. "I can't do that, Fern, but as soon as I get back, we'll go to your place, yeah?"

"I'm ordering you to take me to my place. I own you, remember? And I'm not comfortable here, so you have to do it," I said, my voice growing louder. I sounded like a bitch, but I had no control over that. It was my fear default, and right then, I was shit-scared.

"You're not at risk here, Fern. Leaving you at your place on your own is more dangerous. Now, I've got shit I need to do, and keeping you here is how I'm protecting you."

I charged for the door, but he hooked me around the waist, stopping me. I fought, gasping back my terror. Something else I'd learned over the years was to never, ever scream. I silently fought, my grunts and pants filling the room as Relic manhandled me like I was a rag doll. He pressed me against the wall, immobilizing me easily; one of his big mitts encircled my wrists while his other hand gripped my upper thigh, and his massive body pinned me.

"Stop," he said low. "Take a fucking breath."

"Let me go. I want to go home," I bit out. "You can't do this. You can't trap me here."

A rumbling sound vibrated through his chest and into mine. "I'm not trapping you here—"

"Please ... please, you can't ... don't lock me down here." I was in full-on panic mode now. No, I wasn't screaming or crying or yelling because that was not what I did, but the terror was so vast and so fierce that the panic took hold, and I was close to passing the fuck out.

"Look at me," Relic growled.

I dug my nails into his arm and snapped my teeth at him because I was a demon, and instinct had taken over—scratch, bite, fight.

"Fern," Relic barked, giving me a shake.

I froze and blinked up at him.

"You need to calm down for me, okay? Take a breath, baby, nice and slow ..."

More rumbling vibrated from him to me. It should be terrifying, but something about it was ... comforting. I dragged in a much-needed breath, doing what he'd said—because if I didn't, I would definitely pass out, and then he could leave, and I'd be trapped.

"That's it, Fern, and another one." He pressed a kiss to my forehead, like he'd done to the alpha's female, to that baby, like he cared, as if he cared about me. "Now, I need you to listen to me—really listen," he said roughly.

"I'm not a fucking idiot," I bit out because I wanted him to care, and that scared me even more. "I know how to listen."

His lips twitched, and I barely resisted snapping my teeth again, biting that lower lip hard enough to make it bleed, then I'd lap at it, and—

Stop.

Oh, fuck, now, my body was getting all hot and bothered. I was afraid and turned on at the same time. That was so fucked up. I was so fucked up. *Disgusting.*

Relic breathed deep, and his eyes flashed, getting all glowy before another growl slipped from between his perfect lips, which made me feel even hotter. Oh gods, he could smell it ... *me*. Of course he could. He knew I was scared, and he knew I was turned on. My face burned with humiliation.

"I'm not going to lock you in here, Tink," he said as if he hadn't just scented me, as if he didn't know how hot and slick I'd gotten while I fought against him.

"Put me down," I rasped.

He didn't move; he just held me in place. "I need to do my job, and I can't do that if I'm worried about you. So, I need you to stay here in my room. You'll have the key. You can lock yourself in if you need to, but no one will bother you. You are safe here. I know you're scared, but I need you to promise me you won't leave, that you won't try to go back to your place without me and put yourself in danger."

He was pretending like he didn't know what my body was doing, how it was reacting. He'd chosen not to shame me. I realized that his grip on my wrists had loosened, and if I wanted to, I could slip them free. I took another deep breath because I'd lost my shit just now, and there was no denying it. And as much as I didn't want to stay here, going back to my place alone would be monumentally stupid.

"Who else has a copy of your key?"

"No one but me." His voice was rough as hell. His eyelids drooped, and his irises were still glowing, but he was acting like nothing was wrong. "There's one on my dresser and another with my bike key. That's it, the only two."

What choice did I have?

I blew out a ragged breath. "Okay, fine."

ELEVEN

RELIC

ROMAN FOLLOWED me around the side of the old building. It had been a boarding house back in the day, but it was condemned a long time ago. Now, it had boarded windows and heavy-duty padlocks on the doors. The place reeked of darkness, of fear and blood and chemicals I couldn't name, which singed my fucking nose and prickled at my flesh.

I motioned to the door at the back. The lock was broken. Loth and Fender were going in from the front, so I eased the door open and searched the dark room. Our night vision was excellent; we didn't need any other light to see inside. Rome screwed up his face. The scent was so much worse now. My boots crunched on broken glass scattered across the checkerboard linoleum, and I tilted my head, listening for sounds of life. Nothing.

If Faron had been here, he was gone now, but whoever had been holed up here had caused a lot of damage.

We walked deeper into the room as Loth strode toward us.

"You need to see this," he said.

We followed him down a set of stairs and along a hallway. The carpet was damp and smelled of rot. The farther down the hall we went, the stronger the scent of fear became, overtaking everything else, along with the unmistakable stench of death.

Lothar opened the door to what had once been a utility room at the end of the hall, and Fender looked up from the stack of papers he was leafing through, shoved his red hair back, and shook his head with a scowl. Death, rot, terror—they saturated the room. There was blood streaked on the walls and pooled on the floor—dark, almost black. It'd been there for several days, and it wasn't demon—or not just demon anyway. If it were, we'd be in a room full of ash. No, the owners of the blood in this room had been something else as well.

I walked to the large stainless steel bin against the wall. There was a laundry chute above it. It was covered in a bloodstained sheet. I tugged it off. "Fuck."

"What the fuck is Faron up to?" Roman growled.

I took in the bodies—all female, all mutilated, and at odd angles. The body on top was unrecognizable; they all were.

"Is that ink?" I said to Rome.

"Yeah, and I'm pretty sure ..." He dragged the fabric of the female's shirt up a little, revealing more of her stomach. "It's one of mine."

"You know her?" Loth asked.

"She's a witch." He tilted his head to the side. "She came to me a while back after seeing some of my work."

"They're not just witches though."

"Nah. The blood in here, I scent demon as well," Lothar said. "None of them mated either."

Loth had one of the best noses out of all of us. I was having trouble getting anything past all the chemicals in this fucking room. But when a female was mated, her male's scent was branded on her—claiming her, warning off other males. If Loth said they weren't mated, they weren't mated.

"See if you can find any ID on them. When we know what the fuck is going on here, we can let their families know," he said.

But not before. We didn't need a bunch of witches and their covens getting involved in Lucifer's business, not until we figured this out.

We searched the rest of the place. The scent of chemicals was stronger in several rooms, along with evidence of torture, but nothing else had been left behind. When we finally headed out, I grabbed a steel bar and used it to jam the door shut, and Fender did the same to the front. Then we got on our bikes and headed back to the clubhouse.

By the time we got there, it was the early hours of the morning. I'd forced myself to focus on the job all night, but my mind had repeatedly pulled me back here.

Had Fern been okay without me? She'd been terrified when I left. She'd also gotten turned on when I pinned her to the wall. Fuck. Leaving her had been one of the hardest things I'd ever done.

I crossed the main room, punched in the code by the door, rushed down the stairs, and along the tunnel. Unlocking my door as quietly as I could, I walked into my room. It was dark, apart from the light coming from the TV. She wasn't on the couch or in my bed. I pushed open the bathroom door. She wasn't in there either.

Fuck.

I scanned the room. She'd left. She'd fucking left.

I headed for the door. A whimper came from the couch, and I spun back. My jacket, still tossed over it, moved. Rounding the bed, I eased the heavy leather back, and my breath was punched from my lungs. Fern was curled up under it. So fucking small that I hadn't seen her.

She was asleep. Her blood-red hair was all over her face, and I couldn't resist brushing it back. Her eyes snapped open, and in a flash, her hand jerked up, the knife in it flashing in the light of the TV—

I grabbed her wrist before she could thrust it into my throat.

Her eyes widened.

"It's me. You're okay." I gently uncurled her fingers from around the hilt and tossed the knife onto the floor. Then I scooped her up in my arms. "Go back to sleep, baby. I got you."

She shuddered, then collapsed in my arms. Relief. She was feeling relief again. I fucking liked she felt that way while I held her.

Carrying her to my bed, I laid her down, tugged off her boots and socks, then pulled the covers over her. She rolled, dragging the covers up to her nose, breathing deeply before more of that relief made her features relax. Then, she was out cold again.

My scent—it was on my sheets. That was what had soothed her, and she'd been under my jacket for the same reason.

Possessiveness was a fist in my gut. She had been seeking the comfort of her mate and didn't even fucking know she was doing it.

———

FERN

I felt warm, even my feet—and my feet were never warm—and so comfortable. Every muscle in my body was relaxed. I breathed deeply, and something smelled ... *yummy*. Warmth built between my thighs, a nice ache that had me squirming. I ignored that. I didn't want that. I had to admit it did feel kind of good though. It'd been so long since I had felt like that and wasn't hit with nausea immediately afterward. I hadn't felt nausea when Relic held me against the wall either—no, I didn't want to think about that. Instead, I breathed in deep again.

"Mmm." The sound left me on my next exhale.

The warmth surrounding me was deep in my bones, and I felt out of it, drowsy. I blinked, trying to wake myself up. It was still kind of dark, early morning maybe. I gave up.

The next time I woke, more light filled the room. I blinked again and stretched. My hand brushed something rough. That was when I became aware of the massive hand on my lower back and the boner digging into my stomach.

I jerked up. "What the fuck, Relic!"

He winced. "Fucking hell. Careful, Tink."

"Why are you in my bed again?" I bit out.

"Not in your bed, babe. You're in mine, and I told you, I'm not sleeping on any couch. I will also add—again—I didn't put you up there; you climbed on me all on your own."

He dragged a hand down his handsome face, and I realized he looked tired.

I hadn't really believed him the first time he said I'd done it, but after last night—curling up under his jacket when I'd started to freak out because his scent somehow soothed me—I was starting to. The only explanation for it was that I owned his soul; that had to be the reason for this weird connection I felt growing toward him. I tried to slide off him, and he hissed.

I froze. "What?"

He reached down and covered his dick. "Watch the knee."

"It's not exactly polite to get a ... to get ... like that ... when someone is forced to sleep beside you."

"Polite had fuck all to do with any of this, little demon. Nothing between us has been polite."

I tried to move, and his hand at my back gave some resistance, stopping me for a split second before he released me and let me slide off his body and to the other side of the bed. He was right, of course; basically stealing someone's soul was far from polite, but then neither was stalking.

"Still, I'd prefer if you didn't ... do that when you're with me," I said. "I think we need to lay down a few ground rules."

He huffed out a laugh. "My dick doesn't follow your rules, Fern. I'm sorry if me getting hard while you lie on me offends you, but those curves pressed against me, your body all squirmy, while you made a bunch of sexy little sounds—it got to me. I've got no control over that, babe. You're sexy as fuck and gorgeous, and you smell fucking amazing. My dick's gonna get hard. And, yes, I'm more beast than man, but I'm not a fucking animal with no control. You've got no reason to be afraid of me ... or it."

He was right; his dick did scare me, like everything else fucking scared me. The way it made my body feel—the way *he* made me feel—scared me, and I was so sick of being *fucking scared* all the time.

"You look tired," I said, desperate to change the subject. "Did I keep you awake?"

He shook his head. "Not you. Something else."

I didn't like the look in his eyes. "Did something happen last night while you were out?"

"It's all good. Nothing for you to worry about."

The hound was lying, of course. I could see something was bothering him—something other than me stealing his soul, that was. But I guessed what he did—as long as it didn't affect my safety—was none of my business.

I shoved back the covers and got out. "I need to get to work."

He yawned, stretched, then shoved back the covers as well and stood.

My gaze sliced down his body, and I froze.

He wore only a pair of boxer briefs, and the fucking baseball bat straining the front of them had my eyes widening.

"Holy fuck," I said under my breath.

He turned to me, looked down at himself and his enormous hard-on, then back up. Of course he'd heard me. I expected a cocky smile, but he didn't wink or make some boast about how big he was. No, he frowned before he kind of lifted his hands, as if he was afraid I'd bolt. And I couldn't lie—I was seriously thinking about it.

For a being with limited emotions, he had worry written all over his face. Did he recognize his own emotions right then? Did he know that's what he was feeling?

"It looks bigger than it, uh ... is?"

"I don't think that's how that works," I said, kind of pleased that it was him looking uncomfortable for once, though I didn't really understand why he was being so weird. I kind of felt like I had to make him feel better about his massive dick, which was ridiculous. "No, I wasn't pleased that I woke up with that monster in your pants digging into me, but seriously, don't sweat it. Your dick is none of my business. I'm fine now, truly."

His nostrils flared. "I'm glad to hear it."

"Though, I will say, your dick is terrifyingly large." Okay, maybe I was enjoying it a little too much, him being awkward instead of me.

He froze.

"Question: are you still a virgin?"

He still didn't move; he just blinked at me several times. "No," he said.

"I'm honestly surprised you've had any takers for that thing. If I saw it coming at me, I'd turn and run the other way. No offense." I grabbed my boots and sat on the couch.

Relic tugged on his jeans with jerky movements. "None taken."

I slipped on my boots and noted he looked kind of pissed off now. *Shit*. I'd been joking around—kind of—but I hadn't wanted to hurt his feelings. I mean, after everything, he'd never been unkind to me. I didn't have control over what he said, obviously; he could have been an asshole after what I had done to him, but he hadn't been.

"Sorry, I didn't mean to hurt your feelings—"

"I don't have any, Fern," he said.

But the way he'd said that I didn't believe him. He felt something, in that moment at least, maybe not as much as other beings, but he did, and I'd definitely offended him. I didn't like that.

"Relic, I ..." I took a step toward him as he tugged a shirt over his head.

His gaze came to me, and he waited for me to finish.

Crap.

"You're ..." I motioned to him from head to toe. "All that you've got going on—the muscles, the hair, the face, the ...

145

abs, and that chest—it's all, really good." My face was on fire, but I pushed on. "You're a good-looking male, the whole package."

His brow arched.

"What I'm trying to say is, I'm sorry if I offended you. You can say I didn't, but I can see that I did. You seem like a really good guy—for a hellhound. So, I just wanted to say that some female—with seriously special skills in the bedroom department—will be lucky to have you."

There. I'd thrown the dog a bone, but as I'd said it, an awful feeling had fisted in my chest, then tugged—hard—like it had when he hugged Willow. The idea of another female with Relic, waking up in his bed with him like I just had, didn't sit well with me at all for some reason. Again, I had to assume it was because I owned his soul. That had to cause a certain level of possessiveness, right?

Relic hadn't said anything, and I glanced back up. He was a giant hellhound statue, all except for the muscle at the side of his jaw, which was pulsing, like he was grinding his teeth.

"I feel like I just made it worse somehow." I bit my lip. "I was trying to be nice. I'm, uh … not very good at it." Nice was another vulnerability that I avoided, and it was easy to avoid when you didn't have any friends or family. "Did I make it worse?"

"You know what? I think it's quiet time." He jerked on his leather vest, shoved his feet into his boots, swiped his keys from the bedside table, grabbed his jacket, then took my hand and led me from the room.

The clubhouse was empty when we walked out, and I was more than a little relieved. One grumpy hound was enough for the morning, thank you very much. The parking lot was quiet as well, apart from whoever was working in the garage; the music was already on, and the roller doors were up, the shop open for business.

Relic turned to me, and without a word, he held up the jacket I'd fallen asleep under last night.

"Is that your way of telling me you want me to put it on?"

He narrowed his eyes.

"Fine. Whatever."

I slipped my arms in, and he maneuvered me so I faced him again, then zipped it all the way up. He got on his bike, started it up, and motioned with a jerk of his chin for me to get on behind him.

Okay, looked like he was sticking with quiet time for now. I climbed up, and like always, he reached back and pulled my arms around him, as if he knew I found the intimacy of it difficult, so he made it easy for me by not giving me a choice. I huffed like I was annoyed by his heavy-handedness, like I did when he got into bed with me, because I didn't know how to be close to someone in any way or in any situation. I felt awkward and out of my depth, but secretly, I craved it, and I was thankful that he made it easier on me. Gods, I was so fucked up.

We took off, and I had to admit, I was starting to enjoy our rides. I liked the wind, and the speed was kind of fun, and yeah, I liked how warm Relic was when he forced me to wrap my arms around him, and I was even warmer now in his jacket, which was like a freaking dress on me.

I was starting to love the feeling of freedom I had riding behind him. Even though I had no control over the destination or any of it, sitting back here, holding on to Relic while the wind whipped through my hair, it was like nothing else. I didn't need to think; I could let it all go for a little while. I'd spent too many years of my life not feeling the sun on my skin or the wind on my face, and I couldn't help but love every moment of it.

"I'll never be free again, will I?"

I squeezed my eyes shut to stave off the memory that rushed forward out of nowhere, but it was no use. There was no stopping it.

"You will." I brushed Harks's sweaty hair back from his forehead. "You have to fight this."

He'd told me his name after The Chemist threw him in here with me. He'd contracted the virus two days after he was forced to have sex with me, just like The Chemist had hoped. He was a good male, kind. He never wanted to hurt me, he was just trying to save his brother, but Grady had killed the younger male anyway. Now Hark was dying as well. It was only a matter of time. Somehow, I could hear his heartbeat, and it was growing weaker with every passing hour.

"I'm sorry," I whispered.

"I-it's not y-your fault." A shiver racked through him, and I pulled my blanket around him tighter as he gasped in a desperate breath. "Y-you have to escape here. Promise me you'll f-find a w-way."

"I promise."

I'd only known Harks for a week, but he was the closest thing I'd ever had to a friend, which was fucked up, considering how we'd met.

He struggled to draw his next breath; his mouth opened,

panic filling his eyes—then he went limp in my arms—a moment later, he turned to ash.

I stared down in shock as tears slid down my face.

I didn't know how long I sat there, unmoving, but the sun had gone down when The Chemist finally walked in.

He took in the scene. "The virus works," he said triumphantly. "He had witch blood as well—did you know that? Just like you, yet he died, and you did not." His head tilted to the side. "What are you, Estelle Burnside?"

He didn't want an actual answer. I was a mystery, a puzzle he was desperate to uncover. No matter what he did, I didn't die. And he wouldn't be happy until I ended up like Harks.

Nothing left of me but ash.

The bike pulled to a stop. We'd reached Seventh while I'd been lost in the past. Relic kicked down the stand, and I quickly jumped off.

Relic swung off, his head tilting to the side when he looked at me. "You okay?"

How did he always know? But there was no way I was going to tell him what I'd just been thinking about, so I lied, "Yep."

He stared at me for several more seconds, but thankfully, he didn't push for more and let it go. He did close the space between us though, and instead of taking my hand, like he usually did, Relic's fingers curled around the back of my neck. I jerked and spun on him, but he didn't look at me, just kept walking, scanning the street, that firm grip on me moving me along at the speed he wanted. What he did not do was keep talking. A quiet Relic wasn't natural.

"Relic?"

He looked down and did the brow-raising thing again.

I blew out a frustrated breath. "I'm sorry if I offended you, okay? Can quiet time be over now?" I hated it.

He stood to the side of the door so I could unlock it.

I threw up my hands when he still said nothing. "Why are you so pissed anyway? I thought you'd be proud or something. You have a big dick to swing around and show off. Aren't you, like super stoked?"

I rolled my eyes when he still didn't answer, and that muscle in his jaw jumped again.

"Don't say I didn't try, and that was your last apology." I pushed the door open and stopped in my tracks. "No," I choked out.

Relic's arm was around me a moment later, pulling me back behind him as we entered my store.

Everything had been destroyed. Nothing was left intact.

"My apartment." I pulled from his arms and took off up the stairs.

"Fern! Fucking stop," Relic barked.

He bounded up the stairs after me, hooking me around the waist again and lifting me off my feet before I could get through the kicked-in door. But it was too late, I saw the destruction. All my things that I'd painstakingly collected, things that had given me joy after escaping a living hell— had been smashed to pieces. A gasp of agony left me, and Relic put me down, turning me to him.

"Don't move. Stay right here."

He strode into my apartment, quickly searched it, and then bounded down the stairs. I wrapped my arms around myself.

They'd made their move. They were coming for me.

Nothing could stop them, not even Relic, because, eventually, he would leave me. Eventually, he'd leave me unprotected, and they'd be there, waiting.

I collapsed to the floor as images flashed through my mind like a horror film and I was the main character, but it wasn't a movie; it was my life.

One moment, I was sitting on the stairs, and the next, Relic was lifting me, gripping the back of my head and tucking my face against his shoulder.

"It's okay. They're gone. You're safe."

"I'm fine ... I'm okay," I lied, trying to convince myself as much as Relic, even while I shook uncontrollably against him, sucking in gasp after gasp.

"I got you, baby. Let it out," he said as he rubbed my back.

But no tears came. I didn't cry—I never cried. Crying did me no good. It had never done me any good.

"You need to tell me who the fuck did this, Fern," he growled. "Because I'm going to hunt them down and make them scream."

A shudder slid through me.

No, they'll make you scream. They're the ones who make you scream.

CHAPTER
TWELVE

RELIC

"I DON'T WANT to go with you," Fern said as I led her across the clubhouse parking lot toward the bar.

I'd brought her back here last night and sent a few of my brothers to gather anything salvageable from her place and bring it to my den. Her store had been secured, but she wasn't stepping foot back in that place until I knew what the fuck was going on.

She'd spent the day on the couch, my jacket up to her nose, watching TV. I made room for her stuff and found another set of drawers, but she just stayed under that jacket, not fucking speaking, barely moving.

My female had needed comfort, but she wouldn't let me give it to her the way I needed to, and there was no way I was leaving her on her own again tonight, not while she was like this.

"It'll be fine." I carried on toward the bar. "I got you covered, Fern."

"I should have just stayed in the room."

I felt the tremble move through her when she said that, and she actually clung to my hand tighter—and not just because we were about to walk into a bar owned by hell-hounds. I ground my teeth. She still wouldn't fucking open up to me, and I'd tried all day to get her to tell me something, fucking anything, but she wasn't talking.

"Nah, babe, that isn't happening, not after what happened."

"So chivalrous," she said, trying to be a smart-ass, but I saw her relief in her long exhale, in the way her muscles relaxed, even if she was trying to hide it because I now knew what to look for. "So, how long's your shift?"

"Until closing." I shrugged. "All depends on how busy we are." I could have gotten someone to cover for me, but I needed an excuse to get her out of the room and back to her old, feisty, attitude-filled self.

It was only nine, but the bar was already filling up. I led her around to the barstool I'd had Rome save for her.

"You sit here. You'll be close to me, and if you need anything, just let me know, yeah?"

Fender walked over and held out his fist, and I bumped it. Then, his amber eyes slid from me to Fern, then back.

"Now, I know why you haven't been around much." He leaned against the bar. "Hey, honey. The name's Fender. What's yours?"

"Her name is none of your concern." I slid a whiskey his way.

He held up his hands. "Just being friendly."

Fern's eyes were wide, and I watched as they slid from Fen to Loth, then Jag, before hitting War as they all stood across the room, their leather vests and patches, telling everyone in the room exactly who and what they were. Her entire body stiffened. She was about to bolt. I gave Fender a look, telling him to fuck off without words, and he arched a brow but sauntered off.

I poured her a beer. "Take a breath, Tink. No one here is going to fuck with you, okay?"

"I know. I'm fine," she said, chewing her lip as she glanced at my brothers and back.

She was lying—even I could see that.

Over the next few hours, I stayed busy while the bar filled with shifters—mostly wolf, a couple of crows as well, and a handful of witches. I topped off Fern's beer when it needed it, hoping that might help her relax, but she stayed on edge, scanning the room, as if she expected a monster to walk through the crowd and snatch her off her stool.

Problem was, my female was hot as fuck, even covered from neck to ankle. There was no missing the curves; add in that blood-red hair, those wide peridot eyes, her cute upturned nose, and a mouth like that? Yeah, she drew attention.

Roman had spotted her about ten seconds after we walked in and had instantly headed in her direction. He'd pulled up short when he got a whiff of my scent on her though, and my bared teeth had helped explain the situation further. After that, my brothers had seen the way it was and stayed away out of respect.

The wolves though? Were another story, and one in particular had been eyeing her most of the night. I'd been watching him. Kaleb was young, cocky, and arrogant as fuck. He'd obviously finally decided to make a move, and he was weaving his way through the crowd now, focused on Fern.

"Hey," he said when he stopped beside her, flashing her a grin.

"Hey," she said, not really looking at him.

"I couldn't help but notice you across the room. Can I buy you a drink?"

"No, thanks," she said.

He leaned in and scented her. "What exactly are you, gorgeous?"

I quickly finished pouring a drink for the guy in front of me and handed it over, then strode toward them.

Fern was scowling up at him, and still, the fucker reached out and touched her hair. She jerked back, fire flashing in her now-red eyes for just a moment before she forced them to return to normal because there were humans in this room, and they definitely didn't need to see that. Her hand moved to where I couldn't see it. I assumed she was going for her knife. My female did not like to be touched—definitely not by some random asshole—and I sure as fuck didn't like it either. He reached for her again, and I grabbed his wrist before he could touch her.

The wolf spun toward me.

I gave the little fuck a shake, rattling his shit for brains. "You don't touch her," I growled. "You never touch her."

He paled. "I was just—"

I slapped him in the face with his own hand.

Beer sprayed out of Fern's mouth, and she bit her smiling lips together.

"Relic, man, I was just—"

I slapped him in the face again. "Only one thing I want to hear from you, Kaleb."

His eyes darted between a now barely holding it together Fern and me. "I don't … touch her?"

"That's right," I said, then released him. "Now, fuck off."

He spun around and rushed back to his packmates, and I didn't miss that Lothar, Rome, Jag, and War were all watching and grinning so widely that they looked ready to fucking burst out laughing. I ignored them.

"You good?" I asked Fern.

She was still biting her smiling lips as she nodded. "That wasn't something you see every day. I gotta say, hound, I like your style."

"Thanks, Tinker Bell. I like yours as well."

She seemed to relax a little after that—for the next half hour anyway—until War came over. All my hard work getting her to relax went down the drain when he stood at the other end of the bar, his all-knowing gaze shifting from me to her. Fern instantly stiffened, quickly looking down.

Goddammit.

"There something we should know?" he asked low when I reached him, not that Fern could hear all the way over here, and definitely not over the music and loud voices.

He slid his empty my way.

"She's mine."

He nodded as I poured his drink. "Yeah, brother, we figured that part out for ourselves. You staked your claim. No one here's looking to challenge you. But when you say she's yours, you mean what? You're just fucking for a while or something more?"

He knew, and he was going to make me say it. I had no reason to hide it. I was fucking proud she was mine. I wanted everyone to know, but there was still this niggling feeling inside me that it shouldn't be my turn yet, that Lothar or Jagger or any one of the older hounds was more deserving. Fate had had other ideas though, and who the fuck was I to question fate?

"She's my mate, War," I said, then rubbed at my chest, at the deep ache there. "Only one problem: she's scared of me more than half the time, and I'm pretty sure she hates me."

"Understandable," he said. "You're a hound."

He hadn't missed she was a demon.

"What the fuck do I do?"

"No idea, brother." War grinned wider. "Try and enjoy the ride."

"That's it? That's all you've got?"

He shrugged. "No way I can describe what you're about to go through. All you can do is ride it out and hope like hell you don't fuck it up. Because if you do? You'll have a whole lot of new emotions that will make being without her suck that much harder."

"Good talk." I walked away to the sound of War's laughter.

War had slowly developed a whole lot of new emotions when he met Willow. Somehow, our mates were the key to unlocking all of it, and I couldn't lie—I was fucking terrified.

CHAPTER
THIRTEEN

FERN

RELIC SMILED and chatted with people as he served drinks, and there was no missing the way the female population of this room reacted to him. Lust. All the lust. Females touched his arm and looked up at him with awe. I saw several slide napkins to him with their numbers, and then I watched him toss them in the trash when they weren't looking.

"You need anything?" he asked me when he was at my end of the bar.

"I'm good, thanks."

He asked me that every time he was down here—always checking I was okay, that I had a drink, that no one was hassling me. I was starting to think that perhaps Relic really was a good guy, and that made me feel kind of like shit. I was also feeling a lot calmer. My anxiety had been through the roof, not just from coming in here, there was also the break in, and because of that, my emotions had been getting the best of me. Then, his alpha had eyeballed me across the bar, and I almost peed myself. No, he hadn't done or said anything threatening, but he didn't have to. That healthy fear of hellhounds, built into my DNA, had wailed in my skull, telling me to run. Yes, I'd gotten used to Relic, but the other hounds were another story completely. So I'd done the only thing that would help: I'd taken a small shot of my "courage" potion when no one was looking. I'd pay for it later, but there were too many predators in this room, not only hounds but wolves, and I'd even seen a couple of crows in the corner—a breed you did not ever want to draw attention from. I sure as fuck didn't want any of these beings sensing my weakened emotional state.

"Hungry?" Relic asked, and his gaze dipped to my mouth.

"Nope," I lied.

There was a gnawing in my gut that was constant now, and it wasn't for food. I needed blood. Exhaustion had settled in my bones in a way it never had before. I hadn't been able to get off the couch all day today and it hadn't just been about the rage and sadness I was feeling over losing nearly all of my worldly possessions—and I now knew there was only one thing that would cure it.

"So, I'm curious. Why do you work here? You guys own it, right? Why not just hire more people?"

"I'm not too good to work the bar, Fern. Plus, I like it. When we first left Hell and set up the clubhouse, then the garage and this bar, we had no choice but to work them ourselves. We got to know the people in this town. Good people—humans, not just others. So, we all still like to do the occasional shift and hang out."

That kind of surprised me. "And I guess it's a good way for you all to hit on females," I said, my curiosity getting the better of me.

He frowned a little. "Sure."

His big hands rested on the bar, and I had the crazy urge to slide my hand over his, to feel his rough skin, his warmth. Nope, that was not the kind of courage I wanted from my potion.

"It's also a good way to hear what's happening in the city, to keep tabs on things," he added.

"You seem pretty popular," I said, unable to help myself. I subtly motioned to a human down the bar, watching him. "I wouldn't turn your back on that one. She's barely looked away from you since she walked in."

Relic glanced over his shoulder and frowned, then grunted when she perked up, her smile widening as she waved enthusiastically. He turned back to me. "Fixed her car a few days ago. When she picked it up, she asked me out."

He was watching me closely, and that weird feeling filled me again—that tug in my chest. "So, you're dating her?"

Relic frowned. "Fuck no. Turned her down."

I winked. "Well, don't look now because she's headed this way."

"Fuck," he muttered.

She tapped his arm. "Relic?"

The sudden urge to grab that finger and snap it off hit me from out of nowhere.

He turned. "Hey, uh ..."

"Bethany." She giggled, her eyes sliced to me and narrowed before going back to Relic. "You said you were busy, so I thought I'd come here to see you instead."

"I see that," he said. "I'm working right now."

Her gaze slid back to me, then up at Relic. "You have time to talk to her."

Relic's head jerked back, and his expression hardened. "Said I'm busy, and I'm busy. I also don't owe you an explanation—"

"No, I just mean, you said you were busy, but I've been watching you, and you've been talking to that girl all night. So, maybe you do have time for me after all." She licked her lips. "Just tell her to leave."

"No," he said to her.

"I don't like people playing games—that's all. Tell the girl to leave, and you can come home with me later."

She looked at me again. When her eyes met mine, fear filled them instantly. Humans could sense darkness, danger. My rage spiked, and it was a struggle to stop my eyes from turning red. I didn't know why, but I was barely holding myself back. Unfortunately, her horniness was overriding any sense of self-preservation, and she pressed her hand to his chest.

I gripped the edge of the bar when the urge to leap over there and scratch her fucking face off slammed into me— hard.

Relic swiped her hand away. "I didn't fucking say you could touch me. And as for games? I'm not playing games with you, female. I don't know you. I tried to let you down easy, but now, I see that isn't going to work. Not interested. Don't want to go out or hang, and I sure as hell don't want to fuck you."

"I gave you my number," she said as if that actually meant something.

"And I tossed it as soon as you walked out of the shop." He crossed his arms. "Time to leave."

"But, Relic—"

"Best you find a new garage as well."

Her face crumpled, and she ran from the bar.

Relic shook his head, looking pissed off and kind of bewildered.

I sat there, fighting the feelings swirling inside me, feelings I should not be having. I was irrationally angry, and my skin was hot and tight.

What the hell was wrong with me? Relic was an extremely handsome male—I got that—but I wasn't interested in him, right? I was just confused because of the whole owning-his-soul thing, because he made me feel safe, and I was mixing that all up in my head with something else, something that wasn't real. And, okay, waking up, draped all over him, wasn't helping; it was creating this illusion of closeness that didn't exist. I'd never had any kind of closeness with someone—ever—so I didn't know what to do with it. I was confused. I was just really fucking confused.

Hunger gripped my stomach tighter, and heat hit my face. I quickly slid off my seat.

"Where are you going?" he asked, eyeing me in a way that I didn't like, as if he could see deep inside me.

"Bathroom." Then, I took off before he could round the bar and insist he come with me.

I rushed down the short hall and into the restroom, and as soon as the door shut behind me, silence engulfed the small space like a heavy blanket. I locked myself in a stall and tried to calm my racing heart. The hunger wouldn't subside though. In fact, the silence was making it worse.

I finished up and washed my hands. Then, through the stillness, a heartbeat—no, two—reached out to me, pounding through my skull. I shook my head, trying to get it to stop.

Why was this happening to me now?

Drawn to those throbbing pulses, I walked back out to

the hall and froze when a moan somehow reached me over the loud music and voices out in the bar, as if my senses had zeroed in on the owners of those heartbeats. Instead of going back to the bar, like I should, I followed the sounds of pleasure farther down the hall.

A door was ajar, and I looked through the inch-wide gap. An office. A female was sitting on the desk. She was bare from the waist down, and I recognized the auburn hair of the male crouched in front of her. The hound I'd first met when we got here—Fender. His large hands were gripping her hips, his face buried between her legs. His growls of enjoyment and her cries of pleasure started a deep throb inside me.

I felt out of control, dirty, afraid, and so incredibly turned on that I had to squeeze my thighs together. Fender snarled, and the female fell back, arching against the desk, trembling uncontrollably. The oxygen punched from my lungs when a vision of Relic and me doing what they were doing filled my head. I swallowed thickly.

No.

Nausea tried to creep in, but the hunger inside me shoved it back.

I spun away, rushing back to the bar. The thud of heartbeats, of blood pumping through veins, bombarded me. My gaze darted around the room. I felt cornered, terrified of the deep hunger inside me, gnawing in my gut and throbbing between my thighs.

I didn't know myself at that moment. I didn't know my own mind or my body.

Gasping in a breath, I looked over at the bar and locked eyes with Relic. He was already rounding it, heading for me. My hands came up all on their own, warding him off. I was afraid of what I'd do or say, of my own thoughts and feelings.

One of the wolves howled suddenly, and then someone was tossed across the bar. With a snarl, they jumped up and ran back. The thud of bodies colliding and fists hitting flesh came next, and the room broke out into chaos. The scent of blood saturated the room, and my mind spun, my fangs tingling. Terror washed through me as my hunger deepened, yawning wider. I felt my eyes change, and I tried to change them back, but I couldn't stop it.

"Fern," a rough voice barked.

I looked up, and Relic was staring down at me. He saw my eyes and cursed. He snatched me off my feet when another body went flying across the room and all but tossed me over his shoulder. The hounds were wading in, breaking things up, but Relic strode through the crowd, knocking people out of his way like bowling pins as he went, heading for the exit.

Clamping my eyes closed to hide them, I waited until I felt the cool night air hit my face before I dared open them again. Relic kept walking until we hit the parking lot, but he didn't walk into the clubhouse. He carried me around the side of the garage, where it was dark and quiet. Then, finally, he eased me down his front, putting me back on my feet.

My back was to the wall, and he was crowding me, not touching me, not anymore, but he was close enough that I could feel the heat radiating from his body, making my already-hot flesh burn.

"What are you doing?"

"You were scared, Tinker Bell. Thought you might need some fresh air."

164

And he knew I hated being below ground, so he'd brought me here.

"Thank you."

"It's my job, remember?" he said low—so low that goose bumps rose all over me.

His job because I'd forced him to do it, to be with me.

"Right."

"You're shaking," he said in that extremely rough voice. "You need soothing?"

I knew he was here with me now because he had no other choice, but I did need that. I really fucking did, no matter how dangerous it felt for so many reasons.

"Yes, I think I do."

He moved closer, just the tiniest bit, and my mouth watered, and my pussy ached, and my vision sharpened.

His massive chest expanded, and his nostrils flared. "You're the boss, Fern. Tell me what you need, and I'm here to obey."

He could smell how turned on I was—he was a hound, so there was no way he couldn't—but I was too lost in the turbulent feelings running through my body to care.

"I'm yours to command," he said when I didn't answer right away.

His declaration was like a slap in the face. I was starved, turned on in a way I never had been in my life, but I would never take advantage of the power I held over him. I knew what that felt like—I'd experienced it over and over again—and I'd never do that to someone else.

"I want to go home," I choked out past my scratchy, tight throat. "I'm tired. I don't want to be here anymore."

His golden eyes studied mine, and then slowly, he nodded. "You can't go home, baby—you know that." Then he took my hand and led me to the clubhouse.

By the time we reached his room, I was trembling. The sound of blood pumping through his veins had me salivating, and his ... sweet Lucifer, his scent was making me hot and trembly, and that ache between my thighs wasn't going away—no, it was only intensifying.

I rushed to the bathroom and shut the door.

"Fern?" Relic called through the wooden barrier between us, and that deep, growly voice only made the ache, the need, worse.

"Don't come in. I'm getting in the shower."

I turned on the water, then all but tore off my clothes. My skin was too hot—fuck, it burned. The throb between my legs didn't ache anymore; it hurt so bad that I whimpered. I stepped under the cold spray, but it did nothing to cool me down. My potion had all but worn off, and it sure as hell wasn't helping the out-of-control feelings building inside me.

My hand went between my thighs, and I pressed my palm against my aching flesh. I normally avoided this for more than one reason, but right now, there was no way I could ignore the need pounding through me, distract myself, or exercise until I passed out—not this time. Resting my forehead against the shower wall, I spread my pussy with one hand and worked my clit with the other. Usually, I kept my eyes open so memories didn't invade my mind, but this time, I let them drift closed. I tried to think about Fender and that female and the things they had been doing, but no matter how hard I tried not to think about Relic, that was who kept invading my mind. It wasn't Fender on his knees; it was Relic. It wasn't some random female sitting on the desk; it was me—my thighs held wide, my pussy being licked and sucked.

I bit my lip and tried to hold back my moan so Relic

wouldn't hear when the first orgasm quickly rolled through me, making me shudder and turning my knees to jelly. I cupped myself but stopped rubbing. I kept the images playing through my head, letting my need build once more. My sensitive clit needed to recover for a moment before I carried on. Finally, slowly, I began again, building myself back up until I was panting, rocking my hips, imagining Relic behind me, slamming into me, his mouth at my ear, his growls rumbling through his chest, vibrating through me. I whimpered, gasping for air, so I didn't cry out when I came a second time.

Breathing heavily, I did what I had before, cupped myself without pressure, allowing images of Relic to fill my head because it was the only thing that worked. I knew it was dangerous to think about him like that, but I couldn't stop now. I started again, building back up, but the familiar panicky feeling filled me as I rubbed my clit, trying to get there again.

I was sweaty, hot, desperately trying to come, but I couldn't.

Just wait. Give it a few minutes, then try again.

I worked at slowing my breathing, at forcing down the panic.

Two more. Just two more, then you can sleep.

I started again, gently circling my clit, but it was extremely sensitive, and it wasn't working. Nothing was working.

I shook harder. I just had to wait a bit longer.

Self-loathing filled me, followed by shame.

What the fuck is wrong with you?

Angry tears welled in my eyes as I tried again, until I felt raw and it hurt. I covered my pussy with a washcloth and tried again over the top of it, but it wasn't fucking working.

You stupid fucking bitch. Now, look what you did. You couldn't just not touch yourself? Are you that much of a slut that you couldn't just not play with yourself? Dirty fucking whore.

A sob burst from me, and I collapsed on the shower floor, still rubbing my now-stinging flesh.

Two more times. Two more times. Then, everything will be okay, and nothing bad will happen. You fucking idiot. You dumb bitch.

The bathroom door opened.

"Fern?"

I didn't stop, lost to my compulsion, ruled by it, even more now than usual. The potion hangover was already setting in and making everything worse.

"Get out," I shrieked.

The door to the shower opened. One moment, I was on the floor, sobbing and masturbating like a psychopath, and the next, I was in Relic's arms, and he was carrying me out of the bathroom.

"Put me down," I wailed. "I can't ... I have to ... I need to ..." I whimpered.

He lay me on the bed, and I scrambled up the mattress, my back against the wall, sweating and naked and flustered, while I rubbed at myself like a fucking twisted whore.

"Talk to me, Fern," Relic said, an unreadable look on his face. Not scorn or disgust, just blank.

Thank fuck, he barely had any emotions. I couldn't bear to see those things on his face right then.

"I have to come. I've only come twice. I need to do it two more times, and I ... I can't do it. I can't."

He nodded slowly. "Okay, baby. We'll get you there. Stop rubbing, okay? Right now, you're hurting yourself, and you're not going to get off when you're hurting."

His calm voice slid through me, over me. Somehow, the

panic receded, but the shame grew because there was no stopping now.

"Don't look at me," I choked out.

"You got it, Tinker Bell." He turned away. "You got some toys, babe? Something that vibrates?"

I shook my head, then realized he couldn't see me. "No. I'm not a whore."

"Making yourself feel good doesn't make you a whore, and toys can help get you there easier and faster than your hand. You got some lube?"

"No," I said, dying inside.

"It's okay. We'll figure this out," he said.

He didn't ask me why I was doing this or tell me to stop, or say there was something wrong with me. No, he was going to help me.

I stared at his wide back. "I'm disgusting. You think I'm disgusting, don't you, Relic?"

His fingers curled into fists. "No, baby, you're not disgusting. Far fucking from it."

"I'm ugly and scarred," I choked out. "And depraved."

"If getting yourself off is depraved, then I'm depraved as well, Tink. And if you call yourself ugly ever again, I'll take you over my fucking knee. There's not one thing about you that is ugly. Not one fucking thing."

I felt his words deep inside me, and I couldn't hold in the ones that came out of my mouth next. "If I didn't own your soul, would you want to ... be with me?"

A growl rolled through the room. Then he chuckled without humor, so low that I felt it in the pit of my stomach. "Fuck yes."

I chewed my lip, my heart pounding hard. "Would you know how to ... get me off?"

"Yes."

That was it—one word said with utter certainty. I was desperate. He was kind and handsome, and he'd sworn to protect me, apparently even against himself.

"Then I order you to ... get me off."

His back was still to me, but I didn't miss his sharply indrawn breath.

"Your fear just skyrocketed, Tinker Bell." He took several more deep breaths. "But your pussy—it's hot, and it's getting wet again. I can smell it. You want it, but you're scared as fuck."

He was right; my clit was too sensitive, but just asking Relic to do that for me had that deep ache throbbing all over again.

"I'm more turned on than scared."

"You're still scared of me though."

"A little," I said, giving him the truth.

"You think I'm going to hurt you, sweetness?"

No one had ever called me sweet *anything* in my entire life.

"No."

"But you're scared anyway?"

This was getting too damn deep. I just needed to get off. I needed him to get me off.

"I gave you an order, hound." The demand was ruined, though, by my trembling voice.

He turned slowly, and I yanked the sheet over my nakedness, hiding my scarred body even though he'd already seen everything.

"Then, I guess I'd better obey."

FOURTEEN

RELIC

My female was naked, in pain, curled up at the head of the bed, clutching a sheet to cover herself, to cover those scars on her body. I shook, so full of rage over whoever had done this to her, who had hurt her so much that she was suffering this way. I salivated for their flesh, craved the screams that would come as I tore the meat from their bones.

I didn't know why she needed this, but I'd give her whatever the fuck she wanted if it made the wild, terrified look in her eyes go away. If ordering me to do this gave her the power back she needed, then she could order me about all she liked, but there was no way I'd do anything that she'd hate me for later. I'd die before I did anything to hurt her more.

"I got you, Tink." I moved to the side of the bed. "Keep the sheet over you, and scoot down the mattress for me, yeah?"

The attitude left her wide, stunning yellow-green eyes

now, replaced by other emotions—not all of them I was capable of naming—but it made my gut hurt and chest tight because even I recognized the shame, the hope, the fear. My female felt vulnerable. The word filled my mind—what it was, what it meant—and every one of my instincts demanded I pull her into my arms and soothe her. Fuck, I hated that I didn't know what it was like to feel what she was feeling, that I couldn't fucking help her exactly the way she needed because identifying an emotion was different than experiencing it yourself. I had an understanding because Lucifer had gifted that to us, but that meant fuck all when she was silently asking for something that I had no idea how to give.

"Now what?" she whispered.

My den was engulfed in silence. The only sounds were her quickened breaths and the low, rumbling growls I couldn't seem to stop from vibrating through my chest.

"How do you usually get off, baby? You always rub your clit, or do you fuck yourself with your fingers?"

Her face went bright red. "I ... I, um ... my clit."

"You're pretty raw there now, yeah?" I asked carefully, keeping my voice as soft as I could because she was skittish as fuck.

Her eyes dipped, avoiding mine. "Yes," she said so softly that anyone else wouldn't have heard her reply.

"That's okay. I can fix that." I dropped to my knees on the floor beside the bed. "Can I take your hand, Fern?"

Her gaze sliced up to me, and she nodded. "What are you going to do?"

"A hound's saliva has healing properties. It'll heal you up fast."

I took her hand, lifting it to my mouth, and she watched, wide-eyed, as I dragged my tongue over her delicate fingers, getting them nice and wet. I had to choke down my snarl when I got my first taste of her pussy. Her own healing abilities would heal her fast, but nowhere near as fast as mine.

"Now, I want you to spread yourself, Tink, and gently slide my saliva anywhere it's sore. Can you do that?"

She nodded again, her face still deep red, her breathing growing more rapid. The scent of her pussy reached me, heavier now. She was getting wet again, and my cock was hard as stone, straining behind my jeans. I ignored it, focusing solely on her, on making her feel better.

Releasing her wrist wasn't easy. I wanted to keep touching her, but I couldn't do that, so instead, I watched her hand disappear under the sheet. Her legs spread wider under it, and then she exhaled hard when her hand made contact with her raw flesh.

"Oh, it feels ..."

"Soothing?"

"Yes, it's cooling, but warm and ..." She bit her lip, and I could see her hand moving under the thin fabric.

"A bit more, and you should be all healed." I licked my lips in anticipation. "Give me your hand again, baby."

Her hand slipped back out, and her lids quivered as I lifted her fingers to my mouth. This time, when I dragged my tongue over her digits, her taste was so much stronger, and my fucking eyes rolled back in my head. My balls actually fucking tightened, and my cock pulsed so deeply—that for a moment, I thought I might disgrace myself.

It took all my control not to suck her fingers into my mouth, but somehow, I resisted. This wasn't about me; this was for her—only her. I released her, and she did it again, only now, a little whimper escaped her when she slid her fingers over her abused clit.

"Better?" I asked, my voice so deep that it was all beast now.

"Y-yes. It's not sore anymore."

"That's good, baby. And I know you want this over with, but if you rush it, you'll end up back where you were when I walked into the bathroom. You need to start slow. Be gentle. Your pussy is delicate. The only time it gets abused is when it's the good kind—the kind you want, the kind that makes your eyes roll the fuck back and has you begging for more. You don't hurt yourself, okay?"

That pussy belonged to me, and it deserved to be worshipped at every opportunity.

"You never hurt yourself."

She nodded. Sweet fucking Lucifer, her lips were swollen and dark from her sharp little teeth and fangs. Images of me leaning in and sucking that plump lower one into my mouth and tasting it invaded my mind.

"You usually circle it first or lightly rub?"

She was panting now, and the scent of her arousal filled the fucking room.

"Circles first."

"Okay, good. Start with that, Tink."

Her hand moved under the sheet, and her breath caught.

"Feels good?"

"Mm-hmm," she said, her eyes fucking locked on me.

"No pain, baby?"

"No."

The reason females came back to us over and over again was because we knew when a sexual partner liked what we were doing. We had the ability to register what they were feeling and could zero in and give her exactly what she needed. Yes, I could tell she was getting close by the way

174

she'd picked up speed under the sheet, but I could also sense it and feel it.

"Don't rush. Take it slow."

She nodded, her lashes fluttering as her hand moved faster, ignoring me, chasing how good it felt.

Fuck, she was almost there already.

"You gonna come, sweetness?"

Her hand was moving fast as hell under the sheet now. Then her eyes fucking rolled up, her back arched, and her entire body stiffened. A cry burst from her before she jolted and trembled. Panting, she collapsed back onto the mattress.

"That's it. Fuck, Tink. That's it, baby."

Her face was flushed, her eyes bright, lips swollen. I'd never seen a more beautiful sight than my female after she just came for me—because that was what she'd done. Fern had come for me, looking at me, imagining I was on top of her, inside her—there was no doubt in my mind.

"That was ..." She shook her head.

"Looked pretty fucking good from where I'm sitting," I said before I could stop myself.

A breathless laugh escaped her. "How you doing over there?" she asked.

I knew teasing when I heard it—that, at least, was something I had a lot of experience with, especially since Warrick had mated Willow, and her family became ours. I fucking loved that Fern was feeling lighter after that, especially after the way I'd found her.

"Don't need to worry about me; this is all about you. One more, and then you're golden."

She bit that fucking plump lower lip again, her short fangs sinking in, and I reached out, pulling that sexy lip free before I realized what I was doing. She didn't jerk back or tell me to fuck off though, so I swiped my thumb over it.

"You don't abuse this mouth either—understand?"

She blinked over at me, her delicate throat moving with her audible swallow. "If you say so." Her tongue darted out, sliding over where my thumb had just been.

I felt that stroke, as if it were across the head of my cock. We stared at each other, the silence stretching out. I was so fucking tempted to lean in and kiss her, to take ownership of that hot-as-fuck mouth as the seconds ticked by, but I didn't. I would not risk scaring her away.

Instead, I cleared my tight throat. "You ready to go again?"

"I think so."

"How you feeling? Any pain?"

She shook her head, but then she held her hand out. "Could you? I think it helps."

"You got it."

The taste of her pussy was making me crazy, but I could control myself—because I had to. I curled my fingers around her hand and dragged my tongue over her fingers. I tried to hold it back, but I fucking trembled—a full-body quiver, like I was shaking the water from my fur. I also moaned so rough and loud that Fern actually jumped.

"Sorry," I said thickly and released her.

She blinked over at me. "Are you okay?"

I didn't want her thinking something fucked up over my reaction, so I gave her the truth. "Didn't mean to freak you out, babe, but you taste really fucking good."

"I do?"

Another rough sound, which was pure hound, resonated from deep inside me. "If Lucifer decided to put me in the ground for good, you'd be my last meal, Tinker Bell."

She did that biting-lips grin, like she had at the bar when she was holding in her laughter, and I really fucking liked that a lot.

"You still need my help, or do you want me to leave?" I made myself ask the question. I didn't want to go anywhere, but I also didn't want her to hate me when all this was done, and the lust she was feeling was replaced by something else.

"Oh, um … no. You can leave, if you want."

No, I didn't want that. I wanted to stay. But if I said I wanted to stay now, she'd think I was some fucking creeper when this was over, and if I left, she'd think I didn't want to be here.

"I want to do whatever you want me to do," I said like a fucking idiot.

"I should be okay."

I had no choice but to leave, and I wanted to kick my own ass. "I'll be just outside the door if you need me."

She nodded. I stood and left my den, closing the door behind me, but I didn't go far. I stood right there, facing the door, gripping the doorframe like a fucking dickhead. And not only could I feel her hunger, her pleasure building, but with my superior hearing, I could hear every rustle of the sheet, every panted breath, every whimper. My cock throbbed, and my heart pounded, and I could still taste her on my tongue. I was so fucking pissed off that I was out here and not in there, that I was missing it—missing the most beautiful female I had ever laid eyes on getting herself off—and I wanted to punch a hole through the fucking wall.

Her cry, when it came, pierced my fucking soul, and her

177

drawn-out moan made my cock pulse so hard again that my knees almost gave the fuck out. I listened as she panted, as her breathing finally evened out, slowing when she fell asleep. I should stay out here for a bit longer, but I couldn't stop myself from opening the door.

She lay on her back, her blood-red hair spread over my pillow, the scent of her pussy heavy in the air. I breathed deep as I took her in—so small in my bed, so still, besides her chest rising and falling. One of her hands was still under the sheet between her thighs. The other was up by her face, and there was something dark fisted in it.

I rounded the bed to get a closer look, and when I saw what it was, I bared my teeth and choked down a possessive snarl. My shirt—it had been on the floor. I leaned in and scented it now. I could smell us both. She'd had it by her face. My little female had been sniffing it, breathing in my scent when she got herself off the last time.

Pulling out my phone, I fired off a quick text to Rome. He owed me one, and I was calling it in. I didn't know what caused this, but I'd never let her get in the state I'd found her in ever again.

I should probably give her some space after what happened; I didn't want it, but she might. But I couldn't convince myself to leave, not now. I also knew when she woke, she'd feel even more vulnerable, and I didn't want that. Her waking up naked beside me wouldn't help, so I grabbed my shirt from her hand and eased it over her head.

"Huh?" she said drowsily.

"You're okay, Tink."

She helped me slip her arms through the sleeves.

"Go back to sleep, baby."

She muttered something incoherent, rolled to her side, curled up, and went back to sleep. I stripped down to my boxer briefs and slipped into bed beside her. She immediately wriggled closer; her unconscious mind recognized who I was even if her conscious one hadn't yet.

No, I didn't know what had happened here tonight, what had driven her to that, but I wanted to find out. Somehow, I had to get her to open up to me.

I wrapped an arm around her and buried my nose in her hair. "You're safe now, sweetness. No one will ever hurt you again."

CHAPTER
FIFTEEN

FERN

My eyes flew open when my stomach revolted violently. I blinked into the darkness. I was still in Relic's room, and he was asleep beside me, so close that I felt the heat radiating from his body like a furnace.

Oh, fuck.

My hand flew to my mouth, and I scrambled out of bed as quickly and quietly as I could. Then, I stumbled to the bathroom. I bumped the door shut with my foot and rushed to the toilet. Dropping to my knees, I heaved, emptying the contents of my stomach. Biting back my groan, I gasped in gulp after gulp of air and shook my head, praying this was a one-and-done situation, but I knew I wasn't going to be that lucky when the nausea started to build again instantly.

Idiot. I'd done this to my damn self. *What the hell was I thinking?* I should never have taken the potion last night. I'd let my anxiety get the better of me, like I always did, but between the hunger, and the break in, I'd been seriously struggling. At that moment, when I'd been lost in my fear, imagining the past repeating itself, while sitting in a room full of freaking predators, I hadn't seen another choice. The knowledge that it would make me sick had seemed like a far better option than having a full-blown meltdown in front of everyone in the bar, in front of Relic.

I heaved again, and angry tears filled my eyes. I'd never fucking hated myself more.

Even knowing the nausea would come, that the fear and my compulsions would be worse when the potion wore off, I'd still done it.

In my defense, it didn't usually last that long, but of course, now, out of all the times I'd used it, I could tell this was going to be worse than ever before. Maybe because I'd used it less than a week ago when I went to Agatheena's, and there'd still been traces of it in my system? I could only guess, but I was never taking it again—at least not when I was with others.

I didn't need an audience while my fucked-up mind forced me to complete a list of rituals just so I could function. When I took the potion, old compulsions from when I was younger would rear back up; checking and rechecking that I'd locked doors and windows, switching the light on and off while I counted to four, reading certain things like the names of TV shows or street signs and having to repeat them in my head, only backward, not stepping on cracks, retracing my steps, like there was a rope connected to my back that would get all tangled up if I didn't go back the way I came, whether it was in my apartment or the route I'd taken to the grocery store, the list went on, and all while I counted to four and back, everything in fours—even how many times I fucking orgasmed.

I cringed in shame and horror, remembering what had

happened when we came back here last night, the way I'd behaved, like a sexually depraved psychopath. Groaning, I retched so violently I shook. I wanted to disappear. I never wanted to see Relic ever again. Maybe if I begged, Agatheena would let me stay with her. I'd do whatever she wanted. No one would ever find me out there. Not even Relic could get past her wards.

My face burned hotter, and I gagged, straining as bile burned my throat when there was nothing else left.

I jolted when my hair was carefully lifted back from my face, and tried to pull away, but a muscled arm curled around me, holding me still.

"I got you, Tink. Get it all out, baby."

I shook my head. *No. Sweet Lucifer, no. Not this.* I didn't want him to see me like this as well. "Leave me here," I choked out. "Go away. P-please. Just leave me."

I felt so weak, my limbs heavy and shaky, and despite the nausea, hunger still gnawed viciously at my stomach. I couldn't even shove him away. I couldn't do any-fucking-thing, and right then, I just wanted to disappear and never come back.

"Not going anywhere, Fern," he said roughly. Then, his arm around me slid away a second before I felt his fingers running through my hair.

"What are you doing?"

"Just getting it out of the way."

He was braiding it. A lot of the hounds wore it that way. Relic's had been braided the first time he came into my shop. Tingles prickled all over my scalp—the nice kind that made me feel all drowsy. The last time I'd felt that was when I was a child, when my mom would play with my hair while she read me a bedtime story.

"W-why are you doing this?" I heaved again. I hadn't

thought there was anything left inside me, but apparently, I was wrong.

" 'Cause you got really nice hair, and I didn't think you'd want puke in it," he said.

Out of the corner of my eye, I saw him take a hair tie from the bathroom counter and then used it to secure the braid.

"Good thinking," I said, trying to act like this was nothing, that I didn't care, that I hadn't just begged him to leave when all I wanted at this moment was for the ground to open up and suck me under.

One of his hands, large and warm, slid up and down my back, soothing me. "Don't act so surprised. I'm not just a pretty face, you know," he said, his tone teasing. "I'm kind of offended all you see are the muscles and the good looks."

I huffed out a laugh. "I bet about now, you wish your muscles were the only things I'd taken advantage of since you met me."

"You haven't taken advantage of shit, Fern," he said, all traces of teasing gone.

I shook my head while the elephant in the room loomed over us, stomping its massive feet, demanding attention. I couldn't take it. I couldn't pretend what had happened hadn't. What I'd done was absolutely fucked up. I swallowed past my scratchy throat several times.

"So far, I've stolen your soul, ordered you around, thrown attitude, been a bitch, demanded you protect me, treated you like a servant"—I swallowed again, my throat like razor blades—"and a ... a sex slave last night, and now a fucking nursemaid. So, I don't just see the muscles and the handsome face. No, I know exactly what kind of male you are, Relic—a good one—and I'm ashamed of the things I've done to you—"

"Don't," he growled. "We don't use that word here. Shame does not exist in this place and not between us. So, I'm telling you now, you need to lose it from your vocabulary—understand me?"

"What I did to you ... and last night ..." I heaved again, but not from the aftereffects of the potion, not this time. I'd taken advantage of him, used him like an object to help get me off. I squeezed my eyes closed as I gasped in a breath. "I'm so disgusting. You must hate me; you must hate me so much."

I was jostled suddenly and lifted as Relic sat back, leaning against the wall, positioning me in his lap.

Wriggling, I desperately tried to get away. I didn't deserve to be comforted. "I need to release yo—"

"Shh. It's quiet time." He tugged down the towel from the rail beside him, still damp from his shower earlier, and used it to wipe my face. "No more talking, Tinker Bell, because everything you're saying is not only wrong, but it's pissing me off."

He tossed the towel aside and wrapped his arms around me—not tight, but enough that I knew he wasn't letting me get up. "I told you last night that you're not disgusting, that there's fucking nothing disgusting about you." He smoothed his hand down my back, soothing me again. "No, sweetness. To me, you are fucking perfect."

I recoiled, shaking my head, and opened my mouth to tell him he was wrong, but he took my jaw in his hand—again, not hard or painful, but in a way that told me to shut up and listen.

Didn't he understand that his view of me was distorted? I owned his soul, for fuck's sake. He was confused by the connection it had created between us. I sure as hell wasn't immune to it.

"Everything I've done since the night we made our deal was voluntary."

I shook my head, trying to speak again, and again, he stopped me.

"I know you don't believe that, not yet, but it's true. I'd wanted to protect you before we made our deal, Tink. I told you that—you know I did—so you have to know that I'm more than good with that part. As for the rest of it, getting you a cup of tea doesn't make me a servant, and helping you last night ..."

I tried to look away, but he wouldn't let me do that either.

"Helping you last night did not make me your fucking sex slave, baby. It just fucking doesn't because, again, everything I've done was because I wanted to. And taking care of you when you're sick ... I'm starting to get the feeling that not many people have done that for you, so sitting here with you now—taking care of you when you are at your most vulnerable, knowing that you trust me to do that for you, whether you like it or not—is my fucking privilege, Fern."

I blinked up at him. This male could not be real. Everything he'd said gave me feelings I didn't know what to do with, filling me to overflowing. And the biggest one? Hope. I didn't let myself hope. Ever.

He only thinks those things because you own him.

My head refused to entertain the things he'd said. It was just my poor, neglected heart that wanted to believe a male like him could truly care about me.

"You don't know me," I whispered. "You wouldn't say those things if you did."

I wanted it to be true, for him to truly care about me, but I'd taken enough from him. I couldn't let him think those things; I couldn't *not* warn him. I wasn't the female he thought I was—I couldn't be. If he saw me—if he truly saw me—he never would have said what he had. He sure as fuck would never think caring for me was a privilege.

He held my gaze. "Why don't you try me?"

If I was going to get through this thing with my heart intact, then I needed to protect it. I needed to squash the stupid hope trying to rear its goddamn head. I needed to make him stop looking at me like that.

"I have compulsions," I whispered so low that I wasn't sure he'd hear me. Shame burned my face. "Like ... like last night, but other things too. The way my shoes are lined up, the way my cup is placed by my bed at night. I check things over and over again. I like things in fours, and I count in my head all the time. And all of it gets worse when I'm stressed. My anxiety gets so bad that I made an elixir to help me when the fear and the intrusive thoughts get the better of me, except it makes everything worse when it wears off. What happened when we got back from the bar was the worst it's ever been." I looked away because looking at that handsome face and those gentle eyes was too much. "Then afterward, I get sick. I throw up."

His knuckles slid under my chin, forcing me to stare up at him. "You did this to yourself?"

"Yes."

Yes, I'm that fucked up. So broken that I took something that hurts me because I can't deal with the real world like everyone else can.

Here it came—any minute now, the disgust. It was kind of a relief, honestly, because hope was exhausting and the most terrifying thing of all.

"You should've told me, Tink," he said, his expression unchanging. "If I'd known how freaked you were, how bad it was, I would've gotten you out of there sooner," he said, blaming himself instead of telling me what a fucked-up mess I was.

"Stop saying nice things to me. Just fucking stop."

"I'm not gonna stop, sweetness." His thumb swiped across my cheek. "And you can't make me."

"I'm not sweet, Relic," I choked out, my body trembling as if I were going into shock.

"You are to me," he said, followed by another gentle swipe of his thumb. "And feisty and tough and fucking gorgeous."

I shook my head. "You're wrong."

"Fern, I'm not."

"I'm an abomination," I whispered.

His nostrils flared, and he bared his teeth. "Well then, you're the sweetest little abomination I've ever seen."

"Why are you doing this?" I hated the way my voice cracked, revealing just how vulnerable I was at that moment. "What do you want from me?"

"Don't want anything from you that you aren't willing to give. I just want you, baby, whatever you decide that is."

My heart was pounding wildly in my chest. No one had ever said anything like that to me in my life. My head spun. I was so weak, so hungry, so fucking tired.

Relic was like a dream—a beautiful dream. A nice change from the horror show that usually played through my mind. He made me feel so incredibly exposed. Relic unarmed me, but he was also safe, and for the first time since I'd escaped the twisted prison my grandfather had taken me to, I wanted to let someone in just a little bit.

I looked into his eyes and took several steadying breaths. "I ... I need to brush my teeth," I said, chickening out instead of saying what sat on the tip of my tongue.

I didn't miss the disappointment that drifted through his eyes.

He didn't comment, just stood, holding me up when my legs tried to give out. Guilt and frustration filled me. I'd never felt weaker or more pathetic in my life. I grabbed my toothbrush from the counter, loaded it with toothpaste, and quickly brushed my teeth, but even that felt like too much work. I spat, and he handed me a clean towel to wipe my mouth.

"Ready to leave the bathroom?" he asked.

My stomach still felt iffy. "Not yet."

He sat back down on the floor, taking me with him, arranging me on his lap. Gods help me, I let him hold me in those strong, warm arms with no thought to protest or resist, not anymore.

"I only found out I was a soul collector a couple of weeks ago." I hadn't meant to say it; I hadn't thought I would.

His beautiful beast's eyes searched my face, waiting and hoping for more—I could see it—but he wasn't going to push. Again, I wondered if he realized that he was feeling it, all those emotions that were being broadcast from the depths of his gaze, because surely, he had to be feeling something if I saw it so clearly.

He'd never force me to say or do anything I didn't want to do, no matter how much he wanted me to share with him. Relic wasn't like that. As that truth settled, I realized I wanted to.

"That night at The Vault, that was going to be the first time I drank blood."

His nostrils flared. "You've never fed before?"

I shook my head and licked my dry lips, my eyes drawn to

that thick vein in his throat. "I've had bouts of weakness on and off most of my life—anemia. I thought I knew why, but it's not … the reason I thought. And because soul collectors don't need to feed so often, not like vampires, and because I'm not a full soul collector, I guess I've gotten by without it."

"But something changed?" he asked.

"The weakness, the tiredness has been getting worse, and I'm … I'm just so hungry, Relic. Sometimes, I can't think straight."

His chest expanded. "Then, let me feed you. Let me give that to you."

"I can't ask you to do that."

"You didn't, I offered."

My mouth watered, and my stomach cramped. "What if I hurt you? What if I can't stop?"

I knew how it felt to be on the receiving end of it—being lost to another being's bloodlust—and I'd never wish that on anyone.

He grinned, tucking my hair behind my ear. "First, you're not going to hurt me, and second, you don't think I can stop a little pixie like you?"

"What if I drink too much? What if—"

"If I start getting dizzy, baby, I'll stop you. But FYI, hounds regenerate at a fucking rapid rate. I'll be making more blood as quickly as that pretty mouth is drinking it." His thumb slid over my lower lip. "You don't have to hold back, and you don't have to restrict yourself. You can drink until you're satisfied, Fern. As much as you want, whenever you want it."

A groan slipped past my lips before I could stop it. I realized I was panting. My fangs were tingling, and the cramps in my stomach were growing more intense. The thump of Relic's heart, the sound of his blood rushing through his veins, filled my head now.

"You'd let me do that?"

"You can do whatever the fuck you want to me, sweetness. Whatever you want, I'm yours."

He meant it, and he was making it impossible for me to resist. And I didn't want to, did I? That was why I'd told him those things—because I hungered for him so badly, because I knew he'd offer to feed me. I was still being a selfish bitch, but I couldn't stop this, not now. If I didn't taste his blood soon, I thought I might actually die. His vein throbbed, and I licked my lips.

"Bite me," he said roughly.

The control that I'd been hanging on to by a thread snapped, and I moved with a speed I hadn't known I was capable of. As I straddled his wide hips, my vision went hazy, tingeing red. A weird sound vibrated from my chest— a repetitive purring sound I didn't know I could make.

"If I hurt you—"

"You won't."

"But if I do, promise me you'll stop me. Promise me you'll push me away."

"I promise."

His hands gripped my hips as I dragged my nose up his thick throat, breathing in his delectable scent. My tongue darted out for a taste, and I groaned again, then whimpered when I felt that thick vein, hot and pulsing.

"Do it, Fern. Bite me. I'm yours, baby."

He was mine. The words filled my mind, and at that moment, I believed it. I wanted it to be true. Letting go— finally letting go of everything—I sank my fangs into his flesh. As his blood filled my mouth, sliding over my lips and tongue and coating my teeth, I felt whole for the first time in my entire life. His taste set my body, my nerves, my fucking soul on fire.

"Fuck," Relic grunted, and his fingers dug into my hips, followed by a sound that was impossibly low and gravelly.

If he wanted me to stop, I couldn't do it myself; he'd have to tear me off him because with every mouthful of blood I swallowed down, my body became more alive.

I didn't realize I'd been so numb until, cell by cell, nerve by nerve, limb by limb, I came back to life. The warmth sliding down my throat heated me from the inside out, causing tingles to dance over my flesh. My blood felt hot in my veins, and the pulse between my thighs was deep and wild. As I drew harder on Relic's vein, I felt his cock grow heavy beneath me. The vibrations from his chest—from the animal, the hound—blended with the ones coming from me.

My nipples were tight, and the ache had me pressing my chest against his.

"I got you," he said as he rubbed my back with one hand. "Don't you fucking stop. You drink until you're full."

Dark need curled inside me, untamed and uncontrollable. Between my thighs was swollen and slick, and I felt so fucking empty that it hurt. I couldn't stop myself from pressing down on the hardness beneath me, trying to fill that emptiness, even through his underwear—the only thing between us. I ground down harder, gripping his shoulders, and rolled my hips.

"That's it, sweetness. Whatever you need, you get it from me. You take it from me."

Yes! Yes, I'll take it from him because he's mine. Relic is mine.

I tore my mouth from his throat long enough to cry out as I came hard, grinding on him. Then I latched back onto his throat, rocking against him, feeding in a frenzied way I had no control over. I didn't want to control it. I wanted to feed, and ... sweet Lucifer, I wanted to fuck. I wanted to be fucked.

"Fuck me," I groaned against his throat. "Please, fuck me. I need it."

I ground my clit down on him, bucking and grinding, and I came again, sweating and trembling and crying out, but it wasn't enough. I needed more.

Relic hissed.

"Please," I begged.

One minute, I was straddling him on the bathroom floor, and the next, he was up and carrying me to the bedroom.

"Not gonna fuck you, Tink, not yet."

I growled, rubbing up on him while I slid my tongue over the blood still sluggishly pulsing from his vein. "Please, I need it," I said, knowing I couldn't make Relic do shit, at least not in this, not when it didn't involve my protection or our deal.

A breathless chuckle left him. Then, he dumped me on the bed and came down on top of me. "I know you want it, but you're not in your right mind, and as much as I'd love to get inside that sweet-as-fuck pussy, I'm not doing anything that will make you hate me later. When I fuck you, you won't be blood-drunk; you'll be fully fucking sober. Don't move."

He climbed off the bed, and I protested, spreading my thighs and rocking my hips.

"Hold tight, Fern."

He opened the door, grabbed something from outside, shut the door again, and strode into the bathroom. The sound of running water came next. Then, he was back with something in his hand and lay down beside me.

He pressed it—whatever it was—against my thigh. It was rubbery and vibrating.

"What is that?"

"Something that vibrates to get you off nice and easy so you don't hurt yourself."

A vibrator? He'd gotten me a vibrator.

"When? How?"

Instead of answering, he pressed his wrist to my lips and put the vibrator in my hand. I was too turned on, too hungry still, to resist. I sank my teeth into him, into his vein, and rolled my hips as his blood filled my mouth again. He curled his fingers around my hand and led the toy to my pussy, running it over my clit. I jerked and bit down harder.

Relic growled. "Put it where you need it; put it where it feels good."

I might be blood-drunk, but I knew I'd come twice, that I had to come at least two more times, that for once, I *wanted* to come two more times. I slid it through my slickness, rubbing it over my clit, and the vibrations had my eyes rolling back.

"Oh gods." I rocked against it, panting.

It was too much, and I slammed my thighs closed around it, pulling it back a little bit so it was still touching me but with less intensity. A moment later, I arched off the bed, groaning low, coming a third time, while my inner muscles clenched fiercely around nothing.

"I feel empty," I groaned.

"Then push it inside you, baby. That's what it's for—to make you feel good," he said. "Show me how you like to be fucked, Fern."

His gravelly voice rolled through me. How could I still be turned on?

Holding on to his wrist tight, I drew deeply on his vein, and with my other hand, I positioned the vibrator right where I needed it. I slid it in slowly, and my eyes widened. Then I whimpered when I saw him. Relic was watching me, his eyes glowing gold in the shadowed room.

I lapped at his wrist. The zing of his blood and the feel of being filled—it was more than I knew what to do with. I lost control, sinking my fangs into his vein again as I thrust the vibrator into me repeatedly, my eyes locked on Relic the whole time.

"That's it. Pussy's fucking dripping, Fern. So fucking pretty. So fucking hot. Hold it inside. That's it. Feels good there, yeah? Stay deep. Now faster, short strokes."

It was as if he knew exactly what I needed. Heat flushed my entire body as that dark hunger filled me again. I moaned, squeezing my eyes closed as pleasure built inside me, so high that I was forced to release Relic's vein so I could throw my head back. I screamed as my pussy clamped down hard, making me shake and writhe as I came. I'd never come this way, ever.

My eyes flew open, and Relic was right there, looming over me, his glowing gaze sliding over my face.

Without thinking, completely ruled by instinct, I reached up, slid my fingers around the back of his neck, and drew him to me. His lips met mine, and I moaned as the taste of his blood and his tongue mingled together against mine. He didn't pull away or try to stop me; he kissed me back. It was hot, and deep, and perfect.

I'd wondered what it would be like to kiss him—those full, perfectly formed lips—and it was so much better than I'd allowed myself to imagine.

He slowed the kiss down, taking over as my body calmed, and I loved that even more. His tongue slid lazily into my mouth, sucking lightly on my lower lip before his brushed across mine over and over.

Finally, he lifted his head, his gorgeous eyes on me as he swept my sweaty hair back from my face. "Like I said, Tinker Bell, fucking sweet."

CHAPTER
SIXTEEN

RELIC

SHE BLINKED up at me before she looked away. "I've never kissed anyone before."

My beast snarled, and the growl that left me was deep and rolled through the room.

Her gaze sliced back to me. "You like that?"

"The beast in me likes it very much. I know it's fucked, but I like that those lips are mine and only mine. No one else gets to know how they feel or how they taste but me." There'd been no holding those words in, I hadn't even tried.

Fern was mine, and the sooner she started to figure it out, the better. That new bit of information wasn't going to help me keep my shit together though, not when my cock was hard as fuck, and the beast craved so fucking much more. Yeah, I wanted to flip her over, tug her ass in the air, and mark her while I worked my cock inside her and claimed what was mine. But Fern wasn't there yet. She had no idea what we were to each other, and I didn't know how to tell my skittish female without freaking her out.

She licked her lips. "Well, while we're talking about firsts, I've never had an orgasm like that, uh … last one either," she said. "I've only ever touched … you know, the outside."

My cock throbbed harder, the beast pushing more fiercely against the surface. "You've never fucked yourself with your fingers, Tink?"

She shook her head.

"Why?"

"I just … don't," she said.

She was hiding something from me.

"So, a few firsts tonight then, sweetness?"

"Yes."

I pressed a soft kiss to her cheek, then her lips, and thank fuck, she let me. They were dark, fuller than usual from feeding and kissing, and utterly irresistible. "How do you feel after feeding?"

"I've never felt this good in my life." Her eyes widened and dipped to my throat, then back up. "Are you okay? I didn't take too much?"

Her eyes were bright, her skin glowing. It shouldn't be possible, but somehow, she looked even more beautiful now than before.

I grinned. "You feeding from me had the same effect as a mosquito bite."

She didn't smile back; there was alarm in her eyes. "I couldn't stop, Relic." She almost whispered it, like it was a terrible confession she was afraid to speak out loud. "I didn't want to. All I cared about was satisfying my hunger. Not everyone I feed from is going to be able to regenerate like you or be as strong. I need to learn to control myself when I feed."

I resisted the snarl at the mere thought of her feeding

from anyone else.

I cupped her jaw, running my thumb over her lower lip, brushing over one of those sharp little fangs. "That's not something you'll ever have to worry about, Fern, because I'm the only male, the only being, you will ever feed from."

She huffed out a laugh. "You can't say that. Neither of us knows what's going to happen in the future."

I had to bite my tongue. She was still jumpy as hell and still hiding so much from me. Telling her now that she was my mate might send her running, and with someone out there wanting to hurt her, I couldn't risk it.

"I'm immortal. I'm not going anywhere. We're tied to each other through our deal. You've got an endless blood supply, is all I'm saying."

She gave me an odd look. "Well, thanks for the offer. I appreciate it, but I guess I need to be ready for any eventuality."

I lifted my chin and again bit down my snarl.

Her hand slid up my arm and over my shoulder.

That simple touch had my heart banging harder and goose bumps rising all over me, and the pain in my chest, in my gut, intensified. My feelings for Fern were manifesting in a physical way. War had described it to us once. How it'd felt when he slowly gained his emotions. He'd said it hurt, made him nauseous, and that he had to fight the urge not to do a lot of seriously fucked-up things. Like, for example, right then, I wanted to lick her from head to foot, rub up on her until she was thoroughly marked with my scent, and then lock her in my den until she begged me to mate her.

The beast in me thought that was an excellent idea from start to finish, but Lucifer had made us more than just animals, and I knew that Fern wouldn't be down for that. No, locking her in here would piss her off and scare her.

Then she'd never beg me to fuck her ever again. Was that love? Was I in love with her? I had no idea. I did know that I'd never felt this way before, and it hurt and felt good at the same time, like pleasure and comfort and touch all rolled into one.

"What are these?" she asked, tracing her fingers over the ink on my shoulder.

"Protection runes." I couldn't take my eyes off her lips when she spoke. Fuck, they were pretty.

"Protection from what?"

Her tongue darted out a second time, moistening her lower lip, and again, I leaned in and kissed her softly because I couldn't not. That mouth was fucking mine, and like the last time, she let me.

"From possession. Evil spirits are drawn to us because we make good vessels. We're touched by Lucifer, Hell-born, and"—I stopped myself before I said *soulless*—"strong. A couple of our brothers were possessed a while back when War mated Willow, so we got these."

"Holy shit," she said, still tracing them, making me tingle all over, "that's terrifying."

"We lost one of our brothers, and another chose to remain in Hell after he lost his mate and unborn pup." It had been years, and Maddox still hadn't once returned to the surface.

"I'm sorry," she said. "I know what it's like to lose someone you love ..."

She stopped herself, like she often did, but if I wanted her to keep opening up to me, I had to keep asking the questions.

"Who'd you lose, baby?"

She breathed deeply, and I could see her thinking about it, deciding if she should share.

"My mom," she finally said.

Her gaze grew distant as she shut whatever she was feeling down, and the pain in my chest intensified because I knew that talking about her mother hurt her. But again, I had to keep up that pressure, gently pushing.

"I'm sorry you had to go through that, Tink. How did she die?"

Her throat worked. "She was murdered by a monster when I was seven."

I froze. "A monster?"

"Yes."

"You see it happen?"

She nodded.

"Fern—"

"Do you have a mother?" she asked.

I wanted to ask her more, but this time, I let her change the subject. The more time that passed, the more she was letting me in. She'd tell me the rest of that story—I just needed to wait it out.

"Lothar's my sire, but I never knew my mother."

She frowned. "What happened?"

I shrugged. "No one's ever really told me much about her except that she was a demon. I was the first hound born naturally, well, not created by Lucifer directly, anyway. The first and only born without my parents being mated. His handmaids looked after me when I was a pup, and when I was old enough to train, I joined my brothers."

"So, you're half demon."

"That's not really how it works with hounds. Male offspring are always hounds; female pups always take after their mothers."

She studied me. "So, Warrick's daughter is a witch? She won't be able to shift into a hound?"

"That's right."

And only the males of our young were granted immortality—unless our mates were already immortal, of course. If not? We were forced to watch our females age and die. It was fucked up, and Warrick had been in talks with Lucifer about it. Since Lucifer had granted Willow and any pups they have immortality, War wanted that for the rest of us, but Lucifer was resistant for some fucked-up reason.

"That's kind of crazy." Her finger did the tracing-my-ink thing again. "What about Lothar? Is he a good dad?"

"Loth and I, we've never had that kind of relationship. He's a brother to me, like the rest." Though, for some reason, talking about it now caused a weird feeling in my chest, one I'd never had before.

"Do you love him?" she asked.

"Until a hound mates, we're only capable of feeling loyalty, anger, and lust. We experience pleasure, but love isn't something we're capable of feeling or returning. So, no, but I would die for him, and he, for me."

Her finger drifted down to trace the hound that stood above the words Devil Dogs MC inked on my chest. "Sounds like love to me," she said softly.

"I wouldn't know." And without thinking, I did the same, except instead of ink, I traced over a scar on her forearm. "How did you get this?"

Her entire body stilled, and she pulled her arm away, shoving it under the covers. "I don't remember."

Again, she was obviously lying. My female was covered in scars—so fucking many—and every time I saw them, thought about them, I wanted to tear someone to shreds, to snuff out their worthless life, except there was no enemy to turn my rage on. There was no one to kill. Someone had hurt her though—the marks on her skin were definitely not from some accident. The one beside the scar I'd just pointed out looked like a fucking burn. Those scars shouldn't even be possible.

"I think I'll go to sleep now," she said.

She rolled away, effectively shutting any more questions down, and something thumped on the floor. The vibrator.

Fern stilled, staring down at it, and then she turned to me, cheeks dark pink. "Where did you get that from?" Her eyes filled with alarm. "Have you used that thing on other females?"

"No—"

"Then where did you get it?" she demanded.

"I messaged Rome and got him to pick it up while I waited outside the room last night."

The blood drained from her face. "You got one of your brothers to get it? You told him about me, about what I did, you—"

"No, Fern, I'd never fucking do that. I won't ever talk about you that way. Nothing we do, that you do, will ever leave this room—you hear me?"

She was shaking her head. "You must've told him something. He went sex-toy shopping for you ... for me, for fuck's sake."

She was moving away from me, and I grabbed her around the waist and hauled her back before she jumped out of bed and tried to run away.

"What you need to understand, Fern, is the kind of males we are, the way our emotions are, we do not fucking judge. That's a human emotion. I told you we crave touch, that we need it and the pleasure it gives us, but you've also seen how big I am. Yes, hounds like to fuck, but not all females, especially human, can fuck with a male our size.

So, we get them off in other ways. We use our fingers, our mouths, and sometimes, we use toys. Rome does not give a fuck we used a vibrator; he's used them with females. He owed me a favor, and I called it in, so I didn't have to leave you. Now, the next time you need to get off, you won't fucking hurt yourself. That was what I was thinking, and Rome didn't think any-fucking-thing at all."

She was quiet for several seconds, her mind ticking. She'd at least stopped trying to pull away from me. "What about you?"

"What about me?"

"If you're using your fingers and mouth or whatever to get them off, what do you get?" she asked, surprising me.

I couldn't be honest about what we were to each other, but everything else that came out of my mouth was going to be the truth. "Sometimes, all we want is to feel another being close, so we're not always looking for sex. But if a female is into it, and we're too big for her to fuck, she can use her hands or her mouth on us as well."

Those gorgeous peridot eyes searched my face, looking for something—I didn't fucking know what. "So, before, when I drank from you, when you laid close to me and watched me, did you just do that because you wanted to feel close to someone?"

"No. I wanted to feel close to you."

Thankfully, she hadn't left me to guess what she was thinking this time.

"But you don't want me ... that way? You don't want me to use my hands or my mouth on you? You don't want that from me?"

Her eyes went blank again, and I could literally see her pulling away, just not physically this time.

No way did I want her thinking that shit. "You felt how

much I wanted you, Fern. You were fucking grinding on it, baby. I want you in every way there is. Never think otherwise."

"Are you still … is your …"

"Am I still hard as fuck for you?" I rasped.

"Yes."

I'd been keeping my hips back so I didn't freak her out. "Yes."

Her fingers brushed my stomach, and I hissed. She paused and tried to pull her hand away, but I covered it and put it back. She searched my eyes, and then, finally, she slid her hand lower. I stayed perfectly still while my female explored me. If that was what she needed, I would fucking breathe through it while she checked that I was telling her the truth. Why she had any doubt, I had no fucking idea. Her fingers grazed the head of my cock, and I fucking held my breath. She stayed on the outside of my underwear, and when she gripped my shaft through the fabric, I groaned low—there was no way I could hold it in.

She looked up at me as she curled her fingers around me more firmly. "It's like hot steel."

"You did that. You made me this way."

"I did?"

She was serious—it was written all over her face.

"Fuck yes. How can you doubt it?"

"I guess I don't have much experience with this kind of thing."

"You a virgin, Fern?"

She paled again. "No, I just haven't had a chance to, um … touch a male this way."

I had questions, a fucking lot of them, but I swallowed them down. "You can touch me all you like, sweetness." I was close to hyperventilating and passing the fuck out, but

I'd told her she could do whatever she wanted with me, and I'd meant it.

She slid her hand all the way down to the base of my cock and back, squeezing and testing its firmness. "So, what happens if a hound finds his mate but can never have sex with her? That must happen, right? With your size?"

I curled my fingers into tight fists. "That's never happened. We always fit together; we were made to fit together. Mates are made for each other in every way. We might have to work up to it, but to make our mate ours in truth, we need to claim them, mark them."

"Do you think you have a mate out there?" she asked, her stare sliding from mine as she fucking finally slipped her hand inside my boxer briefs.

A breath shuddered from me as her hand touched my bare cock. "Yes."

"Do you want that? Do you want a mate? Do you want kids?"

I hooked her around the back of the neck and drew her closer. "I do."

She stroked me, and I growled low.

"Does that feel good?"

"Never felt anything as good as your hand on me, Tink."

Fern shoved down the covers so she could watch what she was doing to me. I was already close to coming, which meant my cock was darker and covered in bulging veins. It was also thickening.

Her gaze darted up to me. "What's happening?"

I tried to regain control, but I was fucking drunk on her touch, on the pleasure she was giving me, and rolled to my back so she could work me faster.

"Use both hands, baby." I needed to thrust. If I didn't get to move soon, I'd fucking lose it.

She nodded and did as I'd said, and as soon as she had a tight grip on me, I lifted my hips, thrusting up, and groaned.

"You're getting bigger, Relic," she said huskily.

I gasped in a breath, trying to hold what was going to happen back, but with her taste, her scent branded on me, with my female right there beside me—sated from coming and feeding from my vein—the beast and my body were convinced it was time to mate, and there was no holding the transformation back.

Oh, fuck.

Heat coiled in my gut and burned through my veins, throbbing wildly along my shaft. I was fucking rutting into her delicate hands, lost to it, to her. Panting, I looked down past my now tight-as-fuck abs, so tight that they were almost cramping. It was happening; I was growing longer and thicker; the veins pulsing so fucking heavily now along the shaft while the head grew darker.

"Relic?"

"It's ... it's okay," I gasped out.

I couldn't tell her that this only happened when we were with our mates. That, in six hundred years, this was the first time this had ever happened to me because she was touching my cock, and my body had convinced itself I was inside her, claiming her. I couldn't tell her this only happened when we fucked our fated mates, so we were interlocked, so I'd be planted as deep as I could get, so I could pump her full of my seed and make sure she got every fucking drop.

Fern moved closer, biting her lip, eyes wide, watching, watching my cock, and she was turned the fuck on. Not scared. Thank fuck. Not fucking scared.

The beast roared, and I snapped, my control disintegrating.

Rearing up, I shoved her back and straddled her smaller body so I was up on my knees. I had to be in this position—the beast demanded it.

"Grip it tight," I growled out.

She did, looking up at me—not with fear, but with hungry eyes—as I gripped the headboard and fucked her fists. My balls throbbed, and my cock jerked hard. Shoving up her shirt, I angled my cock down and came all over her stomach with a low groan, emptying myself until I was fucking spent.

Panting, I looked down at her. She was panting as well, watching me. Not afraid though. I didn't sense any fear at all. I stayed where I was, feeling fucking feral as I ran my hand over her stomach, then higher under her shirt, over her tits, smearing her scarred skin with my seed, my scent, marking her the only way I could for now. The beast purred.

"What are you doing?" she whispered.

"Marking you. No one will dare touch you now. They'll know who you sleep beside, who will fuck them up if they dare try and hurt you," I said, telling her in the only way I could right then that she was mine.

My brothers, any fucking shifter or demon, that got near her, would scent me on her skin, and they'd know she was under my protection. Pleasure filled me now, but for another reason. I wanted everyone to know she was mine. Now, there would be no mistake.

"And you want that? You want everyone to know … think I'm yours?"

I leaned in and kissed her, hard and deep, a claiming on its own. "You are, Fern. You are mine."

"Because of our deal?" she asked, her voice husky.

I didn't answer. I couldn't lie, and I couldn't tell her the truth either, so I rolled onto the mattress beside her and pulled her into my arms. "Sleep now, Tink."

She was quiet for several minutes. "Relic?"

"Night, sweetness."

Another pause.

"Night, Relic."

SEVENTEEN

FERN

"I'M gonna need you to tell me why we're going back to the crone's cottage, Tink."

Relic strode beside me through the forest, and for the first time, I wasn't hopped up on my courage potion or freaking the fuck out. I also realized I'd have to share some more with Relic if I wanted him to help me drag an unsuspecting demon through the forest and hand them over to Agatheena as an offering.

Sharing wasn't something I was used to doing or felt comfortable doing, but the more time I spent with Relic, the less terrifying it was becoming.

He hadn't used anything I'd said against me, and he'd taken care of me last night. He'd made me feel good, and I'd touched him. I liked touching him. Sweet Lucifer, the way he'd looked, lying on that bed—so strong, muscles straining, staring at me like … like he truly wanted me, like he truly cared about me—I'd never forget it. I never wanted to forget it.

"Remember, I told you that I'd only recently discovered I had soul collector DNA? Well, that wasn't all."

He glanced my way. "Yeah."

Gods, he really was beautiful.

I cleared my throat. "Agatheena, well, it turns out, she's my great-grandmother, and she has some information about me that could help me—a lot. The type of information that could mean I don't need anyone to protect me anymore. But in exchange for information, she expects an offering."

"What kind of information?" he asked, frowning.

"It's hard to explain. I don't fully understand it myself. I could potentially have some untapped powers, and she might be able to help me ... uh, un-tap them, I guess."

He curled his fingers around my arm, stopping me. "What kind of powers?"

"I honestly don't know. But I ..." I forced myself to say it. "She said I was a triplet, that I was the only one who survived. My siblings died while my mom was pregnant with us, and Agatheena said ... well, she said I absorbed their powers. Only I have no idea how to tap into them." I licked my dry lips and made myself keep going. "I don't want to feel afraid and helpless and out of control anymore, Relic. And if Agatheena can help me stop feeling that way, I'll do anything she asks."

"You feel helpless?"

I dug my nails into my palms when the urge to start counting and tapping filled me. "All my life."

The muscle in his jaw did that little jump that said he was clenching his teeth. "Don't fucking like that, Fern. Don't like that you were so scared that you felt you had to make a deal with a hellhound to feel safe. And I don't fucking like that someone hurt you, that they put those scars all over you ..."

I flinched, and he held up his hands.

"Not asking you to tell me where they came from, baby, not if you're not ready to share, but if seeing the crone will help you with all of that, then I'm on board."

I really liked this guy—like, a lot. Yes, it was dangerous to let myself feel things for him because this relationship wasn't real. Whatever he thought he felt for me was warped by our deal, but still, I couldn't help it. It was impossible not to like him.

"Thank you."

"Never need to thank me, babe. That's what I'm here for." We started walking again. "So, you were telling the truth when you said you were a witch?"

"My mom was Agatheena's granddaughter, but her demon blood skipped over my grandmother. As for my mother, well, it was there, but there was no outward sign. Then, my mom mated a soul collector, and I was the result."

"What did her coven do?" he asked, his gaze sliding back my way.

I didn't talk about this. The first time I had since it'd happened was in Agatheena's kitchen. "When they found out about my father, they killed him before my mom knew she was pregnant. Her family forced her to marry someone else. Then, I was born and eventually, my eyes, they gave me away."

"What happened after that, Tink?"

The words kept coming while goose bumps prickled all over my skin from the memory. "One night, Mom came into my room and woke me. She carried me downstairs and hid me under the hall table. A male walked through the kitchen door. He scared me. He was saying all these things to her I didn't understand. Then, my dad walked in ... well, the male I thought was my dad. I remember thinking, *It'll be okay because Dad will make the monster go away*. But he didn't stop the monster. My dad didn't even try, and then she was gone."

Relic's lips peeled back from his teeth. "Tell me what your dad did after that. What happened to you, Fern?"

Memories filled my mind—memories I tried to avoid—and I flinched again. "Bad things," I choked out. "Really bad things, Relic." I turned away, looking into the forest around me, the dappled light filtering through the trees. For once, it looked pretty, and the shadows didn't scare me because I had Relic, because Relic was with me. "They experimented on me, poisoned me ... they hurt me. I escaped, but they want me back, and they won't stop until they have me."

He growled low, and I wrapped my arms around myself.

Fighting down the feeling of being utterly laid bare, I turned back to him—

He wasn't there.

"Relic?" I scanned the forest, but there was no sign of him.

Someone moved in the undergrowth.

"Relic?"

They stepped out of the trees.

"Hello, Essie."

Grady.

I stumbled back. He'd followed us.

"Relic!" I screamed.

———

RELIC

One moment, I was standing beside Fern, and the next, I was in Hell with Rome and Fender.

"Fucking hate when he does this," Rome growled out.

Lucifer had summoned us. He'd fucking called us back here without warning.

"Fern," I snarled. "I abandoned her in Oldwood Forest."

Fender bit out a curse.

Snatching out my phone, I tried to call her. Nothing. No answer. No messages or missed calls. I shoved it back into the pocket of my leather vest and yanked it off. Then, with a roar, I exploded into my hound form, scooped the vest up in my jaw, and tore off, running as fast as I could through the caverns. My brothers' roars echoed behind me as they shifted as well, following me.

Lucifer had dumped us on the other side of the fire pits because this was where he obviously wanted us, but I needed him to fucking send me back to Fern. It was going to take too fucking long to get to his quarters, even with us running as hard as we could.

Fuck. She'd think I'd abandoned her. Left her all alone. She'd be so fucking scared.

I wanted to tear everything around me to pieces and throw the fuck up at the same time.

Time moved differently down here; in Hell, minutes translated to hours on Earth, hours to days, and she hadn't called or texted since I'd left her in that forest. Not once.

Something was seriously wrong. My mind was instantly filled with horrific things, so many awful fucking things.

Only Lucifer could send me back to the same time, back to the moment I'd been dragged away from her.

"They experimented on me, poisoned me ... they hurt me."

I'd heard it all before I was torn away.

Whoever had done that shit to her, enough time had passed on Earth, they could've already found her. They could be hurting her now.

I roared again, the sound bouncing off the stone walls. Rome and Fender howled behind me, letting me know they had my back, but the only thing that could help was getting to Fern. I was close to madness by the time we reached Lucifer's quarters.

Shifting back, I pounded hard on his door, and I kept pounding so fucking hard that the hinges started to loosen.

It swung open, and Roxy stood there, frowning, her long blade in her hand. The frown dropped, and her eyes widened. "Relic? What's the matter?"

"I need to see Lucifer. He needs to send me back," I snarled and strode in, searching the room. "Where the fuck is he?"

"Lucifer?" Rox asked.

"Yes, fucking Lucifer. Where the fuck is he, Rox?"

She blinked up at me; my lack of respect had thrown her. No one demanded to speak to Lucifer that way, and I'd never talked to her like that ever in my entire life, but right now, I was past control.

"He's not here," she said.

I spun and slammed my fist into the wall with a snarl, panting hard, trying and failing to keep it together. "Where the fuck is he, Roxy? I have to go back; he needs to send me back."

"You need to back the fuck up," Ursula said, her eyes flashing. "You're pissed. Be pissed, but you don't get to yell at Rox. Lucifer isn't here, and he isn't coming back for whatever this"—she waved her hand at me while I snarled and panted and fought not to shift again—"is about."

Roman stepped forward. "His female—she's in trouble. When Lucifer summoned us, they were in Oldwood Forest."

Roxy frowned. "His female?"

I dragged in another breath before I fucking self-combusted. "My mate, Rox. When Lucifer summoned me, I left her alone in a demon-infested forest. She's in danger." The last sentence came out in a roar—a combination of terror and fury.

Her eyes widened. "Oh, no."

"I need Lucifer," I said again, shoving my fingers through my hair. Without him, I was fucked. Without him, I couldn't go back to the precise moment he took me from her.

Ursula cursed. "He's incommunicado. He's journeying, checking on the rest of his lords after Faron's disappearance. It was a last-minute thing. He took Maddox and Gus, which is why he summoned you that way."

He usually gave us more warning if he planned to summon us back or gave us time to get here on our own. Hell was vast, he could be gone for fucking weeks.

"Go," Rox said. "Go to her."

"I'll explain everything to Lucifer when he returns. Go find your female," Ursula added.

"I'll text Loth, let him know what happened," Fender said, pulling out his phone.

I spun and sprinted away, back through the caves.

Fern could already be dead. She could already be fucking dead by now.

CHAPTER
EIGHTEEN

FERN

Gasping, I clawed at the concrete floor.

"You need to be punished, Estelle. You know you do. You were very bad, weren't you?" Grady's boot was on my rib, pressing down. "Weren't you?"

Hissing, I nodded.

"Say it."

"Fuck you," I snarled and coughed uncontrollably. My throat was raw, my mouth full of my own blood.

The Chemist had decided to let Grady loose on me to teach me a lesson. He didn't like getting his hands dirty, not in this way. Didn't like to be the one to dish out the punishments. He did enjoy the aftermath though. He liked to repair the damage done so he could tear me apart all over again *for medical research*.

This had been going on for four days. Grady beat me, and then The Chemist would come in and take pleasure in playing the depraved, psycho doctor.

My mind was fracturing. I could feel myself slipping away.

As soon as Grady had carried me through that door and the smell hit me, a switch flicked. It was like I'd never left, and besides the burned down wing of the building, nothing had changed.

After all the work I'd done to put the shattered pieces of my mind back together, they were falling away, one by one. I felt myself reverting back to that wild thing. The feral little girl The Chemist had to get Grady to tie down before he came into my room.

Grady dropped to one knee and gripped my jaw, his fingers digging in hard. When he leaned in close, I tried to swing, then realized my shoulder was dislocated, so I couldn't do shit. I spat in his face, and he punched the side of my head with a curse.

"Filthy fucking whore." Grady forced my jaw up so I couldn't do it again. "He's still here, you know, Essie." His voice was so cold that it sent ice down my spine. "Ghoul's been down there, chained in that hole in the ground, all alone, since you left. Bet he's really fucking hungry."

I froze, my heart seizing in my chest. Warmth slid over my thighs, soaking my underwear and the drab gray smock they'd put me in. The monster's glowing red eyes filled my mind, huge in his sunken-in sockets, followed by the vicious fangs, the cold, leathery skin, and protruding bones. The long black nails that dug into my flesh, adding to the scars all over my body. When I was young, I'd told myself he was a monster. Now, I knew better; he had to be demon, savage and starved, and the most terrifying being I'd ever encountered.

"You pissed all over yourself." Grady tutted, grabbing

me by the hair, so tight that I thought he'd tear it from my scalp. "You really are a disgusting little bitch," he hissed.

He shoved me away with force, and my head hit the concrete floor. Fisting the front of my smock at my chest, his other hand grabbing the fabric just above my knees, he lifted me roughly before dumping me on the gurney.

"No."

I struggled, but he pushed me back easily, lifted my hands over my head, and I silently screamed, choking on the pain as he chained my wrists to the top, followed by my ankles to the bottom.

He patted my cheek. "The Chemist will be in to tend to you shortly." He grinned. "Oh, and he has something new he wants to test. It's a nasty one." Then he left, shutting me inside, bound and helpless.

Silence filled the treatment room, and minute later I heard it—the slow drip from the sink on the other side of the room. That sound came to me in my nightmares. It filled my head when I least expected it, bringing me back to this room in my mind time and time again.

The last five years, physically, I'd been free, but in my head, I'd never left. I'd been right here. I'd known, hadn't I? It was only a matter of time before I ended up back here in this room, in this place, as The Chemist's creature, to torture and experiment on as much as he liked.

Before, when I'd been here, I'd waited for my chance to escape. That, one day, an opportunity would present itself. And it did. Grady had walked out of the room without securing both my hands after a beating, and I'd taken my chances. I'd set the place on fire, barricaded them in, watched, making sure it went up in flames before I ran like hell.

He'd never make that mistake again. This time, there would be no escape for me.

Gods, I was so fucking stupid. I'd actually convinced myself that Relic cared about me, that he wanted me. Of course, he didn't want a disgusting demon. I'd tricked him into selling me his soul. He saw the real me—the depraved bitch in heat; the twisted wreck who had poisoned herself, then thrown up in front of him just so she could control her fear; the repulsive, scarred whore who'd fed from him, while she'd rubbed up on him, lost to her lust.

He'd asked one of his brothers to get me a sex toy so he didn't have to deal with me—anything to get me to stop pawing all over him—and still, I hadn't seen it coming. He abandoned me in that forest, for fuck's sake. I'd shared more, and he'd bailed, desperate to get away from me. Honestly, I didn't blame him.

But what I really hated was that he was still all I wanted. I'd let him beneath my armor and made myself so fucking weak.

I wasn't sure how to process the loss of him. Could you lose something that never wanted to be yours?

He'd never been mine, not by choice, but even now, I wanted to feel the heat of that big body against mine and the feeling of safety that I'd only ever experienced with him. I wanted to hear that low, rough voice call me baby, and Tink, and sweetness. I wanted it all back, and Lucifer help me, I'd give anything to have it back. I didn't care that it had all been a lie. I just wanted it back.

I wanted Relic back.

The door opened, and I viciously shoved it all down. That was the last time I'd think of him. That was the last time I'd let those emotions in, or I wouldn't survive this. So, I slammed the door and sealed those feelings in tight, and let the numbness come—because I would break if I didn't. My mind would fracture totally, and I'd never come back from it. The Chemist would throw me in that hole in the ground as well and leave me to rot.

"How are we this evening, Estelle?" The Chemist said as he walked in.

My fingers tapped against the cold vinyl beneath me. *One, two, three, four. Four, three, two, one,* as I stared at the ceiling instead of looking at his scarred face. Though seeing the burns covering his cheek and one side of his neck— scars that I'd caused—gave me sadistic pleasure.

"Not in the mood to talk today? That's okay." He slid on his black latex gloves. "Let's see what we have here." He undid the ties at my shoulders and dragged the gown from my body, and I lay there bare, except for my piss-soaked underwear. He studied the raw, weeping, concealment sigil he'd carved into my stomach the first day I was brought back here. Every morning he had Grady reopen it, so it couldn't ever heal. He scanned the rest of my body. "A few superficial bruises and lacerations, broken ribs, a dislocated shoulder. Nothing I can't fix. But first, we need to get a gauge on the strength of your regenerative capabilities. It's been a while since we conducted an experiment on you, Essie, so I'll have to be rather aggressive, I'm afraid."

I knew what that meant. He was going to get me as close to death as he could, and see how long it took for me to recover. The clink of metal on metal sent icy dread through me, but still, I didn't look.

"Open your mouth, Estelle," he said, his excitement making his voice tremble.

I did as he'd said; otherwise, he'd make me, and it would hurt even more.

"Your teeth have always been a good gauge, haven't they?"

Panic filled me, but I fought it down. I didn't scream or cry as he used his pliers and wrenched out the first tooth, and I didn't struggle as more blood filled my mouth, choking me. I wouldn't give him the satisfaction. One by one, he pulled out my teeth, and my fangs. The only sounds in the room were of my teeth hitting the bottom of The Chemist's stainless steel dish, and me breathing heavily through my nose.

As the last tooth was pulled free, the rigidness of my body eased, and I turned my head, letting the blood run from my mouth onto the floor.

"Very good," he said. "But we're not quite finished yet."

He filled a small basin with water and carried it over. Looking at me with that unhinged excitement in his eyes, he began cleaning me up, dipping a cloth into the freezing water and dragging it over my bloody and bruised body. "We need to repair what Grady did before we continue. This needs to be a controlled experiment, and we don't want those injuries to interfere with my results."

I locked my jaw as he dragged the cloth over my wounds again, causing me more pain and enjoying it.

"It appears you've soiled yourself, Estelle." He licked his lips as he slid his scalpel from the small table beside him and sliced through the sides of my underwear. Pinching them between his gloved finger and thumb, he dragged them off and dumped them in the trash. "You'll have to go without."

I lay there, utterly naked in every way there was, while he cleaned between my thighs and down my legs. He hummed to himself as he continued to clean me, waiting until he removed every trace of blood and piss before he finally rested his hand over my ribs. Magic pulsed from his palm, and I choked back a scream when my ribs snapped back into place, followed by my shoulder jerking back into the socket.

Taking a small pot from the table, he dipped his finger into the salt and began the process of rubbing it into each and every new slice, whispering a spell as he did it so that when he used his healing magic, I'd still be left with a scar. He liked seeing the scars. He'd once told me I was a living, ever-changing piece of art. A map of his tests and trials, and that with every mark on my skin, I became more beautiful. Which was why he left the sigil open and raw, it wasn't from one of his experiments and would mess up his living, breathing canvas.

Again, when he finally finished, he checked my ankle restraints, tightening them. I didn't fight it, and I didn't resist because there was no getting away, there was no escape.

"I have a new virus to test on you, but with your rapid healing abilities, we'll need to hinder your body's natural immunity further." He wheeled his table closer, placing another empty dish on top. "For that, we'll need to remove your liver. From past experiments, we know it regenerates fairly quickly, but this way, the virus will have more of a chance to take hold."

Oh gods, no.

There was no fighting down the panic inside me this time. I yanked at my restraints, squirming and gurgling through the blood in my mouth and spilling down my chin.

His eyes brightened. "Fighting will do you no good." He placed a hand on my ribs. "Let's begin."

Searing pain burned my stomach, and I gasped, choking on my blood as he sliced me open.

When the incision was long enough, he shoved his hand up under my ribs, found my liver, and sliced it from my body. I screamed until my throat was raw, then I passed out.

When I came around, he'd already sewn me up and salted the wound.

"You're back," he said as he wiped my bloody mouth. "Nearly done. My new virus is transmitted through sexual intercourse. So, I'll need to place it inside you."

He picked up a large needleless syringe filled with a yellow substance. Pressing one gloved hand down on my stomach, he positioned it, and looking at me with twisted glee in his eyes, pushed it inside me, pumping me full of his poison.

"If administered correctly, you should feel the effects of this one within a few hours," he said, his voice lower, as he slid the syringe from me and tossed it back onto the tray. "But you'll need to stay like this to make sure it works, I'm afraid."

His gaze moved over my naked body, then back, locking on mine. "You know why it has to be you, Estelle," he said, faux contrition rearranging his hateful face. "No one else can handle my experiments like you can."

No, most were permanently disfigured or went mad, and if the virus didn't kill them, Grady did.

"You're special. That blood in your veins is special, there's no one else like you. I tried, you know, many times to replace you."

His voice grated over me while I tried not to writhe in pain.

"Most recently, in the city you made your home. I found an abandoned building, an old boarding house, and Grady brought me test subjects, but alas, they all died. So many females died because of you, because you left me. You won't leave me again, will you Estelle?"

Nausea made my empty stomach cramp and the horror of what he said was a tight band around my throat.

"You won't leave me again, will you, Estelle?" he said more sharply.

I forced myself to shake my head.

"That's right." He shivered and rubbed his tented trousers against the gurney. "It is extremely good to have you back, Essie—you have no idea."

He rounded the gurney, moving to stand above me, and pushed it through the double swinging doors and into the hall. The things that walked these halls—his creations, like patchwork marionette dolls controlled by magic—followed his orders without question. But their eyes said it all; if they could, if his hold on them wasn't so strong, they would kill us all. They turned their beady eyes on me now as I was wheeled by, naked and exposed. Their crude, garbled taunts filled the hall; their grasping hands bruised my flesh, and claws scraped over my skin.

The Chemist let them, and instead of taking me to my cell, he wheeled me into a large room that smelled like rotting flesh. This was where the creatures slept. He was going to keep making me pay for leaving him, for running away. His monsters followed, surrounding me, growling and salivating.

The Chemist turned to them. "My dears, I would like you to take care of my patient. You may come close, but you may not touch her in any way with any part of your body. If she vomits blood, come and get me." Then he walked out.

As soon as he left, they swarmed closer, so close that I could feel their breath on my bare skin, and their stench choked me. I closed my eyes, trying to ignore the perverted things they said, and opened the door I'd told myself I needed to keep locked because if I didn't, I would break completely. Instead, I let my mind take me away to a room underground that was warm and smelled like everything good and safe.

In my mind, Relic lay beside me, his strong arm around me, his voice telling me I was going to be okay. It hurt—gods, it fucking hurt—but I let it. Better that than reality.

Better a fantasy that was lost to me now than what surrounded me.

If this was madness, I welcomed it.

CHAPTER
NINETEEN

RELIC

LOWERING MY HEAD, my leather vest in my jaw, I tore through the forest towards the spots I'd left Fern.

I'd tried to call her again, but still, no answer. Lothar said she hadn't been back to the clubhouse, and there was no fresh scent from her back at her store or in her apartment.

No one had seen or heard from her since I had been summoned to Hell. For me, it had been close to four hours, but for Fern, it had been four fucking days.

My brothers howled in the distance, they were close. I snarled around the leather in my mouth as I broke through the trees and shifted. I didn't know what I expected to find. Days had passed since I'd stood in this spot with Fern, but her scent still remained. With our sense of smell, I could pick up a scent from over a week ago, sometimes longer. Yeah, my female still lingered in the air, but it was different from when I'd left her; now, it was mixed with her fear.

Lothar and Jagger bounded into the small clearing, Loth carrying what I'd asked him to bring in his mouth.

"Still getting nothing?" I asked as they shifted.

Jag shook his head. "Tracking's not working. She's behind some kind of ward—something that's strong enough to block our powers."

I growled. Yeah, I'd figured that out for myself, but I still had to try. "Give it to me?"

Loth tossed me Fern's shirt. I pressed it to my face, dragging in her honeysuckle scent, the stronger her scent, the easier to track her. I closed my eyes, let my powers pulse through me, and searched, but I couldn't see her. No sign. Hounds tracked by scent, yes, but we didn't need to keep our noses to the ground. Once we had a scent, we saw exactly where our prey was in our mind's eye, and when I took in Fern's scent, there was nothing. Just darkness, a blank space where Fern should be. "Fuck," I snarled.

"She say anything about who's after her?" Loth asked.

"Not one fucking thing." My beast's voice was blending with my voice now, making it sound distorted. "She was opening up to me slowly. I was getting her to open up to me, and then Lucifer ..." I roared, spun to the tree behind me and slammed my fist into it.

"Are you mated?" Loth asked. "With the connection, you might be able to—"

"No. She wasn't ready." I shoved my fingers through my hair. "She doesn't even fucking know I'm her mate."

"We'll find her," Lothar said, expression hard. "Whatever it takes. You've waited too fucking long to find her. You're not losing her this way. No fucking way."

I lifted my chin, even as the beast rippled under my skin, contorting my shoulders and vibrating through my chest. I couldn't speak anymore, lost to my rage now—the beast had my throat, full control of my vocal cords now, so I let him lead, and tilted my head back, scenting the air.

My lips peeled back on a growl as I dropped to the ground, breathing her in. She'd been standing a little in front of me. She'd turned away while she talked, sharing more of her past with me, hiding her eyes while she did it. She tried to conceal what bringing those memories to the forefront did to her, but I'd heard it in her voice—

"I got your scent and Fern's," Loth said.

I breathed deeper and rose when I picked up something else. "What the fuck is that?"

Lothar breathed deeply as well and turned, striding to the edge of the track. "They stood there. Male. Demon, but it smells fucking weird."

"I know this scent," I said.

When I'd been outside Fern's store, it had been distant at the time, unimportant, but I knew without a doubt that this was the same. I followed it down the track, and the beast vibrated through my chest. They'd been together, Fern and whoever that scent belonged to. They'd taken her.

My brothers surrounded me, and closing our eyes, we focused on the new scent.

Fuck yes. My mind lit up, showing me the way, leading us right to him.

I was going to tear him to shreds. I was going to make him scream.

With a vicious growl, I shifted and tore through the forest, my brothers right behind me. We made it back to the edge of the forest in record time. Quickly dressing, we got on our bikes and sped away from the city.

The ride felt like an eternity, and the whole way, my mind threw images at me, one after the other, of what was happening to her. My heart was thumping hard, and my blood rushed through my veins while the beast rumbled and snarled, constantly vibrating with rage in my chest.

We finally rolled up to a building an hour later. It was in the middle of nowhere and a similar distance, give or take, from a couple of other bigger towns. The faded sign on the wall said, "Maple Grove Age Care Facility." Going by the washed-out and chipped paint, the broken windows, and the burned-out left wing of the building, it'd been abandoned a while ago. Turning off my bike, I swung off and strode to the front door. With every breath, my chest expanded, and my urge to shift was harder to resist.

"How you wanna do this?" Loth asked me.

I lifted my foot, about to kick in the front door, desperate to get to Fern, but Jagger grabbed my shoulder, shoving me back. I jerked from his hold, and the alpha's second closed in.

"We go in there hot, she could get hurt. You need to get those new fucking emotions under control and play this smart."

He was right, of course, but, fuck, it was hard. The rage felt like a wildfire rushing through me, burning off the hard exterior and exposing all of those new and confusing emotions.

Lothar grabbed the door handle, and his biceps jerked, the veins in his forearm popping. "Warded, but it's weak." He gritted his teeth and twisted the door handle, shattering the lock.

I pushed forward, and every muscle in my body jerked, spasming, as I breached the ward and rushed through. Lothar was right; it was weak, but for anyone else, this would be impenetrable. Whoever this witch was had not been keeping up their wards regularly. Or maybe they were just that fucking arrogant that they thought no one would find them.

The main entrance was dark, but I could see a few flickering lights ahead. Tilting back my head, I breathed deep, and my nerve endings, my blood, fucking lit up like I'd been struck by lightning. Whatever had been blocking her wasn't working here because it didn't need to.

"She's here. I can smell her blood."

Beside me, Lothar bared his teeth, the rage rolling off him, almost as volatile as mine.

"We need to assess the situation before we kill—you hear me?" Jagger said. "Whatever this place is, something is not fucking right. The darkness here is thick, fucking heavy."

I grunted, but if Fern was hurt, I was going to kill anything that moved, consequences be damned. I rushed ahead, Lothar and Jag keeping pace, letting me follow Fern's scent, letting it guide me to her. I didn't need my powers to find her in this place. Her scent was heavy, but it was bitter in a way I'd never smelled on her before. Something was wrong—something really fucking bad had happened—and it was taking all my control not to kick every wall down.

"That smell, like chemicals. The same scent was in that building we tracked Faron to," Jag said.

He was right, it was, but all I could focus on was my female. We made our way down one hall and then another.

"Hear that?" Loth said, tilting his head to the side. "Whispering."

Until then, all I'd been able to hear was my blood rushing through my fucking ears. I forced myself to listen, to tune in—the sound of a low, roughened voice reached me. He was saying evil, sick fucking shit, and I knew instantly who he was directing that fucked-up shit to.

I broke into a run, barreling down the hall and turning into the next. There was a set of doors ahead of me. She was in there. My Fern was in there.

It was hard, but I made myself stop, and instead of busting the doors down, I eased them open as quietly as I could—

The beast lurched forward, snapping beneath my skin, while every muscle in my body contracted and every nerve ending went fucking haywire. Red rage filled my vision as I took in the scene.

Nothing could have prepared me for what was in front of me.

Fern was strapped to a gurney—naked, with a large and raw wound on her stomach and blood coating her chin. She was surrounded by sleeping creatures, the kind I'd never seen before—deformed, stitched together from mismatched body parts—their fucked-up bodies littering the floor. Only one was still awake, and he stood beside her, so close that she'd feel his breath on her skin. Her eyes were closed, her skin flushed and coated with sweat, and she was shaking uncontrollably.

Jag and Loth froze beside me, their rage as hot as mine, like a blast of hellfire.

On silent feet, I moved up behind the fucked-up creature as quietly as I could, and grabbed it, one hand covering its mouth, and twisted, snapping his neck with the other. It went limp, and I lowered him to the floor quietly. Stepping over it, I gently touched Fern's fevered face. Her eyes snapped open, locking with me, but there was no acknowledgment, no recognition. There was just ... nothing.

What have they done to you, baby?

I pressed my finger to my lips, telling her not to make a sound, as I slid off my vest and covered her with it. She'd been through enough; I didn't want her to see what was about to happen next.

"Eyes closed, Tink," I whispered.

"Kill them all," Jag said low.

Whatever these creatures were, they weren't the brains behind whatever this was. They were a fucked-up army created by a sick piece of shit. Loth and Jag shifted, tearing into them, but I stayed in my human form—well, as best as I could because Fern was scared enough as it was, but my poison-tipped claws had burst from the ends of my fingers, my face had distorted, and my mouth was now elongated and full of vicious teeth. I tore the creatures apart, firing my power at them and sending them across the room to smash against the wall, taking out creature after creature, until the place was strewn with blood and body parts.

Jag took off out the door to search the rest of the building, and Loth stood guard at the door as I got to work on Fern's restraints. My fucking hands shook as I undid the ones at her ankles. I moved back up, and she was utterly motionless. She did nothing, said nothing.

"Fern?" I said in a garbled voice around my elongated jaw and fangs because I was seriously struggling to pull the beast back. "Tink, I'm here."

FERN

It was a fever dream or a trick. I blinked, trying to clear my vision, but black spots danced at the corners of my eyes.

Grady was playing games with me.

I wasn't going to fall for it. The monster had Relic's eyes, but the distorted face had a mouth full of sharp teeth. I stayed completely still, waiting, biding my time. The creatures weren't allowed to touch me, but this one's fingers had grazed my skin, and now he was removing my bindings. I didn't want its fucking hands on me. I didn't want anyone's fucking hands on me. Only Relic. Only ever Relic.

That wasn't him; it couldn't be. I was seeing things, seeing what I wanted to see.

He worked on the straps around my wrists, and as soon as they were free, I exploded off the bed. My weak legs immediately gave out, and I fell to the floor. The darkness at the corners of my vision got worse, and the smell of putrid blood filled my nose. Gasping and panting, I scrambled across the wet concrete floor over things—disgusting things I couldn't properly make out. I reached the wall and pressed my back to it, lifting my hands out in front of me.

"The Chemist w-will kill you if you touch me. You aren't allowed to touch me," I said, my speech fucked up without my teeth, and more blood oozed down my chin.

A rumbling sound rolled through the room, and my wild, swinging hands hit something, somebody.

"Stay back," I screamed. As I did, something charged through me, like I was being plugged into an electrical socket, like a dead engine struggling to turn over, suddenly setting off sparks, before dying again.

The rumbling was closer, but I couldn't hear it over the ringing in my ears and the pounding of my heart. My body was burning up; the virus had set in.

One minute, I was pressed against the wall; the next, I was hauled off the ground.

"No! Don't you fucking touch me!" I fought as hard as I

could, but they were restraining my arms and my kicking legs.

With no other way to fight, I reared back and tried to sink my fangs into firm flesh. Again and again, I tried, then whimpered, because my fangs were fucking gone. I was pulled back suddenly, and a moment later, my face was pressed back to that same spot. The scent of blood filled my lungs. I groaned, my tongue darting out, tasting, sliding along a deep slice. The blood was fresh, rich—warm. Not cold and putrid. My starving body ignited, the demon inside me roaring to the surface. Instead of trying to get away, I wrapped my arms and legs around the massive body pressed against me and lapped at the heavy, pulsing vein. It was throbbing and oozing blood, and I sucked hard.

Digging my nails into skin and muscle to hold on tight, I drew deeply on the thick vein, gulping down the fragrant, rich blood, letting it fill me and revive me.

I hadn't eaten at all, and I had only been given a few sips of water since I'd been brought back here. I was so hungry that there was no stopping me. I was jostled, but no one tried to pull me away or shove me off. So, I fed greedily, until my limbs grew warm. I was so weak from my fever that when the adrenaline subsided, I couldn't hang on anymore. My arms fell away, and I braced to hit the concrete floor ... but I didn't.

That was when I realized the solid arms and big hands that had been restraining me were cradling me gently—one arm under my butt, supporting me, the other now at the back of my head, keeping me at that throat, helping me feed now that I was too weak to do it myself.

Now that the ravenous hunger had subsided, a familiar scent filled my senses, and as I feebly sucked, the taste on my tongue finally registered. I blinked several times, and the black shadows in my vision receded. I knew that muscled throat. I knew the runes tattooed on that massive shoulder.

No. This had to be a dream. I'd passed out, and I was still tied down on that gurney, surrounded by monsters.

But even as I told myself that, I whimpered, clawing, trying to hang on to him, to the dream, the delirium. It couldn't be true, yet I was terrified he'd let me go, that this mirage would vanish, that I'd wake and find myself back in that hell.

But I was positive I felt the weight and smelled the comforting scent of worn leather against my back, that I could feel the heat of Relic's skin against mine.

The hand, still at the back of my head, applied soft pressure, and warm breath ruffled my hair. "I got you, baby."

I shivered as that hand moved to the back of my neck, and a comforting, rough-skinned thumb slid along my jaw.

"I will murder whoever did this to you, Tinker Bell, with my bare fucking hands. I will tear their heart out and bring it to you, sweetness. I will lay it at your feet. I promise you that."

I was jostled again, something soft and warm coming around me.

"Get the door open," my Relic dream growled, and I was shifted before I was sitting across his lap.

Gods, this felt so real. I forced myself to blink again. My sight came and went. I was in a truck. I found the strength to tilt my head back, and a pair of gorgeous golden eyes locked on mine.

My Relic dream cupped my face. "I'm so sorry, baby. I'm so sorry it took me so fucking long to get to you."

My limbs felt like they were weighted down by bricks, but I somehow managed to drag my hand out of the blanket wrapped around me and pressed it to his bare chest. His heart pounded against my palm, and his eyelashes fluttered. I let his warmth soak through me, through the blanket, through my skin, into my bones.

"Relic?" I choked out.

"Yeah, Tink, it's me."

Not a dream. Not a mirage. He was here.

Oh gods, he's real.

He'd come for me.

"Who did this to you, baby? Tell me who I need to kill," he growled.

I couldn't say his name, not yet. My mouth refused to form the words.

"Hold me tighter," I said instead. "I need you to hold me tighter."

His arms curled around me even more firmly, trapping me against him, like a warm, violent, protective cocoon.

Right then, at that moment, I was safe.

I let my eyes drift closed, and consciousness slipped away.

CHAPTER
TWENTY

RELIC

Brick opened the door to the truck, and I climbed out, holding an unconscious Fern against me.

He jogged ahead to the clubhouse to open the door for us, and I strode through, Fern still limp in my arms. They'd pulled out all her fucking teeth; they'd cut her open. Fuck knew what else. Fear and burning rage pumped hotly through my veins, making me shake.

Lothar and Jag had stayed behind to search the rest of the building, but I already knew they wouldn't find whoever it was who'd hurt my Fern. They'd stood back while we slaughtered their little army of freaks. We were dealing with a twisted coward who'd run while they had the chance.

I held Tinker Bell close to me, reassuring myself that she was okay with the sound of her heart beating. I pressed my lips to her forehead. Her skin was too fucking hot though. Demons didn't get sick, not like this. Demons who fed on blood could suffer from weakness and wasting if they'd been starved, but not whatever the fuck this was, and definitely not a fever. Yeah, she had witch blood, but the demon DNA in her was strong, predominant—I could feel it. This should be impossible.

Holding her to me tight with one arm, I let us into my den and closed us in together.

I stared down at her. Fuck, I didn't want to put her down, but I needed to clean the blood and gore off her because the stench of those creatures all over her had my body poised to shift. Striding to the bathroom, I turned on the shower and waited for the water to heat up.

"Need to clean this shit off you, Tink," I said, even though she was still unconscious. I tried not to freak the fuck out about that, but it wasn't easy.

Fern was immortal; she should start healing. She should already be showing signs of improvement, but I didn't see it, not yet. If Fern didn't wake soon, I was calling in a healer.

Repositioning Fern's limp body, I let the blanket fall and lifted my leather vest off her. Blood was smeared all over her naked body, and I searched her for further injury. Shifting her in my arms, I hissed when I saw a sigil carved into her stomach beside the new fucking scar, long and jagged. Forcing myself to take a breath, I grabbed my phone from my pocket and took a picture of the sigil. It could help us find the fucker who had done this to her, and I needed all the help I could get.

It took some doing, but I kicked off my boots and managed to get my jeans off with one hand, before stepping into the shower. Fern whimpered and rolled into me, trying to avoid the spray, but she still didn't wake, didn't open her eyes.

"It's okay, baby. Just gonna clean you up." I talked to her

anyway because it soothed the beast, and I hoped like fuck that it soothed Fern as well.

I lathered her up with soap, gently cleaning the blood off with a washcloth. It was too late for the scar below her ribs. I could smell salt. That fucker had rubbed it into the slice. There was no getting rid of it now, but the sigil looked fresh, raw, no salt. That one, at least, I could do something about, and I wanted it gone right the fuck now. Yanking a towel from the rail, I slid to the shower floor, and balling it under her head, I lay her down.

"Gonna make it better, baby," I rasped.

Then I proceeded to lick those slices in her skin as gently as I could, cleaning them thoroughly and letting my saliva start the healing process since hers hadn't kicked in yet for some fucking reason, and mine was faster and more potent.

That twisted fuck had done this. He'd tied her down and carved into her with a knife. When she woke, I didn't want her to be forced to see it.

The skin started puckering around the edges of the wound almost immediately, which meant the healing had begun. I finally felt like I could breathe.

I stayed on the floor, pulling her between my legs so her head was against my chest, and washed her hair.

She whimpered again as I wrung out the last of the shampoo.

"All done, sweetness."

Scooping her back up, I stood and switched off the water. Quickly drying her, I carried her out and forced myself to lay her on the bed. The beast snarled the whole time I wasn't touching her, but with her on the bed, I could see every single scar on her body and all the obvious new ones. Like the rest on her body, they'd been done on purpose. He'd used salt and magic. He'd wanted to scar her body.

I dragged in a breath and another, trying to keep my shit together. She'd been through four days of torture—and fucking years of it before that. It was never happening again. After the way I'd let her down, she wouldn't believe it—I doubted she'd ever trust me after this—but I would prove it to her. No matter how long it took.

I carefully pulled one of my shirts over her head, sliding her arms in the sleeves, and the beast quieted a little. Drying off, I put on some boxer briefs and got under the covers with her. Then I pulled her against me, and with her fevered cheek against my chest, I braided her damp hair so it was out of the way.

Someone knocked on the door.

"Relic?" War called.

"It's not locked."

The door eased open, and my alpha filled the frame.

"Brick said you were back. How is she?"

"They pulled out her teeth, War. They fucking sliced her open." I pressed the back of my hand to her cheek. "She's sick, feverish, unconscious. This isn't fucking normal for a demon." I looked back down at her. "Must be the witch in her causing this. She got both demon and witch blood from her mother's side, but her demon blood's stronger." I glanced up at him. "Her father was a soul collector, and her mother was a Burnside."

War's head jerked up. Everyone knew who Agatheena Burnside was.

Fern whimpered again, and helplessness filled me.

"I don't know what the fuck to do. She should be awake, starting to heal by now."

His gaze slid to Fern, then back to me before he took his

phone from his pocket and tapped the screen. A few seconds later, Magnolia's voice came over the speaker.

"We've got a situation and need some advice," War said.

Magnolia was family—his sister-in-law—and a gifted healer.

"What's going on? You need me to come to the clubhouse?" she asked, instantly ready to help.

"Maybe," War said. "We've got a demon, blood drinker. She's got a little witch DNA in there as well. She's got a fever and is currently unconscious. You got any ideas?"

"So, her demon blood is dominant?"

"Yeah," I answered. "She's immortal—or she should be —but whatever is going on, it's making her really fucking sick."

"I mean, that's not normal. If they're predominantly demon, their own healing abilities should kick in. Where's she been? Who's she had contact with the last couple days?"

"She was held prisoner. We don't know what happened to her, only that it was not fucking good," War growled out.

Mags cursed.

"Gonna send you a pic, Mags." I texted her the sigil from Fern's stomach.

"Got it." She cursed again. "This wouldn't be making her sick, but this is a powerful sigil, a kind of ward. It's not one I've used before because this one's been personalized, corrupted to work specifically for the witch who carved it into her skin."

War's gaze sliced to me. "Witch?"

"Oh, yeah. Whoever did this is definitely a witch. This would make her invisible, not trackable." She was quiet for a beat. "This changes things though. It could be magic making her sick, or it could be something else this twisted fuck has done. There's one sure way to find out though. Feed her. She needs blood, and plenty of it. If it's magic alone, she won't recover. If it's something else? Well, hound blood should do the trick and heal her within a few days."

"And if it is magic?"

"Then you'll need a witch who can break that kind of spell, and unfortunately, that's not my specialty."

"You know anyone who could do it?" I asked.

"I do actually. I'll text you her number," Mags said.

"Thanks, Mags. Appreciate it," I said.

War disconnected and turned to me. "Feed her, brother; make her drink. Get her to feed as much as you can." He planted his hands on his hips. "She's going to be okay, Relic. Whatever this is, we'll make sure she gets better." He looked back at Fern, and his jaw tightened.

I looked back down at her, my gut in knots. Physically maybe. But fuck knew how she would recover from the horror show I'd found her in.

War left, and my phone chimed a minute later. Mags had texted with a name and number.

I wrapped my arms around my female, listening to her slow, even breaths. Then I closed my eyes and prayed to Lucifer. Because the king of Hell seriously fucking owed me.

———

"You need to drink, baby," I said, holding her mouth to my throat.

Fern nuzzled my skin; her body racked with shivers, her skin clammy. She'd been like this all night. I'd fed her twice, it was all she'd been able to manage, and still, she hadn't woken up. Grabbing my blade, I nicked my wrist and lifted it to her mouth to encourage her to drink. She groaned in pain and writhed against the mattress, too weak to drink.

Fuck.

I would not fucking lose her, which was why I wasn't going to wait a moment fucking longer. She should already be showing signs of improvement, but she was only getting worse. So, I'd sent Jagger to get the witch who could hopefully fucking help.

Still, my blood had to be doing something. How much sicker would she be without it?

Slicing deeper so blood flowed freely, I pressed my wrist to her mouth again, and this time, she latched on. She was sucking, but it was weaker now, and blood slid from the side of her mouth and dripped down her chin. I wasn't sure how much she was even getting. She gave my vein one more feeble suck, but her mouth slipped away, her head rolling back. She was panting hard, and her skin was clammy, switching between molten hot and ice cold.

Tucking the covers around her, I got off the bed and paced the room, unable to keep still, feeling fucking useless, helpless.

I finally heard Jagger and the healer coming, and yanked the door open.

The female with Jag wore a long yellow raincoat covered in white daisies. Her fingers were covered in colorful rings, and she had a bunch of shit hanging around her neck. Her hair was honey-blond—some wavy, some straight. There were feathers and beads threaded among it. Her face was flushed, her eyes wide with fear or rage—I wasn't sure which.

She curled her fingers into fists. "I-I don't know who you ... f-fuckers think you are," she stuttered out. "But I don't take kindly to being dragged from my home without explanation for whatever *the fuck* … this is."

My chin jerked back, and I looked at Jag. His eyes were glowing, locked on the witch, his jaw like steel.

"Jag didn't explain?" I could smell her fear, and I got the feeling, especially with all the stuttering and wide eyes, that this bravado was out of character. If we weren't careful, she'd run and leave without helping Fern.

His gaze finally came to me. "I would have happily explained if she'd let me get a fucking word in."

The witch hissed and reached for a knife at her hip.

Jag grabbed her trembling hand and shook his head. "That would be a really fucking dumb idea, female."

"I don't give a rat's ass what you think is a good idea."

"Magnolia Thornheart gave us your details," I said quickly, and she stopped trying to stab Jag and turned back to me. "She said you might be able to help my mate."

The fear instantly receded.

"Why didn't you tell me that?" she fired at Jag.

"Again, I didn't get a fucking chance with all your screeching."

Her mouth dropped open, and her eyes widened. "You kidnapped me off the street!"

"You didn't give me any other choice."

She snapped her mouth closed, her eyes filled with fury, but instead of biting back, she strode past him and into my quarters. She sucked in a breath when she saw Fern.

"Mags said you could—"

"Oh, fuck," she whispered as she rushed to the bed, climbing up beside Fern.

Cursing under her breath, she pressed a finger to Fern's lower lip, exposing her raw gums. Then she carefully pulled back the covers. Fern was still in my shirt, and I hissed when she lifted the sleeves, revealing the new scars there.

"Tell me what condition you found her in."

"Do you know who did this?"

"How did you find her?" she barked.

"Strapped to a gurney naked, in a room full of fucked-up creatures I'd never seen before."

She placed her hand on Fern's chest, and a tear streaked down her face as she nodded, as if someone had said something to her.

"He hurt her," the witch whispered, her voice breaking. "So many times, in so many ways. He healed her but made sure she'd scarred, then did it again and again. His magical imprint is all over her. How long did he have her?"

"Four days."

She shook her head. "The first time?"

This witch had to have the gift of sight or something like it.

"I don't know. But I think she was very young. I think he got to her after her mother was murdered." I wanted to roar at the thought of someone hurting her, of someone hurting my precious female, of taking pleasure from it.

She nodded, and more tears fell as she hovered her hand above Fern, moving it over her, jerking when she reached the long scar below her ribs. "Her liver. He removed it."

My lips curled back in a snarl. *He cut her fucking liver out?*

I didn't know what the fuck to do with myself, what to do with all the rage inside me.

I watched as she carried on, jerking back more forcefully when she reached her hips.

"A virus. He infected her with some kind of virus, but it's all tangled up with magic, a twisted kind, with barbs and hooks. It's sunk in deep and taken hold of her, but she's trying to fight it. She's fighting so hard."

"Can you help her?" Jagger asked.

She didn't look away from Fern. "I think so."

I tightened my fists. "And if you can't?"

"If I can't, she's in serious trouble." She finally looked up, her eyes meeting mine. "If this doesn't work, then you might need to prepare yourself."

Like fuck. I wasn't losing her.

"When can you start?"

"I need some things from my place, and then I'll begin." She climbed off the bed, strode up to Jag, and tilted her head back but didn't meet his gaze. "Let's go then, Prince Charming."

Jag's eyes flicked between moss green and gold. Jaw tight, he motioned for her to lead the way.

———

When the witch—Sutton—returned, she'd brought a large purple polka dot bag with her. She stood by the bed now and placed a wooden box on the bed at Fern's feet. Taking a small clay pot from her bag, she added several oils that had a strong smell, followed by herbs and some other things I couldn't identify, before using a stone pestle to mix everything into a paste while she whispered a spell.

Finally, she looked up at me. "Whatever happens, you can't get in my way or try to stop me. If you think you'll have trouble doing that, then you need to leave."

"I'm not leaving her."

"Then, I suggest you get your brother back in here, just in case."

"Jagger's not seeing my female naked," I snarled.

"Have him turn his back because this isn't happening without him in here as well."

Cursing, I quickly texted Jag, and he replied instantly. He was on his way.

Fern cried out, writhing, panting, flushed, and coated in sweat.

"It's gonna be okay, Fern," Sutton said, brushing her hair back. "I won't leave you like this. I'll take that monster's poison from you; I'll take it all away."

"You know who did this? Did you see something? A vision?" I said, already struggling to hold myself back, and she hadn't even started. She had the sight, she might be able to help.

"I couldn't see him, but I've heard whispers about a witch, and then two of my friends went missing." Fury lit her eyes, and they flashed red.

Sutton wasn't only a witch.

"You know for sure it was the same witch who took them?"

She looked up, those red eyes swirling with black as well now. "We found their mutilated bodies. The magic signature was the same as what I feel coming off Fern."

"Coming in," Jag called through the door.

Sutton quickly covered Fern before he walked in.

"Where did you find them?"

"An old boarding house." Her eyes narrowed. "You already knew that though, didn't you? You and your brothers found them first."

The building we'd tracked Faron to. Her friends had been among the dead there.

"We did," I said, not wanting to lie.

Her hands shook. "And when did you plan on telling the witches council? When were you planning on letting the families, the covens, know about their missing loved ones?"

"It wasn't that simple," Jagger said. "There are other things at play here, things we're trying to figure out, and it looks like whatever happened to Fern is somehow connected."

Her eyes were a swirl of red and black again, and the veins in her throat darkened until they turned black as well. "They were my people; you had no right—"

"We were going to find the families," I said, trying to keep things calm. I needed her to help Fern—that was all that mattered. "We wouldn't have just left them there."

The black veins spread to her jaw. "I despise arrogant males like you. You think whatever you have going on is so gods-damn important. All you care about is yourselves. They were my family, and you left them in a steel bin to rot."

"Like Relic said, we planned to tell the families."

She shook her head in disgust, her hands trembling. "Sure you were."

Jag's eyes narrowed, traveling over her like he was searching for something. "You're not just a witch. How does your coven feel about you having demon blood?" he finally asked un-fucking-helpfully.

Her red-and-black gaze sliced back to him. "The coven I was born into didn't like it much at all. Which was why I found one that wasn't filled with bigoted assholes. Every witch in my new family has been rejected because of their mixed blood or weird powers"—she smiled, but it was more a baring of teeth—"or because they could physically transform in ways that were considered *unattractive*. Coven Ashborne is a family by choice, made up of people who don't judge others for those things, who embrace and love each other for their differences. That is why losing two of my sisters and then finding out what had happened to them the way that we did when you and your brothers could have said something puts you and your pack in the number one spot on my most hated list."

"Terrifying," Jagger said—again un-fucking-helpfully.

He knew loss. We'd lost brothers, but his lack of emotion made it impossible for him to truly understand her pain, and until Fern, I was exactly the same, but he needed to shut the fuck up.

I snarled at him and turned to Sutton. "Please say you'll still help Fern."

"You think I'd leave her like this? That I'd let her suffer because you and your brothers were selfish assholes? Nice opinion you have of me." She shook her head. "I would never leave anyone to suffer like this, especially not her. Fern is one of us. She belongs with us—"

"She's mine," I growled out. "And she belongs with me."

"Well, that'll be up to her when she wakes up." She curled her fingers around Fern's. "I get the feeling she's never had a place where she felt she belonged." She looked up again. "She'll always have a place with us."

Fern arched against the bed, panting and hissing as welts lifted on her arms.

I surged forward.

"Stay the hell back," Sutton bit out. "I need to get to work, and I need to start now."

Her gaze went to Jag. "If he tries to get closer when this starts, you'd better make yourself useful and stop him."

Jagger nodded, and stepped in front of me, turning his back to Sutton and Fern.

As soon as he did, the witch slid the blanket off my

Tinker Bell. There were more welts on her body now—her stomach and thighs.

"Let's make you feel better, sister," Sutton rasped. "It's going to hurt at first, and I'm so sorry about that."

My heart pounded in my ears. The thought of her suffering any more pain had the beast trying to break free and forced a growl from my chest.

"Easy," Jag said. "Lock it down, brother. Let Sutton do her job. Let her help your female."

I nodded, but every muscle in my body was rock-solid, and I was barely holding the beast back. There was no way I was leaving this room though, not a fucking chance, and Jagger knew it as well.

Sutton slipped off her jacket and draped it over the couch. A tiny bat, clung to the front of her shoulder.

"It's okay, Boo," she said, carefully removed it and putting it inside her jacket. "You stay in there. We'll be done soon."

She turned back, and the smile left her face, her expression shifting to one of determination. She rolled up her sleeves, then tied her wild blond hair back into a messy bun. Her eyes closed, and she rubbed her hands together as she muttered words—a spell. The veins in her throat turned black again, but this time, it traveled higher—over her jaw, her cheeks, the darkness pooling below her eyes. When she finally opened them, the whites were stained black as well.

Emotions bombarded me—sensations that were still so new. The biggest was fear that I'd lose Fern. I wanted to shove Sutton away. I didn't know her, and I didn't trust her, but she was all we had. I kept reminding myself that Magnolia wouldn't send anyone here unless she trusted them.

Sutton climbed onto the bed beside Fern, staring down at her with those black eyes and bright red irises, and a magical wind whipped around the witch as she picked up the small pot containing the potion she'd just mixed. Dipping her finger into it, she whispered, repeating her spell, not even stopping when she inhaled, so the words were an unbroken loop of magic.

One by one, Sutton smeared her potion on every single scar on Fern's skin, and with every application, Fern's cries grew louder, more agonized.

"You're hurting her," I snarled.

Sutton ignored me and continued spelling, applying her potion while Fern screamed in pain.

The beast roared. My mate was in pain. She needed me.

"Brick!" Jagger yelled.

The young hound burst through the door, and froze, his gaze locked on the bed. I turned to him and roared again, so loud that he took a step back before he quickly averted his eyes. Jagger barked another order at him, but I didn't hear it because all rational thought had left me. The more my Tink screamed, the more the beast shoved at my control.

My face changed, my fangs elongated, and my claws burst from the ends of my fingers. I was about to shift, and there was no stopping it. Red rage filled my eyes.

Someone shoved me back—hard.

Warrick. He stood in front of me.

Our alpha held me against the wall, his beast's eyes locking with mine. "Stand down," he barked. "You do not fucking shift, understand?"

I snarled, but I had no choice but to listen to War's order and the dominance of his beast pulling me back from the edge. I panted, hissing through my teeth as Fern continued to scream and thrash.

Sutton was straddling her, holding her down as she smeared on more of her potion. "Charming, I need you over here to hold her down."

Jagger cursed but did as she said, and I lost it all over again.

"Let him help," War barked. "He's not trying to take your female from you. You know that, brother. Let him help her."

I knew it. Rationally, I knew it, but the animal in me did not. What I wanted to do and what my alpha commanded were two different things, and it was as if I were being torn down the fucking middle.

Fern cried out again, and this time, power rolled through the room, so strong that it slammed me back against the wall.

Then she opened her mouth and released an agonized scream.

CHAPTER
TWENTY-ONE

FERN

EVERY SINGLE ONE of my nerve endings was *on fire*, sizzling through my limbs, my insides. The tips of my fingers burned hot, and it felt as if hundreds of blades and needles were being pulled from my flesh by a huge magnet, through organs and bones and veins, slicing a path out of me, no matter what was in the way.

I screamed again, trying to fight, but big hands that scalded my skin held me down. There was a heavy weight on top of me, and I gasped as, one by one, those blades and needles popped through my flesh, leaving a jagged path in their wake. Every release from my flesh was agony and relief in equal measure.

Something burned my throat, and warmth trickled down the side of my face. My body was hot, then ice cold, and I wanted to curl into a ball, but the hands holding me down wouldn't let me.

I gulped down breath after breath as something powerful washed through me in ever-increasing waves. Oh, sweet Lucifer, it was unbearable. I needed to release it; I needed to get it out. When I screamed again, it burst from me like a dam breaking.

I fell back, limp, and the weight on top of me and the hot hands holding me down were gone.

"Fern?" a voice I didn't recognize called through the darkness. "Fern? Can you open your eyes?"

I tried to blink, then again.

Something warm and damp was dragged across my eyes with care.

"Now, try again," that same voice said—a kind voice, a familiar voice even though I was sure I'd never heard it before in my life.

I did as she'd said and blinked again. A female with honey-blond hair and demon eyes smiled down at me.

"Hey, you're back," she said.

I trusted no one, but I instantly trusted this female. She'd been here with me—her voice, her warmth. Somehow, I'd seen into the deepest part of her, or maybe she'd shared that with me, but I knew without any doubt that she was good and kind.

A low, rough sound—no, a growl—rolled through the room, but it'd been there the whole time, hadn't it?

I turned toward it.

Toward Relic.

He stood by the door, his glowing golden eyes on me, while his alpha and another male, Brick, held him back. Jagger stood across the room beside the dresser, his eyes averted. That was when I realized I was naked and covered in ... something, some kind of potion. I recognized the scents of several herbs and oils.

The female quickly draped a blanket over me. "What's the last thing you remember?" she asked.

I turned to Relic again. He'd stopped fighting, but his chest heaved, and those eyes were still locked on me.

"I was strapped down, in that room, in that place ..." I squeezed my eyes closed for a moment. "How did I ... how am I here?"

"Relic tracked the male who took you from the forest," Jagger said.

I searched Relic's face, licking my dry lips. "You left me there, all alone."

"No, Tink, let me explain—"

"I turned around, and you were gone."

"Fuck," he snarled. "I was summoned. I didn't have a choice. I would never have left you like that. I would never have done that. Fern—"

"No," I whispered. "Stop talking. I need you to stop talking."

Images flashed through my mind: Grady, The Chemist, and his creatures. My skin crawled.

I didn't want to be here anymore. I knew Relic. He was good; he was a good male. I'd convinced myself that he'd abandoned me, but that was what that place did to me—it broke me down and made me doubt everything and everyone. But now, I was back. Now that I'd seen him, I knew the truth. I believed him. He would never have left me if he'd had a choice.

But right now, I didn't care what happened in that forest, where Relic had gone or why. I just needed to get away from this place. I wanted to scrub my skin, the poison, the twisted sickness off of me.

Relic was suffering because of me. This thing between us was dangerous, toxic. I was toxic. I didn't want to taint him; I didn't want to spread my filth all over the only place I'd ever felt safe.

"Please ... I need to leave," I said to the female.

"You can come with me." She squeezed my hands. "There are others like us. We have a safe place. You're more than welcome, Fern."

I nodded, and she helped me get off the bed. I didn't bother hiding my body; it didn't even feel like a part of me anymore. I felt disconnected from it, like it belonged to someone else. That was how it had been while I was with The Chemist the first time, and when Grady took me back, I slipped back into that numbness like an old, worn coat. It had surrounded me instantly, protected me.

"You are not fucking leaving, Fern," Relic said, voice vibrating. "I won't let you go."

The female helped me dress and gather my things. I couldn't look at him while he raged and fought.

"Go with them," Warrick barked at Jagger. "Make sure they get there safely."

Jagger nodded and ushered us from the room, but I stopped beside Relic.

"Thank you," I rasped. I owed him that—and so much more. More than I'd ever know how to repay him. "For coming to get me. For saving me. But this thing between us —whatever it is—it's not good, Relic, and it's ... too much. I'll find a way to release you. To break our deal—"

"Fuck the deal. You are not fucking leaving me, Fern."

Why did this hurt so much? I guessed this was how people must feel when they broke up with someone. I'd never had a boyfriend, or even a best friend, or any kind of real relationship. What I'd had with Relic for that short time was the closest to those things I'd ever had, and I'd forced him into it. How fucking pathetic was that?

"I'm sorry ... for doing this to you."

"You didn't do anything to me," he bit out. "Do not fucking leave," he demanded.

I'd stolen his soul—that was why he was acting like this. It was the only reason he wanted me around. After all I'd put him through, there was no way he'd want me here otherwise.

"If you're leaving, you need to do it now," Warrick growled, his beast shining in his eyes.

The female wrapped her arm around my shoulders and led me away while Relic roared my name over and over again, shattering me into a million pieces.

CHAPTER
TWENTY-TWO

FERN

COVEN ASHBORNE WAS SMALL, but everyone had been so welcoming, despite the pain they were in. I found out The Chemist had killed two members of their family while he'd searched for someone to replace me, and the guilt of that was a weight I'd never be able to shake. Sutton had reassured me that no one blamed me, but I still felt that guilt.

Unlike other covens, they all lived together in a big, old mansion. It had seen better days but still managed to feel warm and had a really good vibe. I'd liked it here instantly. It'd turned out Agatheena was right; there were more of us with mixed demon and witch blood than I'd realized.

I'd been here for four days. Their house was safe, the wards incredibly strong. Sutton and Phoebe—another witch here—had taken me through the process of creating a ward myself. It was my first magic lesson, and I'd felt power course through me when I completed it.

Something had happened in Relic's den, had been set free, when Sutton cleansed me of The Chemist's magic. I felt the power inside me growing with every passing day. But as exciting as that was, and as much as I liked it here, something was missing. Something felt out of place.

I walked to the window and looked out onto the street. My heart thumped hard.

Relic. He was still down there, leaning against his bike. He looked up then, like he could sense me watching him, and straightened.

I missed him—so fucking much. Jagger had explained when he'd brought us here what happened when Lucifer summoned them to Hell. That Relic couldn't stop it from happening and how time worked differently down there. Even though Relic had come back almost instantly for me, days had passed here.

I chewed my lip. He'd been calling and texting, and I'd forced myself to ignore them all. I hadn't wanted to, but I didn't want to make this harder on him—or me. The connection between us was so incredibly intense.

After the way it had affected him—gods, controlled him —I was never claiming another being's soul for as long as I lived. I'd never do that to anyone ever again.

My phone chimed.

Relic: I'm so sorry, Tink. I would never abandon you willingly.

He'd said variations of the same thing over and over since I had gotten here. Maybe everything was twisted between us, but I couldn't take it anymore, seeing him blame himself for something that was out of his control. I thought I'd gotten that across to him, that I didn't blame him, at the clubhouse before I left, but obviously not. Or maybe this was just all part of our unhealthy connection.

Sutton walked up beside me and bit her lower lip. "He's persistent."

"Any luck?" I asked.

I'd found out that Sutton was not only an impressive healer, but she also worked as a medic. A medical clinic for non-humans had opened a couple of months ago, and Sutton had signed on. They had their own ambulance and everything.

She shook her head. "But Phoebe thinks she's close to finding it. She's feeling brave. She's going to ask Rune for help tonight."

We'd been searching for a way to release Relic from my deal, but since it wasn't safe for me to leave the house just yet with Grady and The Chemist still out there, Phoebe had been poring over the books in the demon library for me.

Sutton's familiar, Boo, poked his head up from the hood of her sweatshirt, and I gave his head a gentle pat. "I seriously owe her one. Rune is ... he's kind of terrifying."

"I try to avoid any interaction with him at all costs. He makes me feel weird, like I'm not in full control anymore, you know?" she said.

I did. It was like he could force you to drop your wall and inhibitions. It wasn't that he controlled or manipulated you; he just removed your filter completely.

She motioned to Relic. "So, what are you going to do?"

I couldn't leave him out there all night, not again. The guilt was too much. "I know this is a big ask, but I think, if I could bring him in and show him around, let him see how safe it is, explain the wards, he might ease off a bit."

She nodded. "You're probably right. Let me check with the others, see if they're okay with him coming in." She fired off a group text, and my nerves went crazy when their replies came back almost instantly. She smiled. "They're cool with it. Just don't let him wander around on his own, and if he starts getting violent, we'll extract him—swiftly."

"He won't." I looked down at him again. "The way he was, when you were with me in his den, that's not him. Not usually."

But if he did lose it for some reason, the ward had a built-in safety mechanism. If his invitation was rescinded by the members of the coven, he would be bound in magic and thrown from the house.

"Thank everyone for me, will you?" I said, then headed along the hall and downstairs.

My heart raced as I unlocked the door. When I walked out, Relic watched me approach through the gate, and he instantly moved to meet me, curling his fingers around the bars.

"Hey," I said.

His gaze did a sweep of me from head to toe. "How're you feeling, sweetness?" He was trying so hard to keep the growl from his voice, to look like he was calm and unaffected, but his voice sounded kind of distorted, like it sometimes did around me, and his chest was rising and falling faster than usual.

"I'm okay." I flashed him my new teeth. "I'm like a squirrel." I tapped on the front ones. "It wasn't the first time I've had to grow a new set."

Relic didn't smile back—no, his nostrils flared, and the muscle in his jaw jumped. "Don't joke about that, Tink. Don't ever joke about that."

"Right, sorry." I slid my hands into my pockets. "I don't blame you, you know? You had no control over what happened. I know you wouldn't have left me if Lucifer hadn't summoned you. You don't need to keep apologizing, and you don't need to worry about me anymore, I promise."

"Not going to stop worrying about you, Fern."

I stepped closer. "I figured you'd say that. So, how about

I show you around, let you see how safe it is here? Would that help?"

He gripped the bars tighter. "It's a start."

"Okay then." I lifted the cover over the keypad beside the gate latch. "You can come in, but you have to be good. No snarling or breaking shit."

"Best behavior." He flashed a grin.

My heart did a stupid fucking flutter, and I couldn't stop my own smile as I tapped in the code for the gate. It beeped, and the lock disengaged. As soon as I pulled the gate open, he strode through, shoved it closed behind him, and advanced on me. I took a step back, and he froze. Then I cursed because I didn't want him to think I was scared of him. I wasn't. It was the complete opposite. And to prove it, and despite knowing I shouldn't, I took a stepped forward. He watched me, and slowly, cautiously, did the same.

"It's been weird being away from you," I admitted.

At my words, he took another step forward, and so did I, and as soon as I did, he closed the space between us with a growl and scooped me up into his arms, wrapping them around me tight.

"You fucking scared the shit out of me, Tinker Bell. Thought I'd fucking lost you."

A feeling rose up inside me, so overwhelming that tears sprang to my eyes. All I could do was wrap my arms around his neck and hold on tight, and for the first time in four days, everything felt right.

He started toward the front door, and I laughed, but it came out shaky.

"You can put me down now."

"Not yet." He carried me up the steps and through the front door.

Everyone had obviously made themselves scarce

because the foyer and main rooms were now empty. Relic pressed a kiss to the top of my head, and I felt his reluctance when he finally lowered me to my feet.

I quickly wiped my eyes and took a step back. "So, um … this is obviously the entrance." I motioned to the wide opening on the right. "That's the living room, where everyone hangs out and watches TV or whatever."

"What is this place?" he asked, looking around.

"The house was owned by a male named Reginald Ashborne. He was like me, mixed blood, witch and demon, like most of us here—and like us, he was rejected by his own coven. So, he formed this one for displaced witches. He passed away a long time ago, but the coven survived."

"Yeah?" He smiled, but it looked a little pained. "You found your people, huh?"

"I did." I rested my hand on his tattooed forearm. "I never thought they existed, people like Sutton. They've been really cool, Relic, so welcoming."

He slid his thumb down my cheek. "Fucking love that for you, Tink."

I smiled up at him, his words filling me with warmth. But why did it hurt as well? Probably because this felt like goodbye, and I guessed it was. The next time I saw him, I'd hopefully have a way to end our deal and release his soul, a way to free him from this insane, ever-growing connection between us. I'd be able to let go of these feelings I had for him and the stupid hope I'd let myself have when I was with him.

"Even after everything, losing two females from this coven because of me, they still—"

"No," he said. "Don't do that. None of that was your fault, Fern. You hear me? It was him. It was all fucking him."

I drew in a shaky breath. "I know, I do. It's just hard, knowing what he did to those females."

"Fern—"

"I'm okay. I promise. Better than I have been in a long time."

"Baby, you don't need to pretend to be strong for me."

I barely suppressed my shiver when he called me that. "I'm not, I promise."

He studied me in a way that made me want to squirm. Time to change the subject. "So, um, Sutton actually found my name in the records at the witches council, in both the Gannon and Burnside family trees." I opened my phone and showed him the picture. "That's me there." I pointed out my real name, not afraid of him seeing it, of him knowing the truth, showing him the red line through it. "When they banish you, like they did me and Agatheena, they cross you out in blood so there's no coming back. I assume it was Gerald, my mother's husband, who did the honors when he realized I wasn't his, and Coven Burnside has already proven they're bigoted and hateful."

"Your name's Estelle?"

I nodded. "But not anymore. I haven't been her in a very long time. I left her behind the first time I escaped ..." I stopped myself from saying *his* name. I didn't want to talk about that monster, not right now.

"Why Fern? How'd you choose it?" he asked, that golden gaze searching my face.

I licked my suddenly dry lips. "The first night after I escaped, I slept under this massive fern in the forest. It made me feel safe for the first time since my mom died. The name just kind of felt right, I guess." I wrapped my arms around myself. "Honeycutt—well, my mom always called me honey, and all I had left of her was this." I pointed to the scar on the tip of my finger, where she'd cut me the day she died. "Stupid, I know, but I wasn't exactly thinking straight at that time, and the name kind of stuck."

"Not stupid, Fern. Not fucking stupid at all."

The intensity he was giving off had me swallowing audibly.

I smiled, trying to lighten the moment a little. "So, you want the grand tour?"

"I'd like that," he said easily, even though his eyes were saying so much more after everything I'd just shared.

I showed him the kitchen, the dining room, and the backyard. And besides him sniffing the air, growling, and asking how many males lived in the house, he'd been on his best behavior. I explained the wards and how they worked as we headed upstairs.

"This is my room." I opened the door.

He walked in after me and shut it behind us, taking it all in. "It's nice. Big."

"Sutton and Phoebe have been teaching me magic," I said, unable to hold in my excitement. "I can only do a few simple spells, but I feel this ... power inside me. It's big, Relic. I just don't know how to reach it yet. Sutton said a lot of us struggle with our magic for a lot of different reasons. Mainly due to emotional blocks."

This was hard, but I wanted to share this with Relic. I wanted him to know I wasn't just the broken, frightened female he'd been forced to look after or the abused creature he'd rescued, that I was sorting my shit out.

"For me, I developed the block when I was a child. I was rejected by my family and my coven. They despised me so much for what I was, believed I was so below them that they sold me to a monster, not caring what happened to me. They rejected me in every way they could, so I rejected them the only way I could—by locking down my powers without even realizing I was doing it."

"They fucking sold you to that monster?" Relic asked, and I didn't miss that every vein and tendon I could see strained under his tattooed skin.

He'd seen me in that place after The Chemist did what he did best—torture me, so there was no reason to hide it, not anymore.

Still, I was scared. I hated talking about this part of my life. I realized I was tapping my fingers against my thigh, and took a steadying breath.

"When I was seven years old, my grandfather drove me out of the city and took me to a big building and handed me over to The Chemist."

"The Chemist?"

"That's what he calls himself. He does experiments. He'd make us sick, but I was the only one who didn't die. No matter what he did to me, I survived. So when I got older, he'd let Ghoul feed on me until I couldn't move, then pump me full of his newest poison, hoping that in my weakened state, his viruses would win out—"

"Who the fuck is Ghoul, Fern?" he snarled. "What do you mean, he fed on you?"

I swallowed thickly. "A blood drinker he kept in a hole in the basement. He'd starve him, then take me down there and he'd ... drink from me. That's why I didn't want to drink from you, from anyone, why I was so scared I'd hurt you—"

Relic's chest was rising and falling rapidly. "Because you'd been hurt."

I nodded, licking my dry lips. "The Chemist couldn't understand why I survived, why I recovered from everything he did to me. If his viruses were strong enough to kill full-blooded demons, immortals, then why not me? He wanted to create the ultimate demon-killing virus, and I guess he decided that I was the ultimate demon."

"That's why you were so sick when I found you—one of his viruses?" he growled, not waiting for an answer. "What else did he do? Did he force himself on you, Fern?"

Humiliation burned my face, even though I knew it wasn't my fault and that I had nothing to be humiliated about. The thought of Relic finding me like that killed me. He'd probably thought he'd already seen me at my lowest, and then he'd walked in on an experiment, on my punishment.

"No, The Chemist never did that, but he's been trying to develop a virus since I was a child, one that's transmitted through bodily fluid. So, he injected his viruses—sometimes directly into my bloodstream, and sometimes, he put them inside me … in other ways." Nausea churned in my stomach.

Relic's eyes turned red, and his fingers were in tight fists. "I'm going to kill him, Fern. I need you to know that, to believe it. Whatever it takes, I will hunt that fucking sick fuck down, and I will make him scream until his throat is raw and he's choking on his own blood. I'll tear his limbs from his body one at a time before I gut him and force-feed him his own organs."

I blinked over at him, my heart slamming in my chest. "That was very, um … creative."

"I'm seriously fucking motivated."

My lips curled up, and warmth filled me. Would he still care once I released him? Once I released his soul? "I appreciate it."

"I need you to stay safe. If anything happens to you —"

"I haven't left the house, and I don't plan to, not until

we know ..." I slid my hands into my pockets. "Not until I know it's safe."

"Good. That's good." His gaze held mine, and his Adam's apple slid up and down his throat. "I've missed you, sweetness."

I wrapped my arms around myself. "I've missed you too," I said, even though I knew I shouldn't. Even though I knew it was pointless, that there was no future here. But for the first time in my life, it felt safe to open myself up to someone else. Relic was a good male; no matter what happened after all of this, I knew that with everything in me. "You have no idea how much."

"I think I might," he said.

I needed him to stop, or I couldn't be held responsible for my actions. His scent filled my lungs, his warmth somehow reaching out and wrapping itself around me. When I was close to him, the numbness dissolved, exposing all my raw edges, and it was terrifying. He made me feel so goddamn strong, but also so incredibly weak. Everything about him terrified me and enticed me.

The silence of the room enveloped us.

"You make me feel warm," I said, unable to keep the words in.

He didn't grin or make a joke—no, an intensity filled his eyes that made me shiver. "And you, Fern Honeycutt, make me feel so many fucking things, things I never thought were possible."

I wanted that to be true—so fucking badly.

"Kiss me." The words fell from my lips before I knew they were coming, but I didn't take them back. I didn't want to.

This was so incredibly selfish of me, but I couldn't help myself. I missed him holding me, touching me, looking at me the way only he could. Relic was the only being who had ever made me feel this way, like I was more than just a broken mess.

He was too lovely, too perfect, too handsome, too strong —just too fucking everything—to resist.

I almost expected him to deny me, to tell me no, to say I didn't know what I was asking for, or that I was too fragile or confused.

He didn't. He growled so low that I felt it in my belly. Hooking me around the waist, he hauled me off my feet, one muscled arm holding me up and tight against him. His other hand went to the back of my head, his fingers thrusting into my hair, and dragged his nose up my throat, scenting me roughly. Shivers slid through me a moment before he tipped my head back, and his mouth came down on mine.

Every part of me came alive.

I was wanted. At this moment, I was truly wanted.

And I was safe in Relic's arms.

CHAPTER
TWENTY-THREE

FERN

Curling my arms around his neck, I hung on tight as he kissed me—no, devoured me. One hand on my ass, holding me in place, the other still in my hair, tilting my head to the side so he could kiss me deeper, harder. Not like I was broken or weak, but like he truly saw me, beyond all the fractures and jagged edges, like he would die if he stopped.

He kissed me until my head spun, until I was panting and slick between my thighs. I ached for him—so badly.

"More," I said, hooking my thighs around his thick waist. "Touch me."

He spun, planting me on the bed. "Tell me where you want me to touch you, baby."

I dragged my shirt off, and he lifted up, giving me room so I could toss it aside. I unhooked my bra, dropping it as well, and his glowing gaze dipped to my chest. He licked his lips before sliding his hand up my waist, curling his fingers around my breast. He squeezed in a way that I really fucking liked before he swiped his thumb over my nipple. I sucked in a breath.

"You want me to kiss you here?"

I nodded enthusiastically.

He chuckled, and the dark, gritty sound had my nipples puckering even tighter. Dipping his head, he sucked one into his hot mouth, and, gods, my hips bucked off the bed. He tilted his head back so his eyes stayed on me as he sucked and licked and teased me. I thrust my fingers into his long, soft hair and fisted, holding him to me while his other hand slid up my body, and he massaged and toyed with my other nipple.

I was panting, squeezing, and rubbing my thighs together to ease the ache, the deep emptiness. He dragged his hand back down my side and gripped my hip as he kissed my stomach, and his rumbles and growls filled the room as he kissed around my belly button.

Oh my Gods. I gasped.

"You good, Tink?"

I nodded again so fast that I earned another one of those dark chuckles.

"You don't like something, you want me to stop, you tell me, and I stop."

"Okay," I said shakily, hungrily.

I bit my lip, waiting for him to come back up and kiss me again. I wanted him to kiss me again, but instead, he went *lower*. I sucked in a breath and held it, freezing.

Was he going to do what I'd seen his brother do to that female in the bar? Heat hit my face, and I tried to slam my thighs closed.

"No," I panted. "Don't."

Relic instantly stopped what he'd been doing. "You don't want your pussy licked, baby?"

I did. At that moment, I wanted it more than anything else I'd ever wanted.

He frowned. "You do."

Not a question. My desire for him was obviously written all over my face, and of course, there was the fact that he was a hound, so he could smell how much I wanted that, how much I wanted him.

"You scared after what happened? Are you"—his nostrils flared, and his eyes flashed red—"sore?"

I shook my head.

"We don't have to do that. You don't want me to touch you there, Tink, I won't. I can get your toy, and we can do what we did last time." It had been among my things when he'd dropped all my stuff off here the day after I left.

I shook my head again, struggling to say the words, feeling frustrated and humiliated. Lost.

He massaged my waist. Patient—always so fucking patient and kind.

"After what you've been through, I get this might not be something you want. I'm so cool with that, Tink. I don't want you to feel pressured into anything, but, Fern, you gotta talk to me. I'll never fucking forgive myself if I scare you or hurt you."

I had to say it, didn't I? I had to say the words because I would not let Relic think he was doing something wrong.

"I'm not scared or hurt. I avoid that part of me because ... because *he* made it something clinical, something that he used to hurt me." I bit my lip and hated when angry tears filled my eyes. "How can you want to touch me there after what you saw? How can you want me at all now that you know what he did to me?"

He flashed his sharp fangs. "There is nothing—not one fucking thing—wrong with you, Fern. I don't see those things. I see a fucking feisty, beautiful, sexy, hot-as-fuck little female. You drive me fucking crazy with hunger. You have no idea, baby, how much I want you. None."

There was no missing the conviction in his voice.

"You really see me that way?" I whispered. "You really want me?"

"My dick is so fucking hard right now, sweetness. Fuck, just look at you. Those gorgeous, round tits. These fucking thighs and an ass I want to take a bite out of. Do I want you?" He blew out a shaky breath. "Again, you have no fucking idea, Fern. Fucking none."

My heart was pounding, and the blood was rushing with force through my veins. I reached down and touched his square jaw. "Then, please, Relic, will you lick me? I need you to show me how good it can be. I need you to give that to me."

I could love this male, if I let myself. I could fall so deeply in love with him, but that wasn't an option for me. So instead, I could let myself have this moment with him now.

His snarl vibrated through me before he gripped my ass in those wonderful hands, dipped his head, and dragged his hot tongue through my pussy. I cried out, arching against the mattress, but Relic held me in place. Covering me with his hot mouth, he sent me into another realm, a realm where only pleasure existed. I lost control completely, and locking my legs around his head, I lifted my hips, rocking against his mouth. The vibrations coming from him told me he liked it—the way I reacted. And the hungry way he sucked and licked me told me that he liked the way I tasted, and that just turned me on more.

When I was panting and shaking, he slid his tongue inside me, licking me deep, while his thumb slid over my clit, and I broke, shuddering and crying out, coming against his mouth.

He didn't let up until I collapsed. Only then did his licks and kisses slow. Finally, he kissed my inner thigh and lifted his head. His eyes were dark and hot, wild.

"You want my fingers for your second one?"

I nodded. Oh, sweet Lucifer, yes. I wanted that badly.

His eyes stayed on me as he slid one long, thick finger inside me.

"Oh, fuck," I groaned at the feel of him filling me before he slid back out. "I-I like that."

"Thought you might. You're fucking dripping, Tink. You want more?"

I bit my lip and nodded, wantonly spreading my thighs wider, and he added another finger.

"Like that even more, don't you, sweetness?"

"Mm-hmm." I couldn't talk as he moved faster, deeper.

In his eyes, there was no hesitation, no disgust, no fear that he was hurting me. He trusted me to tell him the truth, and he loved making me feel good. He truly wanted me at that moment in a way no one else ever had.

He crawled up the bed, those fingers still moving inside me, faster now, and lay facing me. I pressed closer to him, lifting my thigh over his hip, and he curled his other hand around the side of my throat and took my mouth again, kissing me hungrily.

I could taste myself on his lips, all blended with him, and when he nipped my lip as if he couldn't get enough, my pussy clamped down on his fingers. I came for a second time, rocking against his hand, gasping into his mouth, and kissing him wildly.

Panting, I pressed my forehead to his.

"More?" he growled.

"Yes," I said.

I pushed at his shoulder now, wild with hunger for my hound. He rolled onto his back, following my silent order. I sat on my shins and gripped his shirt. He helped me tug it off, and I took in his gorgeous, muscled body.

"You're so beautiful, Relic." I pressed my hand to his tattooed chest, shaking my head. "No one has ever made me feel the way you do."

He reached up and cupped my face. "How? Tell me how you feel."

"Excited, wanted … needed," I whispered, almost afraid to say those things out loud.

"Show me," he rasped.

I licked my lips. "How?"

"Any way that feels right. You can do anything you want to me, Fern. I'm yours to touch, tease, taste as much as you'd like. No limits. No part of me is out of bounds. It's all yours."

The thrill his words sent through me had me trembling.

"I want you naked," I admitted.

"Then, have at it."

I reached for his jeans and shakily undid them. He lifted his hips so I could tug them down. I tossed his boots, socks, jeans, and underwear on the floor, and he lay there, naked, watching me watch him. He was so large—everywhere. His muscles were taut, and the veins in his arms, thighs, and lower stomach all bulged.

"Your body is … it's so perfect."

His lids drooped. "Fucking love your eyes on me."

His cock was so big, angled up, and it looked painfully hard. It was darker than the rest of him, and the tip was glistening.

I knelt beside him, and looking at him like that had me

squirming. I reached out, tracing one of the pronounced veins on his lower stomach, down to his groin, and his cock twitched.

I looked back up, and he was breathing roughly through his nose. I kept my eyes on him as I curled my fingers around his thick cock.

"You're so—gods—so hard."

"Didn't know I could get this hard. You did that to me. Only you can make me this way." He groaned as I stroked him slowly up and back.

He'd enjoyed licking me. Would I enjoy licking him?

Curiosity got the better of me, and I dipped lower and swiped my tongue over the glistening head. A tormented sound rolled from him, and I squirmed again, feeling achy and incredibly wet still. I didn't think I could ever get enough when it came to Relic. I licked him a second time and rocked against my heels, desperate for another release already, but also wanting to make him feel as good as he'd made me feel.

"Come here," Relic ordered. "You need to get off. Can fucking smell that pussy, baby, and it needs attention. Come sit on my face, sweetness."

Oh, fuck. I wanted that. There were so many things I wanted. But right then, I wanted to make him feel good, and I wanted to look at him while I did it. I climbed on top of him, but when he reached for me to pull me up his body, I shook my head. Instead of letting him drag me higher, I ground my pussy on the underside of his cock, trapped between us against his stomach. I knew I could get off this way. He was so hard and hot—gorgeous. I dragged my pussy along his length again, then back.

"Can you … can you come like this?" I asked breathlessly.

"Fuck, yes," he groaned, his fingers gripping my hips and taking over.

He ground against me, making me cry out from the delicious friction. Planting my hands on his chest, I rocked against him in long, sweeping strokes.

"Relic, I ... holy fuck." I groaned.

My hair was all over my face, and he pushed it back with one hand, watching me lose control on top of him. I slid up, then back, coating him in my slickness, utterly wild with need. On the next glide, I went too far, and when I rocked back, the head of his cock pushed inside me, just the wide tip, but that was all it took—that stretch, that heat inside me. My pussy clamped down on the head of his cock, clutching and releasing it as I swiveled my hips, not taking him deeper—not because I didn't want to, but because my inner muscles were so tight that there was no way he was getting any deeper inside me.

I came hard while Relic cursed beneath me. I looked down at him, at his taut expression, at the way his stomach muscles looked as if they'd been carved from stone. His hands were now over his head, gripping the headboard, and I knew it was to stop himself from holding me there and thrusting deep.

He pulsed inside me thickly, hissing and groaning. Hot seed filled me with force, making me come again just from how good that felt as well, how seeing Relic this way made me lose it even more.

I collapsed against him, my face pressed to his throat, breathing hard.

"Don't move," he said roughly.

I shifted my hips experimentally; somehow, he was locked there.

"Oh." I shifted again, and he groaned. "Does it hurt

you?" I couldn't imagine how it would feel to have all of him inside me—as it was, just the head had expanded enough that it locked us together.

"Definitely doesn't hurt. You feel fucking perfect. But if you try to pull away before I release you, you might get hurt."

I nodded against his chest as he rubbed my back.

"You okay, sweetness?"

"Yes," I whispered. I felt more than okay, and right now, I was glad he couldn't see my face because stupid fucking tears were filling my eyes again.

"You're not okay," he said.

"I am."

"Can smell your tears." He forced me to look at him. "Did I hurt you?"

I shook my head. This was just an agonizingly beautiful goodbye.

"You don't know what you've done for me, Relic. You've given me so much, and you … you gave my body back to me. You slowly yet surely helped me take back ownership of a part of me that had been used to hurt and humiliate me. I'll never forget you for that."

A fierceness filled his eyes. "You won't forget me, baby, because I'll always be right here. By your side."

"Relic—"

His phone started ringing, and he growled. We stared at each other for long seconds.

"You should get that," I whispered.

He slipped from me, his body finally releasing mine, and I wanted him back instantly.

He growled again, but snatched his phone off the floor. "What?" His jaw hardened, and so did his gaze. "On my way." He disconnected. "I need to go, but we aren't finished with this conversation. I'll call you when I'm done, yeah?"

"What's going on?"

"Nothing you need to worry about."

He was lying. Something was going on, something that involved me.

"Have you found them?"

His nostrils flared. "I won't know that until we get there."

A shiver moved through me.

"I'll call you when I'm done, and you will answer, Fern. Yeah?"

"Yes," I said, because I got the feeling he wouldn't leave this bed if I didn't agree.

Beyond that, this was hopeless. There was only one way our next conversation could go.

I slid to the side so he could get up, and I watched him quickly dress, locking every second of our time together in my mind.

He planted one hand on the mattress and leaned over me. "I'll call you as soon as I can."

"Okay."

Relic kissed me, deep and hard and hungry, before finishing with one sweet, soft brush of his lips. He swiped his thumb over my cheek, and then he walked out, closing the door quietly behind him.

TWENTY-FOUR

RELIC

"Smells the same," Loth said. "Like chemicals and fear."

"Some other shit as well." I shoved open the boiler room door. The darkness was like a dense cloud. The scent of the foul magic that had been done in here sat heavy in the air. "He was spelling in here." There was a sigil or glyph of some kind drawn in the soot on the floor. "I can smell blood as well."

Lothar had gone back to the building we'd found Fern in and picked up another scent. It was ancient. Demon. And it had led us here, to this vacant house.

"Faron?"

Jag narrowed his eyes. "Yeah, but something else as well. I've smelled it before, a long time ago. There are echoes of it in the back of my mind, but I can't pinpoint it."

Lothar tilted his head back, scenting the air again, and nodded. "Yeah, it's the same for me."

Both were a lot older than me. They'd lived many, many lifetimes, which meant that, sometimes, things that weren't important were pushed to the depths of their memories.

I planted my hands on my hips. "That could've been our last chance to get ahold of that fucker. He knows we're looking for him now. Whatever he did in here with that blood, he was making sure we wouldn't find him again."

He'd be stupid if he weren't long gone by now.

"We're not giving up," Lothar said. "We're not letting that sick fuck get away with what he did to your female."

No, I wasn't giving up. I'd never give up.

We left the building and headed for our bikes.

"You mate her yet?" Jag asked.

They could smell her on me, of course, and that knowledge filled me with possessiveness and pride.

"After what happened to her, I'm not pushing her into anything she's not ready for. I'll wait until she is."

Loth nodded, approval on his face.

I'd never much cared what Lothar thought about the shit I did. He was my sire, yes, but that hadn't meant anything. Now, though, for some reason, his approval felt ... really fucking good. I studied him, and, yeah, I'd noticed our resemblances before—his eyes and hair were the same color as mine, and when he was thinking hard about something, he tilted his head to the side like I did. But, no, he didn't feel the type of connection a father usually did for his son because it had never been that way for us. I wasn't the result of loving mates bringing a pup into the world, like War and Wills, so Lothar hadn't developed the ability to feel. His emotions were still as stunted as they'd ever been. I was Lucifer's experiment, one he'd decided never to repeat. Loth and I, we'd always been tight, but something felt different now—for me anyway—and I wasn't sure what to do with it.

Loth swung his leg over his bike. "You need to bring her home. Your den's the safest place for her."

Jag nodded in agreement. "Mate her, brother, as soon as you can. Get a pup in her. She'll want to stay close to home then." He grunted, "Safe."

I crossed my arms and shook my head. "If it were that fucking easy, I'd be going home to her now."

"You're her male," Jagger said. "Lay down the law. It's for her own good."

I was starting to see why War shook his head at us all the damn time now. He saw things differently since he'd found Willow and gotten the full spectrum of emotions, and I guessed now so had I. I actually laughed, because for being so fucking old, we seriously had no clue.

"Fern would hate me if I snatched her from her place and locked her in my room. It would also scare the fuck out of her."

Lothar frowned. "You're her male. What's to be scared of?"

"First, she doesn't know we're mates. Second, females have minds of their own."

Jag grunted again. "We know that. I listen when they tell me what they want, and I give it to them."

"Not talking about the females you take to your bed, brother. I'm talking about their feelings and their thoughts beyond an orgasm."

"That's where you lose us." Loth grinned.

"No shit." I swung my leg over my bike as well. "I can't fucking wait until you find your own mates."

Loth grumbled and started his bike.

Jagger's expression hardened. "I don't need a female fucking with my head."

"You don't get a choice, Jag. It happens when it happens."

Jag snarled, started his bike, and rode off. Loth followed, and I pulled out my phone and hit Fern's number. I was done playing. Yes, Loth and Jag saw things in black and white, but they were also right about one thing.

Fern was safer with me.

———

FERN

My phone started ringing.

"It's Relic."

Phoebe gave my arm a squeeze. "You got this."

She hadn't talked to Rune—he hadn't been around—but she'd found the book we needed in the library. I finally had the words to set him free. Phoebe gave my arm another squeeze and walked out.

Ignoring the pain in my chest and the sick feeling in my gut, I put the phone to my ear. "Hey."

"I want you to come back to the clubhouse," Relic said by way of a greeting. "I'll swing by now and pick you up."

I shot to my feet. "Whoa. Hang on a minute. What's going on? What's happened? Did you find something?"

He exhaled roughly. "We found where they'd been hiding, but they were gone before we got there. I don't want you out of my sight—"

"I'm safe here. The wards are strong. There's no way he can get through them."

"I fucking love that you've found your people, baby—you have no idea how much I love that for you—but I need you with me, Fern. I need you in my den, in my bed. I know it's fucking selfish—believe me, I know it. But I need to be the one to protect you." Another rough exhale. "I just need you."

This was killing me. Gods, this hurt. I wanted to believe it—I did. But I'd been right; Phoebe had found proof in the texts about unhealthy obsessions growing between those who did deals like the one I had. He wasn't thinking clearly, and I couldn't do this to him anymore. I knew what it was like to be held against your will. Keeping him tied to me would make me as sick and twisted as The Chemist.

"I don't think that's a good idea."

"Why?"

"Because what you're feeling it isn't real. It's just ... not. This connection between us—it's the deal I forced you into."

"No, it's not."

"Relic, it is. You can't see it right now, but there is nothing you can say that would convince me that you would've ever wanted me, truly wanted me, after seeing all you have. The compulsions—gods—what I did to myself, hurting myself, the vomiting, the selfish and reckless way I fed from you. Finding me on that gurney the way you did." I shook my head, even more convinced now than before. "You wouldn't be talking to me now, you wouldn't be so ... so concerned about me, and you wouldn't have been with me earlier today if I hadn't tricked you into selling me your soul."

I felt sick to my stomach. I really was a fucking monster.

He was breathing hard. "How can you think that?"

"It's not your fault. I know what a good guy you are. But I own you, and that has twisted everything between us. Everything."

284

"You don't own shit, Fern," he rumbled. "Everything I've done with you—for you—was because I wanted to."

He was delusional.

"By the power of Lucifer, the lords of perdition, and the fires of Hell, I release you, Relic. Your soul is your own; your mind and heart belong to you alone."

Several beats of silence followed.

"Fern," he said huskily.

"Thank you, Relic, for all you've done for me."

"Fern—"

"You have no idea what it meant to me."

"Fern," he barked louder.

"Have a good life." I disconnected quickly, blocked his number, and slumped back on my bed.

How was I going to survive this? Gods, the pain of it surpassed anything else I'd endured in my life.

How would I live without him?

CHAPTER
TWENTY-FIVE

FERN

"You can't stay in bed all week." Sutton plopped on the bed beside me.

"It hasn't been a week."

"Girl, it's been five days. Time to get up, get out of that smelly shirt, and get in the shower."

It was one of Relic's shirts. I didn't want to take it off. And, yes, it was gross that I'd gone five days without a shower, but I didn't want to wash him off either.

"What's the point? What am I going to do? I can't go to my apartment or my store. I can't do anything. I'm trapped here."

"We can go downstairs, order takeout, and watch a movie."

"I guess," I said, mainly because I was learning that Sutton was sweet, but she was also stubborn.

"Excellent." She gave me a little shove. "Now, get in the shower."

"Fine." I pushed back the covers and got up.

I avoided the mirror when I undressed in the bathroom. I hadn't looked, and I still wasn't ready to see the new scars on my body, not yet. I quickly showered and dressed, and when I got downstairs. Sutton and several other members of the coven were there, eating popcorn, chatting, laughing, and waiting to start the movie.

"She's alive!" Sutton patted the couch beside her. "Come sit. You'll feel better when you lose yourself in ninety minutes of cheesy dialogue and fast cars."

That sounded kind of perfect. Anything to get out of my own head and ease this crushing weight on my chest. The movie started, and I shut down my mind and let myself get lost in it.

I was startled awake when a door slammed. I looked around; besides Sutton, the living room was empty. She was beside me and looked as half asleep and confused as me. We both turned to Phoebe as she all but ran toward me.

"You didn't answer your phone!" She jumped on the couch between us.

"I must've fallen asleep. What's wrong?"

Her gaze slid to Sutton, then back to me. "I went back to the demon library tonight, looking for my headphones. You know I've been looking for them all week, and that was the only place I hadn't been back to check. You know I can't work without them."

Sutton and I both nodded.

"Well, while I was searching the library, Rune came in." Her eyes widened. "He asked what books I'd been there searching for. I explained everything—like, everything— about you making a deal with Relic and claiming his soul so he'd protect you. I'm sorry. I didn't mean to, but it was like he was pulling the words from me, and I couldn't stop."

"It's fine. I know what you mean." I patted her hand. "Don't even worry about it."

She shook her head. "That's not the part I wanted to tell you." Her eyes were still wide. "When I finished talking ... well, first, he laughed—like, a lot. Then, finally, he said ... in that freaky, sexy, terrifying voice, 'No one Hell-born has a soul, lovely, not the kind you mean and not the kind that can be owned.'"

I froze. "What?"

"I don't think you ever owned Relic's soul, Fern," she said, blinking over at me.

"No ... hang on a minute. That can't be right."

Sutton exchanged another look with Phoebe. "Rune would know though, right? He's a soul collector as well. And he's like, Rune."

I shot to my feet and paced away. What the hell did this mean? Had Relic actually ... pretended I owned his soul? Why? Why would he do that?

I'd wanted his feelings for me to be true so badly. I'd wanted the way he touched me, the way he looked at me, to be real, but it was safe to pretend, to want it because it was never going to happen. The deal had been a shield, protecting me from the possibility of real feelings, of real rejection, of again being cast aside for being what I was. For being me.

It hadn't mattered that I was a total mess or how much I'd fucking hated him seeing all my broken pieces, because none of it had been real. I'd forced him to be there with me because of *the deal*, because *I owned his soul*.

Oh gods. I suddenly felt exposed, laid bare in a way I never had before.

But still a voice in my head, timid but hopeful, whispered, *could he really want to be with me?*

I shook my head. No, he couldn't want that. Why would he want that? And even if he did, it would never work, it couldn't. Eventually, he'd get sick of looking after me while I melted down. Eventually, he'd get sick of the compulsions and the weirdness and my feeding off him like a leech and want me gone.

I was finding it hard to breathe. I had to know. I had to know if what Rune had said was true. "I need to go to the clubhouse."

"We can take you," Sutton said.

"We'll make sure no one gets near you," Phoebe added.

I nodded. "Let's go."

CHAPTER
TWENTY-SIX

RELIC

"What do you think?" Roman asked, holding out his sketch.

He'd returned from Hell earlier that day after Lothar went to take his place.

There was still no word from Lucifer.

Besides a couple of brothers playing pool and Brick watching a movie, the common room was quiet.

"Yeah, brother, that's fucking perfect."

The drawing Rome had done was better than I'd imagined. From a distance, you might think it was the Tinker Bell from *Peter Pan*, but up close, not so much. Rome had given my Tink vibrant red hair, cute little fangs, curves for days, and her dress was made of fern leaves.

Rome nodded. "Is your female in your den?" he asked while he loaded the ink.

"I fucking wish."

"Like that, is it?"

"Somehow, I need to convince her to let me get close

again, so I can explain what's happening between us, but I'm not sure that's gonna be easy."

I'd been outside her new place every night, making sure she was safe. I hadn't seen her though, not since she thought she'd released me from her deal, and she hadn't answered any of my texts or calls. I was pretty sure she'd blocked my number *for my own good*, and she had been ignoring calls from unknown numbers as well because I'd tried to call from several other phones.

"She'll come around," he said. "And if she doesn't, we'll grab her and bring her here, and you can keep her in your den until she does."

I had no idea how to convince Fern I was the male for her, and I was getting desperate. The beast was more than ready to tear through the wards at that house, snatch her, and bring her home—but Fern's choices had been taken from her so many times, by so many people. I could never do that to her.

"You want to do the smaller one first?" Rome asked.

I nodded, tied my hair out of the way, and sat in Rome's chair. I wanted this tattoo even more than the Tinker Bell design. The lettering for the neck piece was bold but intricate, just like my female. I tilted my head while Rome transferred the design onto the side of my throat. Where Fern had fed from me for the first time, and also, I wanted it where everyone could see it. I wanted everyone to know I was hers and she was mine because whatever happened, that was the truth.

The buzz from the gun started, and I closed my eyes and let Fern fill my mind—every perfect inch of her—mind, body, and soul. My fucking body ached for her. The absence of her was like a physical pain, sharp and jagged. I thought about her hand on my chest that first time, and the air burst from my lungs. I wanted her hands on me again. I wanted her warmth beside me every night, her voice telling me good morning.

Rage slowly seeped in, and I tried to fight it back, but it was impossible. Her own coven had banished her, cut her out like a disease, because of the blood in her veins and the color of her eyes. They'd sold her to a monster—someone who had tortured her, scarred her, terrified her so badly that she wasn't able to recognize when someone truly loved her, because I did. That's what this huge feeling inside me was. It was love. It was pleasure and agony all rolled into one. A bone-deep wound that only Fern could heal.

The rage grew bigger until time passed in a blur of images in my head—of finding her the way I had in that room, of hunting down the ones who had hurt her and ripping them apart piece by bloody piece. Rome moved from my neck to my chest. My Devil Dogs ink was on one side, and Tink would be on the other, right beside my heart.

I opened my eyes when the buzz of the tattoo machine stopped. Rome held up a mirror. It was her, my Tink; she was under my skin, marking me the way I was desperate to mark her.

"Nice work, brother." I stood, cracked my neck, and tried to shake off the fury pulsing through me.

"You heading to the pit?" Rome asked, not missing where I was at right then.

I nodded, clenching my fingers.

Somehow, I needed to get a handle on this anger before I did something I fucking shouldn't.

FERN

I waved goodbye to Sutton and Phoebe, and Phoebe lifted her phone, reminding me to call if I needed them to come get me.

I gave her two thumbs-up and walked into the club-house, my heart hammering in my chest.

A hound I didn't know had let me through the gates when I arrived. He said Relic was in the dens, then stunned me by giving me the code to go below ground before he went back to the garage. The code wasn't given out to just anyone. The alpha's mate and pup lived down there. Only those the hounds trusted completely were allowed to come and go on their own.

Relic had obviously told them to let me through if I showed up, but he would have had to have Warrick's approval, and the alpha wouldn't just agree to that, not if he saw me as some random female Relic was spending time with, right?

My pulse rushed faster, and my hands shook at what that could mean, at what my heart was trying to tell me it meant.

The big room was empty, which wasn't normal. While I'd stayed here, there were always several hounds up here, drinking or hanging out or whatever. I strode to the door on the other side, feeling like I was doing something wrong and I was about to get caught at any moment. Like the hound who had let me in would realize his mistake, that I wasn't who he'd thought I was, and toss me out. My nerves almost got the better of me.

I almost turned around and left, but instead, I took a steadying breath and punched in the code. Still, I hadn't expected the door to open, that it was some trick. But the sound of the lock sliding free on the other side echoed through the door, and when I tried the handle, it opened.

I tried not to freak out as I walked through before shutting the door firmly behind me. I took the stairs as quietly as I could down to the dens because still, I felt as if I wasn't supposed to be here. I quickly rushed along the main cavern to Relic's quarters, and gathering my courage, knocked on the door.

But no one answered.

I tried the handle. It was locked.

Shit.

I really didn't want to do this in front of an audience, but there was no other choice, obviously, so I headed to the common room, where the hounds often congregated, but I knew it was empty before I walked in. There was no rumble of voices or sounds from the TV or of them playing pool.

A roar echoed down the cavern, and I turned as cheers and howls followed.

What the fuck was that?

It was muted and distant, but it was definitely down here.

Yes, I was afraid, but I knew whatever that was, Relic was a part of it, and suddenly, getting to him overrode everything else I was feeling. I headed down another one of the caverns toward the sounds. I turned time and again, following the roars and growls and cheers, going deeper into the underground maze of caves.

The sounds grew louder. I was almost there.

I rounded a bend and turned into a wide opening that led directly into a huge cavern, big enough for the entire pack with room to spare.

Through the crowd, I could see the edges of a pit dug into the ground. It looked to be several yards across, and the walls were blackened and charred. The hounds surrounded it. Some were yelling instructions, some howling. Others stood with their shirts off, their bodies battered but quickly healing. Brick was across from me; the young hound was busted up pretty bad, and he was nodding while Dirk talked to him. I searched the room full of males for Relic, but I couldn't see him—

A vicious snarl came from the pit.

Goose bumps lifted across my skin and raised the hair on the back of my neck. Without thought, I shoved through the crowd, rushing forward, and sucked in a breath.

Relic was down there. He and Rome were trading blows. Both showing no signs of stopping.

I stepped closer, about to call his name, but a hand landed on my shoulder, stopping me. I spun around. Warrick shook his head as he gently but persistently steered me back from the edge and behind the crowd.

"You need to stop this," I said to the alpha when he was looking down at me.

His expression was unreadable. "Relic needs this, Fern."

Anger sliced through me. "To be beaten bloody?"

"Yes," he said, shocking the hell out of me. "We fight for many reasons, but mostly, it's because, at our hearts, we are animals. That's what a hound does when he feels threatened or afraid or cornered—he attacks. He burns off all the adrenaline pulsing through his veins, blinding him, making it impossible to see the way forward. We fight to see the truth."

I blinked up at him, my stomach knotting. "Why would Relic feel that way?"

War studied me. "Right now, Relic's feeling a lot of things he's never felt before, and after six hundred years of fuck all, it's a lot for him to process." A small smile curled his lips. "You gotta know, Fern, he's in there right now because of you."

"Me?" My heart somehow raced faster, and the nerves grew more intense. "I'm nothing ... to anyone."

His chin jerked up, a look of surprise on his face. Then he barked an order for the hounds in front of us to move before directing me back to the edge of the pit. Relic and Roman were still trading blow after blow, so hard that the smack of fists against flesh echoed through the room. Relic looked, gods, feral. Fury burned in his now-red eyes, but not at Rome. No, his anger was focused inward. This was all about releasing whatever it was he was feeling.

"Take a good look at him, Fern," War rumbled.

I took him in—inked skin slick with blood and sweat, face contorted with rage, those glowing red eyes. His hair was tied back, his square jaw hard, his teeth clenched, canines elongated. He was breathtaking. The most beautiful being I'd ever laid eyes on. My gaze dipped to that perfect mouth again, then down to his throat, veins bulging —I froze, locking onto something on the side of his neck, something new. A new tattoo. Bold, swirly lettering scrawled low on the side of his throat.

Four letters.

Fern.

Sweet Lucifer, my name was inked into his skin—right over the spot where I'd first fed from him.

"I know you've been let down a lot in your life, Fern. I know you've been made to feel unwanted, but you definitely mean something to him," War growled low beside me.

Relic's gaze sliced to me, his red eyes finding me and locking on. That moment's distraction earned him a fist to the face. Relic staggered back, straightened, and shook it off. Then, he walked right past Roman to the edge of the pit and launched himself out.

I couldn't fucking breathe.

Relic advanced on me, and his brothers parted, giving me room as I backed up—not because I was afraid of him, no, because I was afraid that this wasn't real, that it was all a dream and I'd wake up.

This is no dream.

Trembling, I tried to gather my control as he stalked me.

Jagger jumped in the pit with Brick behind Relic, and the hounds turned away, ignoring us, choosing to watch the fight rather than whatever was about to happen between Relic and me.

Relic closed in, until my back was to the wall, and I had nowhere to go and nowhere to look but up at him. He was breathing hard through his teeth, his gaze searching mine. Without a word, slowly, his big body shaking, he dipped his head to my throat and breathed in deep, a low growl rolling from him on his next exhale.

When he lifted his head, his eyes were still glowing, but they weren't red anymore; they were gold.

"Relic?" I whispered.

He cupped the side of my face, the rough tips of his fingers sliding gently down my cheek, making me shiver, and he waited. Waited for me to say whatever it was I'd come here to say.

But looking into his eyes, gods, I thought I knew the answer already. "I never owned your soul, did I?"

Still, he didn't answer, just kept his wide beast's eyes locked on me.

I stumbled on, tripping over my words. "R-Rune said no one Hell-born has a soul, not the kind a soul collector can own. I-I never had any control over you, did I?"

He shook his head.

"And you ... you were with me because ..."

He looked at my mouth, then back up, but he didn't fill in the silence like I desperately wanted him to, to make this easier on me. What he'd said to me on the phone, when I thought I'd released him, filled my mind.

"You don't own shit, Fern. Everything I've done with you—for you—was because I wanted to."

"Because you wanted to ... be near me."

The beast flashed through his eyes, the predator right there, watching me, so goddamn intense.

Finally, he spoke. "You never had control over me, not for one second—at least, not the way you think. Everything I've done with you, every minute I've spent with you, has been of my own free will. Because I wanted to be there."

"Not the way I think?" I whispered. "What does that mean?"

"You tell me," he said, voice pure grit. "Why do you think I couldn't stay away from you, Fern? Why do you think, to me, you are the most beautiful, sweet, lovely, sexy, fucking perfect female to ever exist?"

I opened my mouth, then snapped it shut.

"Say it," he said huskily.

I shook my head. "I can't."

"Why?"

"Because it can't be what I want it to be. It can't be that," I said, voice breaking as tears stung my eyes.

He curled his fingers around the side of my throat. "I'm in love with you, Fern Honeycutt. You are the only one to ever make me feel this way. You are the reason I can feel this way because you were created by the Fates to be mine and I was created to be yours. You are my mate, Tinker Bell. The day I walked into that shop, the first time and saw you standing there, was and forever will be the very best day of my immortal life."

The things he'd just said, it was everything I'd ever wanted to hear.

"I'm scared," I whispered.

"Me too." He brushed his thumb over my jaw. "I'm fucking terrified you'll leave me again."

I reached up, taking that strong throat between my hands, one of them over his new tattoo. "I'm terrified you'll come to your senses and realize I'm not who you want or that this isn't real."

"That will never happen, and I promise you, it's real."

"Are you sure?" I said. This felt too good to be true, like every one of my childhood dreams—that, one day, someone would save me, love me, want me—had become real.

"Yeah, Fern, I'm fucking sure."

"You really love me?" My voice sounded strange to my own ears. My heart was pounding so hard, I was trembling.

"Fuck."

He swiped his thumbs over my cheeks. They came away wet. I lifted my hand and felt my face, and my fingers came away wet as well. I'd had no idea I was crying. I didn't cry. I never cried.

"I'm so fucking in love with you, Tink," he said in his gorgeous, gritty voice.

All the air was punched from my lungs, and I had to drag in a desperate breath. "The last time someone told me they loved me, I was seven years old," I said, still whispering because I was too scared I'd break this spell I'd somehow cast over him or be thrust out of whatever fucking beautiful alternate universe I'd stumbled into.

"Baby, you're killing me." He pressed his lips to the top of my head.

Tentatively, I touched his sides. Then, letting the fear drop, I wrapped my arms around him. "Oh gods, this is really happening," I choked out. "You're really mine."

Relic growled, scooped me off my feet, and holding me close, carried me from the room.

CHAPTER
TWENTY-SEVEN

FERN

RELIC HELD me to him as he strode through the caves, growling sweet, sexy things in my ear.

"Gonna take care of you, baby. Gonna make you feel so fucking good." He nuzzled my neck. "My beautiful little Tink. My perfect mate. Fuck, the way you make me feel."

I clung to him, unable to get close enough. Gods, that night, when I thought I was claiming his soul, the way my world had spun around me, the heat I'd felt, the unexplainable sense of safety that I'd felt and couldn't explain—none of it had anything to do with his soul—no, the moment we touched, a primal part of me had recognized him as mine, my mate, and I'd missed it.

I pressed my face against his throat and breathed him in. His scent was home and comfort and every good thing.

Finally, we reached his quarters, and he quickly let us in, shut the door behind us, and lowered me to the floor.

He was breathing hard as he looked down at me. Then,

taking me by surprise, he dropped to his knees in front of me and wrapped his arms around my middle.

He looked up at me, trembling almost as hard as I was, and I saw the truth in those stunning golden eyes, as if he'd said it out loud.

"You're truly my mate?" I choked out.

"I'm yours, Fern," he said, his fingers flexing against my back. One hand slid up to grip the back of my neck in a possessive hold. "I have always been and will only ever be yours."

I held his handsome face in my hands and decided to jump off the ledge, allowing myself to trust in this, in him. "I'm in love with you, too, by the way."

His nostrils flared, and he flashed his canines. "You love me?"

I nodded. "I never thought this would ever happen for me. I never thought the Fates would give me this after everything they took from me. I thought ... I thought they must hate me, that they saw everything that was wrong with me like everyone else has my whole life." I held onto him tighter. "But if they think I'm worthy of someone as wonderful as you, then maybe I'm not the abomination everyone told me I was."

Relic pressed his face to my belly, and he was shaking harder now. Rage rolled off him as he breathed heavily in and out several times because he didn't see me that way—he never had. When he looked back up at me, his eyes were glowing red again, and his fangs had elongated.

"You never were, baby," he said, his voice rough as hell, confirming it. "To me, you are perfect in every fucking way." He curled his arms around me tighter. "I'm so sorry, my baby, that I didn't find you sooner, but I swear to you, if anyone tries to hurt you again, I will make them pay with their life."

I felt every one of his words down to my soul, and suddenly, I couldn't get close enough to him. I wanted my bare skin on his, his warmth, his scent. I wanted his hands and his mouth on me, his blood on my tongue, and the hard length straining against the front of his jeans buried deep inside me. I wanted it all.

I wanted every part of him, and I wanted to give him every part of me in return.

Leaning in, I pressed my mouth to his, and he groaned against my lips as I slid my tongue over his bottom lip. "I want you to make me yours, Relic."

He groaned. "We have time. We don't have to rush anything."

"But I want it now. I want to be your mate now." My body ached for him, for him to cover me, own me, love me.

"I'll make you come, Fern, over and over, but you're not ready for what I need to do to make it official." He stood, lifting me as he did. "We'll get there, but the last thing I want to do is hurt you."

"You won't," I said, wrapping my legs around his thick waist.

He pressed his forehead to mine. "I could if I don't take the time to prepare you for what needs to happen."

"What do you need to do to me?" I asked. My inner muscles clenched, fluttering, so needy. "Tell me."

"To mate you properly, I'll need you on your hands and knees so I can fuck you from behind ... and when we're both about to come, I have to sink my fangs into your shoulder to mark you," he rasped. "It's another scar, and that mark will be on you forever."

He was worried about causing another scar on my body.

"I want your mark. I want to see it every day." I rubbed my thumb over the tiny scar on my finger. "My mom gave me this the day she was taken from me. Trying to protect me."

Relic took my hand, pressing a soft kiss to the tip of my finger over that tiny scar. Warmth filled me. I lifted my hand to the side of his face.

"Knowing that I have another scar on my body, given out of love and not hatred, having your mark on my skin … will make the rest insignificant. Your mark will prove that my father was wrong, that Grady and The Chemist were wrong, that I'm not worthless, that somebody does want me for their own. That I am lovable. Your mark on my skin will make me the happiest female to ever live, Relic. I don't want to wait another day. I want it now. I want you now."

His big hand was at the back of my neck, and his fingers slid into my hair, fisting lightly. "Then, you'll get me, and I'll make sure it's so fucking good for you, baby. I promise." He shook his head. "But first, I gotta wash off Rome's blood because smelling another male anywhere near you is fucking with me."

He carried me into the bathroom, kicking the door closed after us, and turned on the water. With hands shaking, his muscles twitching, and his teeth bared, he undid his jeans and shoved them down, along with his boxer briefs. Standing naked in front of me, he reached for me, and carefully but urgently, he dragged my shirt off and fired it into the hamper before he stripped off the rest of my clothing.

Taking my hand, he stepped into the shower and pulled me in with him. Quickly lathering up soap in his hands, he worked the suds all over him, then me, removing all traces of the blood and sweat that had coated his skin and inadvertently gotten on me. Directing me under the spray, he washed the soap off, scenting the air as he did before making a growly sound of approval.

Looking down at me, he slid one of his hands over my shoulder and down to my breast, growling again as he swiped his thumb over my nipple, making me shudder.

"You've seen what happens before I come."

I nodded.

"That transformation only happens when our mates are near, when you're close to me. It's only ever happened with you, and it's gonna happen when I come inside you. I'm gonna be locked in place, like last time, for a while. So, I need to prepare you for that." He gave my breast another squeeze and continued to stroke the rough pad of his thumb over my nipple as he talked. "You can take all of me though, sweetness, because that's how this works." His other hand slid down over my hip. "I'm gonna need to use my mouth and my fingers for a while first, get you nice and wet and ready for my cock."

I licked my lips. "Okay."

He cursed. "You're so fucking gorgeous. Fuck, Fern, I've been desperate to get my mouth on that pussy again."

He dropped to his knees, and I thrust my fingers into his thick, wavy hair. A whimper slipped from me when he kissed his way down my belly, licking and sucking my skin. He gripped my waist and lifted me, sliding me up the slick wall, and when he leaned in, I automatically hooked my legs over his wide shoulders. With a snarl, he swiped his tongue through my pussy, and I cried out. Relic gripped my ass, yanking me closer, licking me like I was the best thing he'd ever tasted.

All I could do was hang on, my fingers tangled in his hair, while he feasted on me, driving me wild, working my clit over and over until I was flailing against the shower wall, not sure what to do with myself as the pleasure built and built, and finally broke. My cries echoed off the tiles, mixed with Relic's hungry growls.

I'd barely caught my breath when he lowered my legs and stood. Before I could speak, and with his eyes locked on mine, he slid a thick finger inside me.

"*Oh, fuck.*" I gripped his biceps.

"Can't wait to feel you gripping me tight, Fern," he said. "Gonna live in this hot little pussy for fucking days. Gonna make you mine, and then I'm gonna cover you in my scent so every male who comes anywhere near you knows exactly who you belong to."

He slipped in a second finger, and the moan that came from me was a sound I'd never made in my life.

"And w-will my scent b-be on you?"

His nostrils flared. "You'll be all over me, sweetness. Your scent will tell everyone that I'm taken, that I have a mate who is fucking everything to me."

His thumb slid up, rubbing my clit steadily while his fingers pumped in and out. And, sweet Lucifer, it felt so fucking good, and the things he said were so perfect that I followed the urge to rock my hips forward, seeking out more.

"I need you," I said, pulling him down for a kiss.

He devoured my mouth while he fucked me with his fingers. "You got me, baby," he said against my lips. "Need to make you come again before I give you my cock though."

He wouldn't have to wait long because every time those long fingers slid inside me, he hit a spot that had me gasping and my hips rolling.

"Oh, fuck." I pressed my head to his chest, digging my fingers into his biceps as he rubbed my clit faster.

"You gonna give it to me, baby?"

"Mm-hmm," I groaned as the feeling built inside me, but this time, my fangs tingled, and the need to bite was overwhelming. My fangs grazed his skin.

"Bite, Fern. You bite me if you need it."

I did. I needed it—badly.

My pussy clutched at his fingers as I sank my fangs into one of his muscled biceps, and as his blood filled my mouth, I came all over his fingers. I took one final suck and dragged my tongue over the puncture marks I'd made, and panting, I tilted my head back.

He leaned in, and his tongue lapped into my mouth, making my head spin. The shower was turned off, and I was lifted out, quickly dried, and on his bed before the haze of satisfaction could even begin to lift. I blinked, and Relic was hovering over me, his golden gaze moving over my face.

I gripped the side of his throat before he could even think about denying me. "Now, can you make me yours?"

He licked his lips, leaning in, nuzzling the spot between my shoulder and neck, as a rumbly growl rolled from him. "I'm going to mark you right here." Another needy growl, and then he lifted his head. "If you have any reservations, Fern, you need to tell me now. Once it's done, there is no undoing it—understand?"

"I don't have any reservations."

He smiled, gentle, gorgeous. "Love that you feel that way, baby, but if you need me to stop at any time, you say so, and I'll stop."

I nodded. "I won't want you to stop."

"You remember what I told you? What I'm gonna do to you, Tink?"

"Yes." I shivered.

How was I still so turned on? But I was. I was hot and achy and so fucking empty.

He brushed my damp hair back. "Are you scared?"

I shook my head and took his face in my hands. "I know I'm safe with you, Relic, no matter what. I know I'm always safe with you."

He pressed kisses along my throat and my jaw before sucking and nipping at my lower lip. "I need you to remember that when I'm fucking you, sweetness. I'm gonna try to be as gentle as I can, but the beast is fucking itching to claim you. I might have rock-solid control most of the time, but not when it comes to you. I'm going to try like fuck to keep it locked down, but things could get a little rough."

I shivered again, but not from fear. He watched as I swallowed convulsively and then licked my lips.

"You said I was made for you and you, for me."

"Yes," he said.

"Then, I'm thinking ... I'm gonna love it any way you give it to me."

He stilled for several beats, his chest pumping hard. "Fuck," he finally gritted out.

The beast leaped forward in his eyes, and they flashed brightly before he bared his teeth, lifted me, and flipped me over.

"Hands and knees," he ordered as he gripped my hips, lifting my ass in the air before I could do as he'd said.

Excitement thrummed through me, and I jumped, squirming when he pressed a kiss to my side, then across my lower back. His hands slid up, cupping my breasts, squeezing as he continued to kiss and rub up on me. He was marking me with his scent, letting the animal take the lead, and when he leaned over me, covering my body with his, I could hear—*feel*—the beast vibrating through his chest.

His cock nudged my rear, and my nerves shot higher. I wanted this. I wanted it more than anything. I wanted to belong to him and me to him. But for me, sex had never been about pleasure; it had been something used against me, something to get through, something I and the person I was with had never wanted. I knew it wouldn't be like that with Relic, but muscle memory had me jerking forward.

Relic stilled, his mouth at the side of my throat. "Talk to me, Tink."

"Don't stop. Do not stop. I want this. You have no idea how much. Please, Relic, don't stop."

"Not gonna stop if you don't want me to, baby, but maybe we do this another way to start with." Then, he was gone from behind me, positioning himself beside me on the bed. "Climb on, sweetness. You start, and when you're feeling ready, I'll finish."

He wasn't put off, not treating me like I was broken, and instead, he'd come up with a way to make this good for us both. Trusting me. Always trusting me.

I could do that.

Gods, he was utterly gorgeous, lying there. Still, nerves fluttered inside me. He was trying to look relaxed, but every muscle in his body was tight as hell, and his long, thick cock strained against his stomach.

"What if it doesn't fit?" I said before I could stop myself.

"We were made for each other, remember? It's gonna fit."

"The Fates seem to love fucking with me. What if this is another one of their cruel games? What if we can never be together like that? Then what? I won't be your mate," I rasped, starting to spiral.

This had to be too good to be true, right? The Fates wouldn't give me this. They wouldn't.

Relic hooked me around the back of the neck, snapping me from my freak-out. "You will be my mate," Relic growled. "Nothing will change that. And if we can't fuck that way, then we don't. We love each other, and we do all the other shit that feels fucking amazing."

"You really mean that, don't you?"

"Yeah, I fucking mean it. I know you're scared. I know you're used to people hurting you and throwing you away, but that will never be me." A smile curled his gorgeous mouth. "But maybe instead of assuming the Fates are fucking with you, Tink, how about you try and fuck me first?"

I could definitely do that. I nodded and straddled his muscled body.

"That's it. Now, start like last time, working that pussy against my cock until you're nice and wet again—can you do that?" he said.

I couldn't wait to do that. Planting my hands on his chest, I did what we had last time, trapping his thick cock against his stomach and grinding down so my pussy spread around his length. A shudder rolled through me when I started working my clit against him. It didn't take long before I was soaking again, sliding up and back along his cock, while pleasure coiled low in my belly.

"You look fucking gorgeous up there." His hips lifted a little off the bed.

Leaning forward, I kissed him and let my hunger for him take over. I kissed him like it was the end of my world, and it was—the end of the hell I'd lived and the start of a new life, where I belonged to someone, where I was loved and cared for, where I was safe. Where I had a future spread out before me that I'd never dreamed possible.

I couldn't believe it, and yet I knew it was real, that this was real.

"I love you," I choked out as I slid forward. Instead of sliding back, I let the head of his cock notch just inside me. "And I'm going to make you mine," I said, the words coming from a primal place inside me that was every bit as possessive as his beast.

I pushed back, and he stretched me wider as he slid deeper.

"You are mine," I said with a hiss.

"Yeah, I fucking am," he said, holding my hair back so he could see my face as I took a little more of him. "That's it, baby, nice and slow."

My mouth fell open as I wriggled my hips and worked in another inch.

Maybe this was all some messed-up game the Fates were playing; maybe they wanted to hurt me again, but I wouldn't let them win. They would not win, not this time.

I worked my hips, swiveling them and rocking on that big cock, working him in one hot inch at a time. When he stretched me wider, I ignored the pinch, so fucking determined.

Panting, I eased up and back down, taking more each time, until I could take no more. I was shaking and sweating and had bitten my lip so hard that it bled, but I'd done it.

"I won," I gasped out. "I beat them," I said as a hot tear streaked down my face.

Relic reached up and swiped it away. "Yeah, you fucking

did, Fern." He was panting as well, his stomach muscles impossibly tight, his chest and arms straining.

"I made you mine," I hissed from a mix of pleasure and pain. I slowly swung my hips forward so he was almost all the way out, then pushed them back, stuffing myself full of him once more.

"Not letting you go," he said, his hands gripping my hips. "Never letting you go."

"I won't let you," I said brokenly as more tears slid down my cheeks. "If you leave, I'll follow you."

He chuckled, dark and gritty. "If I had a soul to give, baby, it would be yours. Neither one of us is going any-fucking-where without the other."

I nodded and moved faster, and every time I took him deep inside me, shocks of pleasure jolted through my body. I was so wet now—there was no resistance—and, gods, I was close to coming again. I stared into his eyes as I moved on top of him, gasping and sobbing as I got closer and closer to the edge. His long, thick fingers gripped my hips tighter, and he hissed a breath through his teeth as he lifted his hips again, filling me more deeply.

Oh, fuck. I dug my nails into his chest and moaned low. "I'm ... I'm going to—"

"Not yet, baby. Hold on." Relic lifted me off him, flipping me onto my belly again, then dragged my ass in the air.

As he hooked me under the hips, holding me up, I whimpered, trying to impale myself on the head of his cock. Desperate to feel him inside me again. He slid back inside me, this time in one smooth thrust, filling me easily.

"Oh gods, yes," I moaned.

He slid out, and when he thrust inside me again, all the air was knocked from my lungs. I barely managed to drag in a breath before he was *taking me.* His growls and snarls filled the room as he claimed me—as the animal, the beast, claimed his mate. Fisting the sheets under my hands, I gasped for breath and shoved back into him, wanting every huge inch inside me. Everything about it was wild and raw and so fucking perfect.

The way Relic wanted me, the way he was claiming me, made me feel loved and wanted and utterly out of control. But for once, I didn't have to be scared because my mate held me tight, and he'd never let me go.

He growled lower. "That's it, Tinker Bell; fuck me back, show your hound how you like it deep," he said in a distorted voice. "You're gripping me so fucking tight, baby."

I groaned and lifted my ass higher, pushing back harder, and he roared like the beast he was. I loved it. I wanted him to feel as out of control as I did. I fisted the sheets tighter as I felt my orgasm build inside me. My pussy fluttered wildly, and Relic barked out words in a low, guttural language I didn't understand.

He grew larger inside me. "Oh, fuck."

"Only you do that to me," he said in that otherworldly, resonating voice. "Only you'll ever know what this feels like." He gripped the back of my neck and pushed my upper body down to the mattress.

He thrust deep, and when he tried to slide out the next time, I was tugged back with him. We were locked together. My head spun, my body vibrating with pleasure.

Relic's groan was so guttural that it lifted goose bumps all over me. He lapped at my shoulder, and I shivered when his canines scraped my skin.

"Don't try and pull away when I bite," he said, then sank his fangs into me, moaning against my shoulder and rotating his hips.

I cried out as his cock throbbed heavily inside me,

pumping me full of hot seed and sending me over the edge. I shuddered and moaned, my pussy fluttering and spasming as I came around him. His canines in my flesh didn't hurt—no, it tingled, felt warm—and as one orgasm waned, the next built.

He released my shoulder. "That's it, Fern. Come again for your mate," he growled like the beast he was.

His rough demand was enough to push me over the edge, and I came again. His roar echoed through the room, the beast letting everyone know that he had claimed his female. That I was his.

While we were still locked together, he gripped my hips and rocked and ground into me, filling me so thoroughly, and all I could do was breathe through it.

"You did so fucking good, Tink," he said low, gently, rubbing my back and massaging my hip.

His rocking turned to shallow thrusts, and then he was able to slide in and out of me again. He leaned over me and lapped at the bite he'd given me several times, and the rasp of his tongue made me shiver.

Finally, he slid out, and his arms came around me so he could carefully position me where he wanted me on the bed. I couldn't have moved even if I wanted to. I was warm and weak-limbed and, gods, dazed. Relic climbed in behind me, wrapping himself around me so I was fully cocooned by his heat and scent and comfort.

"My mate," he said in a voice full of reverence, and my eyes stung. He nuzzled his mark on my shoulder and lapped at it again. "Mine."

TWENTY-EIGHT

RELIC

I SLID my hand up and down Fern's back, still catching my breath, while my little female lapped at the bite she'd given me while she'd ridden my cock. She lifted her head, looking down at me, her pretty peridot eyes heavy-lidded and soft with satisfaction.

My blood stained her lower lip, and I loved that so much that my heart fucking clenched when I reached up and wiped away the little bit that had trailed down her chin.

Her cheeks darkened, and she smiled in a shy, sexy-as-fuck way that had me curling my fingers around the back of her head and pulling her down for a kiss.

Feeding her somehow satisfied the beast even more than fucking her. Knowing I could sustain her in that way —knowing that no matter what, she would never go hungry, that she would always be full—provided me with the kind of peace and fulfillment I hadn't known was possible.

"Have you had enough?" I said against her perfect lips.

"I have," she said back. "Thank you."

"Told you, Tink, you don't ever thank your male for feeding you." I nuzzled her jaw. "I also fucking love it."

She was warm and soft, relaxed in a way that I knew she had never been before, and I fucking loved that as well.

We'd been holed up in my den for the past few days, and I never wanted to leave this room or this bed.

She wriggled so she was on her side, facing me. She rested her head on one hand while the other stayed on my chest, where I liked it, idly tracing my Tinker Bell tattoo. "So, I'm going to suggest something, and I'd like you to hear me out before you get all growly and possessive and say no —because then I'll have to do something you won't like, we'll argue, you'll lock me up in your room, and I'll get super pissed and give you the silent treatment until you let me out. Do you want that?"

I fought back my grin. "It's not like we've been doing much talking anyway. Maybe we should jump straight to the silent treatment, and I'll eat your pussy while you get over it."

Her eyes widened, and she bit her lips together in that way I had quickly learned meant she was amused, turned the fuck on, or both.

"Stop trying to distract me from this very important conversation," she said as she slid her thigh over mine.

I couldn't hold back my dirty-as-fuck laugh. "You're thinking about it."

She rolled her eyes. "Of course, I'm thinking about it. You're good with your mouth, hound, and your fingers … okay, fine, you play my body like an instrument you've been studiously practicing for centuries, but we do need to talk about a couple of things before we get back to making more beautiful music together," she said with a cute grin.

"But I love making you hit those high notes, baby." I smirked.

"No more talking, only listening." She pressed her finger against my lips.

I grabbed it and nipped the tip. "Are you sure you want to talk right now?" Because now, I had my heart set on eating out my mate's fucking delicious pussy.

"I'm sure." Some of the teasing had left her eyes.

I didn't like that. "Okay, talk to me."

"You promise to be reasonable?"

"I'm always reasonable, Tink."

"We'll have to agree to disagree on that one. Though mating my hellhound stalker has been the highlight of my entire life and an excellent title for a romance novel, I can't just stay in this bed for the rest of my life, having mind-blowing orgasms and feeding from you—"

"Why not?"

Her gaze slid to my mouth, and she sighed, her lips going all pouty and making me want to kiss her again. "Because I have a business to run and clients who rely on me."

She was right; I was going to say no.

"You know why you can't do that. It's too dangerous for you to leave the den."

"I know, but this isn't a permanent solution. I can't live down here like a mole person for the rest of my life."

"A mole person?"

"Relic—"

"You don't like it here?" I swallowed thickly.

She leaned over me, cupping the side of my face. "I love it here, but I still need sunlight and contact with other people. I love my store, and I have new friends. Maybe it's selfish of me, but I want it all. I want to be here with you, and I want my store back, and I want to spend time with my new coven. I want to live."

If anyone deserved it all, it was Fern, and I wanted to give it to her more than anything. "I promise I'll find him, and when I do, I'll put him down screaming. Then, when I know you're safe, you can have it all."

"I know you want to do that for me." She pressed a gentle kiss to my lips. "But without me, you won't find him." She lifted her head and held my eyes. "You have to let me help. I want to help."

Everything in me rejected the idea. "Fern—"

"Which is why I need you to take me to see Agatheena."

TWENTY-NINE

FERN

Agatheena eyed Relic. "You're not coming in, hound."

He stared back, eyes blazing, teeth bared. "You think you can stop me, crone?"

I stood on the other side of the ward. "You need to stand down. Agatheena isn't going to hurt me—"

"Where you go, I go."

"You try it," Agatheena said coldly.

Relic charged forward, hit the ward like a brick wall, then was propelled back and knocked to the ground. He bounded back up and charged forward again, this time slamming his shoulder into it once, twice ...

He was airborne a moment later, crashing to the ground again.

"Please, Relic, stop."

Agatheena snorted at him when he charged back. "You might have broken through the wards of lesser witches, but you won't get through mine. Growl and snarl all you like, but it won't make a scrap of difference." She muttered something under her breath, shaking her head, and headed back down the path. "If you're coming, then move it," she said to me. "Or I'll toss you out with him."

I turned back to Relic. "I'll be right back—"

"That female fucking eats demons," he growled. "Don't you dare go in there without me."

"She's not going to eat me. I'm her family."

"I said no—"

"Are you coming, or am I tossing you out?" Agatheena called.

"I'm coming," I said, my eyes on Relic's, pleading for him to understand.

"Don't do it."

"Please, don't worry; I'll be right back," I said, then turned and sprinted up the path to the cottage with Relic's roars following me. I ran up the stairs and through the door, and it slammed shut behind me.

I didn't want him to be afraid for me, but I had to do this, and there was no time to make him understand. In fact, I didn't think he was capable of it right then. He'd told me himself how possessive newly mated males were, how irrational they could be at times, and how insanely protective. So, I knew this was my only option. Still, I felt sick to my stomach, leaving him out there to worry.

I turned to Agatheena, who stood by the fire, her eyes burning into me. "I'm sorry for what he said. He didn't mean to offend you."

"He's not the first delusional male I've had out here, and I have a feeling he won't be the last," she said.

Relic roared again, and it sent a shiver down my spine.

"You're mated to the hound," Agatheena said, not a question.

I nodded.

"If you want him to calm down, you need to do the same. He can sense your unease whether he realizes that's what it is or not."

"I'm not uneasy," I said, lying through my teeth.

She tilted her head to the side. "If you continue to lie to me, child, this visit will be very short."

Fuck. "Sorry, I won't lie again."

She huffed out a sound that might be her version of a laugh. "So, spit it out. What do you want?"

I straightened and worked on calming myself, for Relic's sake. "I need to find the one who hurt me, and I was hoping, if you'd found any information about me, about what I can do, then maybe—"

"Then maybe you could use your powers to find him?"

"Yes."

Delores cawed and landed on the back of the chair beside Agatheena. She took a piece of meat from a small plate beside the fire and tossed it to her.

"He's powerful, child. I feel echoes of his magical imprint all over you; it's seeping from your pores. Whoever cleansed you did a good job; it's almost all gone. In a week or so, there will be nothing of him left."

"My friend Sutton worked on me, and when she did, I felt it—my power. I just ... I couldn't hang on to it."

"There's a reason you couldn't hang on to your magic— we still need to unlock the power that simmers inside you, not truly."

I curled my fingers into tight fists. "Have you found something? Do you know how?"

"Yes."

Hope and terror filled me all at once. "Whatever it takes, I'll do it. I want him gone—for good."

She nodded. "I can help you, but it's not going to be

easy, and it's going to hurt." Her gaze held mine. "Skin-being-flayed-from-flesh kind of hurt."

I stared back. "I'm not afraid of pain. I've lived with it my whole life."

She nodded. "Then, when you find him, child, you make him feel the pain you suffered. You make him feel every moment of it," she said, quiet fury vibrating in her voice. "They hurt us, but in doing so, they make us stronger. So much stronger than they could ever hope to be."

If fury fueled power and magic, I'd scorch the earth beneath my feet. "What do you need me to do?"

"You need to bleed for your craft. You need to offer your blood to the mother and beg her forgiveness for forsaking her for so long, and you need to ask her to finally accept you as one of her children."

Mother Nature, the Great Goddess Terra, was the Creatress of all life and was often referred to as the mother by the witches who worshipped her. Not many had seen her true form; some didn't believe she had one because, more often than not, when she needed one, she chose to inhabit her pet serpent.

I'd only prayed to her once, when I was taken to The Chemist by my grandfather, but she never answered, never came. I never prayed to her again after that. I'd assumed she felt the same way about me as the evil, twisted fucking witch who'd been hurting me.

"Your mother was a witch, as were your grandmother and your great-grandmother," she said as if she were reading my mind. "Yes, we are also demon, but the mother's gifts reside in you. You are a witch, child, and to ignore those gifts is blasphemy in the eyes of the Great Goddess. To receive your magic, you must atone."

"She never came for me when I was a child; she left me

to suffer. Why would I ask her forgiveness? Why would I pray to her when she ignored my prayers for help?" My voice shook with anger.

Agatheena closed the distance between us. Her hand lifted, and her eyes rolled up so only the whites were visible, and a strange lightness shifted through her features. "I feel her, you know, all around you." Her eyes rolled back. "Your mother. Before she was murdered, she cast a spell, didn't she?"

I stilled, rubbing my thumb over the scar there, where she'd cut my finger. "How did you know?"

"You're surrounded by a protection spell. It's as if ... as if her arms are wrapped around you, even now. If you hadn't been taken to that place, the monster never would have found you. When you escaped, that spell was the reason it took so long for him to find you again."

I always believed she'd been trying to protect me, and now, I knew for sure.

"The mother is like any one of the gods, child; she sees us and the realms in a way we can only hope to. The gods are omniscient and powerful beyond our imagination, but they, like us, are beholden to the Fates. Your life, as unfair as it was, has unfolded as the Fates intended."

"Well, the Fates are fucking bitches," I bit out.

Agatheena chuckled. "That might be so, but in the end, they always get their way."

"So, you're saying I need to suck it up?"

She shrugged. "I'm telling you to not let what happened to you define who you are. No, don't ever forget those who hurt you and never forgive them for their evil, but don't let the hatred you feel for them blind you either; don't let it erode and poison the good that's to come."

When I'd allowed myself to drop my guard, to go after

what I wanted, I'd been rewarded with Relic. How much more could there be?

"I think I've had all the good there is to be had."

She shook her head. "It's boundless, great-grand-daughter."

My heart hammered at her calling me that, at what her words implied, because I wanted to believe her so badly. "And to receive more, I need to invite the mother into my life?"

"You must worship her to receive all of her gifts"—she grinned, and it was wicked as hell—"and then you can kill your monster and make him scream for mercy. You are more than one of Lucifer's demons; you are a witch—you are a daughter of Terra—and to become all that you can be, you must embrace both."

I wanted that. I wanted to embrace both sides of myself. "How do I begin?"

There was a dark mahogany dresser on the other side of the room, and she shuffled over, opened one of the drawers, and took something out.

"Some witches use blood when they need an offering or for binding and warding or to cement their spells. The witches in our line are no different. When a witch like us turns fourteen, our mothers gift us with a special blade, especially for those times, and we carry it always for the rest of our lives." She closed the space between us.

"If your mother hadn't been stolen from you, child, she would have given you one." Her fingers curled around my hand, and she placed a small jeweled knife in my palm. It was silver and studded with emeralds and sapphires of varying shades, and it had a thin blade with a sheath made of the same worn silver.

Her features actually softened. "This was my mother's. I

never got to give it to my own daughter, but I am proud to give it to you."

The softness vanished as fast as it had come. "As you know, my girl, there are witches who will condemn you, who will try and harm you, but we are Terra's children, just like them. We belong, great-granddaughter. *You* belong. You deserve to be here." Her face hardened further. "Are you ready to take back what's yours, Fern?"

I curled my fingers around the jeweled hilt, and they trembled as my eyes changed, now glowing red, the same way hers were. "I'm ready."

"Then, remove your jacket and kneel before the hearth," she said.

I quickly did as she'd instructed.

She slid the blade from my fingers and unsheathed it. "Give me your right arm."

I lifted it to her, and she held it in one hand.

"Do not scream. Cutting is what we do, who we are. The mother is the earth, abundant with power, and the blood we shed for her are the roots, reaching out to her, reaching out for her gifts. This is her blessing to us, so we do not cry out in pain. We relish it. We thank her for it."

I nodded, clenching my teeth when she ran the razor-sharp blade down my forearm. Relic roared again, as if he could feel it, as if he knew what was happening in here. A thud and crash came next, over and over. He was trying to break through again.

I turned to the door, about to get up to rush to it to show him I was okay, but Agatheena gripped my chin and made me look at her.

"He is immortal. Whatever damage he does will heal. You need to focus."

My heart hurt. I was desperate to go to him, but the future we both wanted couldn't happen if I didn't do this.

I nodded. "I'm focused."

She held out the blade like she was handing over a mantle. "Now, you," she said.

I took it, gripping the knife in my hand.

"Repeat after me. *Mother, I am your humble servant, your child, and I offer you my blood.*"

I said the words as I made an identical slice along my left arm.

"*I have forsaken you. Please grant me your forgiveness and gift me with your blessings,*" Agatheena said.

As I repeated the words, a surge of power rolled through me almost instantly. Then, a crash came from deep in the forest. I spun to the door again.

"She comes," Agatheena said.

As I stood on shaky legs, the power inside me grew wilder, and a voice echoed through my mind.

"*Come to me, child of coven Burnside. Come to me now.*"

"She's in my head," I choked out.

Agatheena smiled, flashing her pointed teeth. "Go to her. Now."

THIRTY

RELIC

THE GROUND SHOOK under my feet while the beast rolled under my skin.

Fern was in pain.

And something fucking huge was coming toward the cottage.

The door opened, and Agatheena walked out. When she stepped aside, my heart slammed against the back of my ribs. Fern's vibrant red hair flew around her face as she made her way down the steps. Her arms were at her sides, and blood slid down her forearms, pooling in her palms and dripping on the path as she moved toward me. Her red eyes were unfocused, and her entire body trembled.

"Fern!" I roared, but there was nothing, no recognition. I roared her name again, and as soon as the sound left my mouth, my body was thrown back and slammed against a tree.

The crone. Her hand was raised and aimed at me, her magic coiling around me and forcing my mouth shut.

The trees near me shook as Fern walked through Agatheena's ward and out the other side. She was so close, but still, it was as if she didn't see me. I struggled as hard as I could, but there was no breaking free from the crone's magic.

Fern's head tilted back, and I looked beyond her as a massive serpent slid out from between two shuddering trees and toward my mate.

I strained against my invisible binds.

The serpent hissed, its black eyes focused on my female as it stopped in front of her. Fern nodded as if she understood it. The snake's forked tongue darted out, tasting the blood sliding from the slices down her arms, and it hissed again.

"Yes, Mother," Fern said. "I promise to worship you for the rest of my days."

The huge serpent's eyes flashed to white, glowing bright, and Fern cried out as her body lifted from the ground, bowing and jerking midair. I fought harder to get to her.

Fern jerked one more time, and then she dropped, landing on the ground in a heap. Unmoving.

The serpent swung around and slithered back into the forest, and as she did, the crone finally released me. Cursing, I sprinted to Fern, dropping to the ground and pulling her into my arms.

"Fern," I roared.

"Stop the dramatics, hound. If you want to be helpful, heal those cuts on her arms."

I turned to the crone, now standing at the end of her path and watching from behind the safety of her ward. "What have you done?"

"What I've done, what the mother has done, is give her

the magic that was denied by her coven and by the monster who hurt her. She is finally whole."

I looked back down at Fern, and she blinked several times.

"Fern? Fuck, talk to me."

"I'm okay." She sat up, and I held her to me. "I'm okay, Relic," she said again, and looked up at me. "I'm sorry if that scared you, but it had to happen."

The scent of her blood was driving me crazy, and I grabbed one of her forearms and did what the crone said, licking each of the slices to start her healing.

"You scared the shit out of me." Another scent hit me then. Witch. Even after I knew she was witch as well, her demon blood had dominated everything else, and I hadn't been able to detect it. I did now.

Her phone vibrated on the ground beside her, where it had fallen out. Sutton's name was on the screen. The witch had texted several times while we were caught up in each other, asking Fern to come over.

Fern picked up the phone, and as soon as she did, her entire body froze, and her eyes rolled back.

I shook her. "Fern?"

"She sees something," Agatheena said. "Leave her."

"What the fuck are you talking about?" I snarled.

"A vision," the witch said.

Fern gasped suddenly, her eyes rolling back down.

"Tink?"

She looked up at me, horror contorting her face. "He's got them."

"Who? What are you talking about?"

"The coven, Sutton ..." She struggled to her feet. "The Chemist, Grady—they're there, at the coven house."

"You saw them?" Agatheena asked.

She nodded. "And I heard them. I fucking smelled that monster. I smelled his poison." Fern grabbed my arm. "We need to help them."

"Your power is still unstable, child," Agatheena said. "More than someone as unskilled as you can handle. It could manifest in ways you're not expecting. You need to be careful. Always be on alert and speak with care and caution. Anything can be a spell with the right motivation." Her eyes slid to me. "Protect her with your life, hound, until she learns to do it herself, or I will cut you into pieces."

I nodded, but the threat wasn't necessary. I would always protect Fern.

"We need to go," Fern said, fear vibrating through her. "We need to get to them before he kills them."

"We'll get there faster if I carry you." I quickly texted Jag for backup.

"I'm okay. I can run," she said.

"Not what I meant, Tink." I pulled off my vest and shirt, and shoved down my jeans.

"Relic?"

I gave her a quick kiss, and let the hound explode from my skin. My mate stared at me, eyes wide, and I nudged her with my snout, before lowering to the ground, urging her to get up.

"Holy shit," she whispered, unmoving.

I made a huffing sound and pressed my snout into her hand. She jolted, snapping out of it, and quickly scooping up my clothes, scrambled up onto my back.

I growled and gave her a shake when she didn't hang on tight enough, and she quickly wrapped her arms around my neck. I huffed my approval, and took off.

Instead of heading back to my bike, I swerved to the left and exploded through the trees. We'd get there faster, cutting through the forest. Fern lay against me, her arms locked around my neck, gripping my fur. There was no way she was coming off, so I dipped lower and picked up my speed. I would not let her lose her friends. She'd just found them; she needed them, and I would not let her suffer their loss.

But more than anything, I wanted to hear that sick fuck scream for mercy while I shredded him with my claws.

————

FERN

My mind spun as we flew through the forest. Relic ran so fast that the trees were a blur. I clung to his thick neck, my face pressed to his fur, while images bombarded me. When I'd grabbed my phone, the world had spun around me. I saw the coven house, but it was dark. Someone had screamed, and then the smell had hit me: chemicals, blood.

My friends were in pain. Their cries still filled my head, the scent of warm blood and poison making me dizzy.

He was hurting them.

I had to stop him.

The spinning in my head grew wilder and had me fisting Relic's fur tighter.

My body was yanked to the side, but Relic's fur was still in my hands. I hadn't moved. I was yanked again. Then, he was gone, and I was falling.

I hit the ground hard. Winded, I coughed and gasped for air.

Rolling, I climbed to my hands and knees and blinked down at my fingers. Not in dirt. Concrete. There were no trees or dappled light coming from the setting sun. And no

Relic. It was dark and cold, and the only light filtered in through a small frosted window in the door beside me.

I wasn't in the forest anymore.

I stumbled to my feet.

What the fuck?

I was at the coven house. I'd seen this room, I'd smelled it, and now, I was here.

There was a muffled sound from the shadows.

I spun around, snatched my phone from my pocket, and I turned on the light.

Phoebe.

Oh, fuck. She was strapped to a gurney, bloody welts all over her exposed skin.

She opened her mouth, but no sound came out.

"Phoebe?" I whispered.

I didn't know how I was here. I'd been thinking of this place, and now, here I was.

My powers, it had to be because if The Chemist had somehow done this, he would have been waiting. Oh gods, Relic would be frantic.

"It's going to be okay," I said, rushing to my friend. Hands shaking, I quickly undid the straps. "Can you talk?"

She shook her head and shuddered.

"Are all of you down here somewhere?"

She nodded.

He'd magically gagged them so they couldn't use the wards here to toss him out.

"Is it just The Chemist and Grady?"

She nodded and shuddered again when a scream of pain echoed from somewhere else in the basement. A tear slid down Phoebe's face.

Sutton.

That fucker was hurting her.

There was a storage cupboard on the other side of the room. I quickly helped Phoebe over to it. It was big and full of coats and a few sleeping bags.

"I need you to hide."

She limped in.

"Help's coming. They'll be here soon. I need you to stay still and quiet, no matter what, okay?"

She nodded again and tucked herself into the back corner, wrapping her arms around herself. I covered her with coats and stacked several of the sleeping bags and camp equipment in front of her. As I shut the door, I hoped like hell she survived this. Whatever he'd infected her with was already taking hold.

Rushing to the door, I listened for movement beyond it. Power throbbed through me while I stood there, power that I had no idea what to do with. All I could hope for was that The Chemist felt it, that he sensed the strength flowing through me. Because it was so incredibly vast and wild, there was no way that monster wouldn't feel it pouring from me on the waves of my hatred.

Sutton screamed again, her pain and horror so raw that tears sprang to my eyes.

Get it the fuck together. Your friend needs you.

Gritting my teeth, I yanked the door open and strode out into the hall. There was another one at the end, and I didn't think—I couldn't think, not when my friend was being tortured. If nothing else, if all else failed, The Chemist seeing me walk into that room would stop him hurting her. I just had to stop him from hurting her, and then Relic and his brothers would be here. I just had to buy some time.

As the fear in my gut swirled faster, it twisted into rage, and I let it feed the power simmering inside me. It could be a monumentally stupid thing to do because I had no real control over my magic. And the way it felt? Shit, if I let it, it could bring down this entire house. So, I thought of an iron door, of locks, so many of them, holding some of my power back to try to restrain the magic spiraling and surging inside me. It seemed to work—for now anyway.

Throwing up my hands as I approached the doors, I let a little of it slip free, and they burst open, buckling and snapping under the force.

The Chemist spun toward me, a bloody scalpel in his black latex-covered hand.

"Stop," I cried out, and my voice seemed to resonate through the room.

The Chemist froze, his eyes widening.

Sutton was strapped to a table in the middle of the large room while Boo went crazy in a cage beside it, crashing repeatedly against the bars to try to get to her.

"Step away from her," I ordered, my voice sounding far stronger than I felt.

The rattle of chains, hisses, and snarls came from one of the shadowed corners. Ghoul. The Chemist's most horrible creature, a demon, broken and starved, was right there. I forced down the fear that instantly hit me and aimed all my hatred at the twisted witch holding the scalpel.

Shock and surprise moved across The Chemist's face when he struggled, trying to move, to fight it, but he was forced to take a step back. "Ahhh, there you are, Estelle," he said, the surprise replaced with excitement. "There is my very special demon." His head tilted to the side. "I've waited for so very long for you to show me who you truly are. You're powerful."

"Yes, I am, and I'm not here to show you anything," I snarled. "I'm here to fucking kill you, you twisted fuck."

He grinned, and it sent cold dread down my spine. "You

can't hurt me, Essie—you must know that. You've seen my very special sigils."

Yes, I'd seen the sigils branded into his flesh while he'd fucked his favorite mannequin in front of me.

A howl echoed in the distance, and my heart leaped.

I smiled. "Do you hear them? Hellhounds—they're coming for you, Erwin."

He bared his teeth, fury lining his face. He didn't like being called by his name. "They won't get through my ward, not this time."

"I hate to burst your bubble, but you have no idea how strong they are."

He was powerful, but nowhere near as strong as Agatheena. Relic had already proven he could get through one of The Chemist's wards before, and this one, with him and his brothers battering it, would be no match.

Grady burst into the room, saw me, and immediately charged. I threw up my hands instinctively, and he stopped so hard and fast that something snapped—several bones in his body breaking or dislocating. He flew across the room, slamming against the wall before hitting the ground hard.

As soon as he did, Ghoul's chains rattled, and his bony arm shot out of the shadows; long, tattooed fingers grabbed the only part of Grady he could reach—his hair—and dragged him into the darkness with it.

Grady's screams filled the room, and The Chemist stared into the corner, breathing hard, his eyes wide with shock. Then I felt it—his fear. And it was bright and sharp and wonderful, feeding my burning rage.

The Chemist's gaze sliced back to me, and I slowly circled him, until I stood between him and Sutton. She was unconscious—at least, I hoped that was all she was—and when I saw the extent of the damage he'd done to her, my rage and power shot higher.

Vicious barking, growls, and snarls echoed in the distance, but quickly grew louder.

The Chemist looked up, but he shook his head, a furious expression on his face. "Even if they manage to breach the ward, they can't touch me."

The sound of the door splintering upstairs came next.

"You were saying?"

A roar came from upstairs, so thunderous and violent that goose bumps rose all over me.

The Chemist tried to step back, and this time, he could —whatever I'd done, whatever spell I'd cast was wearing off. He turned to the door behind him, but I wasn't letting him leave. No fucking way.

I flung up my hands. "You will not leave this room."

A massive hound—my hound—burst into the room, then another and another. The Chemist spun back to the door. My powers were as volatile as Agatheena had said they'd be. I didn't know how to direct them, and now they weren't stopping him. He ran for the door—

Relic leaped from one side of the room, landing in front of the exit. He shifted, looming over the smaller male, and The Chemist stumbled back.

My mate grabbed for the monster who had tried to break me over and over, and as soon as Relic's skin made contact, it started to bubble and burn from the power of The Chemist's sigils. Relic hissed, but he didn't let go—no, his eyes met mine. Asking what I wanted him to do. I could let Relic kill him—he wanted to. It would be so easy for him to crush my torturer, but when I looked at my friend, so badly hurt, and thought about what he'd done to Phoebe and gods knew how many others, my hatred manifested inside me, pushing outward.

I lifted my arms, and as I did, my rage and hatred radiated from me, dense and vibrant, forming a kind of shield, sparking from my skin like a live wire. I walked toward them, relishing the look of horror on The Chemist's face. He hated touch, germs, and contact of any kind. Relic holding him was making him freak out already, but I kept coming as Agatheena's words filled my head.

"Then, when you find him, child, you make him feel the pain you suffered. You make him feel every moment of it."

The force field around me sparked brighter as image after image of the things he'd done to me filled my head. I fed my magic with that pain until fire ignited, dancing over my palms, just like my mom had done the night I was taken. It didn't stop there, though; it engulfed me, the hot wind whipping around me.

I kept walking, closing the space between us, and wrapped my arms around The Chemist's struggling body as tight as I could.

Relic stayed right there, not letting him get away as I poured all that savage fury inside me into my tormentor, my torturer, my abuser. He screamed, and I lifted my head, looking into his eyes as his scarred face bubbled and burned.

"You deserve this. You deserve to die screaming," I said, my voice shaking with the force of my power and the fury in my heart.

His face melted away, and he went limp in my arms. My power burned higher, and I screamed, releasing all the pain and fear inside me as the rest of his body melted away.

Then, there were massive arms wrapped around me while the fire raged.

Relic. Oh gods.

I cried out, trying to pull away, terrified I'd hurt him, but he just held me tighter.

"You did it, baby. He's gone. Let it go. Let it all go."

The power inside me—the magic—slowly subsided, and the fire died down. Shaking, I frantically searched him for burns, but the welts from The Chemist had already healed, and the fire hadn't touched him.

"You're okay ... you're okay."

He flashed his teeth. "Hellfire can't touch me, sweetness."

"Hellfire?"

He nodded and pulled me in against him.

Witch and demon, I was both, and my powers had manifested in a way that included my demon blood.

I took in the room around us. The three other hounds crowding it. Jagger was holding Sutton in his arms, and he was licking my unconscious friend's wounds, growling under his breath, trying to heal her, while Dirk and Roman closed in on the corner where Ghoul had dragged Grady.

"No, don't go near him," I cried out.

Grady's body was tossed from the corner, leaving a smear of blood and gore on the concrete floor. Rome was now within striking distance. Chains rattled, but Rome didn't attack—no, he cursed in surprise, then reached down, helping the demon, pulling him from the shadows, and holding him up. I stared over at him—at the threat that had been held over me most of my life, Ghoul, the evil *thing* who had drunk my blood while The Chemist watched, eyes glittering with glee.

The demon looked different now that he'd drained Grady. He was still thin, but his inked skin clung to flesh and muscle; he was no longer just skin and bone.

Ghoul's gaze slid to me and locked on, and I stumbled back a step.

Relic caught me, but he was looking at the demon. "Lukan?"

"You know him?" I choked.

"He's one of Lucifer's lords," Rome said. "He's been missing for a really long fucking time." He turned back to my nightmare. "Brother, Lucifer's been looking for you for decades."

Hand trembling, Lukan shoved his long, tangled hair back from his face, before his eyes met mine, a vibrant yellow-green. "I-I'm so sorry," he rasped, "that I h-hurt you. When he brought you to me, I was blinded by hunger. I would never have ... your mother and me ... I loved her."

I knew who he was instantly. The bony, hissing, starved creature that The Chemist had kept chained, taking him wherever he went, was my father.

"I don't understand."

He straightened, looking a little stronger now. "Erwin trapped me with a hex knot a long time ago, and he's kept me imprisoned since before you were born."

"What?" I choked out.

"Your mother's coven found out we'd mated, and they captured me. Erwin was hired by your coven. At first, their goal was to take out Lucifer and bring about the apocalypse. It's written in ancient texts that Faron and I are the only two who know Lucifer's one true weakness, and with that knowledge, he could be destroyed. So, they held me and tortured me, and when I wouldn't tell them what they wanted to know, they brought you here to force my hand. They starved me until I didn't know what I was doing or who I was feeding from ... and then they'd bring you in. Afterward, Erwin would show me what I'd done, who I'd hurt." He shook his head. "I wanted to save you. I wanted to make it stop. I wanted to stop them from hurting you, but even if I could get free, my choice was saving my daughter or bringing about the end of times." He leaned more heavily against Rome. "I don't expect you to ever forgive me, daughter, and I'll never forgive myself for what I did to you either."

I held Relic's hand tighter. "And when he realized you'd never talk, he focused on developing a magical virus that would kill us all instead," I choked out.

"Yes."

"Is Faron here as well?" Rome asked him.

Lukan nodded. "When I was moved, I had a moment where the hex knot slipped. I was too weak to escape, but I reached out to Faron. He came for me, but that little fuck, Grady, was ready. He'd let the knot slip on purpose. He knew I'd call for my brother, and I fell for it like a fucking fool. I guess they thought they could make him talk since I wouldn't and they'd lost you. He's being held here, but they've kept us apart."

His gaze came back to me, and I couldn't look away. My father was one of the lords of Hell.

"Sutton needs a healer," Jag growled out.

I snapped out of my shock. "And Phoebe—she's hiding in the closet in the other room. There are others locked down here as well."

Everyone jumped into action, freeing the others in the coven, who were thankfully unharmed, and like I'd thought, they'd been magically gagged by The Chemist so they couldn't eject him from the house.

Grady had followed us when Sutton and Phoebe dropped me off to see Relic at the clubhouse, and then he snatched them, and he and The Chemist had forced them to grant access to the coven's house.

The hounds found Faron in one of the other rooms, bound by a hex knot as well. He was thin and pissed off, but he was fine.

Healers were brought in to come and take care of Phoebe and Sutton, and the hounds stayed here to guard the house.

Only then did I let the exhaustion set in.

Relic hauled me into his arms and headed upstairs, knowing I wouldn't want to leave my friends—not yet, not until I knew they'd be okay.

He pressed his mouth to my hair. "You've done everything you can, baby. Now, it's time for your mate to take care of you."

"I'm okay."

"Well, I'm fucking not. After today, I'm far from okay, Tinker Bell. So, you're going to let me take care of you before I lose my fucking mind."

"Okay." I wrapped my arms around his neck and pressed my forehead to his. "I think, after everything, I need that as well. I need my mate to hold me and not let me go."

"Never," he growled.

CHAPTER
THIRTY-ONE

FERN

My phone lit up, and when I saw Sutton's name flash on the screen, I snatched it up. I rushed to the bathroom so as not to wake Relic and shut the door. "Sutton?"

The sound of her breathing echoed down the line. She was having another panic attack.

"Breathe, babe, slow and steady. You're okay. He's gone. He's dead. You're safe now."

She didn't reply, just whimpered, then hissed. I felt her fear, followed by her anger, and there was nothing I could do to make it go away. Her breathing finally slowed.

"T-thanks," she whispered down the line. "Fuck ... sorry."

"I'm here for you, day or night. You don't need to apologize to me, not ever." I shook my head and sat on the edge of the bathtub. "If I hadn't—"

"Don't," she said. "Don't you dare blame yourself. You did nothing wrong, and neither did I. That twisted fucker did this. This is all on him."

"Yeah," I whispered back.

It'd been two weeks since I'd killed The Chemist and since Grady had been drained dry and killed by the demon who had turned out to be my father. Recovery for all of us was slow-going. Phoebe had finally started to heal—thank the gods. The welts on her body had been horrific. The healers who came to tend them didn't know what to do. If it wasn't for Agatheena and her potions and elixirs, both Phoebe and Sutton wouldn't have survived. They'd both been left with scars though. Inside and out.

Thankfully, they had a coven to surround and care for them.

The sound of rustling came down the line, and I could tell Sutton had gotten out of bed. A bond had formed between us and had grown in such a short time. We weren't just friends; we were family now, and I would be here for her whenever she needed me.

"Charming just showed up," she said, obviously looking out the window.

The hounds had been taking turns watching the house, staying close, not because there was any real danger now, but to make sure everyone felt safe while they healed and regained their strength. Jagger seemed to volunteer a lot.

"Is that okay?"

She blew out a shaky breath. "Yeah. Now that he's here, I'll be able to sleep."

"I'm glad. Has he spoken to you yet?"

"No, not since ..." She swallowed audibly. "He just stands out there, scowling, then takes off early." She blew out another breath, and this one was more even. "Why does he come here if it pisses him off so much?"

Jag had been scowling and stomping around the clubhouse as well.

"I think what pisses him off is what happened to you and Phoebe, not that he has to be there. Hounds really don't like it when females are mistreated."

"Right," she said, sounding unconvinced, then yawned. "I think I'll try and sleep now."

"Night, Sutton."

"Night, Fern."

I disconnected and looked up when the bathroom door opened. Relic walked in, chest bare, his hair back in a messy braid. He looked so impossibly handsome that I was still struggling to believe this was my life, that he was mine.

"How's she doing?"

Relic cared not only about me, but about the people I cared about as well. Though, I would say, he was still seriously wary of Agatheena.

"She had another panic attack."

He nodded. "It'll take time."

"Yeah." I knew that firsthand.

He watched me for a few seconds, then crossed his arms. "Lukan called me earlier to see how you were doing. I told him I'd only give him updates if you were cool with it."

My father had given me space since that night, but sometimes, I sensed that he was close, and I wasn't sure how I felt about that. He was a victim of The Chemist like I was, but it'd take time to shake the fear I had of him that was so deeply ingrained.

"It's fine. You can tell Lukan I'm doing good, better than good." I stood. "But I'm not ready to talk to him yet."

Relic closed the space between us and pulled me into his arms. "You don't have to do anything you don't want to, baby. Not one fucking thing. I'll make it clear he doesn't talk to you, doesn't approach you, unless you give him the green light. Anyone wants to get near you, they'll have to go through me."

I smiled up at him. "I love you—you know that?"

He grinned. "Yeah, sweetness, I know it. At least the Fates knew what they were doing when they sent me into your store." He tucked my hair behind my ear. "Though, even if I hadn't come in that day, it was only a matter of time before I found you. I only wish it'd been sooner."

"Now, we have an eternity."

He dipped his head, pressing his forehead to mine. "Yeah, we fucking do."

Then, he hauled me off my feet and carried me back to bed.

EPILOGUE

RELIC

THREE MONTHS LATER

GERALD GANNON WAS A FUCKING coward and today he would die screaming.

I watched the male who had thrown Fern away, who had given her to pure evil, move around inside his house. It hadn't taken long for word to reach him, for him to learn that Fern was alive, and that she was mated to a hellhound. He'd packed up and run before I could get to him—but not fucking far enough.

It hadn't been easy to find him, not with the piece of shit doing everything in his power to conceal himself. I could feel the ward around his new place vibrating with magic.

I grinned. That wouldn't fucking save him.

Fern didn't know I was here. She had no idea where this fucker had gone, and she never would. I didn't keep things from my mate, but right now, she was happy. She didn't need to be burdened with this. My precious Tinker Bell didn't need to carry the weight of this fucker's death on her shoulders.

Pulling out my phone, I stared down at it. My hand shook with rage, I was seeing fucking red. And as much as I wanted to be the one to end this motherfucker's life, there was someone who deserved that honor more than me.

Lukan deserved this, he deserved to relish Gannon's screams. The witch was the reason his daughter had been imprisoned and tortured. He'd had Lukan captured and starved, and because of that, the male had hurt his own child—something that had seriously fucked him up. All that was bad enough, but Gannon was also the reason Lukan had lost his beloved mate.

If anyone should get to kill the witch, it was him.

I took a picture of Gannon through the window and sent it to Lukan. A moment later, the powerful demon appeared beside me.

Physically, he'd recovered. He was dressed in jeans and a faded T-shirt. His inked arms were no longer skin stretched over bone. He looked like the male he once was, young, fit, powerful—except for his eyes. There was a disturbed, crazed look in his eyes that never seemed to go away. His eyes narrowed on the witch, and he grinned, the expression on his face one of pure evil. "But I didn't get you anything."

"All I ask is that it's not quick."

He dragged the back of his hand across his mouth. "Oh, no. It won't be quick. I have ways to make sure old Gerry boy is suffering for years."

Good. That's what he deserved. I turned to leave.

"How is she?" he said, stopping me. His voice had changed, a pained note making it rougher.

I turned back. "She's good, Lukan. Really fucking good. She's got lots of good friends, a new coven, and she's got me."

He nodded. "I'm really fucking glad to hear that, and for what it's worth, Relic, I'm glad she has you. I know I've never been a father to her, but if I'd gotten that chance, after some fucking with you and making you sweat..." he grinned. "I would've given you my blessing. I'm glad she has a male who loves her the way she deserves, someone who can protect her the way I never could."

I nodded. "She doesn't hate you, you know, and she doesn't blame you."

"My daughter is terrified of me," he said, his gaze sliding back to Gerald.

"It won't always be that way. It'll take time, but we have plenty of it," I said because I felt bad for the male. I got to be with Fern and he didn't, and my mate was fucking amazing.

"I hope you're right." He glanced back at me and flashed me a grin. "Now, if you'll excuse me, I have a house call to make."

He strode to the front door, and as I walked away and swung onto my bike, the sound of wood splintering echoed through the night.

FERN

Phoebe laughed at Sutton's imitation of her super-surly new boss, and it was so incredibly good to hear.

My friends were still recovering after what had happened to them. Sutton had gone back to work a few weeks ago, and she said she was fine, but I knew she was just trying to make me feel better. She had a ways to go, but I wasn't going to push. She knew I was here for her if she needed me and she still called me at night sometimes when she couldn't sleep.

"More wine?" Sutton asked, topping off her glass.

I went from having no one to having a mate, the hounds, a coven, and Willow and her family had become good friends as well. Even Agatheena and I had grown closer—well, as much as a female like her would allow.

"I'm good." I curled my feet up under me on the couch.

We had a couple of drinks here at the coven house most Friday nights.

"So, has Relic calmed down about the whole work thing?" Phoebe asked.

I grinned. "Yes, he has. Well, he still calls and texts me a million times a day to check on me, but he's stopped sending Brick to secretly watch my shop."

After I'd called him out on his overprotectiveness and told him that he needed to calm the hell down, he'd sent Brick to "guard" me instead.

"I have a feeling it'll take time after everything that happened for him to relax a bit, especially about my safety." I winced. "Though, according to Willow, hounds only get worse, and when you have pups, the overprotective thing reaches a whole new level."

"Pups? Are you—"

"Noooo. Not looking to add a baby into the mix just yet. I've barely lived, you know? I just want to be with Relic for a while before we have kids."

"Makes perfect sense," Sutton said, pulling her phone

from her pocket when it chimed. She stilled as she looked down at it, her eyes widening.

"What is it?"

She looked up. "Jagger just followed me on Nightscape."

"He did what?" Phoebe said, looking as shocked as I felt.

Sutton held up her phone, showing us his profile, and Phoebe and I leaned in to check it out. No profile picture, no posts, no followers—and he was now following one person. Sutton.

"Is he back?" Sutton asked.

I shook my head. "He's still in Hell."

Jagger had been in Hell for two and a half months, helping Maddox with some training for the younger hounds, apparently, and not even Relic knew when he was coming back.

"I can't believe he did that. It's almost as if ..."

"As if he created the profile just to follow you," Phoebe said, taking the words right out of my mouth.

Sutton frowned, and her cheeks turned pink. "Why would he do that?"

Relic and I had a theory, but he'd told me not to say a word, that these things had to unfold on their own. "He likes you," I said because that was obvious, right?

She huffed out a laugh. "The guy scowls and snaps at me whenever we're in the same room. I piss him off more than anything."

He'd also held her in his arms like she was his whole world, desperately licking her wounds to heal her after we had found her in that room, after the torture The Chemist had put her through. I didn't know if she remembered, but she'd made it clear she didn't want to talk about what had happened during those days with The Chemist, so I hadn't shared what Jag had done while she was unconscious.

"Are you going to follow him back?" Phoebe asked. "I kind of feel bad for him."

Phoebe was far too sweet for her own good.

"Why do you feel bad for him?" I asked her.

"He obviously doesn't know how Nightscape works. His account isn't even private, and I get the feeling Jagger's a private male. I also doubt he knows we can see that Sutton's the only person he's following."

I thought she was probably right.

"Should I follow him back?" Sutton asked, biting her lip. She had a major thing for him, but wasn't admitting it, not even to us. "I should, right? Fuck it," she said. She hit the Follow button, then quickly put the phone on the coffee table like she was afraid it would bite.

There were so many things I wanted to say, but I held them back, for now anyway. "Right, well, I'd better get going. Relic's taking me for a ride tonight."

That had become a tradition as well, one I absolutely loved, which included a ride through the city, before finding a secluded spot on the way home so we could tear each other's clothes off. Our very first ride had been a bit different, though. That time, we'd ridden out to where The Chemist had kept me prisoner for so much of my life, and I'd watched as Relic blasted it with hellfire, flames pouring from his palms until the place was completely engulfed. He'd held me in his arms, and we'd watched it burn.

My friends walked me to the gate, and Sutton's phone chimed with the distinctive Nightscape notification sound. One guess who that was. As I opened the gate, I bit back my smile.

We said our goodbyes, and I closed my eyes, visualizing the clubhouse, and embraced the sensation of falling. My feet hit pavement a moment later, and I opened my eyes. I was getting better at it every time I did it. A few more weeks, and I was sure I'd be able to land in our den.

Tonight, though, I'd landed just outside the clubhouse gates. "Hey, Brick."

He grinned, opened up for me, and I headed up to the main doors and inside. Friday night was often a party night, and the hounds were blowing off steam. Magnolia, her cousin Jasmine, and their mates were there as well. Mags waved me over.

I grinned. "Relic's waiting for me, but next time, for sure!" I called over the music, and she gave me a thumbs-up.

I headed down to the dens and along the cave. When I opened the door to our den, I found Relic standing in the middle of the room, and as always, when I saw him after being parted from him for any length of time, my heart skipped a beat.

"Hey."

He grinned wide and closed the space between us, pulling me into his arms. "Hey, baby. Missed you."

"Missed you too."

He was fresh out of the shower, dressed in jeans and his leather vest, his chest bare underneath. Now that it was warming up, he did that a lot, and I wasn't sad about it.

"You ready for our ride?"

"Can't wait."

I sat on the edge of the bed, and he sat on the floor, his back to me. I slid my legs around him and under his arms, then took his damp hair in my hands and sectioned it off.

"You have a good night with the girls?" he asked as I started braiding.

"Yeah, really good." I rested my chin on his shoulder. "Jag followed Sutton on Nightscape."

"Jag's on Nightscape?"

"Well, it looks like he just signed up, and Sutton's the only person he follows." I tied off his braid.

"Fuck." A low, sexy laugh rumbled from my mate. "Though I'm not surprised. He's probably getting fucking desperate."

"What do you mean?"

"After I met you, staying away from you was impossible. Jag's been in Hell for close to three months. He's tasted her blood, seen her hurt and at her most vulnerable. Being away from her has to be torture for him."

I straightened. "Then why is he staying away?"

Relic stood, and I got off the bed.

"Fuck knows. No idea why he's holding out. Unless we're wrong about those two?"

My mate led me out of our room, through the party, and out of the clubhouse. We got on his bike, and I wrapped my arms around him.

"Ready, Tink?" he said, his voice so full of love and rough with hunger.

"Always," I said, sliding my hands up under his vest so I could feel his skin against mine.

We tore out onto the street. A laugh of pure joy burst from me, and I felt Relic laugh as well. Gods, I loved when he laughed.

If Jag was Sutton's mate, I didn't know why he was holding out either. Resisting was a waste of time, but then again, some of us needed time to realize we were worthy of love.

Relic sped around a corner, and I stopped thinking and hung on tight to my mate—my home, my whole world.

And I would never let go.

ALSO BY SHERILEE GRAY

Rocktown Ink:

Beg For You

Sin For You

Meant For you

Bad For You

All For You

Just for You

The Smith Brothers:

Mountain Man

Wild Man

Solitary Man

Lawless Kings:

Shattered King

Broken Rebel

Beautiful Killer

Ruthless Protector

Glorious Sinner

Merciless King

Boosted Hearts:

Swerve

Spin

Slide

Spark

Axle Alley Vipers:

Crashed

Revved

Wrecked

Black Hills Pack:

Lone Wolf's Captive

A Wolf's Deception

Stand Alone Novels:

Breaking Him

While You Sleep

ABOUT THE AUTHOR

Sherilee Gray is a kiwi girl and lives in beautiful New Zealand with her husband and their two children. When she isn't writing sexy contemporary or paranormal romance, searching for her next alpha hero on Pinterest, or fueling her voracious book addiction, she can be found dreaming of far off places with a mug of tea in one hand and a bar of chocolate in the other.

To find out about new releases, giveaways, events and other cool stuff, sign up for my newsletter!

www.sherileegray.com

Printed in Great Britain
by Amazon

51538862R00207